PRAISE FOR ROBERT BEVAN

"Love these books. I think Robert Bevan does a great job with characterization and he is slowly adding characters to the story. I think this has the best ending yet. I wish he cranked these out quicker. I really can't wait to see what happens and I forget some details between books."

—James Noyes, Goodreads Review

"I hate this series. It makes me want to play RPGs again. One could say that it's more of the same, but it's not. Bevan manages to evolve the humor and up the stakes with every book. If you're reading this you're likely already up to your beach in the series. Be a Denise and get some more sand in your "vegetables" because this another great book that is right for you and not for everyone else."

—Jon, Amazon Review

"The splitting of the party was something I particularly enjoyed as it allowed some lesser characters the chance to shine on their own, giving us a chance to get to know them better."

—Morgan Hobbes, moganhobbes.com

CRITICAL FAILURES V

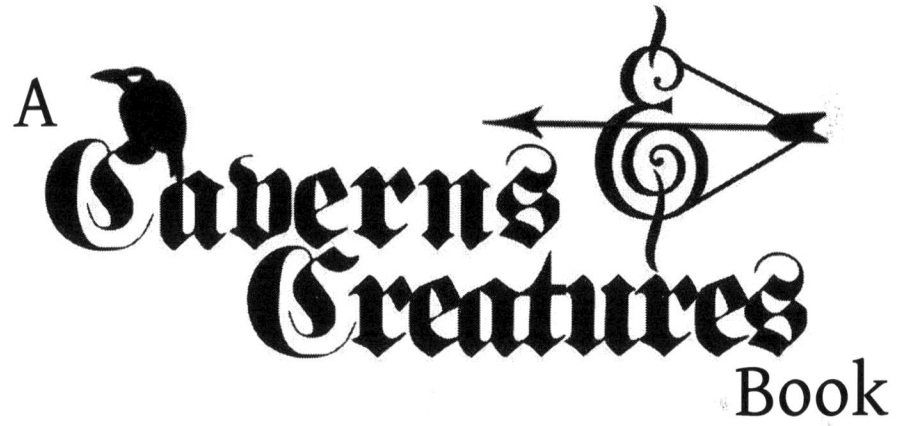

V IS FOR FIVE

A Caverns & Creatures Book

by

ROBERT BEVAN

All content edited by Joan Reginaldo.
Layout design by Christopher Dowell.

ISBN: 1545363617
ISBN-13: 978-1545363614

SPECIAL THANKS TO:

My editor, Joan Reginaldo.

My wife No Young Sook.

My cover designer, No Hyun Jun.

My ARC team.

CHAPTER 1

"Go fuck yourself," said Tanner as he held up Tim's silver scroll tube.

"Excuse me?" Tim gave up on his fruitless effort to scrub the hardened black grime off the steel serving tray. There was no way that shit had accumulated in one day. If it was good enough for the dishwasher before him, it was good enough for Tim. He dropped the tray into the rinse bin and accepted the scroll tube.

Tanner shrugged. "I apologize. The gnome would only surrender your character sheets on two conditions. The first was that I personally tell you to go fuck yourself upon delivery."

"What was the second?" Tim began twisting the cap off his tube. "And why's this thing so fucking heavy?"

The latter question was answered when a clumpy brown liquid flowed out of the tube into the rinse bin. The smell was like releasing a genie who'd been farting in a lamp for a thousand years.

"Jesus Christ!" Tim dropped the tube. The relatively clean water of the rinse bin grew murky and brown. He looked up at Tanner. "What the fuck, man?"

"That was the second condition."

"Any surprises in my tube?" asked Katherine. She was sitting on the stained wooden floor against the back wall, sucking back a bottle of The Piss Bucket Tavern's cheapest vintage and stroking Butterbean's fur.

"I don't think so." Tanner took a step toward Katherine, tube in hand, but stopped as her wolf picked up his head and growled at him.

"Stop it, Butterbean!" said Katherine. "We don't judge people by the color of their skin."

Tim reached into the poo water for his character sheet. "I think he's just a little distrustful of your taste in men. Your last boyfriend tried to eat him, after all."

Katherine hugged Butterbean around the neck with one arm and held out the other to accept her scroll tube.

To Tim's surprise, his character sheet came out of the water dry and clean. Not even the ink or pencil marks were smudged. He was less impressed with the actual stats on the paper. He was a Level 4 Rogue, with about a quarter of the Experience Points required to reach Level 5. That meant he probably hadn't gained a whole lot since they'd returned to this world. Still, he was able to confirm that his Dexterity score had risen to 18, so that was something. He rolled up his sheet, returned it to its tube, and pulled a dish out of the sludge-filled wash bin.

"I don't understand this," said Katherine, looking at her character sheet. "Druid 2 means I'm still a second level druid, right?"

"Yeah," said Tim. "Sorry, that sucks."

"So what's Fighter 3?"

Tim stopped scrubbing. "You've got three levels of Fighter? How the fuck did you..." Then it occurred to him. She couldn't gain levels in Druid while she was a vampire, but she was still getting Experience Points. They had to go toward something. The game must have credited her with Fighter levels for all the animals and monsters she'd beaten the shit out of. "You're a fifth level character now. I'm still only fourth. This is bullshit."

"I guess you don't get a lot of Character Points for getting drunk and pissing yourself."

"See what I mean? They're called Experience Points. You don't even know what you're talking about."

"I don't know what either of you are talking about," said Tanner. "What are these papers you sent me to retrieve? Why are they so important?"

"You wouldn't understand." Tim deemed his current dish clean enough and dropped it into the rinse bin.

"What the hell do you think you're doing?" asked Katherine.

"The fuck does it look like I'm doing? I'm doing the same goddamn thing I've been doing for the past seven fucking hours. I'm washing dishes."

"Your rinse bin is full of shit water."

Tim frowned at the rinse bin. "It's more water than shit." He pulled out a dish. It still looked clean. "See? You can't even tell."

Katherine shook her head. "No way, little bro. You have to fill that with clean water and wash all those dishes again."

"No fucking way! Why don't you get off your ass and help out?"

"I've been waiting tables all day. My ass has been grabbed more times than a Tickle Me Elmo on Black Friday. And apparently tipping isn't a thing in this world."

"Come on, Kat. I'm exhausted. I need a drink."

"You should have thought about that before you murdered Mordred... again."

"I understand you're pissed, but punishing me with extra bullshit work isn't going to change our situation."

"Bullshit work?" said Katherine. "The dishes are literally swimming in shit! How long do you think it's going to take Morty to figure out why everyone in his tavern is puking and shitting themselves the day after we start working here?"

"Have you seen the quality of the food in this place? Trace elements of half-orc shit aren't going to make any difference."

"I'm not taking that chance. We are homeless in a fantasy world because you're an insecure little drunk shit. If Morty comes in here and sees you putting dishes in shitwater, he's going to kick us out of here. How many other places do you think are going to board a wolf and a black man?"

Tanner cleared his throat. "Half-drow."

Tim wiped the sweat from his brow. "You've got your druid powers back, right? Don't you have a water purification spell or something?"

Katherine looked at the back of her character sheet. "Purify Food and Water. It's a Level 0 spell." She looked up at Tim. "You think that'll work?"

"It's worth a shot."

Katherine stood up and walked over to the rinse bin. "So what do I do?"

"Did you prepare your spells like I told you?"

"Yes, but all I've ever done is summon a wolf."

"Just touch the water and say something like 'purify'."

Katherine grimaced at the brown water. "I can't believe I'm doing this." She touched the surface with the very tip of one finger. "Purify."

The water instantly turned crystal clear. A faint scent of shit, which Tim supposed he'd just grown accustomed to, was now noticeably absent. Not only that, but the dishes were clean as well. Like, dishwasher detergent commercial clean. They were so clean beneath the surface of the water that the stark contrast above the surface only served to illustrate what a piss poor job Tim had been doing this whole time. Even that hard black shit on the serving tray had vanished. Well, half of it anyway.

"Holy shit!" said Tim. "That's incredible." He started putting the clean dishes back into the wash bin with the ones he hadn't washed yet.

"Tim!" said Katherine. "What are you doing?"

"We're better off serving food on shitwater dishes than these two-tone dishes. Get ready to fire up another spell." Once he'd stuffed all the dishes back into the wash bin, Tim scooped clean water from the rinse bin and dumped it into the sludge in the wash bin.

When all of the dishes were completely submerged, he raised his eyebrows at Katherine.

"Purify." As soon as she spoke the word, a shockwave of cleanliness blasted out from her finger, wiping out every last scrap of uneaten food, every bit of dried blood, phlegm, and whatever, which Tim had been working for hours to scrub away, in the blink of an eye.

Tim stepped back and admired Katherine's handiwork. "You could serve a fucking god on these dishes."

"What a peculiar thing to say," said Tanner.

Stupid NPCs. They always take everything so literally. "That was hyperbole," Tim explained. "I just meant that the dishes are very clean."

"I know what hyperbole is." Tanner's tone suggested that he didn't appreciate being condescended to. "I'm interested in learning more of this other world that you claim to come from. The other night was the first time I'd ever heard of anyone eating the flesh of a god. I've never even thought to consider it. But you speak so casually of the act, going so far as to suggest serving them on dishes. Is this so common a practice where you come from? Are all your gods made of food?"

"That's not what I –"

The door leading out to the bar and common area swung open. Morty's hoofsteps and bovine eyes were heavy with exhaustion. Given the recent improvement in the smell of the back room, the stench of cow sweat was all the more salient when he entered.

"That's the last of them." He set four glasses down on the table, each with the dark remnants of 'well-sludge', the beverage of choice for those patrons who commonly stayed out this late at night, clinging to the bottom.

"Rough night?" asked Katherine.

Morty grabbed his horns and used them to twist his head left and right until his meaty neck cracked on both sides. "Any night I don't have to kill anyone is a blessing from the – Good gods!" He gawked at the dishes in the wash bin. "Those are the cleanest dishes I've ever seen!"

Tim dried his hands on a towel which he wished he'd thought to throw into the bin before Katherine cast her spell. "Any job worth doing is worth doing right." An asshole boss of his, from before he'd started at the Chicken Hut, had always said that.

"I'm impressed," said Morty. "You've done a fine job. Katherine, you were very popular with the customers as well."

Katherine raised her wineskin. "That's one way of putting it."

Morty looked at Tanner. "And you did a fine job of... well... staying out of sight."

Tanner smiled. "We all have our gifts."

"No offense intended. It's just that my patrons have a distrust of..."

"Do you distrust me?"

"I distrust everyone who walks into my tavern," said Morty. "I'm an eight hundred pound minotaur. Whether I trust you or not is inconsequential as long as we both know I could kill you without breaking a sweat."

"I certainly can't argue with that."

Morty frowned. "That came out wrong. I didn't mean to single out you in particular. I mean any of you."

Tim and Katherine exchanged a nervous glance.

"No no no!" said Morty. "This is why I can never keep good help. I meant to say that I'm grateful for all the hard work you've done. Why don't the three of you join me for a drink out front?"

"Fuck yes," said Tim.

Morty led them to the table where he sometimes sat with special guests of the tavern.

"What'll you boys have?" asked Katherine, reverting back to server mode.

"You sit down, dear," said Morty. "You've worked hard enough for one night. It would be my pleasure to serve you."

Katherine took a seat at the table. "If you insist."

Tim emptied his bag onto the table. "You should pack your character sheet at the bottom of your bag," he said to Katherine. "Keep it safe."

"I'll do that tomorrow." Katherine opened Tim's pouch of caltrops and dumped them on the table. She rolled the pouch into a tight ball and wrapped the cord around it. Tossing it up into the air, she grabbed a caltrop before catching the ball with the same hand.

"Those aren't jacks," said Tim. "They're caltrops."

"I know what they are. But I'm using them for a different purpose. You should see Tanner at work. He's like MacGyver."

"What's a MacGyver?" asked Tanner. "And what purpose are you using those for?"

Katherine tossed her ball up and scooped up two caltrops before catching it again. "It's just a game I used to play when I was a little girl."

"Were you raised in a mercenary camp?"

"No, I went to a Catholic school." Katherine failed her attempt to scoop up three caltrops, knocking a few of them off the table.

"Nice going, Kat," said Tim.

Katherine picked up the caltrops off the floor and placed them on the table. "You think you can do better with your tiny little bitch hands?"

"Of course I can. I've got an 18 Dexterity."

Katherine smiled. "Let's make it interesting." She looked over at Morty, who was filling a pitcher with beer. "Can you bring us, like, twenty shot glasses?"

Morty's nostrils flared briefly. "Glad to see you're not shy about taking advantage of my generosity. What would you like in them?"

"Beer is fine." Katherine sat across the table from Tanner with Tim's caltrops and balled-up pouch. "We take turns around the table. Toss the ball in the air, pick up a jack, and catch the ball. Everyone else drinks one shot of beer."

Tanner frowned. "This seems like an overly complicated means of not getting very drunk."

"Toss the ball in the air again and scoop up two jacks." Katherine demonstrated. "Everyone drinks two shots."

"I see how this could escalate."

Morty returned with two pitchers of beer and a tray full of shot glasses, also full of beer. He sat on the larger, reinforced stool opposite from Tim, pushed the shot glasses to the middle of the table, and kept the pitchers for himself.

"You're not playing?" Katherine asked.

"Minotaurs do not play children's games, nor do we drink beer from tiny glasses. I shall observe, and drink as I please."

As Tim, Katherine, and Tanner took their turns, growing steadily more intoxicated, a flaw in the game revealed itself. Caltrops are sharp. When trying to scoop them up, the drunker they got, the more frequently they punctured their hands.

Before long, the old dried blood from the countless bar fights of years gone by was painted over with fresh streaks of red. The shot glasses soon became smeared with red fingerprints.

"Son of a bitch!" said Tim, resisting the urge to fling away the four caltrops digging in to his bleeding hand.

Morty snorted like an enraged bull. For whatever reason, he seemed to find Tim's injuries – and subsequent swearing – the funniest of anyone's.

"Tim, are you okay?" Katherine's head swayed as she struggled to focus on Tim's hand. "That looks pretty bad."

"I can barely even feel it," said Tim. It was half-true. His hand was torn to shreds, but it didn't hurt nearly as much as those initial pricks had. "That's four shots each. Drink up, motherfuckers."

Morty laughed even louder. He pounded the table with his fist and wiped tears from his big cow eyes. It must have been the novelty of a halfling swearing. Well, that and the booze. After his two pitchers of beer were gone, he'd switched over to stonepiss, but was still drinking it out of a pitcher. For as much as he was doing for them, Tim could live with this small indignity. In fact, he'd even ham it up for the big guy. It was nice to hear some genuine hearty laughter, and to know that he was the cause of it. Morty was laughing at his performance, rather than at his existence.

"Get ready for five, you shit-nosed pigfuckers!"

Tanner looked at Katherine, then back at Tim. "That seems uncalled for."

But Morty didn't think so. He was choking on his stonepiss.

Tim stood on his stool, threw the balled-up bloodied pouch, then brought his hand down quick to scoop up his five caltrops. The table was a little higher than he'd remembered, and his hand came down hard on three caltrops.

"FUCK!" he cried, this time unable to resist jerking his hand away. The caltrops flew upward as something wet and squishy hit Tim in the face from above.

"The fuck?" said Tim as he lost his balance and fell off his stool. He landed on his backpack, which he hadn't closed properly, and his shit spilled out all over the floor.

"Stop! Please!" Morty wheezed between snorts. "It's too much. I can't..."

Tim didn't begrudge Morty his good time, but his head and ass hurt from where he'd hit the floor, and he was starting to get some feeling back in his hand. It would probably be a good idea for him to switch over to stonepiss himself, to dull the pain and to tolerate Morty's obnoxious bovine laughter.

"You're not going to be laughing when you get a caltrop in your hoof," said Tim, picking himself up off the floor. "Would you guys mind helping me find the ones that fell on the – Goddammit!"

Katherine stood up. "What's wrong?"

"I found one." Tim winced as he plucked the caltrop out of his foot.

Morty slammed his empty pitcher down as he wheezed

with his wildest and most obnoxious laughter yet.

"Screw you, dude," said Tim. "That fucking hurts."

"I found the second one," said Tanner, rising to his feet from the other side of the table. "I cheated and used my eyes instead of my foot."

Tim gave him the finger. "Laugh it up, Fuck-o. Real fucking funny."

Morty seemed to think so. He was wheezing even harder, pounding the table with both fists.

Tim had had about enough. He needed either to suck down some stonepiss or kick Morty in the nuts. He climbed back up on his stool and grabbed one of Morty's stonepiss bottles.

"As long as you're feeling so fucking jolly, I think I'll help myself to some of your – WAH!"

Just as Tim grabbed the neck of a bottle, Morty grabbed the neck of Tim. Still wheezing, he lifted Tim into the air by the throat. His cow eyes were mad and terrifying.

"Sorry!" Tim croaked. "It's... empty..." Tim dropped the bottle.

Morty didn't drop Tim. He opened his mouth wide, showing teeth like a forest of spikes in his black gums, and pulled Tim toward it. His grip on Tim's neck was firm, but not actually squeezing.

"Katherine! Help!"

"Let go of him!" shouted Katherine. Morty's mouth backed up about six inches as Katherine pulled at Tim's feet.

Tanner grabbed Morty's other arm. "Come on, Morty. We've all had a lot to – Yaaaaahhhhh!" Morty threw him across the room.

Tim's neck felt like it was being stretched to twice its normal length as Morty pulled him back toward his gaping maw. His breath was hot and boozy like a creepy uncle's. With his free hand, he pointed to the inside of his mouth.

"I don't want to go in your mouth!" said Tim. He was making a considerable effort to neither cry nor piss himself. "Katherine! Do something, please!"

"I'm doing my best," said Katherine, still pulling at his feet. "I don't know what else I can do."

"Kick him in the junk!"

Morty shook his massive head. His eyes looked both mad and pleading. He pointed even more frantically at the inside of his mouth.

"Fuck that!" said Tim. "I'm not going in there. Katherine, hurry!"

"Aack! Aaaaaccccckk! Aack!" said Morty frantically.

Tim's head lunged into Morty's mouth as Katherine let go of his feet. He shut his eyes and waited for his head and torso to be bitten off, but that never happened.

"Hnnnnnngggg," said Morty. From the inside of Morty's canyon of a mouth, Tim could feel the inarticulate sound as well as hear it. It was the sound a man's heart makes when he's been kicked in the junk.

Morty's grip loosened, and Tim felt the welcome pain of crashing onto the floor. When he opened his eyes, Morty lay next to him, a puddle of blood and drool forming near the corner of his mouth, eyes lifeless.

"Jesus, Katherine," said Tim. "How hard did you kick him?"

Katherine frowned down at the dead minotaur. "Not hard enough to kill him." She looked at Tim. "Are you okay?"

Tim sat up. As strange as it seemed, he was okay. He was better than okay even. "I feel great."

"So glad to hear that," said Tanner. He was bleeding from a gash in his head, but didn't look too bad otherwise. "We really should do this more often."

Tim looked down to find that the scroll case holding his character sheet was between his legs like a big silver dong. He unscrewed the cap and pulled out the otherworldly paper. He was a fifth level rogue.

"What's wrong?" asked Katherine.

Tim looked up at her. "I think I killed Morty."

“That’s ridiculous. How could you have killed him? By starving him to death? I’m the one that kicked him in the nuts.”

Tanner swirled around the residual stonepiss at the bottom of Morty’s pitcher. “There’s blood in here,” he said. “I think Morty found the third caltrop.”

CHAPTER 2

Frank sulked over his sweaty beer mug, his eyes too heavy to look angry anymore. "Do you think filling the tube with dog shit and pee was going a step too far?"

"Not far enough, if you ask me," said Tony the Elf. He didn't look quite so tired as Frank. But that might have had something to do with elves and their weird sleep thing.

"I agree," said Stacy. She had plenty of anger left to burn. "I would have pissed in it myself if I didn't think that little creep might keep it to sniff and whack off to."

"That's pretty gross, even for one of them." Frank looked over at Cooper, sleeping face-down on the floor. The back of his loincloth fluttered. "Do you think he'd really –"

"The fact that you're asking the question means you know it's within the realm of possibilities." She sipped her beer. "I've seen it before, and I wasn't even as hot as I am now."

"So you've mentioned," said Rhonda.

"You know what I'm talking about. Back in college, when you had a guy in your room, how many pairs of panties went missing every time you stepped out to use the bathroom?"

Rhonda looked down into her drink. "It wasn't so much of an issue for me."

Frank and Tony the Elf glanced awkwardly at each other.

Stacy sucked back her beer a little faster, trying to think of something to say other than, "Oh."

Rhonda set her glass down on the table a little harder than necessary. "I went to an all-girls school."

"Ah," said Tony the Elf.

"Of course," said Frank.

"That explains it," said Stacy. "You didn't miss out on anything. You wouldn't believe how low some of those creeps would stoop. But to the best of my knowledge, none of them have ever killed a guy over me. Before now." She looked at Frank. "Is there honestly anything Tim could do that would surprise you?"

Tony the Elf's almond eyes went round. "Stacy, you're brilliant!"

Stacy smiled. "Why thank you!"

Rhonda rolled her eyes. "And strong, and hot. We've been through this."

"I've got an idea," said Tony the Elf, rising from his stool. He carefully stepped over sleeping bodies as he made his way to the cellar door.

"You might want to rethink going down there," said one of the elves who passed their sleepless nights playing a meta-game of Caverns & Creatures. "She's down there."

"This can't wait."

"Suit yourself." The elf turned back to his group and rolled a handful of wooden dice.

Julian was sitting near the game table, but facing away from it, staring at the wall. He was most likely in his elf trance that passed for sleep. He didn't seem to enjoy the game too much, but he'd been spending more of his nights over there since all the shit went down with Tim. And he'd been spending more of his days suddenly remembering errands that needed running whenever Stacy came around.

Tony the Elf knocked gently on the door leading down to the cellar. "Excuse me, Denise? I need to come down there." He opened the door a crack.

"Give it to me good, Dwayne!" Denise's voice echoed up the cellar stairs. "I smell what The Rock is cooking!"

"Hello?" said Tony the Elf, loud enough to try to get Denise's attention, but not so loud as to wake anyone up. It was a fine line. "I'm coming down th–"

"My oven is preheated, honey. Insert that eggplant parmesan!"

Tony the Elf looked down and shook his head.

"Set the timer for thirty-five minutes!"

"Eggplant parmesan?" said Frank. "Is that a racial thing?"

"That was my first thought," said Stacy. "But now I'm starting to think she's just reading a recipe."

Tony the Elf stomped down the stairs, clearing his throat continuously as he did so.

"Then turn me over and – Goddammit! Don't none of y'all know how to knock? Wait! The fuck are you... I was using that!"

"I'm sorry, Denise," said Tony the Elf. "This is important. Please let go."

"Who are you to judge me, motherfu–"

There was a snap of breaking wood, followed by a loud crash of wood, stone, and steel, then some sobbing.

"Fine," said Tony the Elf. "You can keep that much. But I'm taking the rest."

"This is natural!" cried Denise as Tony the Elf's footsteps quickly grew louder up the staircase. "I got needs!"

Tony the Elf emerged with a three-legged wooden chair and slammed the cellar door behind him, silencing Denise's throaty sobs.

"Do we want to know?" asked Frank.

Tony the Elf frowned. "Denise is... using the other leg."

"Isn't there a more appropriate... device down there?" asked Stacy.

"Would you use it, knowing what you know?"

"She could wash it."

"Even then, would you?"

Stacy frowned. "No, I suppose not."

"It's probably a good idea to give all those weapons a good boil," said Rhonda. "She spends an awful lot of time down there."

"What's with the chair?" asked Frank.

Tony the Elf's eyes lit up. "All that talk about panty-sniffing got me thinking about that little guy we had tied up in the cellar."

"That may be the most fucked-up sentence ever uttered in the history of language."

Tony the Elf paused to replay the sentence in his mind. "Yes. I can see how that may be misconstrued out of context."

"Please waste no more time getting to that context."

"We're all in agreement that our former prisoner was very likely one of Mordred's avatars in this world, right?"

Stacy nodded. Rhonda shrugged.

"Yes," said Frank, bitterly.

"Well he spent a lot of time with his ass firmly planted on this seat." Tony the Elf held up the chair and pointed to the seat. "And no one can sniff out an ass like Dave."

Stacy focused through her beer buzz. "The stocky guy with the beard?"

"No," said Tony the Elf. "The other Dave. My Animal Companion."

Rhonda's jowls sagged. "It's a nice thought, but I wouldn't get your hopes up. He could be anywhere by now."

"Ass is a powerful scent," said Frank. "And I think there's a decent enough chance that he might still be nearby." He looked up at Tony the Elf. "Good work. We don't have any time to waste. Separate the four planks of that seat. Wake up three more people who have dogs or wolves as Animal Companions or Familiars. Partner up, fan out through the city, and see if any of you can pick up the scent. If we're lucky, we'll be able to hone in on that little bastard while Mordred's in one of his other bodies."

Stacy smiled at Frank. "It's good to see you excited about something. But Rhonda's right. Maybe hold off on getting too optimistic until we actually find the little guy."

"After the past couple of days of crushing disappointment, I'm going to allow myself the luxury of a bit of optimism. We'll find that little fucker all right. And when we do, we know how to coerce him into rolling these –" Frank's face turned pale.

"What is it, Frank?" asked Stacy. He was frozen with his hand over his pants pocket. She thought he might be having a stroke. "Frank, what's wrong?"

Frank seemed to snap out of a trance, smiled to himself, then took a long swig from his glass. "Remember when you asked me if there was anything Tim could do that would surprise me?"

Stacy had a strong feeling that she wasn't going to like what Frank was about to say. "Yes..."

"The drow."

"Who?"

"The dark elf who came in here earlier to get Tim and Katherine's character sheets."

"What about him?"

"He wasn't here to get the character sheets. He picked my pocket." Frank climbed up to stand on top of his table and patted his empty pocket. "They're gone."

Rhonda gasped. "You don't mean..."

Frank hurled his glass down on the table, where it shattered in an explosion of beer and shards. "They're gone! They're fucking gone!"

Bodies began to groan and rise from the floor.

"Dude," said Cooper. "What the fuck? Is it morning already?"

"I'll tell you what the fuck," said Frank. "Your little shithead friend stole my dice."

The crowd on the floor became suddenly much more awake. Groans gave way to angry murmurs.

"Calm down, everyone," said Julian, apparently out of his trance. "Let's get a clearer picture of what we're actually deal–"

"Shove your Diplomacy up your ass, Julian," said Frank. He looked like he wanted something else to throw, balling his fists up in frustration. "Tim's as good as dead, and so is anyone who gets in my way."

Julian shut his mouth. Frank's warning was obviously intended for those closest to Tim.

"What about the other halfling?" asked Tony the Elf, not bothered in the least by Frank's sudden authoritarian takeover. "Shall we put that plan on hold for now?"

Frank shook his head. "I'll get someone else on it. You go after Tim. Check out the pubs in the Lantern District. Take Cooper with you."

Tony the Elf's face looked like the doctor just told him his father didn't survive the surgery. "Come on, Frank. Anyone but –"

"NOW!" Frank stomped on a piece of his broken glass, crushing it into the table.

Stacy stood up and strapped on her sword. "Julian and I will ask around at some of the seedier inns near Eastgate."

Frank regained his composure and scratched the back of his head. "I don't know. Considering Tim's feelings for you, we might be able to use you to lure him into a trap."

"I'm done being used as bait, Frank. That's how I wound up here in the first place. I was paying you a courtesy by informing you of my intentions. I wasn't asking permission."

CHAPTER 3

"It's weird," said Katherine, switching focus between her bleeding hand and various blood smears around the tavern.

SMASH

Another bottle of liquor exploded against the wall. Tim had been standing on the bar throwing them since shortly after he'd killed Morty. Katherine sensed he was upset about something.

"You don't realize how many things you actually touch until you start bleeding from the hands." Katherine hiccoughed, re-calibrated her train of thought, and continued. "For example, that chair over there. I don't even remember going –"

SMASH

"Hey! Are you listening to me?"

"No," said Tim.

Katherine grabbed the nearest thing she could throw, a blood-caked shot glass, and hurled it at her brother. She missed pretty wildly, but not so much that he didn't notice.

"What the fuck was that for?"

"For being an asshole. I was just trying to cheer you up."

Tim looked at her, then at the bottle in his hand, then at her again. "Can you not see I'm in the middle of something?" He threw the bottle against the hearth, causing an explosion of shimmering glass shards, and leaving a purple stain running down the stone.

"I'm pretty drunk," Katherine admitted. "But it looks like you're just throwing shit against the wall."

"I'm prepping this place to burn. We need to cover our tracks."

SMASH

"Well don't smash all of it."

"I've packed as much of the best shit as I could into our bags already."

"The upstairs rooms are empty," said Tanner, hurrying down the stairs. He was wearing a thick hide traveling cloak that Katherine was sure he hadn't come in here with.

Katherine downed two of the shot glasses least murky with blood, which was ironic considering that she'd been a vampire only a few short days ago. It was also weird that she was able to get so shitfaced on beer so quickly. Going without for a while really did a number on her tolerance. Or maybe it had something to do with all the blood loss. She wanted nachos.

"Katherine," said Tim. "Get Butterballs ready to go. We need everyone at the front door when we set this place alight."

"Butterbean!" Katherine called out in a random direction.

Butterbean barked. He'd been right there beside her the whole time. The fur on his face and neck were red and sticky with blood, like he'd been going down on a –

Ew, no. Stop that train of thought at the next station please. I'm getting off here.

Still, this wolf was in dire need of a bath.

"I don't want to tell you how to go about your business," said Tanner. "But could you remind me why we're burning this tavern to the ground?"

SMASH

Tim grabbed another of the decreasing supply of liquor bottles from one of the shelves behind the bar. "This creates confusion. If we just ditched this place with the dead minotaur owner on the floor, there will be questions asked. Not a lot of people saw you or me, but Katherine would be fucked."

"And how is adding arson to her list of crimes supposed to help her?"

"Fires happen. Who's to say Morty here didn't have a little too much to drink, knock over a candle when he passed out, and succumb to a painless carbon monoxide-induced death while the tavern burned down around him?"

Tanner thought for a moment. "What's carbon monoxide?"

"It's the shit that's in smoke that makes you dead. Any more questions?"

"The fire could explain the dead minotaur. But what explains the fire? Between all the broken bottles along the base of the walls and the empty till, this looks to me like a clear case of burglary, murder, and arson."

Tim bit his lower lip like he'd forgotten something. "I didn't empty the till."

"I did," said Tanner.

Katherine took another shot and threw the empty glass against the wall. Why not at this point?

"We could sweep up the glass," said Tim. "And Morty could have emptied the till before he started drinking."

"I'm just thinking out loud here," said Tanner. "Couldn't we just bury the body somewhere like normal people? Maybe he got called away by some sort of family emergency. We clean the place up a bit, and no one would immediately leap to thoughts of foul play. By the time his absence grows suspicious, we'll all be the hazy recollections of a few drunks."

"Where would we bury him? How would we get him there? He's eight hundred fucking pounds of man-cow."

"We could chop him up."

Tim grabbed another bottle. "That would take forever. We'd likely be caught in the middle of the process."

A thought bubbled up to the surface of Katherine's boozy mind. "Oh, I know! We could drag him down to the secret room that leads into the sewer and let the dire rats eat him."

Tim stopped his arm half-cocked. "What secret room?"

"The one Morty showed me when you were hogging the bathroom for so long."

"It wasn't that long."

Tanner frowned. "It was pretty long."

"I'm so fucking sorry!" said Tim. "I didn't realize there was a goddamn line of you waiting outside the door. Griffon gumbo was a lot easier going in than coming out, okay?" He looked at Katherine. "Why didn't you mention this 'secret room' before?"

Katherine shrugged. "Nobody else was waiting to use the bathroom."

"Jesus, Kat. I meant as a way of getting rid of the body."

"I didn't know we were brainstorming."

Tim uncorked the bottle he was holding and took a drink. "That's a much safer plan. We'll have to do a little cleaning, but it should give us plenty of time to –"

"Fuck!" said Tanner.

"Hey! You keep your dirty little dick away from me and my sister, hear?"

The room suddenly got a lot brighter. Katherine shielded her eyes. "Did somebody pull up the shades? Wait, is it morning already?"

"Shit!" cried Tim. "Everybody get on the floor!"

Katherine noticed flames reaching from the floor to the ceiling. "Oh hey, the room's on fire. Thank god. I thought I'd blacked out at the bar."

Tim tugged on her jeans. "Get down here!"

Katherine joined Tim and Tanner on the floor. She glance back and forth between them. "What are we doing?"

"Marine crawl to the front door."

Tanner shook his head. "No good. It's more on fire than anywhere else."

Tim frowned. "That makes sense. I concentrated most of my effort there."

"Why would you concentrate most of your effort on our only way out?"

"I wasn't planning on lighting this shit up until we were outside. I was going to toss in a torch after we'd left, and I wanted to make sure it got a good start. How the hell did it already start anyway?"

Tanner jerked his head back. "It fanned out from the hearth. Some liquor must have seeped in and caught an ember."

"That's some high-octane shit," said Katherine. "Did you pack any of that in our bags?"

Tim nodded. "Try not to catch on fire."

Tanner cleared his throat. "You mentioned something about a secret room?"

Katherine started crawling to the back of the tavern, which was also on fire, but less so than the front. "It's behind one of these sections of wall."

"This one here," sad Tanner, staring up at smoke seeping out through a crack near the ceiling. Grabbing a non-burning section of the right side of the panel, he slid it aside to reveal a wooden staircase leading down into darkness. The air was musty and smelled faintly of sewage, but at least it was relatively free of smoke. "Ladies first?"

Katherine and Butterbean led the way down the stairs. The darkness subsided after the curve of the stairs revealed the secret room, which had a glowing stone hanging from the ceiling.

Tim sat in a corner and pulled out a bottle he'd salvaged from behind the bar. "So we hole up here until the fire dies down, then make a break for it?"

Tanner shook his head as he examined the walls. "Bad idea. This room will only remain a secret for as long as it takes for the rest of the building to burn away. We're not hiding. We're escaping."

"Through the sewer?"

"Yes."

"The dire rat infested sewer?"

Tanner removed his cloak and started folding it. "I'm not any more excited about it than you are. It'll be next to impossible to keep this from getting ruined."

"Who gives a shit about your cloak?" asked Tim.

"It's a nice cloak," said Katherine. "It looks good on you."

Tanner smiled at Katherine. "Thank you. It's a little flashier than what I'd normally wear, but it was worth taking Murkwort for everything he had on him. Greedy old wizard would have given me his undergarments as well if I'd pressed him a little more." He removed a fancy leather scroll tube, a jewel-hilted dagger, two heavily-laden coin pouches, and a few more innocuous items out of his bag before carefully stuffing his cloak into the bottom.

"Who's Murkwort?" asked Tim. "Where did you get all this shit?"

"He's one of my connections in town. I like him because he doesn't ask questions, and he likes me because I'm usually in a hurry to dump my stolen loot. He thinks he's taking advantage of me, but I recognize it for what it is. The cost of doing business in the industry I'm in."

"And what industry is that?" asked Katherine.

"Thieving."

Katherine shrugged. "I guess it's got more potential than fried chicken."

"If you know what you're doing. The only reason the industry remains so robust is because too many would-be master thieves fall into the same traps time and time again."

"What traps?" asked Katherine. Being fugitives, she thought it a good idea to take whatever kind of wisdom anyone could offer. She hoped Tim was paying attention.

"The most common are greed and a lack of self-awareness as to how skilled a thief you are. It's better to steal a single pie to keep you going another day than it is to get caught trying to steal the king's crown."

"It's probably not so easy to unload a king's crown anyway," said Katherine.

"You make an excellent point, and one which many an amateur thief would have done well to know earlier in their short-lived careers."

"What's that?"

"Keep things moving. Do you know how most thieves get caught?"

"They talk too much?" asked Tim. Katherine was glad he was paying attention, even if it was just to be a dick.

Tanner smiled at Tim. "In a manner of speaking." He picked up the ornate dagger. "Take this dagger."

Tim's eyes lit up with sudden interest. "Okay."

"As an example."

Tim's interest turned back to his bottle. "Oh."

Tanner shifted his attention to Katherine. "As you can see, the craftsmanship is exquisite, the jewels are authentic, and..." He pulled the dagger slightly out of its sheath, exposing an inch of blade, which glowed with faint purple light. "It's imbued with magic."

"It's beautiful," said Katherine. She glanced over at her brother. His attention was once again on the dagger.

Tanner pushed the dagger back into the sheath, extinguishing the glow. "Now imagine you were to steal this from me."

"One step ahead of you, buddy," said Tim.

"Now let's say you take it to a fence who specializes in exotic weaponry. How much would you demand for such a fine piece as this?"

Katherine had no idea. She threw out a random figure. "Five hundred bucks?"

Tanner's smile faltered briefly. "In this world you claim to come from, you still barter in wildlife? How very quaint. But I was referring to a monetary value."

"It would depend on the magical enchantment," said Tim.

"Wrong."

"I give up," said Katherine. "How much?"

"Whatever you're offered."

Tim pulled the bottle away from his lips long enough to say, "Fuck that."

"That's just the kind of thinking that will land you in a cell for the rest of your life."

"So if some asshole offers me five silver pieces, I'm just supposed to bend over and take it?"

"If that happens, you've failed long before then. You need to cultivate relationships, establish something akin to trust, prove yourself to be a discrete supplier of quality merchandise. A quality fence is one who knows and understands the risks we all go through, and who will offer you enough to keep you coming back. Too much haggling, too much back-and-forth between fences trying to squeeze every last copper piece out of the highest bidder, and you'll only make yourself known as a pain in the ass whom nobody wants to deal with."

"So wait," Katherine had another question bubbling to the top. "The cloak, the scrolls, the magic dagger. Did this Murkwort guy extend you a line of credit for the money you were going to swipe from Morty's till?"

"No," said Tanner. "While I was out, I had no idea we would be engaging in murder, theft, and arson. This all came from whatever was in the sack I nicked off the gnome."

"Frank?" asked Tim.

"I believe so."

"Good. Fuck that guy."

Katherine grew cold with apprehension. She took a bottle out of her bag to help combat some sobering thoughts which were now occurring to her. "What sack, exactly?"

Tanner shrugged. "I don't know what they were. Some kind of black gemstones with numbers etched into them. They glowed red in the center, so I figured they were magical. Murkwort deals in magical oddities, so I thought he might be interested." He looked at Tim as if to continue his lesson. "Now maybe I might have been able to get a better offer somewhere else, but in the long run, nurturing my relationship with –"

"Tanner," said Katherine. "Please shut the fuck up for a minute."

The crackle of flames from above filled the brief silence

that followed.

"What's wrong with you, Kat?" asked Tim. "You're pale as shit. Did the Jesus blood wear off? Are you vamping out again?"

"Black gemstones."

"That's right. I was paying attention, just like you told me. It's a lot easier when he's talking about ripping Frank off."

"Can you think of nothing that Frank might have been carrying on his person that someone might mistake for black gemstones with numbers etched into them?"

It took a minute, but Tim's wandering gaze went to razor sharp focus.

"Oh fuck."

Katherine nodded. "Uh huh."

"They're going to think I..."

"Uh huh."

"I'm sorry," said Tanner. "I can't help but feel like I'm missing something. What seems to be the –"

A crash sounded from above. Katherine hoped that it was just the building collapsing, but the heavy footsteps that followed snuffed that hope right out.

"Morty? Morty!" It was Tony the Elf. He had a lot more anguish in his voice than Tim felt the death of an NPC warranted. "That little son of a bitch killed Morty!"

"Why did he immediately jump to that conclusion?" asked Tim. "I mean, it's true, but given the data that –"

A dog started barking wildly, very close to the top of the staircase. Butterbean growled and barked back before Katherine could wrap her arm around his muzzle.

"Shit!" said Katherine. "Do you think they heard –" Tim snatched the bottle out of her hand and ran up the stairs. "Hey, what are you doing?"

Tim walked backwards down the stairs dumping the contents of his own bottle and Katherine's in front of him. "What does it look like I'm doing? I'm setting the stairs on fire."

"Is that your answer to everything?"

When Tim reached the bottom, he hurled both bottles into the stairs and pulled a set of two bars out of his bag and started clanking them together. They produced sparks, but not enough to ignite the staircase.

"There's no time for that," said Tanner, standing next to Tim, his hand on the lever which made the magical floor disappear, effectively "flushing" the secret room into the sewer. "We have to go now!"

The din of flames and barking suddenly got louder. The secret door was sliding open.

A rush of heat blew back Katherine's hair as the sudden increase in the intensity of light nearly blinded her. The shifting air had brought the flames to the stairwell.

Tim packed up his flint and steel. "That was easier than I'd expected."

"Tim?" a gruff piggy voice called down through the flames.

"Cooper?" Tim called back.

"They just want the dice back, man. Don't make this worse than it is."

"I don't have the dice!"

"Bullshit! That black dude you left with grabbed Frank's sack." Cooper snorted at what he'd just said. Of course he did.

"I don't know what you're talking about."

That was interesting. Tim had moved from half truths to bald-faced lies.

"Give us the dice, Tim," Tony the Elf shouted through the crackle of flame and billowing smoke in the stairwell. "Or I'm going to... I'm going to kill Cooper."

Cooper snorted. "The fuck you are. Here, say that again with a mouthful of my balls. I'll kick your scrawny elven – Oh, shit. Right. Sorry. Help me, Tim! He's totally going to kill me. He gained, like, ten levels yesterday."

Katherine raised her eyebrows at Tim. "Can we go now?"

Tim nodded, then looked up at Tanner. "Flush us."

Tanner pulled down hard on the lever, and a large rectangular area of the secret room's floor faded until it disappeared entirely, revealing a stagnant river of liquid filth below. Katherine tried to brace herself for the smell, but it was overpowering.

"I can't go down there," said Tim. His eyes were wide with terror.

"What's wrong now?" asked Katherine.

"It's a dire rat."

Katherine followed Tim's gaze. There was indeed one of those giant-ass rats lurking in the river of sludge like a hungry crocodile waiting for some fresh meat. But considering all they'd been through, a big rat shouldn't have been all that frightening.

"Don't be such a little bitch. It's just a rat. Watch, I'll take care of it." She leaped down into the sludge, landing harder than she'd expected, but managing to keep her balance.

Butterbean jumped in after her and growled at the rat.

The rat ignored the wolf and hissed at Katherine threateningly, but she shut it up with a good solid kick to the face. While it was distracted, she grabbed it by the forelegs, slammed it against the wall, and lunged at its throat with her mouth, stopping just short of biting into it.

"Jesus, I can't believe I almost did that. That would have been so fucking gross." Katherine shook the thought out of her mind, kept the rat pinned to the wall with one hand, and punched it in the head until its blood and brains started seeping down the ancient brickwork of the wall. It wasn't hard, exactly, but more of a workout than she'd been prepared for. More shit-air invaded her lungs as she breathed heavily and thought about investing in a weapon.

She dropped the rat carcass and smiled up at her little brother. "Better now?"

Tim shook his head, then looked at his feet as clear water and broken pieces of dishes and cutlery flowed past them into the sewer.

"Tim!" said Katherine. "They're putting out the stair fire. You have to come down here right fucking now!"

Tim continued shaking his head. "I just can't. I've got a thing about rats. I – FUCK!"

Tanner scooped up Tim and jumped down into the sewer. The ceiling materialized above them, blocking out all the light.

"I can't see! I can't see! I can't see!" Tim sounded like an accidentally tripped car alarm at a funeral. It was embarrassing.

"Take it easy," said Tanner. It was a gentler approach than the 'slap the shit out of him until he calms the fuck down' approach that Katherine had just been about to employ.

Tim's freak-out session was interrupted by a sound like a snapping tree branch, and a faint light radiated from a stick in Tanner's hand.

Tim reined in his shit and got his breathing under control.

"Would you feel better if you held the tindertwig?"

For once, Tim didn't seem to mind being treated like a toddler. He nodded enthusiastically.

"We need to move," said Katherine. "They'll be right behind us."

Tanner smiled at her. "I don't think so." He held up a rod that had been floating next to him in the sewage.

"What the hell is that?" asked Tim, his voice just about back to normal.

"It's the lever that opens the floor."

CHAPTER 4

Julian nearly had to jog to keep up with Stacy's pace. He had no idea where they were going, but she seemed to be in a hell of a hurry to get there.

"Can you slow down a bit?" He determinedly avoided looking directly at several seedy-looking characters who were staring at them, then picked up to an actual jog in order to get close enough to whisper. "This doesn't appear to be the friendliest of neighborhoods."

Stacy slowed down, but just barely. "If you're hunting rats, you look in the sewer."

"Is that, like, some down home Mississippi wisdom?"

"I don't think so. I just made it up."

"It's very clever."

Stacy stopped in her tracks and spun around to look at him. "Something on your mind, Julian?"

Shit. She was onto his Diplomacy attempt, and she didn't seem any less ready to stab someone.

At the risk of making himself an even better candidate, Julian cleared his throat and said what he'd been meaning to say since they left the Whore's Head.

"I'm not going to help you kill Tim."

Stacy blew her hair out of her eyes and laughed mirthlessly. "You and I are that little shit stain's best chance at surviving."

"But you told Frank –"

"I've spent the past couple of days cozying up to Frank and talking shit about Tim. He thinks of me as part of his inner circle. You, on the other hand, he sees as too close to Tim."

"I barely knew him before we –"

"It doesn't matter. Consider it from Frank's perspective. You guys all came in together. Frank's in an us-vs.-them frame of mind right now, and you're them. Do you remember how he insisted that Tony the Elf bring Cooper along? He needs one of you to help find Tim, and he needs one of us to keep you in line."

"That's very insightful."

"I'm wise as shit."

"You seemed pretty pissed off too. At least as much as Frank."

"I am. Tim's a selfish lowlife piece of shit, but that's not justification for murder."

Julian breathed out a long sigh.

"Have you soiled yourself, sir?" asked Ravenus, flapping down to perch atop Julian's quarterstaff.

"What? No!" Julian looked down at his crotch for a wet spot. There wasn't one. "Why would you ask that?"

"I sensed a sudden surge of relief."

Though the empathic link he shared with his familiar had saved their asses on more than one occasion, Julian sometimes wished it came with a toggle switch.

"We need information," said Stacy. "And for that, we need money. How much have you got on you?" She held out an open hand like she expected him to dump out his coin bag in full view of all the leering eyes around them. "Just the gold and platinum. Don't bother with any small change."

Julian leaned toward her and whispered, "Maybe we should be a little more discreet?"

Stacy glanced around. "You're right." She grabbed him by the shoulder and pivoted him toward a dark alley. "In there. Hurry up."

Stumbling over piles of rubbish and through puddles of what smelled like liquor which had already been enjoyed and expelled through various orifices, Julian wondered if the alley was really the safer option. He spotted something cylindrical and furry poking out from under a mildew-blackened sheet of canvas which he hoped was a rolled up and discarded shag carpet.

The sense of gluttonous ecstasy he felt when Ravenus flew ahead and tore into it with beak and talon confirmed what he was pretending not to already know. It was some poor creature's leg.

"Okay, I think we've gone far en–" When he turned around, Stacy was nowhere to be seen. The faint light from the street looked a lot further away than he was comfortable with. "Stacy?"

"Looks like she ditched you, friend." The voice had a forced air of confidence to it, like the speaker was deliberately trying to use his Intimidation skill. It was working. "Let's hope, for your sake, that she didn't snag that coin purse of yours."

A small, wiry humanoid figure stepped out from the shadows, still barely visible but for the two blades he wielded. Each was about the length of a shortsword, but they were two completely different styles of terrifying. The blade in his left hand was round and narrow, like a miniature lance, or a giant novelty icepick. The blade in his right hand was something between a sword and a sickle, like an incompletely flattened question mark, sharpened on the inner curve.

How these two blades might be used to complement one another was immediately obvious to Julian. You pin your subject to the wall with the former, and casually hack off his limbs with the latter. Whether or not that would work in practice, the mere suggestion was extremely effective.

Julian sensed Ravenus was alert and ready to strike.

"Take it easy," said Julian, hoping that his message was received by both his familiar and his mugger. He reached under his serape like Enzo the Baker.

"That's it. Pull it out and toss it here."

Well, shit. Julian's attempt at Intimidate was interpreted as unconditional surrender. This guy just assumed he was reaching for his coin bag.

Julian weighed his options. As usual, it came down to casting a Magic Missile, whacking a guy with a stick, or summoning a horse and hoping for the best. His hand found the coin bag. If this guy was just after money, Julian could just dump the bag and make a run for it. He wasn't carrying a fortune, but what he was carrying didn't belong just to him. He'd helped bring down a red dragon only a few days ago. Was he really going to throw his friends' money at some lowly street thug? He took a step back to keep his options open for a few more seconds.

"You don't want to go that way," said the mugger, taking a larger step forward than Julian's step backward. "That way's dangerous." His cold grey eyes briefly focused on something about as far behind Julian as the sound of heavy boots stomping through the trash.

Keeping his hand under his serape, Julian took a quick glance to his rear. A second mugger was approaching, his means of intimidation more straightforward than his sneaky companion's. Built like five sides of beef held together by a leather diaper, the brute made no effort to hide himself or the weapon he brandished in front of him, which appeared to have been crafted from half a telephone pole and some railroad spikes.

Throwing money on the ground was looking more and more like the best option available. He'd still need a way to get around this guy though. No... not around. Through.

Julian pulled out his money pouch and threw it into the air. "Come and get it, motherfuckers!"

The smaller mugger's greedy eyes followed the shimmering fountain of copper and silver coins.

"Horse!" Julian shouted. His skill with this spell had improved to the point where he could anticipate where the beast would show up with such accuracy that he was able to get one foot in the stirrup as it materialized. He'd barely swung himself up onto the horse when it vanished from between his legs.

The next thing he knew, he was on the ground, staring at

the heavy-bladed throwing knife Stacy had helped herself to from the cellar of the Whore's Head Inn. The blade was slick with horse blood. He looked up.

His would-be mugger looked decidedly less confident with Stacy standing behind him, a fistful of his hair in her left hand, and the edge of her sword at his throat.

"Drop your weapons," said Stacy.

The straight pointy blade and the long curved blade clanged against the alley floor simultaneously.

Julian picked up Stacy's throwing knife. "You appear to have dropped one of your weapons as well, right into my horse's throat."

"That was meant for him." Stacy nodded past Julian.

Julian turned around just in time to see the big mugger fleeing around a corner at the other side of the alley. "You missed."

"How was I supposed to know you were going to summon a goddamn horse?"

"I always summon a horse!"

"I thought the coins were supposed to be the distraction."

"They were."

"So what was the horse for?"

"I didn't know we were working together. All I knew was that you ditched me in an alley with a couple of muggers."

"I didn't ditch you. I was hiding, waiting for you to provide a distraction."

"How was I supposed to know that? You just disappeared without telling me anything."

Stacy shrugged. "You're too nervous and expressive. You would've blown my cover."

The mugger cleared his throat. "Are we done here?" Stacy let go of his hair and guided his neck to the wall like it was an extension of her sword. "We're done when I get some information out of you. Now are you going to spill your guts, or am I going to do it for you?"

"Whoa, hey! No need for that. Just tell me what it is you

want to know?"

"Who are you working for?"

"What makes you think I'm working for someone?"

Stacy raised the tip of the blade up to where his lower jaw met his neck. There wasn't much bone to block the path from there to his brain.

"The Rat Bastards."

"Who?" Stacy pulled the blade back about a centimeter.

"I'm not working for them yet. I'm still trying to pass the initiation. It involves a sizable donation to the guild as well as a finger from whomever it was stolen from."

"Wait," said Julian. "You were going to cut off my finger?"

"Of course not."

"Don't you of course not me! You needed a finger, and I was your mark. You were totally going to cut off my finger."

"Were you going to cut off his finger?" asked Stacy.

"No!"

Stacy shrugged. "I believe him."

Julian felt like his stomach had been kicked in the nuts. "Why?"

"I don't know." Stacy pressed the blade into the mugger's neck again. "Why do I believe you?"

"I swear by the gods!" He sounded sincere enough, but anyone could sound sincere with a sword at their throat. "Check my bag. I've already got a finger."

Julian had to admit, that would be a pretty lousy bluff, what with it being immediately verifiable.

Stacy eased up again, leaving a second bleeding prick in his neck. "Where did you get the finger?"

"I know a guy at the mortuary. I'm still working on the sizable donation part."

That reminded Julian that all of his and his friends' money was still scattered on the ground. He started picking up coins and putting them back in his pouch.

"How much is a sizable donation?" asked Stacy.

"I don't know. They leave that intentionally ambiguous."

"What were you aiming for?"

"My goal was ten gold pieces. That sounds okay, right? I mean, that and a finger."

Stacy nodded slowly. "If I wanted to be a Rat Bastard, who would I need to talk to?"

"Ask for Dolazar at the souvenir shop in Shallow Grave."

Julian knew that place. He stopped picking loose change out of the filth and stood up. "Shallow Grave? Isn't that kind of a... um... rough neighborhood? Who buys souvenirs in Shallow Grave?"

Stacy and the mugger both gave him a 'What the fuck is wrong with you?' look.

"Nobody buys souvenirs there," said the mugger. "It's a front."

Julian wanted to ask how a front was supposed to work if there was no legitimate commerce taking place, but he thought it might earn him even harsher looks. He squatted back down to search for glimmers of copper and silver amid the piles of trash.

"Ask around," said the mugger. "You can usually find him in the early afternoon."

Stacy pulled the blade away from his neck. "Leave your bag. Get out of here."

His grip tightened on the shoulder strap of his satchel. "Show some mercy, huh? Everything I own is in this bag."

"From what you've already told me, that amounts to less than ten gold pieces."

"And a finger," added Julian. "At least that shouldn't be too hard to replace. There should be nine more where that one came from."

"What about my weapons?" He was talking directly to Stacy, not even glancing Julian's way. "A guy's gotta make a living."

"You're lucky I'm letting you live," said Stacy. "You tried to steal from my man."

She couldn't have said 'friend'? Even 'boyfriend' would have been okay. 'My man' made it sound ironically emasculating. The mugger must have thought so too, because he stifled a laugh.

Julian stood up. "I was actually doing fine on my own."

The mugger dropped his bag at Stacy's feet and backed away. "Here, take it. If Dolazar doesn't like the finger, you can offer him the set of elf balls you keep in your own bag."

CHAPTER 5

A disconcertingly banal electric chime sounded as the door opened. A short pointy-eared monster walked through, tightening the rope that held up his khaki shorts.

"Shaggy!" The young ponytailed woman behind the counter glared at the creature, her eyes burning in the shadow of her Arby's cap brim.

The monster looked up at her as innocently as its yellow eyes could manage.

The woman – Jennifer, according to the plastic tag pinned to her shirt – brandished neither weapon nor magic. She was armed only with the air of someone not to be fucked with. "Did you wash your hands?"

"I..." The creature looked at the floor.

"Do you want to be a fry cook for the rest of your life?"

"No, ma'am."

"Fred and Velma are already on registers. Look at their hands."

Two similar creatures who were almost certainly not born with the names Fred and Velma displayed their green, clawed hands above the counter. Clean as they may have been, Dave didn't relish the thought of them having touched the food he was eating.

"Yes, ma'am," said Shaggy.

"Now get your little goblin ass back in there and use soap like I showed you."

"Yes, ma'am." The chime sounded again as Shaggy hurried out the door.

"And tuck in your shirt!" Jennifer called after him. "This

isn't Hardee's."

Dave swallowed his mouthful of roast beef sandwich. "She seems to be adjusting well to being dragged into a fantasy world against her will."

"Hmph," said Professor Goosewaddle. "She ought to be, with what I'm paying her." The wrinkles in his forehead deepened between his fluffy white eyebrows. "The girl is robbing me blind, but she runs a tight ship."

"She certainly has a way with the goblins," said Murkwort, an associate of Professor Goosewaddle's who had popped in for a visit and an order of curly fries. He was human, but clearly from this world. He had a long forked beard, one side white and the other side black with streaks of grey. His black cloak covered his feet and dragged behind him when he walked, giving his lower half the appearance of a serpent or slug.

"You should see what she has me paying them! It's preposterous."

Murkwort grinned, showing off his platinum and gold-plated teeth. "You pay goblins, with coin?"

"More than I ever got paid as an apprentice wizard." Professor Goosewaddle shrugged. "Incentive, she calls it."

"Would it not be more... incentivous... to throw one of them into the boiling potato oil as an example to the rest?"

"You are truly a disgusting human being," said Rhonda, applying Horsey Sauce to her open sandwich.

Murkwort's eyebrows, colored identically to the forks in his beard, raised as the sides of his mouth drooped.

"Naturally, I'd replace the oil before I resumed cooking. I would have thought that much was obvious."

Dave had to agree that Murkwort wasn't the most pleasant person in the world to listen to. Even when he wasn't speaking openly of throwing another living creature into a fryer, he was boastful and mildly obnoxious.

Even Professor Goosewaddle seemed to be put off by him. Dave caught him rolling his eyes as his guest bragged about getting twenty percent higher than market value for a scroll of Whispering Wind which included a musical background with the message. And as much as the professor normally enjoyed a good chat, his participation in the conversation since Murkwort had arrived had mostly been limited to short to-the-point answers to Murkwort's direct questions, his little rant about having to pay goblins notwithstanding. But Dave sensed that Professor Goosewaddle just wanted to vent, even if it involved talking to someone he desperately wanted to leave.

For all of Murkwort's faults, at least he wasn't boring. Dave hadn't been thrilled to be partnered with Rhonda, even if the assignment was as simple as hanging out at Arby's and waiting for Tim to show up. She was a prickly one, who seemed to be constantly lying in wait for someone to say something she could be offended by. Trying to have a casual conversation with her was like taking a stroll through a minefield.

Shaggy hurried back in through the door, quickly tucked in his shirt, and ran to the back of the restaurant.

A few seconds later, Jennifer re-emerged. "Paul!"

The other fish-out-of-water human employee, who had recently gone on break, looked up from his salad. "What?"

Jennifer crossed her arms and gave him the same look she'd used to bring Shaggy in line.

Paul put down his fork. "Yes, ma'am?" His voice had an unmistakable trace of bitterness.

"There's something called a shocker lizard drinking out of the toilet in the men's room. Go take care of that, would you?" The hint of smug satisfaction in her voice seemed to complement the bitterness in his. Dave sensed a recent turning of tables in their professional relationship.

"But I don't even know what that is!"

"Neither do I. Maybe bring a mop."

"Jennifer," Paul pleaded.

"Excuse me?"

Paul looked at the floor. "Miss Hutchinson."

Jennifer smiled and nodded for him to continue.

"This is a grievous abuse of authority."

"Like making someone come into work on the day of her grandfather's funeral?"

Dave and Rhonda glanced at each other and sank lower into their booth.

"I was understaffed!" said Paul. "Ronnie and Thomas both called in –"

"I've got a stack of applications in my office, Paul. A bunch of folks would love to replace you as assistant manager. People with more brains, more charm, more legs. If you want to test the job market out there," She at the window to a world outside of Arby's, full of demons and vampires and dragons. "then by all means –"

"Fine, I'm going. I'm going."

"I'm afraid I must be off as well," said Murkwort. "I have some very important business to attend to in the Crescent Shadow."

Professor Goosewaddle closed his eyes. "Yes, you've mentioned that."

"What do I owe you for the coiled potatoes?"

"Keep your money. You are my guest here, not a customer."

Dave was a little miffed that he didn't qualify for guest status.

"Don't be silly," said Murkwort. "You need something to pay the goblins with, after all." He reached out and placed five shiny platinum coins on the table.

"You are very generous, but that's far too much."

Murkwort flashed his shiny metallic grin again. "Worry not about me, old friend. I expect to come into a sizable amount of money very soon."

"Best of luck with that."

"I've recently acquired some valuable merchandise, you see."

"Very nice."

Murkwort patted a bulge on his hip. "Some really high-end stuff."

Professor Goosewaddle appeared to be struggling to find an alternate response to politely express his disinterest. "Okay."

"It's a bit of a secret, which is why I haven't spoken of it in any more detail."

"Oh?" said the professor. "I assumed it was because I hadn't asked." He gave Dave and Rhonda a quick wink.

Murkwort shuffled out of the booth and stood. The bottom of his robe pooled around his feet like spilled ink. "Fare thee well, old friend. Best of fortune with your little restaurant. May it work out better for you than your previous business ventures."

With his left index finger, he traced a circular pattern in his right palm. A funnel cloud of swirling green vapor grew out of his hand, and soon obscured his whole being. When the storm calmed and the vapor cloud dissipated, Murkwort was gone.

Professor Goosewaddle let out a long sigh. "I really don't like that guy."

Blue light flashed in the windows, accompanied by a sound like someone shoving a fork in a wall socket. Three pulses over the course of two seconds, then darkness and silence resumed.

Jennifer gawked at the window, her eyes wide and panicked.

"Son of a bitch!" Paul shouted from outside.

Jennifer exhaled, then turned her attention back to the employee scheduling whiteboard.

CHAPTER 6

"Please tell me that was your stomach," said Tim.

Katherine nodded and rubbed her belly. The sewer walls had amplified the sound so much that it might have been an angry bear. "I'm starving. Do you remember where that Arby's is?"

"Sure. Only problem is that I don't know where we are." Tim held Tanner's magical dagger in front of him as far as his little arm could stretch. Since the light from the tindertwig had gone out, the magical glow from the dagger was their only source of light. He supposed that was better than no light at all, but he could probably piss farther than he could see.

"How can you two think about food?" asked Tanner. "Do you not know what we're trudging through?"

"I know all too well," said Katherine. "I've thrown up, like, five times already, and I was completely empty after the second. I'm not saying I want to have a picnic down here. I want to get the fuck out of here, rinse as much shit off of me as I can, and fill my stomach with some crappy fast food."

"We've been walking forever." Tim knew he sounded whiny, but he was waist deep in waste, and felt entitled to a little whining. "We should be far enough away from the Piss Bucket by now. Let's climb out through one of these manholes."

Tanner looked up at the manhole he was standing directly under. "And how do you propose we get up there?"

"I don't know. We could stand on each others' shoulders or some shit."

Tanner resumed walking. "There's no point wasting that kind of time until we find a cover that isn't magically sealed shut." When faced with the option of continuing ahead and turning right along a perpendicular tunnel, he turned right without hesitation. "The king had all the covers magically sealed after the shenanigans which brought about the current state of your former neighborhood of residence."

"Do you know where we're going?" asked Katherine.

"Not in the slightest." Tanner paused briefly under a manhole, then continued walking.

"You seem to be very confident in your direction."

Tim agreed that Tanner was exuding a great deal of confidence for someone who had led them to three dead ends already.

"I'm merely keeping to the right," said Tanner. "It's the simplest method of covering the most ground in the shortest amount of time when lost in a labyrinth, provided you're not continuously walking in a circle."

Katherine looked disgustedly at the wall. "How can you be sure we're not?"

"You were kind enough to leave a mark on the wall. If we happen upon a conspicuous smear of rat brains, we'll know it's time to try our luck on the left."

Tim had been playing 3D shooters all his life. He was no stranger to the 'stay to the right' trick. But in this situation, he had what he thought was a better idea. "Wouldn't it be smarter to just continue in one direction until we got to the edge of town and travel along the perimeter until we found the Collapsed Sewer District? Maybe it's not wise to surface that close to the Whore's Head, but at least we know it's open. We could get out of the sewers, keep our heads low, and make for a different part of town."

"That would be a plan worth considering if the sewers weren't, as I've already mentioned, a labyrinth."

"I didn't realize you meant that in the literal sense."

Tanner glanced down at Tim curiously before looking ahead into the pitch black darkness again. "How is it that you've never heard of Mad King Lidon and his twisted sewers?"

"We're not from this world," said Tim. "As we've already mentioned."

"Yes, of course. You're from this other world, where it's perfectly natural for a halfling and half-elf to be brother and sister."

Tim truly didn't give a thimbleful of fuck whether Tanner believed him or not, but he volunteered further information to keep his own mind occupied with something other than walking barefoot through rat-infested shitwater. "Our bodies changed when we arrived. In our world there are no halflings or half-elves. Everyone is human."

"Interesting. Many an ancient king or queen claimed to seek lasting peace through the annihilation of all but their own race. How's it working out for your world?"

"Not great. We just hate each other based on religion and skin color."

"The ignorant masses are easy to control if you give them an easily identifiable enemy to unite against. In the absence of more substantial differences, it's not so far-fetched to think a leader could breed hatred based on something as trivial as –" Tanner stopped in his tracks and looked up at a manhole cover which, to Tim's strained eyes, seemed no different than any of the others they'd passed.

"What is it?" asked Tim.

Tanner squatted to Tim's level and gestured for Katherine to join them. Even Butterbean seemed interested.

Tanner wiped a finger on his cheek and held it in the glow of the dagger. He grinned as a single teardrop shone in the faint light.

Tim sighed. The last thing they needed right now was for their most competent adventurer to start cracking up. He took a deep breath and faced Tanner.

"Listen, man. There's a lot on the line here. We are in some of the deepest shit we've ever been in, both figuratively and literally. We're all counting on you to keep your shit together until we get out of this goddamn sewer."

"What does it look like I'm doing?"

"Grinning and crying," said Tim. "And it's kind of freaking me out."

"What are you..." Tanner looked at his finger. "This isn't mine. It fell from up there." He pointed up to the manhole.

Tim was in no mood to get his hopes up just to have the rug pulled out under him. "I guess that makes it a little less weird. But still, why are you so giddy about having some hobo piss on your face?"

"The seal is broken on this one. That's our way out!"

Butterbean growled and bared his teeth.

Katherine crouched down and hugged him. "Would you prefer a different exit?"

"He's not objecting to the exit," said Tanner. He followed the wolf's gaze beyond the dim magical glow of the dagger, and seemed to be alternately focusing on multiple targets. "We should go. Katherine, sit on my shoulders. Tim, can you climb up the both of us?"

"You bet your ass I can. And I'm about to whether you want me to or not." Tim had a pretty good idea where this sudden sense of urgency was coming from.

Tanner crouched down to allow Katherine to grab his head and hook her legs over his shoulders. When he stood up again, the hisses and squeaks began. They came from every direction. With echoes bouncing off the slippery walls, it was impossible to tell how many there were.

"Fuck," said Tim.

Butterbean waded in a tight circle around Tim and Tanner, looking outward and snarling.

"Are you balanced?" asked Tanner.

"As much as I'm going to be," Katherine replied. "Come on, Tim. Put the dagger away and get your ass up here."

Tim didn't want to extinguish his only source of light. He

thought about holding the dagger between his teeth, pirate style, but he didn't know if the magic would slice his mouth open like the Joker. He could hold the hilt in his mouth, but that seemed kind of blowjobby. He might be able to –

"Let's hurry this up, shall we?" said Tanner. He grabbed Tim by the arms and picked him up. "You're heavier than you look."

"I'm wearing a bag full of booze and pants full of other people's shit."

With some effort, Tanner lifted Tim up to Katherine, who strained to pull him up further by the wrists. Tim caught hold of Katherine's shoulder with his foot and helped her help him the rest of the way up. He wobbled at first, fearing a long and painful drop, but managed to steady himself by grabbing hold of one of the two iron handles on the underside of the manhole cover.

From what he could tell, it opened kind of like a submarine hatch. One side of the cover was attached to hinges, presumably so methheads couldn't steal it and sell it as scrap metal. The part that the handles were attached to had a little give to it. He was able to jiggle it slightly clockwise and counterclockwise. That probably meant he had to turn it one way or the other to unlock it. With a couple of initial test turns, he found that neither way budged easily. He was going to have to put a little muscle into it, but he didn't want to risk tightening it further.

He called down to Tanner, "Do you guys do lefty loosey righty tighty in this world?"

"I don't know what that means!" Tanner's voice sounded strained. "I'd like to remind you that time is a factor here."

Tim needed a better grip. He slid the magical dagger into its sheath on his belt, putting himself back in total darkness. That seemed to embolden the rats; they sounded a bit louder and closer now.

"Tim!" cried Katherine. "Hurry the fuck – AAAHHHH!"

Katherine's shoulders were suddenly no longer supporting Tim's feet. He was hanging by the manhole cover above the squeaks, grunts, growls, and the occasional four-letter word.

Tim convinced himself that continuing to attempt to open this cover was the most productive use of his efforts, rather than an act of extraordinary cowardice. He jerked his body clockwise, then counterclockwise, neither direction getting him anywhere.

Then he found some footholds on the edge of the cover, pulled his feet up, and used the leverage to give the cover a proper turn. He turned the cover counterclockwise as hard as he could. It turned easier than he expected it would, and even went as far as to pull him right out of the sewer. A thick steel spring was attached to the hinge which worked similarly to a mousetrap, making the cover go upright when the lock was released.

"Ha ha!" cried Tim. "It's open!"

"A fine lot of good that does us," said Tanner. He grunted while a rat squealed in agony. "Would it be too much of a bother for you to throw down a rope?"

"I'm working on it!" Tim pulled off his backpack and opened it up on the dark street. He carefully removed liquor bottles until he was able to reach his coil of rope. He tied one end to the hinge of the manhole cover.

"Tim!" Katherine shouted.

Tim looked down into the sewer. Katherine was directly below him, lying on her back with a dire rat on top of her. Her face was barely breaking the surface of the sewage as her efforts were divided between not drowning in shit and keeping the rat from biting her face off.

Tim tied the other end of the rope around his waist. He pulled out the magical dagger, gripped it firmly by the hilt with both of his tiny hands, blade pointed down, and jumped back into the sewer. "Sneak attack, motherfucker!"

The rat hissed and disengaged with Katherine, who sat upright as quickly as the spring-loaded manhole cover had, leaving only about a foot and a half of shitwater to break Tim's fall. He shut his eyes, held his breath, and braced himself for impact.

Pain surged out from his ass bone, up his spine and down his legs. He lay still for a moment, completely submerged, to allow the initial shock to subside. As the explosion of pain settled down to a dull, throbbing ass ache, he reflected that a sneak attack was probably something that was best left unannounced.

The next sudden pain was one he was wholly unprepared for. His left foot burned with the sensation of being swallowed whole by a vagina full of acid-covered barbed hooks. His mouth and eyes opened involuntarily, and his lungs filling with liquid sewage took his attention away from his foot being torn to ribbons by a giant rat.

After a few seconds, the rat stopped tearing his foot off, and someone was holding him up out of the water by his armpits, but he was still blind and choking on shit.

Through the sound of himself hacking and vomiting the rancid water from his lungs, he heard the conversation taking place around him.

"Let him go!" What a fucking dickhole.

"I can't." Please don't leave me down here, Kat.

"I need you." Oh, like you two would have such a rosy future after you talked her into leaving her brother to be eaten by shitrats.

"What about Butterbean?" Wait, what? That's your fucking negotiation?

"That's why I need you." I don't quite know what to make of that.

"Okay, let's go." No, Kat, please! How fucking insecure are you? I'm your goddamn brother!

Tim continued coughing up the shit from his lungs, but when he felt his sister's hands abandon him for the rope, he was ready to succumb to the shitrats. Perhaps that was the fate he deserved.

Something grabbed his wrist and he nearly shit his pants. It was a hand. It placed the hilt of a dagger in Tim's hand.

"Hang on a little longer," said Tanner.

Tim coughed up some more shitwater and tried to stand up and shove the business end of the dagger into Tanner's black heart. Hang on a little longer? What was that if not just dumping salt in the wound? If he was going to die down here, at least he could take this smug bastard with him.

Shit. Bad foot. No he couldn't. Tim fell face first back into the sewage.

Trying hard not to inhale until he was able to push himself back out, he coughed out some splattery bubbles and pushed his palms down hard against the gritty floor. Once his head surfaced, he resumed hacking normally.

"Watch out, Tim!" cried Katherine from street level. "There's one right behind you!"

So it wasn't enough to ditch him down here. She was going to watch until the bitter end, like he was some kind of midget gladiator? That almost made it worth surviving for, just to spite them. His foot was still screaming with pain, but he managed to get on his knees and spin around.

He jabbed with his right hand while using his left to stay balanced. His dagger found nothing but putrid air.

Several rats hissed. They were near, ready to strike at any moment. His hacking was suddenly interrupted by something tight around his belly, like a python trying to give him the Heimlich maneuver.

"We've got you, Tim," said Katherine as Tim felt himself leave the water, vomiting booze and stomach acid.

Once Katherine and Tanner sprawled him out on the street, his stomach and lungs had given up pretty much all they had to give, and he was breathing relatively normally again. He didn't bother to wipe the shit out of his eyes, because he feared seeing the state of his foot.

"Pass me a bottle of stonepiss," said Tanner.

That sounded like a fine idea to Tim. He started to say so, but discovered that his stomach still had one left in the chamber. He puked up a glob of bile.

His injured leg, which already felt like it was on fire, suddenly felt like it was being dipped in lava.

"FUUUUUUUUCK!" cried Tim. That was just what he needed to clear the residual shitwater from his lungs and the turdcakes from his eyes. He saw Tanner pouring stonepiss onto the hamburger meat that used to be his foot. "Jesus Christ! Give me that!" Surprising himself that he had the energy to do so, he sat up and snatched the bottle out of Tanner's hand.

"One shouldn't invoke the New God in anger," said a soft female voice behind him.

Careful not to move his leg, Tim stretched his neck and torso to look behind him. A petite young human woman gazed sympathetically at him from beneath a tattered grey shawl.

"Can you cut me some slack, lady? I've been through some shit today."

"Your wounds are too deep. If you want to keep your leg, it must be properly cleaned and treated."

"I'm sorry," said Katherine. "But who the hell are you?"

The small woman bowed her head slightly to Katherine. "My name is Lissa. I am a Sister of Healing."

Katherine narrowed her eyes. "Well isn't that fucking convenient."

Tim couldn't drink fast enough to dull the scorching pain in his foot. He extended his finger toward the woman. "Whatever. I'll take it."

She stared at him confusedly. "I don't understand. Why are you pointing at me?"

"I'm in a lot of pain here, lady. If you've got a healing spell memorized, just touch my finger and cough up an incantation, will you?"

"I'm afraid you've mistaken me for a cleric. The Sisters of

Healing rely on more traditional methods of treatment."

"What, like herbs and shit?"

"Herbs, yes. As for... We should really get you off the street."

Tim winced as Tanner scooped him up off the ground, one arm supporting his neck, and the other under his knees. He couldn't judge the distance they walked, being repeatedly jolted awake with pain and lulled back to sleep with booze.

Eventually, he woke up good and hard to the all-too-familiar sensation of having his foot gnawed off. This time was different, however, as he couldn't move his upper body. He opened his eyes.

On the bright side, his foot wasn't being gnawed off. Lissa was scrubbing it hard with an old sponge and some noxious-smelling purple liquid. It hurt like a son of a bitch, which likely explained the leather restraints keeping his torso and arms firmly fixed to the bed.

On the not-as-bright side, Tim could feel a dull throbbing burn in his leg all the way up to his knee. The combination of rat spit and liquid shit had caused an infection, and it was spreading.

Katherine wiped some sweat off his forehead. "Are you feeling any better?"

"F-f-f-fuck no!" said Tim, suddenly realizing he also had a chill. "I'm cold, the nerve endings in my foot are being scrubbed raw, and I've got Cooper squirts running up my leg."

Lissa stopped scrubbing. She frowned and jabbed his red puffy leg just below the knee.

"FUCK!"

"That hurts, does it?"

Tim shivered and spoke through clenched teeth. "What do you think?"

"It's just as I feared," Lissa said to Katherine. "The disease is spreading. With the herbs I have here, I can slow the spread. Give the halfling two, maybe three more days before his fate is in the gods' hands. But to reverse it, I require fresh fenberries."

"What the fuck is a fenberry?" asked Katherine. "And where the fuck am I supposed to..." Her eyebrows furrowed in confusion for a moment. "Why do I know exactly what the fuck a fenberry is, where the fuck to find them, and what their medicinal properties are?"

Tim groaned. The pain in his foot was being caught up to by an overall feeling of shittiness. "You're a druid. You made a good Knowledge Nature roll. How far away are those berries?"

"There's a swamp about a day's ride north of here. Fenberries should be plentiful there around this time of year."

"The Swamp of Shadows," said Tanner. "Near the Borderlands. If we leave now, we should be able to make most of the trip by day. Depending on how quickly and easily we acquire the berries, we could –"

"Stop," said Katherine. "I need you to stay here and look after my brother."

"It's too dangerous to go alone. The lizardfolk who inhabit the swamp are wild and unpredictable."

"I can handle myself. And I won't be alone." Katherine scratched Butterbean's head.

Tim stayed out of the argument. He didn't like the thought of her being in danger, but he knew she wouldn't be reasoned with, and that arguing would only keep her around longer, making it all the more likely that her eventual decision to go alone would be for nothing.

Tanner offered her a small coin pouch. "At least take this. Buy a fast horse, and whatever weapons and provisions you require."

Katherine snatched the pouch out of his hand. "Thank you." She kissed her fingertips and pressed them against Tim's forehead. "Stay strong, little brother. I'll be back before you know it."

Tim gave her a nod and a weak smile. When she exited the room with Butterbean hot on her heels, he sucked back what was left of his bottle and drifted off to sleep wondering if he'd ever see her again.

CHAPTER 7

Chaz felt a little insulted at not having been deemed important enough even for hanging-around-at-Arby's duty.

"People are nervous right now," Frank had told him when he asked what he could do. All night, Frank had been barking orders left and right, red-faced like a boil about to pop. But he spoke to Chaz in his kindly fatherly voice. "Play the folks a song. It'll be good for morale."

Chaz didn't need a Condescension-to-English dictionary to translate what he was really saying. "Get this fucking bard out of here. The grownups are talking."

Chaz's future was as much on the line as anyone else's, but he sipped his beer and strummed his lute for an audience of exactly no one. People were panicking, and all the Tom Petty covers in the world weren't going to help.

He'd almost fallen asleep in his chair when he was jolted awake by a sharp knock on the front door.

Gus, the big gay half-orc, was on door duty. He checked the window, then quickly opened the door. A green-robed sorcerer whose name Chaz couldn't remember hurried inside and Gus shut the door behind him.

Frank looked to him with wide desperate eyes. "Tell me you've got something, Gilbert."

Gilbert. That was it.

"We spotted the sister leaving through Northgate."

"Was she with anyone? Tim? The half-drow?"

"She was alone on horseback. Her wolf ran alongside her."

Frank stroked his beard. "What about bags?"

Gilbert frowned. "She could've had the dice on her. From that distance, it was impossible to tell."

"I meant like saddlebags. Something large enough to hide a halfling?"

"Oh no. Nothing like that. She was traveling light. Light and fast."

Frank drummed his fingers on the table and looked at Chaz.

Chaz had been expecting as much and was doing his best to feign complete and utter disinterest, strumming his lute, singing softly to himself, and only observing through his periphery.

"What is she up to?" asked Frank. "Maybe she's got a lead on one of Mordred's avatars?"

Gilbert shrugged. "I won't know anymore until I get close enough to reestablish my Empathic Link with Barney."

Barney was Gilbert's familiar. Chaz remembered that much because he was named for being a barn owl.

"He's following her from a discreet distance above," Gilbert continued. "He'll do so until he loses her, he's discovered, or she returns to Northgate."

Frank cradled his head in his hands. "I guess that's the best we can do. If we can keep track of the sister, she'll lead us to Tim sooner or later. Hurry back to Northgate so you can pick up Barney's signal when he comes back."

Gilbert left quickly. Gus shut the door behind him.

The next time Chaz was suddenly awakened from a slumber he hadn't realized he'd drifted into, the noise came from the other side of the room.

"Woo wee!" said Denise, emerging from the cellar with an axe in one hand and a glistening, moist-looking chair leg in the other. "I slept like a motherfucker!"

Chaz didn't realize it was so late in the morning. People who'd actually slept properly through the night were now beginning to wake up.

Denise sauntered over to the front door and glared up at Gus, who was blocking her exit. "Move out of the way, fudgecock. I got shit to do today."

"I'm sorry, Denise," said Gus. "I can't let you leave, as much as I'd love to."

"Love to watch me walk away, you mean?" Denise turned around and waved her broad dwarven ass at Gus. "You like what you see? Come on down to the cellar and I'll straighten your ass out."

"No, thank you. I'm, uh..."

Denise held up her chair leg and waved it around in Gus's face. "Go on, boy. Get a good whiff. Tell me that don't stir somethin' inside you."

"Please stop that." Gus looked to Frank for guidance.

There was no reason to keep feigning indifference now. Doing so would probably seem more suspicious than not doing so. Chaz looked over at Frank, who was grimacing and waving for Gus to just open the door and let her out already.

There was something so genuinely vile about her that she could neither be considered useful nor a credible threat.

Gus gratefully stood aside, and Denise exited the Whore's Head to get started on whatever business she had planned for the day.

Chaz had no specific business in mind on the outside. He didn't like the idea of being confined, but the world outside the Whore's Head, at least for now, was considerably less dangerous than inside it. Perhaps his purpose was here, paying attention to developing factions, keeping abreast of their comings and goings, gathering intelligence which might prove valuable when shit hit the fan.

Then again, no one had explicitly told him he wasn't allowed to leave. Perhaps he was pre-capitulating to a non-existent demand out of extreme cowardice.

Chaz was willing to give himself the benefit of the doubt.

CHAPTER 8

"This doesn't feel like the New God's work," said Wettle. He dropped the bundle of bricks he was carrying, stretched his back, and wiped a quart of sweat from his balding head. "It just feels like work."

Randy set down his own bundle more gently, then sat on it. "We're rebuilding our community. When folks see the good works that we do, they'll be inspired."

"Or take us for fools. We're not even being paid for this."

"The Lord's work is its own reward. Ain't nobody gonna be inspired by watching men work for money. You can see that anywhere."

Indeed they could. In the wake of the devastation brought on by dragon fire and the seismic footfalls of a giant bread monster, the part of the city near Southgate was positively abuzz with construction, like ants rebuilding a hill that had been stepped on.

Wettle sat down on his pile of bricks. "I get what you're saying, but we're not exactly rebuilding what was lost. Most of these properties were scooped up by opportunistic merchants preying on shop owners who couldn't afford to rebuild. Do you remember there being this many bakeries on this street before?"

Randy frowned at a row of buildings under construction. At least two thirds of them had signs out front featuring the cheerful smile of the Pillsburg Doughchild. Those which had been rushed to completion already had lines flowing out of their doors.

"Do you know what Jesus was before he started preaching?"

"Sure, everyone does. A heavenly mixture of flour and water, with just a pinch of cosmic salt."

"Who told you that?"

Wettle shrugged. "That's what I've heard."

"Well you heard wrong. He was a carpenter."

"And he worked for free?"

"No. Not exactly. But the point –"

"Forgive my insolence, Grand Baguette, but –"

"Please don't call me that."

"But I only seek to make sure that your generosity is not taken for granted and used for unscrupulous ends."

Randy felt lower than he'd felt in a while. He wasn't fit to lead anyone. Wettle was probably right, but Randy felt backed into a corner. If unscrupulous men were taking advantage of them, did that mean they should just stop working? That didn't seem right either. Sometimes it's just better to let yourself be taken advantage of, right? Wasn't that in the Bible somewhere?

"Blessed are the..." None of the beatitudes that came to mind seemed appropriate for this set of circumstances. "... poor of heart?"

Wettle stared at him blankly. "Oh. Okay."

"I appreciate your advice, Wettle," said Randy. "I really do. I got to say, I'm feelin' a bit lost at sea myself. I don't want you to never feel like there's somethin' you can't say to me."

"I'm happy to hear you say that, Grand... Sir Randy." Wettle looked back at the other eleven men who had chosen to follow Randy. "There has been talk of late. The men had been expecting a lot more smiting of evil, and not quite as much manual labor."

Whether he was fit for the task or not, Randy had a responsibility to keep this band of criminals who had been released to his charge from going off on some misguided killing spree.

"The truly righteous seek neither adventure nor excitement." The fact that he was now badly misquoting Yoda rather than Jesus did little to bolster Randy's self-confidence.

"You best take it down a notch, Holy Poly," said Denise, waddling onto the construction site. "Eternity's a long goddamn time, my friend. I reckon you'd be more comfortable in the queer section than with the blasphemers."

"Excuse me, Wettle," said Randy. He hurried to intercept Denise between In Gods We Crust and Loave Thy Neighbor, far away from his disciples for them not to be overheard if they used their inside voices. The air was already heavy with the scent of spoiled wine and yeast, but it seemed to intensify as he got closer to her. "Is there something I can help you with?"

"I just came by to fill you in on the latest developments with the little piece of ass you betrayed me for."

"I don't know what you're talkin' about."

"I'm talkin' 'bout the little boy toy you was chauffeuring around while he was choppin' my nuts off."

"You believe what you want, Denise. I have a different recollection of those events."

"We go back a long way, you and I," said Denise. "And you just up and threw me under the goddamn bus for some of that sweet sweet toddler ass."

"I did no such thing! You're the one who tried to –" Randy felt the blood rushing to his cheeks. Denise was trying to stir him up. "You know what? I ain't gettin' drawn in to no argument with you. If you got somethin' to say, I suggest you say it and get on your way. We got work needs doin'."

Denise folded her arms over her puffed-out chest and cocked an eyebrow up at Randy. "Your new BFF stole Frank's dice. He's gonna ditch us all here in this bullshit world."

That took Randy by surprise. He wasn't expecting Denise to have any actual news. "Tim?"

"That's the one. Sweet little innocent Tim, with his sweet little puckered asshole, just waitin' for –"

"Would you please shut up?" Tim was selfish and petty, and had some self-destructive tendencies, but Randy didn't think he'd betray his friends like that. "I call bullshit."

"You're a terrible judge of character. That's the problem with you folks. You catch one whiff of little boy butthole, and all the blood from your brain rushes straight to your dick."

"Damn it, Denise. It weren't never like that!" Randy took a breath to calm himself down. "Did you actually see him steal the dice, like with your own eyes?"

"Hell no," said Denise. "He ain't done the deed himself. He's too chickenshit, and couldn't have gotten close enough if he'd had the balls anyway. He sent that nigger elf to –"

Slapping Denise across the face was just what Randy needed. He felt better about this whole encounter now. "I warned you 'bout using that word 'round me."

"Fine," said Denise, rubbing her cheek. "That African American elf. Better?"

Randy wasn't sure if it was. "It'll do for now. What about him?"

"Your BFF sent Homey the Elf to the Whore's Head with the stated intention of retrieving his and his sister's character shits."

Randy thought for a moment. "Do you mean character sheets?"

Denise scratched under her left boob and nodded. "That probably makes more sense, come to think of it. But the point is, they ain't all he retrieved."

"That don't mean for sure that Tim put him up to it." Randy didn't want to believe that Tim would abandon them all, but he had a harder time believing the words coming out of his own mouth.

"Clear the shit out your head, Randy. He fucked us over good, and it's up to you and me to stop him."

That was unexpected. "You and me? What about everybody else?"

Denise scoffed and spit on the ground. "They's all sniffin' chairs and chasin' their tails. Ain't none of them got two brain cells to rub together. What we need is a network of trained professionals to root out that little turd proper like."

"Are you referring to my...?" Though they liked to identify themselves as such, Randy couldn't bring himself to call his twelve new companions his 'apostles'. Instead of saying the word, he just looked over at them busily constructing the city's latest bakery.

"Goddammit, Randy. No! Them twelve faggots couldn't find nothin' that weren't hidden up each other's assholes. I'm talkin' law enforcement." Denise leaned in closer. "The biggest advantage we got right now is that we's in a big city. That little shit will think he's safe to move around, so long as he keeps his distance from the Whore's Head. He won't be expectin' every guard in the city to be lookin' out for him."

"And how do you aim to get every guard in the city lookin' out for him?"

Denise grinned at Randy. "That's where you come in, old buddy. I reckon the king owes you a favor."

CHAPTER 9

Cooper grunted extra loudly, but the portcullis remained down.

"Are you even trying?" asked Tony the Elf. "Why don't you use your Barbarian Rage?"

Cooper turned around and coughed out a gob of phlegm. "It wouldn't make any difference." Technically, he wasn't lying. Between the rusted bars of the portcullis, the rotting wooden frame, and the fire damage, the thing was likely to fall loose under its own weight at any moment. He'd felt a lot of crunch with his first half-assed attempt to lift it, and all of his effort since then had been focused on trying to make sure it stayed upright while attempting to appear like he was trying to do the opposite. That was some complicated shit.

Tony the Elf folded his arms. "Do you know what I think?"

"If it has anything to do with me giving a fuck what you think, you're mistaken."

"I think you're not really trying to open the gate. I think you're faking it to buy your little murderous friend time to escape."

Damn you, Bluff, for being a Charisma-based skill.

"Tim's a lot of things, but he's not a murderer."

Tony the Elf's jaw hung open. "We all watched him slit a guy's throat a few nights ago."

Shit. Tony the Elf made a compelling argument. Arguing was likely an Intelligence-based skill. Also not Cooper's strong suit.

"That was different. He was upset." The pressure of Tim's life hanging on Cooper's wits built up in his stomach, then escaped through his anus. The portcullis had reached its threshold of suffering, and clanged against the stone floor.

"You stupid fool," said Tony the Elf. "You can bet your foul ass that Frank is going to hear about this. Now get out of the way." He cautiously stepped past Cooper.

Cooper allowed him to pass. "Frank can eat my ass. He wants to kill my friend."

Tony the Elf stepped into the room beyond the stairs, but seemed perplexed. "Your friend is on a killing spree. And he took the only means we have for getting back home, just to spite us. I personally don't give a damn what Frank does with him. I just want those dice back."

"He said he didn't have them."

"You can't possibly be that stupid. I don't care what your Intelligence score is." Tony the Elf was knocking on random parts of the walls. "Open your eyes, Cooper. Tim doesn't give a shit about you. If he gets his hands on another Mordred, he'll ditch us in a heartbeat. All of us, including you."

"Sticks and stones, fuck-o. I don't believe that. He's my friend, and he's going through some rough shit right now." Cooper swallowed hard, feeling a sudden pang of guilt for having abandoned Tim. He should have left the Whore's Head with him. He shouldn't have left him alone on the south road. He should have maybe beat the shit out of him and dragged him along, but he shouldn't have left him. Tim's too self-destructive to be left on his own.

Cooper stared despondently at a conspicuously smooth hole in the scorched door frame.

Lever.

It was something like a thought. It came from inside his head, but he didn't think it was his. Another something-like-a-thought occurred to him as to what he might stick inside the hole, and the fact that it wasn't his dick made him all the more suspicious.

His hand found his axe handle, and he was overcome with

an irresistible urge to shove the handle into the hole. Seeing no reason to bother resisting, he gave in to the urge. It was a good snug fit.

Another urge followed, as innocent as an itch wanting to be scratched. Cooper scratched his balls and pulled down on the axe.

"Shit!" cried Tony the Elf as the smell of concentrated ass filled the air. There was a shallow splash, then Tony the Elf shouted "Shit!" again. Also, there was a big rectangular hole in the floor where there hadn't been one just a second ago. Dave, Tony the Elf's sheepdog Animal Companion, was looking down into the hole and barking.

"No, Dave! Stay! STAY!" Dave jumped into the hole. "Damn it!"

"Tony the Elf?" Cooper called into the room.

"Cooper! What the hell did you do?"

"Nothing. I was just scratching my nuts."

"Get us out of here!"

Cooper walked over to the edge of the hole and looked in. Tony the Elf was soaked in liquid shit from the waist down. His dog was completely covered in it.

"Dude, what the fuck are you doing down there?"

"The floor just vanished out from under me. Stop asking me stupid questions and lower a rope or something."

Cooper pursed his lips. "Why do you want to get out?"

Tony the Elf balled up his fists. "Why the hell do you think? I'm in a goddamn sewer!"

"Well, well," said Cooper, rubbing his chin thoughtfully. "That presents quite the condumbum... cumyumyum... condom drum?"

"Conundrum?"

"That's the one."

Tony the Elf put his fists on his hips and tilted his head. "What are you getting at?"

"I'm no scholar, but it appears to me that we've discovered

where Tim and Katherine and that other dude escaped to. Are you suggesting we abandon the hunt?"

Leave him. Go!

"I'm getting to that, voice in my head."

Tony the Elf's expression changed from disgust and annoyance to genuine concern. "What are you talking about?"

"I don't know. It's just this thing. Hang on a minute." Cooper walked back toward the stairs.

"Cooper!" cried Tony the Elf. "Where are you going? Don't you leave me down –"

Sudden and absolute silence. That was weird. Cooper looked back. The floor of the room was solid again. His axe was still sticking out of the hole in the door frame, but it was tilted upward.

Cooper nodded slowly. Interesting. I guess it works like a toilet.

He didn't want to leave Tony the Elf to die alone in the sewer. That shit wasn't cool. But he couldn't risk being followed either, especially since he didn't know where he was planning to go.

He raced up the stairs to tie up one loose end.

The fire hadn't spread like Cooper had feared. He imagined he'd be rushing into a blazing inferno, but the place actually appeared to be less on fire than it had been when he'd first arrived. Judging by all the broken glass on the floor, he guessed Tim had tried to use booze to light the place up. As Cooper knew from personal experience, the effects of that were hit or miss. Sometimes you get a big initial flare-up, but it burns itself out before the wood really gets going. That looked like what had happened here. The beams were too robust, and separated by too much brickwork.

It was still smokey as fuck though. Whoever took the place over was going to want to air it out a bit first.

Back to the task at hand. There was a big-ass minotaur corpse on the floor, whose death Tim may or may not have had something to do with. Cooper needed to get to Tim and shake the shit out of him before the king issued an arrest warrant on him. This body had to go.

Cooper grabbed it by the horns and dragged it back toward the secret door leading down to the sewer dump. Dude was heavy as fuck.

The body proved to be much easier getting down the stairs, so much so that Cooper nearly gored himself on the horns.

He tested the floor with his toe, making sure it was solid, before dragging the minotaur's body onto the middle of it, then retreated back to the staircase to pull the axe handle down once more.

"–OOOOOOPEEE–" Tony the Elf's shout blared out of the reopened floor until it was interrupted by a dead minotaur. "Jesus Christ! What the hell?"

"Sorry, dude. If somebody found that, they might think Tim was responsible."

"Tim was responsible!"

"Tim's just a halfling. That's a fucking minotaur. No way Tim did this. I need to go find him before he gets himself hurt." He started back up the stairs.

"Cooper! Please don't leave me down here. Come on, man. Come ba–"

As he was trying to figure out his next move, it occurred to Cooper that Tony the Elf might think he was abandoning him right now. He could go back and tell him just to sit tight for a second.

Nah, let him sweat.

Cooper returned to the bottom of the staircase with a short stool from one of the nearby tables, and a longer bar stool. Just as he'd hoped, the short stool's legs were about the same girth as his axe's handle, and fit nicely into the hole in the door frame. He pushed down on the stool.

"–orry!" Tony the Elf was shouting hysterically. He might have even been crying. "Okay? I'm so so sorry!"

"Dude," said Cooper. "You're making this weird."

"Cooper! Thank God you're back. You've got to help us. We're not alone down here."

"'We' kind of implies that, dumbass."

"No, I meant something besides me and Dave."

"Well there's –"

"And Morty," said Tony the Elf. "There's something alive down here. I can hear them squeaking and hissing."

"They're probably just dire rats. You're in a sewer."

"I know I'm in a fucking sewer. I need you to let me out of the fucking sewer."

Cooper wedged the bar stool into place so that it held the smaller stool in the down position. "What the fuck do you think I'm doing?"

"I honestly don't know. You're almost certainly making this more complicated than it needs to be. All I need you to do is throw down a rope and pull me out."

Cooper grabbed his coil of rope from his bag, along with two flasks of oil. "I'm going to rub the rope down with oil, then I'll tie one end to the portcullis and throw the other end down to you."

"May I ask why you're doing that?"

"So you can climb out, dumbass."

"No." Tony the Elf took a deep breath, like he was trying to maintain his cool. "I meant why are you rubbing it down with oil first?"

"So you'll have a harder time climbing up. You're lucky I remembered the oil. My first idea was just to piss all over it."

"Why do you always have to be like that? And don't give me any bullshit about your low Charisma score."

"Dude. I'm trying to help you out."

"You would be decidedly more helpful by throwing down a rope without first slathering it in oil or urine."

Two flasks may have been overkill for the amount of rope required for the task at hand, but too much was better than too little. “I need to find Tim. I can’t have you follow me.”

“Believe me, I have no intention of following you anywhere. Go on and run back to that tiny sociopath. You deserve each other, and I’ll be thrilled to be rid of you. We have gone from bad to worse since your lot showed up. You may very well be the Everest of stupid assholes, but your friends are the rest of the Himalayas.”

Cooper frowned. “You know what?”

“What?” snapped Tony the Elf.

“I think I’m gonna go ahead and piss on the rope after all.”

When his business was complete, Cooper lay the portcullis diagonal on the other side of the door frame so that Tony the Elf wouldn’t just pull it into the sewer with him. He started up the stairs when the strange intruder inside his head cleared its throat.

He noticed his axe leaning against the corner of the stairwell. He picked it up and ran up the stairs. After making sure the secret door leading downstairs was closed and looking as secret as he could get it, he ran out of the tavern, directionless, into the night.

CHAPTER 10

The rhythmic pattern of hooves pounding against hard-packed dirt hadn't been interrupted since Katherine passed through the city walls. More than one group of travelers had moved aside to allow her to pass.

The small pouch of gold coins that Tanner had given her went further than she'd expected, and she hadn't been stingy about using it. She bought the most formidable-looking horse the stable master had available, and replaced her old sickle with a hefty scythe, wearing it strapped on her back such that the long curved blade was very visible.

Despite the fact that she could once again enjoy the sun's warmth on her face without bursting into flames, losing the powers and near-invincibility of a vampire made her all too aware of her vulnerability as a half-elf. She hoped the horse and weapon would continue to keep opportunistic would-be attackers at bay, as she felt less like a confident warrior, and more like a wad of glue holding a few badass accessories together.

Her jeans-and-turtleneck combo did little to aid her intended visage as a Reaper of Asses, so she'd invested in a sturdy black cloak as well. The shadow of its hood would conceal the fact that she was a half-elven woman. But when the chill of the morning wore off, it started to get hot in there. She told herself that was reason enough to lower the hood, but she knew that if she was honest with herself, she kind of wanted a fight. Maybe she hadn't quite shaken her vampire mentality, or maybe it had something to do with the three levels of Fighter Tim had mentioned. She had a new weapon and she was itching to use it.

With the hood lowered, the wind on her face and in her hair was refreshing. She let herself enjoy the sweet fresh air, and tried not to think about the pain her brother must be going through right now. About ten minutes later, she spotted a mule-drawn cart on the horizon. She bit her lower lip with anticipation that someone might fuck with her.

What are you doing, Katherine? You're intentionally trying to lure someone into giving you justification to murder them. That's kind of fucked up, don't you think?

Yeah, maybe it was a little fucked up. But on the other hand, why should she need to hide who she was. If some motherfucker tries to pick a fight with her, that's on him, right?

Tim doesn't have time for this.

Katherine growled to herself and yanked the hood back up over her head. The traveler steering the mule cart pulled completely off the road as she passed. The fat little fucker even looked the other way when she approached, as if there was something more interesting than her on this all-but-featureless stretch of road.

"Asshole!" she shouted as she passed him. Butterbean barked in agreement. When they had put enough distance behind them, Katherine pulled her hood down, shook out her hair, and rode on.

A few smaller roads branched off to the left. Even fewer to the right. But somehow, though she'd never been this way before, she knew that none of them would lead her where she needed to go... until she found the one that would.

Katherine reined in her horse to a stop. Butterbean looked up at her expectantly, his tongue hanging out. He was panting heavily. Exhausted, but eager to keep serving. She was exhausted too, and all she'd been doing was sitting on a horse. She closed her eyes and rubbed her temples.

Butterbean let out a small whine.

"It's okay," said Katherine. "This game's just fucking with

my brain, that's all. I can't explain why I know exactly where I am. It's something to do with my character's knowledge, I think. She – or I – might have grown up around here or something." She sighed. "And now I'm talking to a dog."

Butterbean barked.

"Sorry, wolf. Jesus I need some sleep."

Her Animal Companion lay down on the road.

Katherine laughed. "No, not here. It's too dangerous. Besides, we've still got work to do. You ready?"

Butterbean growled.

"Yeah, me too. Let's get moving."

They traveled east while the sun began to set in the opposite direction. This smaller road wasn't as well-kept as the main one. The forest loomed close on both sides, threatening to obliterate the path completely with branch and vine. Part of Katherine felt comforted at being so close to nature, but she was also keenly aware of what dangers might be lurking just a few yards beyond her ever-shrinking field of vision.

Butterbean and the horse, however, didn't seem to mind the slower pace they were forced to travel at.

The thick tangle of twisted oaks and gnarled elms began to thin out a little as the light faded into darkness.

Eventually, it grew too dark even for Katherine's enhanced half-elven night vision to see the path in front of her. She dismounted her horse and pulled a torch out of her bag. She was about to search for her set of flint and steel, but remembered she knew a spell that was just as effective and less likely to burn down a forest.

She could cast it on anything, but since she already had the torch out, why not?

"Light," she said, touching the business end of the torch. It instantly glowed with a soft white light, illuminating her surroundings. They weren't exactly what she was expecting.

Just beyond the edge of the path, a scum-filtered image of herself holding a lit torch stared up at her. A reflection. The path was an artificially raised dirt mound with stagnant water on both sides. She was in the Swamp of Shadows.

Cypress knees poked out of the water. Purple vines hung like the entrails of impaled giants from the trees' great branches. Here and there, the still film of green scum coating the surface of the water was disturbed by something moving underneath it.

Katherine swapped out her magically lit torch for her scythe, holding the latter and strapping the former to her back so that the glowing head peeked out over her shoulder. She looked down at Butterbean.

"Stay close."

Leading her horse on foot, she kept a wary eye out for anything that might want to jump out and eat them while scanning her surroundings for signs of a fenberry vine.

Fenberries, also known colloquially as deadberries in regions where they flourish due to their high toxicity, are not actually true berries. Like strawberries and raspberries, they are an aggregate fruit, developed from the merger of several ovaries in a single –

"Jesus Christ, I don't give a fuck!" said Katherine. "Is there any way to turn off Knowledge Nature? I just need to find the goddamn berries and get the hell out of here!"

A few moments later, that very same Knowledge Nature skill allowed her to recognize the slender, three-pointed leaves of the species of vine she'd been seeking. The vine itself was wrapped around the trunk of a particularly tall cypress tree about ten yards away from the path she was on, but didn't appear to have any berries growing on it. That was odd. It should be bursting with fruit this time of year. Was it an unhealthy vine? Or was someone, or something, foraging for fenberries around here?

She could keep going and try to find a more productive vine, or she could investigate this one more closely in the hope of finding some fruit. Both options felt simultaneously like they could be wasting time that her brother didn't have.

Fuck it. Her indecision was certainly an even greater waste of time. She set her bag and cloak down next to Butterbean.

"Stay here and watch the horse. I'll be right back."

Butterbean growled his halfhearted obedience.

Katherine stepped into the stagnant water. It was warm and gritty as it soaked her jeans and filled her boots. Breaking the surface released a more pungent smell of centuries-old rot and death, but it was a natural smell that she found almost pleasant. The piled-up dirt forming the path sloped down at a fairly steep angle, but leveled off to a squishy floor when she was about waist deep. At least that would allow her to keep both hands on her weapon.

When she reached the tree, she examined the fenberry vine more closely. It had been fruitful after all. Broken stems revealed where clusters of fruit had been torn away. Who would do that? Could it have been the lizardfolk that Tanner had mentioned? Were they making poisons, or might they be using them for some ceremonial purpose?

Who gives a shit? Stay focused, Kat.

She traced the vine up the trunk until she spotted a cluster of those piss-yellow motherfuckers, ripe as could be and bursting with juice that could make an elephant shit itself to death.

Standing on her toes, holding her scythe by the very end of the handle, she still couldn't quite reach the berry cluster.

Not a big problem. The vine was thick enough to support her weight easily.

She used her scythe blade to cut the vine where it submerged into the water, then unwrapped it around the tree trunk until she reached the part with the fruit.

The climbing was easy but slow. Leaf stems provided enough resistance such that her hands didn't slip. But her boots were too slippery to gain traction on the trunk. She had to shimmy up with her thighs.

About halfway to her goal, she spotted a disturbance on the

water's surface scum. A slow-moving log, though not so slow as the nigh-imperceptible current of the swamp.

She smiled to herself. She'd fallen for one of nature's oldest tricks, even after having grown up on the Gulf Coast. That was no log. That was a gator. And a pretty fucking big one, by the looks of it.

No, that wasn't quite right. This was clearly a crocodile. From her vantage point above it, she could see the disturbance on the water's surface was made by a V-shaped snout as it passed beneath her. Besides, alligators are not indigenous to –

"Shut up! Shut up! Shut up!" Katherine rammed her palm repeatedly into the side of her head. Priorities having been set straight, she resumed climbing the tree. She had just about reached the fenberries when another thought about the crocodile popped into her head. It was moving, slowly but with purpose.

"Butterbean!"

Even if she let herself fall, she wouldn't be able to trudge or swim through that water fast enough to reach the crocodile in time. And without her vampire powers, running into a straight fight with a beast that big was suicide. Somehow, she had to find a way to outsmart that prehistoric piece of shit.

A light bulb shone above her head. Not so much a light bulb, but a yellow aggregate fruit reflecting light from her magically lit torch. She had an idea.

The vine could carry her Tarzan-style to cut off the croc. When it opened its big mouth to attack, she could throw in the fenberries. Brilliant.

Katherine plucked the cluster from the vine, wrapped the vine around her right forearm, and let go of the trunk. She sailed straight over the crocodile, hardly believing how flawlessly her plan was working. That is, until it came time to land. Her path was leading her in a trajectory that would send her crashing straight into her horse. Let go too soon, and she'd fall in the water between the animals and the giant crocodile. Let go too late, and –

"Shit!"

The horse wasn't as soft as she'd hoped it might be. She hit it with both knees, flipped over its ass, and splashed down into the swamp on the other side of the path. When she picked her head out of the slimy water, she found the smell less naturally refreshing, and more... just slimy and gross. The horse was staring down at her accusingly.

"Well you could have fucking moved, couldn't you?"

An explosion of water sprayed out from the other side of the horse just before a massive set of reptilian jaws grabbed it by the saddle and belly. The horse screamed as it fell to its knees and started sliding off the path.

"Hey! No!" shouted Katherine. "I need that!" She scampered up onto the path, but didn't fancy her chances of winning a tug-of-war game against this thing. Its head was nearly as long as she was tall.

"Fuck." She looked down at her left hand, still holding the cluster of fenberries. That was her only chance.

The crocodile's mouth was locked tight around the horse's midsection, leaving it both occupied and open enough to shove her arm in with relative confidence in being able to keep it.

She pushed the fruit back as far as she could into the crocodile's mouth, hoping that her horse wasn't about to split in two.

A slimy lump pushed against her hand, freaking her out. She dropped the fenberries and pulled her hand back. It was the crocodile's tongue. It was rejecting the fenberries.

"Uh uh," said Katherine. She took the torch off her back and pushed the cluster of fruit back in just as they were about to drop out of the side of its mouth.

The tongue didn't flap around. It was more of a lump moving around under a membrane than an appendage. She was able to keep the fenberries in the croc's mouth, but the tongue-lump kept them from being swallowed.

After a little back-and-forth, the crocodile disengaged with the horse, prioritizing ridding its mouth of this fruit that its kind must have evolved to recognize as being extremely dangerous.

The horse fell flat as the crocodile's jaws snapped shut, and Katherine did the only thing she could think to do. She jumped onto the crocodile's head and wrapped her arms around its lower jaw.

Like with any animal, the muscles that close a mouth are much more developed than the ones that open it. Still, this was a huge fucking animal, and those opening jaw muscles were pretty powerful as well. Katherine was barely able to keep hold of her wrist with her elbow locked around the mouth.

Butterbean, who had been barking, snarling, growling, and otherwise following Katherine's non-suicidal lead up to that point, jumped into the water and attacked.

"You swallow that fruit, you scaly son of a bitch!" Katherine kicked her heels into the croc's eyes. That may have proved to be a mistake. Or the head-thrashing that followed may have been inevitable. She held on as the giant beast tried to shake her off, slamming her left and right into the muddy water. "There... are starving... children... in India... who would love – FUCK!"

The crocodile reared high, then came down in a barrel roll, pinning Katherine under the water and into the squishy mud below. Motherfucker was trying to drown her. She didn't kick or try to push herself up. This was now a waiting game, and any effort she exerted beyond keeping the croc's mouth closed would only take vital seconds off her clock.

The crocodile seemed to be following a similar strategy, as it was no longer thrashing wildly about. It was alive and forceful, but its movements seemed to be limited to and concentrated on keeping her down. The occasional jerks and wiggles she felt were probably the crocodile's attempts to swat its little legs at the pestering wolf that was trying to bite through its hide.

Bless his heart, but Katherine knew that Butterbean wasn't going to be able to save her. And though the crocodile's nostrils were submerged down there with her, she knew she would drown long before it did. Her only hope was that –

And just like that, the big bastard stopped moving. Katherine tentatively loosened her grip, ready to pull tight again in case this was a ruse. But crocodiles weren't that smart, and she didn't have much more time. She let go completely, and the giant head pinning her into the mud remained immobile. She pushed it off her and sat up. Her head was still underwater. It must have really pushed her down deep. She stood up, surfaced, and took a deep breath of kinda-fresh air.

Butterbean stood proudly atop the crocodile's lifeless belly, his muzzle red with blood. He'd managed to do more damage than Katherine thought he could have. She didn't know what kind of reproductive organs crocodiles were supposed to have between their legs, and she wouldn't be getting that education today. Being softer and more vulnerable than the rest of the animal's tough hide, the junk was where Butterbean had focused his attack. The entire area between the hind legs and tail was a mess of blood, shredded flesh, and claw marks.

Katherine hugged Butterbean as they both took a couple more moments to breathe. "Good boy."

The wolf tensed as the giant croc shuddered between Katherine's legs. Had that fucker been faking dead after all?

"Shit! Butterbean, run!" Katherine and Butterbean scrambled up the side of the raised path. Wet, slippery, and panicked, they weren't being very quick about it. Katherine clawed at the dirt, fearing she was seconds away from being bitten in half.

When they finally made it up, Katherine looked back. The crocodile was still upside down, its head still submerged, and neither its tail nor its legs were moving. There was, however, a distinct tremor running up and down its belly.

Then, with a sound like vomiting into a toilet, a gush of reddish brown liquid exploded from the opening that Butterbean had either created or widened. What scum had survived the creature's thrashing on the water's surface fanned out in a circular pattern, leaving a ring of black water, and an inner circle of shit and blood radiating from the croc's asshole.

Katherine looked down at her horse. Its guts were spilled out over the side of the path and into the water. Transportation was going to be a problem.

Butterbean shook his body vigorously, spraying swamp water in every direction. If only she could dry herself off like that. She was wet and cold, and so fucking tired.

She picked up her cloak, sat on the path, wrapped it around herself and Butterbean. Her clothes were still wet, and they both smelled like swamp ass, but the cloak managed to hold in some of their combined body heat.

Time to think. How the hell was she going to get back to town?

She hadn't slept in two days, and the crocodile fight had just sapped what little energy she had left. Her brain was far too exhausted for problem solving right now. She just couldn't go on any longer.

But she'd found the fenberries ahead of schedule. Tim still had at least a day left in him. She just needed a little nap, then she'd be able to find a way to get back to him. Maybe magic could help. She could summon a big bird or some shit to carry her. Was that a druid spell? Maybe she could...

Just a quick nap. She'd figure out what she needed to do when her brain was fresh and rested.

*

Katherine woke up to a buzz in her ear and a slap to her face. The slap was from her own hand, and the source of the buzz was splattered all over her palm.

"Blegh. Fucking mosquitoes." She opened her eyes to find the swamp awash with sunlight. The swamp was far less spooky during the day, a wild medley of vibrant shades of green. Frog croaks had been replaced by birdsong. It was all kind of beautiful.

"Shit! What time is it?"

Judging by her stupid Knowledge Nature skill, it was pretty late in the morning.

She scratched at the left side of her face. It seemed the mosquito on her hand hadn't been her only visitor during the night.

Still, she'd fared better than her former horse, of which only the head and one hoof remained on the path. What the hell was she thinking going to sleep in a crocodile-infested swamp?

She stood up quickly and checked to make sure all her and Butterbean's pieces were accounted for. Thankfully, everything was there, but her right hand was red and swollen to about fifty percent larger than her left hand. Some of the fenberry juice must have leaked onto it. Hopefully, that was something she could recover from.

On the bright side, if she could call it that, all the previous night's action had shaken a few clusters of fenberries from higher up on the vine. There were three clusters of them lying on the path.

She emptied the few remaining coins from the pouch Tanner had given her into her backpack, then carefully scooped one berry cluster into the pouch.

Now that she'd procured what she'd come for, it was time to work on that transportation problem. For that, she'd need to waste even more time praying for her spells, and hoping that one of them would get the job done.

She sat down and crossed her legs, placing her hands palms up atop her knees and closing her eyes.

"Mother Nature, or whatever. Please hear my prayer."

As she mumbled nonspecific words of generic prayer, her mind cleared, and her choices became known to her. The options available didn't look good.

The most obvious choice was the Longstrider spell, which would increase the speed with which she could run. But she still wouldn't be as fast as a horse, and even if she prepared it as many times as she was allowed, the duration of the spell was much too short for it to get her back to Tim in time to save him.

Most of the spells she had available to her were either likewise too limited in duration to be of any use, or completely useless for her current needs to begin with.

Having ruled out the more obviously useful-looking spells one by one, she focused her attention on trying to get creative with some of the shittier ones.

Suddenly the stars aligned, peace came over her being, and she knew what she had to do.

"Thank you, Mother Nature... or whatever."

Katherine remained sitting, but turned around to face Butterbean. She grinned, giddy with excitement, but just a bit sad as well for their imminent parting. "Come here."

Butterbean faithfully obeyed, wagging his tail and tongue.

"Now sit."

Butterbean sat.

"Stay."

Butterbean stayed.

Katherine licked her lips and rubbed her hands together, feeling the magical energy flow through her. She placed her hands on Butterbean's head. "Now Speak!"

"Hello, Katherine," said Butterbean.

Katherine crab-walked backward a foot. "H-h-h-holy fucking shit!" She breathed heavily as her heart pounded against her ribcage. "Why didn't I ever think to do this earlier?"

"You've been busy." He wasn't actually speaking like a person. It was a mixture of barks and whines and growls, typical wolf noises. But Katherine could understand them as perfectly as if they'd come from any person she'd ever spoken to.

"I'm going to use this spell a lot more in the future, I promise. But it's got a short duration, and I need to ask a favor of you."

"Of course, Katherine. You know I'd do anything for you."

Katherine rubbed the fur on Butterbean's neck. "I know you would. Do you think you can remember how to get back to that place where we left my brother?"

"Who?"

"Tim."

"The halfling?"

Katherine nodded.

"That guy's your brother? But how –"

"I'll explain all that when we have more time. Can you find the place?"

"Of course. It's bound to still smell like shit. But I don't want to leave you alone out here."

"Don't worry about me. I'll be right behind you. Just a little slower. I need you to take these berries to him."

"Berries?"

Katherine rolled her eyes. "Fine. Technically, they're an aggregate fruit."

"I don't know what that means. But... Are we trying to kill your brother?"

"Of course not, silly." Katherine smiled at her friend. "These have medicinal properties as well. We need these to save his life."

Butterbean sighed. "Okay, good. You had me a little weirded out there for a second."

"Hmm..." said Katherine. "I don't know how much more time we have with this spell, but we might as well use it up. Is there anything you'd like to ask me?"

"I notice you turn away sometimes when I lick my balls. Does that make you uncomfortable?"

Katherine shook her head. "Nah. I grew up with a brother. Christ knows if he could do that, he'd never leave the house. It's just instinctive for me to want to give you some privacy.

Anything else?"

"One more thing."

"What is it?"

"There's a naked man in a tree behind you."

"What?"

Butterbean growled. The spell had timed out. Shit.

Katherine stood up and turned around slowly, hoping against any reasonable probability that 'There's a naked man in a tree behind you' was some kind of figure of speech among dogs meaning 'Safe travels and let's talk again soon.' The naked old man staring down at her from a nearby tree suggested the meaning was more literal.

He stood about five feet tall and couldn't have weighed more than seventy-five pounds. He was bald on top, but long scraggly grey hair hung down to his shoulders. A matching tangle of pubes hung down to his knees. His eyes were wild, mismatched, and unnerving as they seemed to move independently of each other.

Without taking her eyes off him, Katherine crouched down and put her arm around Butterbean's neck. She placed the drawstring of the pouch in his mouth.

"Go now."

Butterbean growled some more at the man in the tree.

"I've got this," said Katherine. She looked into Butterbean's eyes, hoping he remembered their brief conversation and could make out something that she was currently saying. "Go save my brother. Save Tim."

His eyes shifted to meet hers when she said the word Tim, and his growl turned to a whine. He didn't want to leave her, but he understood.

"Go!"

Butterbean turned around and started running back down the path. A yellowish brown blob splattered down where he'd just stood.

"The fuck?" Before she could look away, Katherine noticed

little white studs – fenberry seeds? – in the... shit? She looked up and saw that the old man had another handful ready to fling.

"Do you eat fenberries?" she asked.

"Intruder!" screamed the old man, and launched his payload at her.

Katherine dodged the shitball easily enough. It splattered on the ground next to her.

"Why are you flinging shit at me?"

If the man heard her, he made no attempt to answer her question. He merely squatted down to reload his hand.

"Intruder!" he shrieked again. Katherine prepared to dodge, but he launched his load at a target above her, up in another tree branch. This one connected, and a plump little barn owl, covered in shit, fell to the ground with a thud.

"What the fuck is wrong with you? It's a fucking owl! How's that an intruder?" Once again, Katherine's Knowledge Nature skill kicked in to remind her that this species of owl was not native to the swamp. And once again, Katherine did not give a fuck. She bent over to pick up the poor terrified bird. It clawed at her fat right hand as she scooped it up under each of its shit-smeared wings. "Goddammit, bird. I'm trying to help you!"

"Intruder!" cried the old man just before Katherine felt a large splat on the back of her cloak.

"Will you please knock that shit off?" said Katherine. She'd had enough of this swamp, but she had to go back for her bag. The stupid owl was still trying to claw into her hand. She tucked it under her right arm like a football, dodged a couple of shit grenades, scooped up her bag, and shouted, "Longstrider!"

She'd prepared that spell as well in case her chat with Butterbean didn't work out like she'd hoped. It was a better-than-nothing last ditch effort spell, which would have cut her travel time down by minutes instead of hours, and probably would have been too little too late. But as long as she had it ready, she'd happily use it to flee a shit-flinging crazy old naked man.

She ran down the path with the effort of a casual jogger and the speed of an Olympic sprinter. It felt amazing. Useful or not, she was determined to try out a lot more spells in the future, just to see how cool they felt.

After about half an hour, when the ground started to dry up and cypress trees mingled once again with oaks and elms, Katherine remembered that the owl she had tucked under her arm was still covered in shit that likely contained a lot of fenberry juice. She stopped running and looked at her swollen hand.

"Shit."

Carefully, she took the owl out from under her arm. She gasped. The fat little bastard looked like a feathered basketball.

"Oh my god, you poor thing!"

With its added girth, its little legs no longer had the reach to scratch at her. It didn't even try. It must feel like shit.

The path she traveled on was no longer raised out of the swamp, but there was still plenty of water around. She dunked the owl and scraped as much shit from its feathers as she could manage.

When it was as clean as she could get it, she pulled it up out of the water. "How's that? Do you feel better now?"

The owl blinked.

"Don't you worry. I'm going to take care of you, okay? The first thing we need to do is get you dried off. And since I'm in kind of a hurry, we can kill two birds with one stone. No offense."

Katherine held the owl in front of her with both hands and resumed running. She ran until she reached the main road, hung a right, and kept on running.

Eventually, she started to catch up with a horse-drawn wagon. Perfect. She hadn't even considered hitchhiking. Not knowing how much more time this spell had left in it, she ran as unnaturally fast as her legs could take her.

When she was just behind the wagon, she shouted, "Excuse me!"

The driver turned around. His eyes went as wide as the owl's. "Gods have mercy!" He turned back around and whipped the reins. "Yah!" The horses started speeding up.

"Hey, motherfucker!" said Katherine. "Stop those goddamn horses right now!" She considered how she must appear, having slept in a swamp. Her hair was a filthy mess. Her face was covered in mosquito bites. One of her hands was twice as big as the other. She smelled like swamp water and shit. And it couldn't have helped that she was running inhumanly fast while holding a deformed owl in front of her.

She tried a different approach. "Please!"

The man looked back at her, then at the horses, then back at her again. Whether pity got the better of him, or whether he reasoned that his horses wouldn't be able to outpace whatever the hell she was, Katherine didn't care. He reined them to a stop.

When the wagon had come to a stop. The man folded his hands and bowed down to Katherine. "Spare me, merciful swamp hag!"

"Fuck you!"

"I am but a humble potato farmer. I have a family!"

"I don't want to hurt you, and I'm not a fucking swamp hag. I'm just a woman who's had a really shitty night and needs a ride into town."

The man bit his lower lip, apparently weighing the option to just get the horses moving again.

"I can pay you," said Katherine.

The man frowned. "What's wrong with your owl?"

"He's had a shitty day, too. Can we please have a ride."

"Well, I suppose if you intended to kill me, you could have done so by now. Climb on up."

CHAPTER 11

If there were two things the quad in front of the Great Library of Cardinia didn't lack for, they were delicious snack foods and entertainment. Food carts lined the perimeter selling pickled eggs, various meats, and so many different varieties of beer. While a lot of the merchants had their kids standing in front of their carts holding signs to advertise their wares, some of them had hired performers to play an instrument or juggle. None of their half-assed measures held a candle, however, to Captain Pyre's Dire N' Fire.

They must have been paying a small fortune to run this operation. It occupied at least eight times the space of any other plot. A roasting dire boar rotated on a spit about two stories high. Atop each support holding up the spit was a wooden platform. Signs hanging from the platforms identified the dwarves standing on them as Ditto and Wimbly. They were dressed in brightly colored robes and pointy hats, flinging insults and spells at one another in a fascinatingly dangerous-looking vaudeville act.

Though they were caricatures of wizards, Julian suspected Ditto and Wimbly were actually bards. The spells they cast at each other came from wands rather than from within them, and their vocal and acrobatic talents were more remarkable than their magic. Any real wizard would see the phony Fireballs and Lightning Bolts for what they really were, impressively rendered manifestations of the harmless 0-Level Prestidigitation spell.

But the real star of the show was the man behind the counter, Captain Pyre himself. He was almost certainly neither a military figure nor the owner of the establishment. He was a first class carnival barker though. Full braided beard. Big ass helmet with what looked like mammoth tusks on either side. Eye patch. Skin riddled with tattoos of mysterious symbols. The works. Even the fire behind him doubled as a backdrop, giving the effect of a blazing battlefield. He berated and insulted his customers as he served them the only thing he offered, boar meat on a stick, and the customers loved him for it.

After twenty minutes in line, it was finally Julian's turn.

"And what have we here?" Captain Pyre shouted as Julian stepped forward. "Did ye roll around in pixie shit on yer way here?" Julian guessed the joke had something to do with his colorful, yet admittedly filthy, serape. The crowd of customers laughed politely but expectantly, like they were waiting for a bigger punchline.

The captain shrugged and spoke in a normal tone to Julian. "What'll ye have, lad?"

"Two please," said Julian.

"Yer wee elven mother had two." Captain Pyre paused dramatically as the crowd hushed in anticipation. "Two of me fists up her arse!" He brought his forearms together and punched upward suggestively.

That's what the crowd had been waiting for. They roared with laughter and slapped each other on the backs. Julian forced a smile, but he was reminded of Cooper, and that reminded him of Tim. How did they get in this big mess? He hoped his friends were all okay.

"That'll be a silver piece, lad."

Julian placed a gold piece on the counter. "Keep the change."

"Much obliged, sir." Captain Pyre handed him two sticks of dire boar meat chunks slathered in some kind of brown sauce.

Stacy and Ravenus were in the middle of the quad, right where Julian had left them. Ravenus was idly scratching at the ground while Stacy was lying on her back, tossing a dagger and staying perfectly still as it pierced the ground extremely close to her.

"That's really impressive," said Julian. "But I feel I should warn you. In this game, you always have a five percent chance of failure no matter how good at something you are."

Stacy sat up. "Is your curiosity sated?"

"Yes."

"Was it everything you'd hoped for?"

"He said he fisted my mom."

"Nice. I hope he washed his hands before returning to work."

Julian waved one of the skewered dire boar meat sticks at Stacy. "I got an extra one."

Stacy hopped to her feet and accepted Julian's offer. "As long as we can eat and walk."

The meat was tender and smoky. The sauce reminded Julian of Heinz 57 with some habanero peppers thrown in for a bit of spice.

"You win," said Stacy through a mouthful of meat. "This was worth the detour."

Ravenus flapped down to land on Julian's shoulder.

Julian could sense his familiar's curiosity. "It's really good. Wanna try it?"

"No thank you, sir!" said Ravenus. "They've gone and burned all the flavor out."

"That's called cooking."

"I prefer my meat raw and properly aged."

"I know that," said Julian. "You just seemed curious, so I thought I'd offer."

"I was curious, sir. Not by your barbaric food-ruining rituals, but by something you said earlier."

"What's that?"

"What does it mean to 'fist one's mum'?"

Stacy started to choke on a piece of meat. She held her hand to her throat, concentrated, then swallowed. "Wow. This must be what having a kid feels like. So how about it, Julian? Is it time to sit Ravenus down and have the ol' 'fisting your mum' talk?"

"Is something amiss, sir?" asked Ravenus. "You seem somehow... uncomfortable."

Julian raised his wrist to his shoulder for Ravenus to step on to. "I'll explain it when you're older. Go find a dead cat or something. Let us finish our lunch." He launched Ravenus into the air.

Stacy smiled at Julian as Ravenus flapped upward. "They grow up so fast."

As good as the meat was, neither Julian nor Stacy was able to finish the entire stick. In addition to creative marketing, unconventional yet effective customer service, and quality food, generous portions were apparently a part of Captain Pyre's business model. Tim might learn a lot from him if they ever made it home before he went too much further off the rails.

Shallow Grave was about as pleasant as the name suggested. It was the part of town that one was advised to avoid unless they had specific business there, and usually even then as well. The recent influx of residents, who had tried to sack the city only a few days earlier, did little to improve the neighborhood's reputation. The place was crawling with orcs who had been training since birth for the day when they could mercilessly slaughter the people of this city. Every movement felt like a threat. Every glance felt like a dare to make the first move. Julian stayed close to Stacy. He'd never felt whiter or elfier in his life.

"Will you calm down?" said Stacy. "Nobody's going to hurt you. These people were all just saved by Jesus."

"In my experience, those are the ones you most want to look out for."

"This is different. You know what I mean. I don't know much about Meb'Garshur, but from what I've gathered, it's possible that some of these people might never have seen an elf or a human before. We're exotic. So just chill out and – Does that wolf look familiar to you?"

Julian followed Stacy's gaze. A block ahead of them, a grey wolf was crossing the street. A small pouch dangled from its mouth by the drawstring. It looked enough like Katherine's Animal Companion, but Julian wasn't confident that he'd be able to pick Butterbean out of a lineup of other grey wolves.

"It's just a wolf," said Julian. "There's nothing to suggest –"

Stacy grabbed him by the back of the head and forced his eyes back on the wolf. "Look at what he's got in his mouth. That's Frank's dice bag."

Julian had to admit that the circumstantial evidence for this being the specific wolf in question was piling up. A hierarchy of thinning doubt flashed through his mind.

Wolf.

Grey wolf.

Grey wolf with a bag.

Grey wolf with a bag matching the description of the bag they were looking for.

Grey wolf with a bag matching the description of the bag they were looking for wandering unaccompanied in an urban setting.

Grey wolf with a bag matching the description of the bag they were looking for wandering unaccompanied in an urban setting in the specific neighborhood Stacy had been seeking one of the people known to be traveling with said wolf.

Grey wolf with a –

Stacy shook Julian's head. "What are you doing?"

"I was thinking. And I think you're right. Should we follow him?"

"If we can get the bag now, our situation will be vastly improved. We can take it back to Frank and everyone can calm the fuck down. He'd recognize you as an ally, right? Call him."

Julian licked his lips, then swallowed. "Butterbean!" he called out.

The wolf stopped and looked back at him. There was no mistaking that. Julian started to sigh, then sucked his sigh up in a gasp when Butterbean turned back around and bolted away.

"Shit!" said Stacy, preparing to run after it.

Their path was blocked by one of the biggest and baddest-looking orcs Julian had ever laid eyes on. His body was covered in enough scars to suggest that he'd been stabbed at least five times a day since birth. The lower tusk on the right side of his mouth had been sawed in half and capped with silver. He glared down at Julian with his one functioning eye, the other being just a blood-red orb. "What did you call me, elf?"

Julian scrambled for an appropriate response. "Huh?"

"He wasn't talking to you," said Stacy. "I'm his Butterbean." She pinched Julian's cheek very hard. "Isn't that right, Honeylamb?"

Julian felt his head being guided up and down by the cheek until he got the hint to start nodding voluntarily.

The orc grabbed a handful of Julian's serape. "Are you mocking me, elf?" he challenged.

Stacy tugged Julian's cheek from side to side.

He slapped her hand away. He'd collected himself. "No, sir. My heart was overwhelmed with joy at reuniting with my true love. I was compelled to shout her name." Was this a bad Diplomacy roll? This felt like a bad diplomacy roll.

The orc turned to the companions he'd been sitting with at a table outside of a little shop. "Does he speak truth?"

The only orc at the table not covered in scars was calmly

sipping coffee from a tin cup. He shrugged. "It's a different culture here than what you're used to."

The orc looked back at Julian, breathing heavily through flared nostrils. He let go of the serape and smoothed it down the front with both hands. "I apologize. I am new here and your ways are strange to me. I'm afraid I misunderstood." He bowed low.

Julian grinned nervously. "No harm done."

"Time to go, Sugarbunch," said Stacy. "We don't want to be late for that... thing."

"Go, new friend," said the orc. "Attend to your thing. And may the New God watch over you."

"While I'm attending to my thing?"

Stacy grabbed Julian's arm and yanked hard. "Let's go!"

Julian was grateful to no longer be staring horrible violent death incarnate in the face, but Butterbean's trail had gone cold.

Ravenus caught up to them a few minutes later, panicked about Julian's sudden shift in emotions, but even aerial reconnaissance turned up no sign of any wolves in the vicinity.

"Sorry I panicked back there," said Julian. "It's my fault we lost him."

Stacy shook her head. "We can't outrun a wolf, and he clearly didn't want to be followed."

"I thought you'd be more upset."

"Not at all. You think it's a coincidence that Butterbean turned up in this neighborhood? The neighborhood where you and I are about to have a meeting with an organized crime boss? I'm telling you, we're right on top of that little jerk."

The shop where the appointment was scheduled was nearly indistinguishable from any of the surrounding structures. The windows were boarded up. The brickwork was crumbling. The area in front of it was littered with garbage.

The only two things that set it apart from the others were that it had what looked like a relatively new front door, and a hastily painted sign hanging over the door which read “GIFTS”.

“I’ll do the talking,” said Stacy.

That was just fine with Julian. He was more than happy to unload the burden of being ‘the face of the party’ onto someone else. But he would have felt better knowing that they were going in with some kind of plan. “Do you know what you’re going to say?”

“I’ll adapt as the situation progresses. Trust me. I’m, like, crazy smart.”

“That’s very reassuring.”

“Your role is silent partner,” said Stacy. “You’re mysterious and unpredictable, but not outwardly threatening. Can you do that?”

“Sure. I guess.”

“Good. Let’s do this.” Stacy didn’t even bother knocking. She turned the handle and walked right in the door.

Julian followed behind as silently, mysteriously, unpredictably, and not outwardly threateningly as he could.

The interior of the shop wasn’t any more inviting than the outside. The flaky remnants of paint suggested that the walls had once been blue. Now they were dingy grey, most of the paint having succumbed to neglect or whatever creature had scarred the walls with claw marks.

One wall – the only one Julian recalled from the outside as having had a window – was obscured by a large dusty bookcase. A random assortment of trinkets sat on what shelves were left of it. A bronze cup, a stringless lute, a broken ship inside a glass bottle. It was like they were trying to meet some minimum legal requirement to be able to call the place a gift shop.

A half-elven woman in a satin magenta blazer sat behind a desk which appeared to have come with the building, given that one of its legs was a stack of old books. She’d been speaking to a human assistant in a light green cloak when Stacy and Julian barged in on their conversation.

She folded a small piece of paper and tucked it into her

breast pocket under her right lapel. Turning back to her assistant after a brief glance at her guests, she said, "Snaketongue couldn't be bothered with it, so they passed it on to us."

"Seems that way, ma'am," said the assistant.

"Send word to our contacts in the west. Find out what it is."

The assistant bowed, then walked briskly toward Stacy and Julian. Stacy stepped to her left, and Julian followed suit, stepping to his right. The man in the green cloak walked between them without even sparing them a glance and left the room.

Three more assistants remained, all of them silent, mysterious, and unpredictable, but not outwardly threatening. Each of them was lean and wiry, about as physically intimidating as Julian. If scowls were an inherited trait, he supposed they could all be brothers.

"Close the door, please," said the woman behind the desk.

Stacy nodded to Julian. So that's how it was. He was subservient to her now. This shit had better just be part of the act. He closed the door.

"I'm here to see Dolazar," said Stacy.

The half-elven woman smiled and spread her hands wide. "Take in an eyeful. What can I do for you?"

"You're Dolazar? I was expecting..."

"A man?" said Dolazar. "So was I. Only one of us, however, was supposed to be surprised. What is your business here."

"I have something for you," said Stacy. She took a step forward and reached into her bag, glancing at the men in the green cloaks as she did so. They didn't even flinch.

"Come come," said Dolazar. "Time is money. Step forward and let's see what you've got."

As they approached the desk, Julian spotted a charcoal drawing of a face that looked a lot like Tim's lying among some other papers on the desk. Stacy didn't appear to notice at all.

When they reached the desk, Julian nudged Stacy with his elbow and looked at her, repeatedly moving his eyes from her face down to the desk. She responded with a hard, tight-lipped glare.

Julian went back to being silent, mysterious, and unpredictable, but not outwardly threatening.

Stacy emptied her prepackaged offering onto the desk. Specifically on the picture of Tim. Julian took that as a subtle way of saying, "Yes, I saw the fucking picture. Chill your goofy ass out."

Julian chilled his goofy ass out.

Dolazar frowned at the finger wrapped in bandages sitting atop the pile of coins. "Take this away."

One of her green-cloaked assistants immediately hopped to the task, removing the finger and exiting the room.

"So you want to be a Rat Bastard."

"That is correct, Ma'am," said Stacy.

"What is your name?"

"I'm Stacy, and this is my assistant, Julian."

Julian wondered how wise it was for her to use their real names. It probably made little difference, but it felt like Stacy was giving away more information than she was getting, as he was almost certain that the half-elven woman's name wasn't actually Dolazar.

"It's a pleasure to meet you."

Stacy thrust her hand forward enthusiastically. "The pleasure is all mine."

Dolazar accepted a brief handshake, seemingly just to get Stacy's hand out of her face. "You realize, of course, you must provide a sizable donation to the guild. And there is an initiation test to be passed."

"Haven't I just done those two things?"

"You have done neither," said Dolazar. "All I see here is someone else's donation and someone else's failed test."

"You're saying you want more money and another finger?"

"The tests are tailored to individual candidates. Do you take me for some finger-collecting savage?"

"Do you take me for a sap?" snapped Stacy, less diplomatically than Julian was comfortable with.

Dolazar laughed in disbelief as she stood up to speak to Stacy face-to-face. "I take you for the least qualified candidate ever to walk into my office. May I please have my ring back?" She put out her hand.

Practically trembling with contempt, Stacy reached into her pocket, then placed a ruby-studded ring onto Dolazar's open palm.

Dolazar shook her head. "This is a business of subtlety, restraint, and measured risk. You tried to steal from your would be boss, during an unscheduled interview, and with the grace of a herd of oxen. And look at you. In the middle of the day, dressed like some burglar whore, stringing along a strange elven mute wearing a Prismatic Wall."

Stacy grabbed Dolazar by her blazer lapels. "Listen here, you uptight long-eared bitch!"

"Stacy!" cried Julian. "What are you doing?" He tried to pull Stacy back, but she was strong as shit.

Stacy shook the shit out of Dolazar. "Listen here, you uptight long-eared bitch! I'm the rogueiest rogue in Roguesylvania! Do you understand what I'm saying to you?"

"I honestly do not!" Dolazar's eyes were wide with genuine terror.

By this time, the two remaining assistants were helping Julian try to restrain Stacy. Julian was thankful that they hadn't opted to just stab them both to death instead.

"Sleep with one eye open, lady!" screamed Stacy as she was dragged back toward the door. "Because I'm subtle as fuck, and I'm coming for your soul!"

Stacy writhed and screamed like a banshee as Julian and the two men in the green cloaks escorted her.

They threw Stacy out the door and gave Julian an unfriendly shove.

"You'd do well to keep that lunatic in a cage," said one of the cloaked men. "Don't ever let us catch you around here again."

Stacy stood up, brushed herself off, then gave them the finger. But they'd already shut the door.

When they were far enough away, Julian stopped walking. "What the hell was that back there?"

"Relax. Plan A wasn't working out. I had to adapt."

"You call that adapting?" said Julian. "Because to me, it looked like you just completely lost your shit."

"That's what it was supposed to look like. We bungled the initiation thing, leading her to believe I was an incompetent rogue. So I went with that. I used a bit of misdirection, grabbed what I could, and cut our losses."

"You are an incompetent rogue. You didn't misdirect shit. You got caught stealing the ring, and you almost got us killed."

Stacy smiled. "Getting caught with the ring was the misdirection. My real target was this." She pulled a scrap of paper out of her pocket.

"What's that?"

"Fuck if I know. Let's see." She unfolded the paper, revealing a series of symbols that Julian couldn't comprehend.

"Is that a language? Can you read that?"

Stacy shook her head. "Nothing I'm familiar with. Looks like some kind of code."

Julian didn't know if the scrap of paper was worth anything at all, but he felt at least a little relieved that Stacy's recent display of violent batshit insanity probably wasn't symptomatic of an actual mental health problem.

While Stacy stared at the symbols on the paper, Ravenus flew down to perch on the sign of a long-abandoned shop.

"Good news, sir! I've located the wolf."

"Seriously?" asked Julian. "That's excellent. Where is he?"

"Follow me."

Ravenus led Julian and Stacy to yet another abandoned building a few blocks away. "Just in there, sir."

The smell of rot, decay, and something like raw sewage wafted out of the open doorway.

"Ugh," said Julian. "That's horrible."

"Indeed, sir. Finding the wolf was quite accidental. I had hoped to find something to eat in here."

The building was small, with only two rooms. Julian found Butterbean lying on his stomach in the back room, the drawstring of Frank's dice bag still in his teeth. The only furniture in the room was a blood-stained wooden bench. Bloodied rags littered the floor. The bugs crawling all over them might have indicated a certain degree of freshness, but Julian was no forensic investigator.

"Hey there, Butterbean!" said Stacy, leaning down and reaching for the bag. "Who's a good boy?"

Butterbean reared up to a crouch and snarled at her.

Stacy looked at Julian. "Katherine and I aren't exactly the best of friends. Maybe he'll take kindlier to you." She backed up behind Julian.

Julian approached the wolf slowly and cautiously. He had a high Charisma score, and he thought he remembered having a couple of ranks in the Handle Animal skill.

Be cool, Julian. If he growls or snarls, just back off.

He tentatively reached out to pet Butterbean on the head and met no resistance. In fact, the wolf seemed to really welcome the affection. He even rested his head on Julian's knee once Julian felt comfortable enough to sit next to him.

Their trust established, Julian continued stroking the wolf's filthy fur with his right hand while reaching slowly and cautiously for the dice bag with his left, wary of any change in Butterbean's demeanor.

Julian got as far as wrapping his hand around the bag and giving it a small tug before he got a low growl from Butterbean.

"Come on, Butterbean. We need this bag."

Butterbean refused to let go.

Julian tugged a little harder. Something was wrong. It didn't feel like a bag full of dice. It was squishier than that. He squeezed it with both hands, feeling all around for any solid lumps, but coming up empty. Some yellow liquid oozed out of the opening. He looked up at Stacy.

"There aren't any dice in here."

"Then what's in it?"

Julian shrugged. "I have no idea. Ectoplasm or snot or something."

"Why would Butterbean be carrying around a bag full of snot? Do you think Cooper has anything to do with this?"

"I guess that's possible," said Julian. "But it doesn't explain why Butterbean is defending it so vigilantly, and why he brought it here to this particular place."

Stacy scratched behind her ear. "The plot thickens."

Julian let go of the bag and stood up. "So where do we go from here?"

"We focus on what clues we have available. The most obvious one being trying to figure out what this secret message is." She pulled the scrap of paper out of her pocket again and peered at the symbols written on it.

"That could be anything. What makes you think it has anything to do with Tim or the dice?"

"I know you noticed the picture of Tim on Dolazar's desk. They're in on this somehow. Maybe this is nothing, but it's all we have to –" Her gaze flickered up from the paper for a fraction of a second. She offered it to Julian. "See what you can make out of it. I have to pee."

Julian took the paper as Stacy walked out the back door.

There was a triangular spiral, a Q, something that looked like a vaguely familiar Japanese symbol, and a whole bunch of other random crap. There was nothing for him to make out. You either know the code or you don't. This was just another dead end in a string of – Something thudded from outside.

"Stacy?" Julian called, probably too quietly for anyone beyond the other room to hear him. "Stay here, Ravenus." The sound came from the front of the building, so Julian tiptoed into the other room and peeked through the front doorway.

He was somehow not entirely surprised to see Stacy dragging a body toward him.

"Give me a hand with this guy," she said. "He's heavier than he looks."

It was one of the green-cloaked men from Dolazar's office. He would have a bad headache and a nasty lump when he woke up. Julian took one of his arms and they dragged him into the room where Butterbean and Ravenus stared blankly at them.

"Getting a bit crowded in here, isn't it sir?" Typical Ravenus. He'd blurt out questions about fisting moms on a crowded street, but tried to maintain a sense of discreet propriety when inquiring about why Julian was dragging a body into the room.

"This guy was following us. He might have some answers. Or not. I don't know, but here we are."

Stacy got right to work tying up the man's ankles and wrists, then tying the ankles to the wrists. When she was satisfied with her knots, she separated the three strands of a four foot section of rope that she'd cut from the rest. She wrapped two of the strands tightly around the four fingers of each of his hands, leaving only the thumbs to wiggle freely. With the remaining strand, and the balled up sleeve of his green cloak, she made a gag.

"Get Ravenus to perch on his head," Stacy instructed. "You're still going to be silent, mysterious, and unpredictable. But you can be threatening this time as well."

"Should I stand with my hands on my hips?" Julian put his hands on his hips and squinted.

"No. You look like you're annoyed by a late bus."

"What if I cross my arms?"

"Too chill."

"I could lean against the wall and casually sharpen a dagger."

Stacy shook her head. "That's going overboard. You know what? Just stand there. You're doing fine."

Julian asked Ravenus to perch on the man's head, then stood

out of the way, hoping things weren't about to turn really ugly.

Stacy let water trickle from her waterskin onto the man's face until he began to stir, then took a step back.

When he regained consciousness, his eyes opened wide with terror at first, then softened with recognition of Stacy, and finally glazed over with resignation at his situation.

"I've got some good news and some bad news," said Stacy. "The good news is that you're not going to die today. The bad news is that you might wish you were dead." She glanced at Julian.

Julian nodded his approval. Good stuff.

"If I take this gag out, do you promise not to scream?"

The man nodded. Stacy removed the gag.

He cleared his throat, spat out a bit of lint, then looked up at Stacy. "If it's all the same to you, can we skip the torture routine?"

Stacy looked at Julian again. He shrugged.

"This is standard protocol for getting captured," the prisoner explained. "I'll happily tell you everything you want to know if you promise not to hurt me."

"What kind of protocol is that? You expect me to believe you'll just sell out your fellow guild members as easy as that?"

"As our organization takes into account a certain level of mutual distrust for occasions such as this one. I'm not privy to any information which could be particularly damaging if leaked."

Stacy nodded. "That sounds fair."

"You can get off his head, Ravenus," said Julian.

Ravenus hopped down to the floor.

"Thank you," said the man. "Now how can I help you?"

"You can start by telling me everything you know about the halfling."

"What halfling?"

"Oh come on," said Stacy. "I thought we were going to skip the whole torture thing."

"I'm sorry. That was a very vague question. You'll have to be more specific."

"The halfling on the picture on Dolazar's desk."

The man bit his lip and thought for a moment. "Oh, are you talking about the wanted poster?"

"Wanted poster?" asked Julian. "What is Tim wanted for?"

Stacy glared at him. He realized he was both breaking character and prematurely giving away information. She kept the glare, but directed it toward her captive.

"A whole list of things. Murder, arson, theft, indecent exposure, blasphemy, rape, –"

Julian and Stacy gasped.

"I made up the rape part. I was curious to see what it would take to get either of you to look surprised."

"Where did you find the poster?" asked Stacy. "And why is Dolazar interested in him?"

"She's interested in all matters involving criminal activity. I ripped that one off a lamp post. The kingsguard began posting them all over town this morning."

Julian leaned over and whispered to Stacy. "Ask him about the message."

"I was getting to that." She pulled the coded message out of her pocket, unfolded it, and held it up for the bound man to see. "Can you read this?"

"Yes."

"Please do so."

The man cleared his throat. "Overheard at Arby's. Major transaction going down at Crescent Shadow. Goods unknown."

Stacy nodded slowly. "He's going to make a deal with Mordred."

"I still don't think he'd screw us all over like that," said Julian.

Stacy glanced at her prisoner, then dragged Julian by the arm into the other room and spoke in a whisper. "I don't think so either. I think he's trying to be a hero to make up for screwing us over before. He wants to save the day and bring all of us back home."

"Well that sounds nice," said Julian. "Why does your voice still sound like you think he's a piece of shit?"

"Because it's still all about him. He's like that friend with a gambling problem who steals your life savings to bet it all on a 'sure thing' at the racetrack. He's telling himself that you're going to thank him when he pays back double what he took from you, but he knows that if he fucks up, he hasn't really lost anything."

"You think he's going to fuck up?"

Stacy looked into Julian's eyes. "Julian. Look deep inside yourself and find the answer to that question."

Julian frowned. "Shit."

"I don't know how this whole 'multiple Mordred' thing works. But if he's retaining memories from all of his avatars, then he saw all the shit that went down at the Whore's Head right up until Tim slit his throat, and can probably guess what happened shortly thereafter. He knows Tim is in a desperate spot right now, so he made him an offer too good to pass up. Tim steals the dice for Mordred, and Mordred promises to set him and all his friends free."

Julian didn't want to think that Tim would be that gullible, but what Stacy was saying made a lot of sense. The stolen dice. The major transaction. Arby's. Tim's sudden crime spree.

"Shit," Julian said again.

"We need to get to Crescent Shadow and intercept those dice before Tim makes contact with Mordred."

"Sounds good. Where is Crescent Shadow?"

"How the hell should I know?"

Julian nodded toward the other room. "Do you think he knows?"

Stacy marched back into the rear room. "We've got one more question, and I suggest you give me a straight answer, lest I have my companion's bird peck your eyes out."

"That's really unnecessary," said the man. He looked down at Ravenus.

Ravenus, startled at being the focus of anyone's attention in a conversation he didn't understand, looked at Julian. Julian shook his head.

"What's the quickest way to get to Crescent Shadow?" asked Stacy.

"Teleport."

Stacy frowned. "Okay. Fair enough answer. I should have phrased the question differently. Where is Crescent Shadow? And what's the best way to get there on limited funds?"

"I suppose you might hire a griffon rider to take you up there. But the tricky part is wandering around the desert trying to find it."

"It's an island... in a desert?"

"Above," said the prisoner. "Crescent Shadow is a floating island. It meanders above the Fertile Desert, never staying in one place for too long."

"That sounds really cool," said Julian. Stacy didn't glare at him this time. Now that the interrogation was running along smoothly, there wasn't much point in maintaining his threatening façade.

"On the contrary. It's one of the hottest and most unforgiving places in the world."

"I meant the island."

"Ah, well yes. I suppose there's probably more of a breeze up there. I've never been myself."

"I'm sorry," said Stacy. "I feel like I've missed something again. Is Fertile Desert a contradictory name, or is there more to that than what you're telling us?"

"I apologize. I mean to keep no secrets. I thought you might have some knowledge of the history of the world." He paused and thought over his words. "Again, I apologize if that sounded condescending."

"You're doing fine. Feel free to explain things to us as if we were little children from a different world. Tell me about the Fertile Desert."

"The legend goes back to the time of the First Men."

Stacy rolled her eyes. "Of course it does."

"Excuse me?"

"Nothing. Please go on."

"Humankind was the final creation of the gods, and we were meant to be their finest. But since the elves and dwarves and halflings and such had already established themselves, the gods chose to give their newest creation a place of their own where they could thrive until they were ready to join the rest of creation. They created a garden so abundant with life that their newest creation would want for nothing, and be able to focus on forming a civilization of their own."

"An Eden myth," said Julian. He knew in the back of his mind that this was all just stuff that Mordred had ripped off from ancient myths he was familiar with, but it was fascinating all the same.

Stacy looked less fascinated. "Let me guess. There was this one particular tree, the fruit of which the gods explicitly told the First Men not to eat."

Their prisoner looked puzzled. "No. They were supposed to eat the fruit. That's what the gods put the fruit trees there for."

"So there wasn't, like, a talking snake or anything?"

The prisoner looked like he was starting to get worried about being tortured again. "There might have been. I can add a talking snake if you like."

"No," said Stacy. "You're doing great. Keep talking."

"Instead of building a civilization and preparing to find their way in the world as the gods had intended, humans grew lazy and complacent. Knowing they were the gods' favored race, they also grew arrogant and demanding."

Julian shook his head. "Here we go."

"The gods sent emissaries from each of the other races to

demonstrate to the humans what wonders were possible with a bit of effort. They were sent to introduce art and literature and magic."

"Whew," said Julian. "For a second, I thought that was going to go in a different direction."

"The humans raped and/or ate the emissaries."

"Oh." Julian frowned. "A minor detour, but we're back on the road I thought we were on."

"Naturally the gods were incensed. They cast an eternal drought upon the land. It is a desert, but the soil itself remains abundantly fertile. Spill only a few drops of water on the ground, and you can see vegetation sprout forth. But when the water stops, the insatiable barren earth drinks it away and the plants wither and die."

Stacy looked at Julian. "Change of plans. We need to find Cooper."

"Oh right," said Julian. "Because he's got the... the thing. The water thing."

"Thank you for your time and cooperation sir." Stacy placed the gag back in the prisoner's mouth, which he opened wide to accommodate her. "I think you understand we can't have you follow us."

The man nodded understandingly.

"So we're just going to leave him here?" asked Julian.

"Someone should be along shortly to meet the wolf here, I would think."

"That looks really uncomfortable."

"Well I'm sorry I don't have a pillow handy."

Julian spread the arms of his serape wide and channeled his sorcery.

"You're not going to summon a horse, are you?"

Julian ignored her, placed his hand on the man's forehead, and whispered, "Sleep."

The prisoner's head lolled to the side as he fell instantly to sleep.

CHAPTER 12

Where would I go if I were Tim and on the run?

Cooper realized the second part of the question was probably unnecessary. Tim would go to a bar. He'd tell himself that he needed to clear his head and think, but he'd just wind up getting shitfaced and passing out.

There were only two problems with this insight. Cardinia was crawling with taverns and pubs, and Tim was in a sewer.

Cooper stopped running and tried to think of which direction Tim and Katherine might have gone after they escaped the Piss Bucket Tavern. No, that was impossible to determine. He didn't even know what direction he was headed in.

Wherever he was, he had this part of town pretty much to himself. The street was quiet. He took a cautious glance up and down the street before trying to remove a manhole cover.

Another dead end. He could barely get a grip, and the thing just wasn't even pretending to budge.

Shit. Back to square one.

In a moment of zen, all of Cooper's anxiety and tension and worry and self-doubt coalesced in his mind and sunk down into his bowels, then noisily out of his butthole.

If Cooper couldn't move these fuckers, there was no way that Tim or Katherine could. As far as he knew, there was only one publicly accessible way in and out of the sewers. If they could fight their way through whatever horrible creatures lived in other people's shit, Cooper would be able to find them at the edge of the Collapsed Sewer District.

That was a good bit of thinking. He wished he had someone to high five.

It was indeed a good bit of thinking.

"Thanks, voice in my head."

Let us make haste to this Collapsed Sewer District.

"Dude. I'm fucking going already. Keep your pants on." The voice in Cooper's head was just a little bit demanding, but he was grateful for the company. He might even miss it once he got some proper rest and sleep deprivation stopped fucking with his mind.

He took a roundabout way to the Collapsed Sewer District, both because he wanted to avoid running into anyone from the Whores Head Inn, and because he began his journey without the faintest idea of where he was. By the time he reached the rubble-strewn exposed tunnels, it was nearly dawn. The first hints of light were beginning to silhouette the buildings to the east.

Filthy vagrants huddled around fires fueled by the remains of what was once one of the more prosperous parts of the city. If he played his cards right, he might just be able to fit in.

"Alright, boys," said the hobo in charge. "The fire's good and strong now. Roll out the cauldron and start filling her up."

Four men rolled a large iron cauldron out from where it had been hidden behind some rubble. Two others carried out the carcass of a freshly slaughtered dire rat. Everyone else got to work scooping up water from puddles and dumping it into the cauldron.

A younger man, one of the four who had rolled out the cauldron, frowned at the giant dead rat. "Doesn't it seem wrong, that we should be eating rat?"

Cooper was at least as hungry as he was tired. A bellyful of rat gumbo sounded great to him. He wasn't sure, but he sensed the voice in his head was hungry as well.

"Don't be such a sissy," said the leader. "It'll keep your belly full and warm. And besides, I nicked enough garlic to mask the taste." He pulled two bulbs of garlic, each about the size of a softball, out of his satchel and tossed them into the empty cauldron. "What else have we got?"

"We stole a bag of rice," said one of the other cauldron movers. He and a companion hefted up a heavy burlap sack and dumped dry rice into the mix.

"Aye, good lads. That'll thicken it up nicely. Anything else?"

"I've got carrots," said one of the puddle scoopers. He removed a seemingly empty scabbard from around his waist and dumped four scrawny carrots into the cauldron.

The leader frowned. "A weak effort, but every little bit helps." He pointed to two of his hobo underlings who were slacking off. "You two, up off your asses. You can skin and gut the rat."

Cooper kept his distance, knowing he was charismatically challenged, trying to think of some way he could contribute so that he might be invited to share their meal while waiting for Tim and Katherine to surface.

The guys on rat gutting duty finished their job quickly enough, and were reassigned to puddle scooping. This was going to take forever, and Cooper strongly suspected that those puddles had more hobo piss than water in them.

Hunger and exhaustion must have a way of kindling the imagination, because Cooper suddenly had an idea that was sure to endear him to these men.

He stepped out into the open. "Excuse me, gentlemen. I couldn't help but notice that what you're cooking is fucking disgusting."

Everyone stopped what they were doing and glared at Cooper. To be fair, his words had sounded more endearing before he spoke them aloud.

"Well well," said the leader. "Look who's too good for boiled dire rat. Lucky for you that nobody asked you to join us."

"I'm sorry. That came out wrong. I'm totally cool with eating rat. I just thought you might enjoy some clean water."

"What know you of clean water? You don't appear to have made its acquaintance for months." His subordinates laughed.

"Hey," said Cooper. "Not cool, man. I have, like, glandular problems and shit."

"You best be on your way, half-orc. You might have noticed we're not so finicky about what we boil and eat. With enough garlic, it all tastes the same." The leader put his hand on the pommel of his short sword, prompting everyone else to reach for their weapons as well."

Cooper raised his hands as a gesture of peaceful intent. "Whoa. Take it easy. I'm not here to start any shit. I'm waiting for some friends, and I thought I'd offer you something in return for your company, and maybe a little rat soup."

The leader licked his lips and eyed Cooper warily. "I'm listening, half-orc. What's your offer?"

Very slowly, and as non-threateningly as he could, Cooper approached the cauldron as he reached into his bag and pulled out the Decanter of Endless Water.

The leader removed his hand from his weapon and raised his eyebrows. "My my, but wherever did you come by such a... shiny... receptacle?"

That was more like it. Cooper grinned as he held the decanter over the cauldron. "It does more than shine." He tipped the vessel forward, and crystal clear water poured out from the top. Long after it should have emptied, the water just kept on flowing.

The crowd gathered around in hushed awe. They were impressed.

"What's your name, half-orc?"

"My friends call me Cooper."

The leader's nose twitched as he offered Cooper a wide grin. "Well I have some good news, Mr. Cooper. I've decided to accept your offer. You hand over the shiny pitcher, and we'll share soup and stories around the fire."

Cooper snorted. A fleck of snot shot down and him in the nipple. "I think you mistook my offer. My bad. I don't always communicate well. The offer I was making was just for the water."

The hobo leader laughed in a way that made Cooper begin to feel uncomfortable. His underlings joined in the laughter, from well within Cooper's personal space. They took a step back and coughed when Cooper had another sudden buildup and release of anxiety.

"Sorry," said Cooper. "Empty stomach."

"I'm afraid it is you who are mistaken," said the leader. "if you think you're walking away from here with that shiny bit of treasure in your hand."

Shit.

Cooper was in enough trouble already. Katherine would be pissed if he surrendered her Decanter of Endless Water to a bunch of hobos.

I'm hungry.

"Goddammit, this is not the fucking time. I'm in the middle of some shit right now."

The leader's smile faltered. "Your personal problems are no concern of mine, Mr. Cooper. I can assure you that, if you wish to remain alive, now is most certainly the fucking time to hand over the pitcher."

"I was talking to someone else. He says he's hungry, like I've got time for that shit right now."

Some of the men crowded around him craned their necks to check out the surrounding area.

"Listen," said their leader. "You seem like a nice enough fellow, if a bit slow. Mind games are not your strong suit. Give me the pitcher, and you and your imaginary friend can consume all the rat soup your bellies can hold. How does that sound?"

I feed on blood and the souls of the wicked.

"Dude, there's, like, no nutritional value in that."

"I put carrots and garlic in the soup." The hobo leader's voice was growing impatient. "It's very healthy. Now give me the pitcher!"

"Can one of you please shut the fuck up for a minute?" said

Cooper. "I can only handle one conversation at a time."

Feed me.

"This is your last chance, half-orc."

Give in to your rage.

"Hand over the pitcher at once."

FEED ME!

"FUCK YOU!" Cooper needed to end at least one of these conversations, and only one of the voices was coming from a discernible mouth. The choice was clear. "Geyser!"

"Very well, Mr. Cooper. Have it your –" The hobo leader flew backward when a torrent of water hit him square in the face.

"I'm really angry!" said Cooper. His vision turned red as the hobos drew their weapons. He swung the decanter sideways, catching the nearest one in the side of the head, dropping him to the ground.

Use me, you fool!

Cooper tore his axe from the straps on his back and shoved the decanter into the cauldron, where it continued to spew water straight up in the air. The axe glowed bright red, which the small functioning part of Cooper's mind thought might be a trick of his rage-fueled vision. But it appeared that the hobos could see it as well, because they all backed away.

"There are a dozen of us, and only one of him!" cried the leader, who had somehow just turned into some weird hybrid of man and rat.

"Master Splinter?" Cooper needed some food and sleep. This shit was getting fucked up.

"Kill him!" Master Splinter was kind of a dick.

Some of the men remained men. Others followed their leader in morphing into man/rat hybrids. Those without weapons went full rat. All of them rushed Cooper at once.

His axe blade cleaved through hobo-rats, felling them like saplings made out of meat. Cooper felt a sensation not unlike the first beer after a long and shitty shift at work as he painted the ground with blood.

Cooper felt a few stabs and jabs here and there, but they didn't hurt nearly as much as they probably would once he came out of his Barbarian Rage. One thing that did catch his eye, however, was the fact that whenever he killed a hybrid or full rat, they morphed back into their human form. The gashes his axe left in their rat forms doubled in size as their dead bodies changed. Both fascinating and gross.

When only three of them remained standing, all in hybrid form, the leader ordered their retreat. The three rat men ran into the sewer tunnel, and Cooper was ready to abandon his Rage and let them run off.

They will return with more of their kind. Bury my blade in their chests, so that I may drink directly from their still beating hearts!

As fucked up as that sounded, Cooper had to admit the voice in his head had a point. Adrenaline still pumping, he gave chase into the sewer, and chopped through the two underlings with ease. The leader was faster, but not by much. He turned around and begged on his knees.

"Forgive me, great warrior! I beg your mercy!"

Cooper raised his glowing red axe above his head. "MERCY SHALL BE GIVEN AS BELHANNA SEES FIT!" He brought his axe down hard, slicing through the rat man's head, neck, and deep into his torso. The body changed back into human form. Even the insides, bones and brains and parts that Cooper couldn't identify, morphed in subtle ways.

His enemies defeated, Cooper deflated back into his flabby exhausted self. "What the fuck did I just say?"

In the darkness of the sewer, his axe still glowed with a faint red light.

My hunger is quenched for now, Cooper. Take me and satisfy your own.

"Are you the axe?"

I am.

"You're the one who's been talking to me inside my brain?"

Correct.

"And now you want me to eat you?"

What? No. The voice paused for a moment, then sighed. I meant that you should take me with you, and then go eat some of that rat soup. Two separate instructions. I should have been clearer.

Cooper removed the axe from the dead body, but wasn't quite ready to strap it onto his back. He held it in front of him, less like a weapon and more like a picket sign, as he made his way back to the cauldron.

You needn't be afraid, Cooper. I sense the good within you. That's why I chose you as my new keeper.

"Who the fuck are you?" asked Cooper. "I mean, aside from a talking axe."

My name is Nabi.

"Knobby? As in, 'like a knob'?"

No. Nabi. It's the Old Sylvan word for butterfly.

"That's a pretty name, I guess." Cooper exited the tunnel. The sky was quickly lightening the dead bodies and red pools of watery blood as the decanter continued shooting water up into the air.

"I should probably clean this up." He set Nabi down and hauled the bodies, one by one, out of sight into the tunnel. He could hide them better later if he needed to.

The cauldron was about half full from geyser water that had fallen back down into it. The top of the decanter was cool to the touch, but the water inside the cauldron was beginning to heat up.

By the time Cooper was done hosing the blood away as best he could, the water in the cauldron had come to a boil. He didn't know the proper way to cook giant rat, but he supposed there couldn't be much more to it than chucking the carcass into the pot.

After having done so, he considered that the rat might not

even be necessary. Garlic and carrots might have been enough for flavor, and the rice would have made it filling enough. But fuck it. The deed was done, and the only thing keeping him from falling flat on his face to sleep right now was the promise of sweet sweet protein.

There were a number of factors that made it unlikely that Cooper would ever write a cookbook, the two biggest of which were that he could neither cook nor write. But if he did, he would include one tip in the boiled giant rat recipe which he was quite pleased with himself for having discovered.

Let the tail hang over the side of the cauldron. That makes it easy to pull up the meat and test whether or not it's sufficiently cooked.

That was pretty fucking clever. Cooper hoped that he hadn't recently leveled up and inadvertently blown an ability score point on Intelligence.

After about thirty seconds, Cooper pulled the skinned rat out by the tail. He wasn't sure what rat meat was supposed to look like when done, but he was pretty sure this wasn't it.

He'd have to be patient. With little else to do, he sat back against the wall of the sewer tunnel, rested his eyes, and thought about what other recipes might go in his fantasy cookbook.

What about fried –

He had the weirdest fucking dream about a fairy paladin, her face smeared with blood, staring icy-eyed at something Cooper couldn't see, against a backdrop of a raging forest fire. Her butterfly-like wings fluttered uselessly, as she was weighed down by heavy full plate armor. She wielded a long slim blade in one hand, and a bright blue ball of magical energy in the other. It was like Tinkerbell had finally had enough of Hook's shit.

Sleep well, new friend. Our work has only just begun.

CHAPTER 13

Katherine parted ways with the driver outside a festival taking place in the city center. He'd seemed a little less on edge since they passed through Northgate, most likely figuring that she was less likely to murder him in a crowded city. But he seemed even more relieved to now be rid of her for good.

"Good day, ma'am," he said, tipping his hat as his horse pulled away. "Peace of the New God be with you."

He was facing away from her, so she gave him the finger. "And also with you."

She hadn't drunk any of the booze she'd swiped from the Piss Bucket Tavern during the ride, because she felt like it might be a breach of etiquette. What if he didn't approve? This was an old-timey place. What if they had weird views about women drinking in public? Or open bottle laws? The ride was already awkward enough as it was.

But now that it was over, she thought she'd more than earned a swig.

Getting the Bag of Holding open was a little tricky, given that her left arm was wrapped around Scratchy the Overplump Ungrateful Owl.

Still, her left hand was free enough to at least hold the lip of the bag. She reached in with her right hand and was just about to say the word "liquor" when two copper coins dropped into the bag.

"The fuck?" Katherine looked up. Captain Righteous was staring down at her, his familiarly judgmental eyes shining through his Kingsguard-issue visor. He and a younger, fatter Kingsguard were on horseback. The other one didn't even glance her way, his attention alternating between the crowd on the streets and the piece of paper he was holding open in front of him.

"The New God is watching," said Captain Righteous. "He'll know if you spend that on wine. Now run along and let gentler folk enjoy the festival."

"You motherfucking son of a fuck!" Katherine didn't say. Instead, she bowed her head and croaked out, "Thank you."

Was one night in a swamp enough to make her completely unrecognizable? She walked away with a hobble to reinforce his assumption that she was... well, whatever he was assuming she was.

There would be time enough to drink after she'd reunited with Tim. When she was far enough away from Captain Righteous, she straightened her gait and picked up her pace. It was dark now, and she remembered that getting Tim patched up was only the first item on the list. She also needed to track down whoever Tanner sold those dice to, get them back, and return them to the Whore's Head before the three of them were hunted down like –

Shit.

Tim stared at her from a lamppost. It wasn't really Tim, of course. It was just a charcoal sketch on a wanted poster. Some of the features were less than perfect, but it was totally Tim. She rushed to the post and ripped the paper down. In immediate retrospect, that was almost certainly illegal. She looked around for any sign of the Kingsguard.

The only people who seemed to have taken notice of her were two men with heads like hyenas. Katherine bared her teeth and hissed at them, and they continued on their way.

When they moved, Katherine spotted an identical wanted poster on the wall just behind where they'd been standing.

She looked more closely at the listed charges on the poster she was holding. "Who the fuck was that minotaur? A senator or something?"

Scanning the area, she found Tim's picture hanging everywhere, now that she was looking for it.

Now she had to get Tim out of town and hide him somewhere safe. Just add that on to the growing mountain of impossible shit she had to do.

Finding the area called Shallow Grave was easy enough, but finding the exact building where she'd left her brother proved trickier. Every dilapidated shithole building looked just like every other.

The deeper into Shallow Grave she got, the more deserted the place became. Not that anyone was giving her any trouble. Far from it, the residents of this part of town were giving her plenty of space. She really needed a mirror and a shower.

She'd left Tim in a pretty deserted area, so she hoped she was getting closer. She thought she recognized a few signs on some boarded up shops, but she could've just been conjuring memories to make herself believe she was going in the right direction.

"Butterbean?" she called out. A sharp bark came from somewhere ahead.

After running about twenty seconds toward the bark, she suddenly knew exactly where she was. The building where Tim was being cared for was directly in front of her. She ran across the street and went inside.

In the back room, there was no sign of Tim except for the bloodied rags which the Sister of Healing had cleaned his wounds with. Likewise, there was no sign of the Sister or Tanner either. Just Butterbean, who still had the fenberry bag in his mouth, and some poor chump tied up and gagged on the floor.

"Who the fuck are you? Where's my brother?"

The man on the floor made a show of looking down at his gag.

"Oh, right." Katherine leaned over to remove the gag, then stopped. She knew exactly who this was. It was another Mordred. It must be. Who else would Tim have left tied up on the floor?

She set the owl on the floor, which rolled onto its back and blinked helplessly.

Mordred stared at the owl with eyes nearly as wide and round as its own.

"I'm going to remove that gag," said Katherine. "If you utter a single sound that isn't a direct response to one of my questions, I will slit your throat from ear to ear, just like we did to that other one of you. Do you understand?"

Mordred nodded. Katherine removed the gag.

"Please," said Mordred. "There's no need for all that. I'll tell you whatever it is you want to know."

"Tim was here before. What happened to him? Where did he go?"

Mordred looked at Katherine's ears. "Might you be referring to a half-brother?"

"That's real fucking funny. You're about to be laughing through a gaping hole in your neck."

"I'm sorry! I meant no offense. He was here, with a woman. It couldn't have been that long ago."

"Was he... healthy?"

"I suppose so. I've not studied the healing arts, but –"

Katherine flicked him in the nose.

"Ow! What was that for?"

"Cut the nerd shit, fatty."

"Fatty?"

"Did Tim's legs work?" Katherine readied her middle finger and thumb for another flick.

"YES!"

"And he was walking around on them okay?"

"He looked fine to me."

A thought occurred to Katherine. Mordred had identified Tim and the Sister of Healing. He made no mention of Tanner. Had he ditched her? She couldn't remember the word that black people liked to be called in this world, but she didn't have time for any PC bullshit.

"Was there no one else with them? A black companion?"

Mordred looked puzzled at first, then his eyes lit up with recognition. "Oh yes, of course. I don't know how I forgot to mention him. He was sitting on my head!"

That was weird. Probably some kind of interrogation technique. That wasn't the sort of lie you made up to sell your story.

"Where did they go?"

"They were headed for the Shadow Crescent, in the Fertile Desert. If you hurry, you may be able to catch up to them."

Katherine put the gag back in Mordred's mouth. She didn't like having to trust his word, but it was all she had. Besides, her gut told her he was being truthful. She folded her arms and tried to fill in the missing puzzle pieces.

Tim is touch and go. If the Sister of Healing doesn't act fast, he's going to die.

She finds some expired fenberries, or some substitute herb, and does an emergency procedure, which works miraculously well. Maybe she dug up an old healing potion or something.

Mordred hones in on their location with magic or some shit.

Tanner gets the jump on Mordred, and they tie him up and interrogate him.

Under duress, Mordred tells them that they can find the dice at this Crescent Shadow place.

Tim doesn't recognize an obvious trap because he wants to redeem himself, or because he's shitfaced.

They keep Mordred tied up here, knowing Katherine will be along shortly. She's supposed to deliver Mordred to the Whore's Head, and let them know that Tim will be back with the dice soon.

"Well, Mordred," said Katherine. "It appears you have me in quite a pickle."

Mordred looked up at her confusedly. "Hnnnggg?"

"I can't take you with me. So that leaves me two choices. I can either run to the Whore's Head, and let Tim walk into the trap you've got waiting for him."

"Hnnnngggg!"

"Or I can catch up with Tim, giving you more time to escape, or for one of your other Mordreds to come rescue you."

"Hnnngg hnnngggg hng hnnnnngg!"

"I'm not gonna tell you. You can sit there and stew on it. Come on, Butterbean." Katherine removed the bag from Butterbean's mouth, picked up her swollen owl, and walked out the front door.

"Barney!" cried a vaguely familiar looking man in sorcerer robes. A glowing arrow hovered by his side, aimed at Katherine. She'd seen Julian cast that spell enough times to recognize it as a Magic Missile.

"Stop right there, Katherine," said Frank. He was pointing a crossbow at her.

It wasn't as friendly a greeting as Katherine would have liked, but it solved her conundrum.

"I'm really glad to see you guys."

"Cut the shit," said Frank. "Hand over my dice bag, nice and slow."

Katherine looked at the bag in her hand.

"What have you done with my owl?" screamed the other guy. "You sadistic bitch!"

Katherine looked at the owl in her other arm. "Your owl? Have you been spying on me?"

"You and your brother stole my dice," said Frank. "I suspect Tim was the mastermind behind it, and he might not have even told you what he was doing, which is the only reason I haven't shot you yet. Give me the dice, and we can all walk away."

"Listen, Frank. I know how this looks. But I don't have your dice. Neither does Tim."

"I really didn't want to have to shoot you, but now I kinda do."

"Just hear me out first, okay? There's another Mordred tied up in the back room behind me. Tim is trying as hard as he can to get your dice back, but he's walking into a trap. I need you to keep Mordred in custody while I go rescue my brother. Then we can focus on finding the dice."

"Why should I believe a single word of that horseshit story?"

Katherine sighed. "Because I'm not going to give you any other choice." She flung Frank's dice bag as high into the air as she could, and tossed the bloated owl to the sorcerer.

"Barney!" cried the sorcerer. His Magic Missile fizzled out as his concentration broke.

"Are you insane!" cried Frank. He dropped his crossbow as he prepared to catch the falling sack.

Katherine picked up the crossbow and aimed it at Frank just as he caught the bag, as well as a faceful of fenberry goop.

"Oh my god it burns!" Frank desperately scraped the yellow goop from his eyes, wiping it on his shirt and pants.

Katherine almost felt sorry for him. The way he was spreading that shit around, he was going to be worse off than that fucking owl.

"Sorry, Frank. That's gonna sting for a while. It should wear off after a couple of days." She turned to the sorcerer, who was holding his fat familiar with both hands, his expression a mix of shock and fury. "Get Mordred back to the Whore's Head. I'll send word when we get the dice back."

Before anyone could answer, she ran off to find someone who could tell her where the hell this Crescent Shadow place was.

CHAPTER 14

The king's Arcane Minister frowned down at Denise, the strands of his long white beard swaying gently in the arid desert breeze. "Do you understand why you've been sent here?"

"Because the king's gayer than five fags in a barrel of lube?"

Randy nudged Denise with his elbow. "Ain't you got us in enough trouble?"

"And you, Sir Randal," said the Arcane Minister. "The king has granted your request. Posters have been placed on every corner of the city. If the halfling still resides in Cardinia, he shall be apprehended shortly."

Denise snorted. "Good one, Minister."

"The minister glanced down at Denise, then addressed Randy. "Your insistence on sharing this wretched woman's punishment is the only thing that saved her from being hanged. Truly, you are a fine representative of the New God. Few men would show such courage in the face of certain death to spare the life of such a lowly creature."

"Listen here, motherfucker! Who are you callin' a lowly –"

With barely a flick of the wrist, the minister sent Denise five feet backward to land ass-down in the sand.

"So..." said Randy. "All's we need to do is walk out of the desert and back to town, and all is forgiven?"

"The Path of Penance is more treacherous than you think. It is no mere stroll through the sand. Many who begin the journey come to find they would have preferred a quick and simple hanging instead."

"Well shit," said Denise. "If I wanted to die in the desert, I wouldn't have paid them niggers to break my legs before I was deployed to Iraq."

Randy shot Denise a warning glare.

"Sorry. Colored gentlemen."

"Pray to the New God," said the Arcane Minister. "Repent for your sins against the Crown and basic decency."

Randy bowed respectfully. "May the peace of –"

"How about one quick roll in the sand before you get on your way?" asked Denise. "Ain't no one got to know." She twirled the end of her wispy beard between her fingers in what Randy assumed was supposed to be a seductive manner.

The minister cringed. "The desert holds many hidden dangers. It would be wise to conserve your energy."

Denise smirked and nodded. "Can't get it up no more, huh?" She spit in her palm and rubbed her hands together. "Why don't you hike up that pretty dress and whip out the ol' Dumbledong. I'll show you magic like you ain't never seen."

"Um..." The minister was visibly uncomfortable. "I have some... urgent business to attend to back at the palace. Good luck to you both." With a snap of his fingers and a puff of grey smoke, he was gone, leaving Randy and Denise alone in an expanse of rippled white sand that stretched out as far as they could see in every direction.

Denise thrust a middle finger at the dissipating smoke. "Fag!"

"Damn it, Denise!" said Randy. "That's exactly the kind of behavior that got us sent here in the first place."

"Don't give me none of your homo-liberal bullshit, Randy. I'll say whatever I goddamn well please. Freedom of speech is the cornerstone of democracy."

"We're not in a democracy!" shouted Randy. "This is a monarchy, and you called the king a cocksucking queer right to his face!"

"Yeah, well whatever. You say potater, and I say tomater."

"You got to stop throwin' yourself at folks like that, Denise. Have a little self-respect." Randy looked away from her. "And maybe a little... self-awareness?"

Denise cleared her throat. "And what, exactly, is that supposed to mean?"

"I just don't think you're as attractive a woman as you seem to think you are."

"The fuck would you know about it, Cockophile Dundee?"

"I'm just tryin' to give you some constructive criticism. Everybody's got gifts. I'm sure you got some good qualities in you. But maybe outer beauty just ain't your strong suit."

"Them's some hurtful words, Randy."

Randy looked down. "I'm sorry. I was just upset is all."

"Fuck it," said Denise. "It's all water under the bridge once we get out of this goddamn desert. You got an empty bottle or somethin' I can piss in, just in case we need to drink it later?"

Randy frowned. "No, my waterskin is full."

"So is mine. You mind turnin' 'round so's I can take a squirt?"

"All right. But be quick about it. We don't want to waste no more time than we got to." Randy squinted and peered in every direction that didn't include watching Denise take a piss. There was nothing to see. No cacti. No dunes. No tumbleweed. Just hot, sun-bleached sand. Even if he knew which direction to travel, he didn't know if they'd make it.

"Goddammit," said Denise. "I just got piss on my skirt. I ain't got nothin' to aim with. I s'pose it'll dry quick enough. Ain't like we gonna see no one out – SON OF A MOTHER–"

Randy turned around. Denise was on her back, her battleskirt wrapped around her ankles, piss spraying out from between her legs. But the strangest thing he saw was a vine growing out of the sand. Healthy, green, and thick, it supported a bunch of pink juicy-looking grapes.

"Where'd that come from?"

"Fuck if I know," said Denise, scooting back from smaller plants rapidly sprouting out of the sand in a pattern that seemed to be following her. "I was just mindin' my own business, takin' a piss in the desert, when all of a sudden, I feel this vine ticklin' my cooch." She scooted back on her bare ass. "And now it's followin' me!"

Sure enough, the sprouting greenery was growing thick in a straight line headed directly toward Denise's nether regions. Stems sprouted leaves and flowers, which in turn swelled up into berries of various colors. Finally, they gave up the chase, and Denise was able to rest and pull her skirt up.

"Goddammit, I got sand all up in my vag."

Randy plucked a grape from the first vine. "You reckon it's safe to eat?"

Denise shrugged. "Only one way to find out. Go for it."

Randy went for it. The grape's sour juice burst out between his back teeth.

"What's it taste like?" asked Denise, reaching up under her skirt to further sort out her sand issues.

"Tastes like a grape." Randy cringed a bit at an unpleasant aftertaste. "And maybe a little bit like pee."

Denise stopped fiddling under her skirt. "That's it!"

"What's it?"

"This shit all started growing when I started pissing. And then it stopped when I stopped." She grabbed Randy's left arm with both hands. Her left hand was conspicuously moist and sandy. "It's just like you said. Everybody's got a gift. Maybe my gift is magical piss. Like Rapunzel's hair in that Tangled movie. Except, you know, with piss."

"That ain't exactly the sort of gift I was thinkin' about," said Randy. "But who knows?"

"Aw shit," said Denise. "Look at that."

The grapevine blackened and fell under the weight of the bunch, which shriveled into a cluster of raisins before withering into dry grapeskin scabs in the sand. The other plants soon followed, withering, shriveling, and falling over as if invisible vampires were sucking the life out of them.

"Well how about that." A means of testing Denise's magical piss theory occurred to Randy. He spit on the ground and watched the spot closely. The sand soaked in his spit almost instantly. A set of leaves sprouted out from the spot, and a stem began to shoot up between them, but the whole plant withered and died before it could really get going.

"I guess magical piss ain't my special gift after all."

"It's all right, Denise. You'll see. The good parts of some people are just buried a little deeper than in others. We'll just keep digging, and I bet we find... Wait, hang on a second... When did you ever see Tangled?"

Denise glared at him. "It was on... I was... Shut the fuck up, Randy! Need I remind you that we're still lost in the fuckin' desert?"

"That's a good point. Any idea which way the city's most like to be in?"

"Now how the fuck would I know that, Randy? I only been here just as long as you have."

Randy thought for a moment. "I suppose that since neither of us know which way to go, our best bet is to travel with the sun. We'll get more daylight that way."

"I suppose your mama must have dropped you on the head when you was a baby."

Randy frowned. "I don't see –"

"Do you recall Cardinia having a big fuckin' ocean directly to the east?"

"Okay, now that you mention it, I –"

"The sun travels from east to west. And while there's no guarantee we're on the same continent, it makes more sense to assume we are than to just up and add a potentially unnecessary ocean voyage to our itinerary."

"All right, Denise," said Randy. "You made your point. So you think we should travel east?"

"Yeah, Randy. I think we should travel east."

Randy nodded and took a step away from the setting sun.

"At least, that's what I'd think if I had a head full of dog shit."

Randy stopped. "Did you have some more insight to share?"

"Think for a minute. What causes a desert to exist?"

"Um... sand?"

"Jesus Christ, Randy." Denise took a deep breath. "Think about the deserts back home. The ones in Mexico, Africa, Saudi Arabia. What do all of them have in common?"

"Um... sand?"

"Goddammit, Randy! It's like tryin' to teach a rock to swim."

"Well I'm sorry! I ain't studied deserts as extensively as you, I guess."

"Studyin' don't enter into it. It's just common sense. A desert is the result of climate patterns which are more likely to follow certain latitudes than they are longitudes."

Randy kept his mouth shut.

"Climates change more predictably as you go north and south," Denise continued. "That's why it's hot at the equator, and colder as you go farther north or south."

Randy gave a small nod to show he was following along so far.

"Goin' east and west, you never know how long the same pattern might go on. So if you're stuck in the middle of a desert you don't know shit about, you're better off traveling north or south."

"Thank you for explaining that," said Randy. "I didn't know you was such a survival expert."

"You makin' fun of me?"

"Uh uh. Like that stuff about drinkin' your own pee."

"That ain't nothin'. I seen Bear Grylls do that on Discovery. Motherfucker really chugged it down."

"How 'bout that stuff you said about lattertudes and such?"

"Everybody knows that, Randy."

Randy shook his head. "I don't think so. You got real knowledge. Maybe that's your special gift."

"You reckon?" Denise twirled the end of her beard between

her fingers. "Come to think of it, it does seem odd that I'd know that so readily. Maybe it is my special gift."

"So which way do we go?" asked Randy. "North or south?"

"Don't matter. You pick one."

"South?"

"Excellent. We'll head north."

"Then why'd you even ask me?"

"'Cause I may not know which way to go, but I do know that your instincts are shit."

CHAPTER 15

The crowd at the Whore's Head had thinned out significantly. Each time Dave returned from Arby's duty, he found that a few more people had abandoned the place as Frank added more names to his growing list of "The New Horsemen".

Dave couldn't blame anyone for wanting to leave. The atmosphere had become decidedly less chill in the past few days, and Frank's paranoid speculations about deserters allying themselves with Mordred to launch a second attack on the Whore's Head probably had the opposite effect of the one he'd been going for.

Some just went out on patrols and never came back. Others left more dramatically.

"Gus!" Tony the Elf called out from behind the bar. "Relieve Scar on door duty." When Frank was out on patrol, Tony the Elf took to calling the shots. He tended to be a little less diplomatic when doing so.

Gus grabbed his crotch. "Relieve this." That earned him a few weak laughs from people who hadn't had much to laugh about lately.

"Is there something in the rulebook that says half-orcs need to reference their genitals every time they open their mouths? Seriously, you"re no better than Cooper."

"I don't claim to be," said Gus. "That dude was cool."

"Cool? So murderers are cool now? Need I remind you that he threw me in a sewer and left me to die?"

"You don't look dead to me."

"You know what? Fine. If opening and closing a door is too complicated for you, I'll just find –"

"No, man. It's cool. I think I've got the hang of it." Gus walked over to the door and pulled it open. He made a gesture like Vanna White showcasing newly turned letters, then gave Tony the Elf the finger. "Peace out, motherfucker." He stepped outside and closed the door behind him.

Tony the Elf shook his head and sighed. "Add him to the list."

Rhonda scoffed. "Gus? Come on. He's just blowing off steam. He'll come back."

"I have no doubt," said Tony the Elf. "He'll come back with the rest of them to kill all of us."

"You need some sleep, Tony the Elf, or whatever it is you elves do instead of sleep. You're talking nonsense."

"Nonsense? You just heard it for yourself from his very own mouth. He sided with Cooper for trying to murder me."

"That's one way to interpret it."

"This isn't up for debate," said Tony the Elf. "Frank left me in charge, and I said put Gus on the list."

"And that's the problem," said Rhonda. "That you and Frank seem to believe that either of you are in charge of any of us."

"I don't have time for this. Do whatever you want. I'll put his name on the list later."

Rhonda crumpled the paper into a wad and threw it at Tony the Elf. "You can put my name on there, too. I'm out of here." She started rolling up a scroll she'd been working on.

"If you walk out that door, don't even think about coming back!"

"I won't!"

Chaz leaned over and whispered to Dave. "This shit is getting out of control."

Dave nodded. "You need a refill?"

"Oh yeah."

As Rhonda finished packing her bag, Dave walked up to the bar with his empty stonepiss bottle and Chaz's empty beer mug.

Rhonda had almost made it to the door when it was kicked in from outside. The first person to enter was unidentifiable, as he had a bag over his head.

Gilbert, the sorcerer whose owl familiar had been tailing Katherine, followed Bag Head inside with his owl tucked under his arm. The poor bird was swollen to the size of a basketball.

Finally, Frank waddled in. Like Gilbert's owl, his face and hands were swelled up like a Macy's Thanksgiving Day parade balloon.

"Jesus Christ," Dave said under his breath.

"Frank!" cried Rhonda. "What happened to you?"

Frank's squinty eyes looked sideways, then up at Rhonda. "Kaffwin. Wist."

"Get him up here," said Tony the Elf.

With such a sudden and bizarre emergency unfolding, Rhonda seemed to forget the little squabble she'd just had with Tony the Elf and did exactly as he said. She picked up Frank and placed him gently on top of the bar.

"Ow, ow, ow, ow, ow, aaaah." Frank sighed with relief when his ass touched down on the bar.

"Who did this to you?" asked Tony the Elf.

Frank looked to Gilbert.

"Tim's sister attacked us," said Gilbert, a hint of courtroom drama in his voice. "We tracked her down to an abandoned building in Shallow Grave, consorting with this man, one of Mordred's avatars." He shook Bag Head by the shoulder. "When we confronted her, she flew into a rage and threw a bag of poisonous slime at Frank before fleeing the scene. She got away, but we managed to capture a Mordred."

Dave didn't buy it. Something didn't add up. They had a prisoner who they claimed was Mordred, and there was no question that someone had fucked up Frank pretty bad. But Gilbert talked too fast, like he was trying to spit out all the details of a story he'd rehearsed before he forgot them.

Still, Dave wasn't about to stick his neck out and accuse

anyone of lying based on that. He'd just refill his beer and see how things played out.

"You!" said Frank, aiming one of his fat hands at Dave. He looked like he was trying to point, but was unable to move his fingers. "Baw's cwosed!"

Dave could tolerate a lot, but this was going too far. "Come on, Frank. You can't close the bar. That's the only thing keeping people here anymore."

"Awe you fweatening me?" challenged Frank.

"Am I what?"

"Take it easy, Frank," said Rhonda. "He's just telling you the truth. We're losing a lot of people as it is."

"The twaitows wiow wetun, and we must keef our wits and weddy ow defwense!"

"Slow down. I'm having trouble understanding you. We must Keefer Wits and wetty our Depends?"

Dave was doing his best not to laugh, but cracks were forming in the dam. He thought he was doing a good enough job of hiding it, but Frank noticed.

"You fwink this is funny? Wook at my face! Wook at my swowen wifs!"

More laughter snorted out from Dave's nose, and his eyes started to tear up. The worst thing Frank could have done, under the circumstances, was to call even more attention to his giant lips. Others in the inn were starting to laugh as well.

"It's not his fault, Frank," said Rhonda. "If you could see or hear yourself right now, you –"

"Fwis is no waffing mattaw! We aw aw in sewiwous twubbaw!"

Dave covered his mouth and tried to fake a cough, but he knew it wasn't even close to convincing.

Frank was furious. "Tony the Ewf! Wonda! Wock Dabe uf in the cewa!"

Tony the Elf looked at Rhonda, then back at Frank. "I'm sorry. Could you say that one more time?"

"You want us to whack Dave off in the sewer?" asked Rhonda. "That can't be right."

The background laughter had grown louder. People weren't even trying to hide it anymore. Dave felt a little bad for Frank, even though Frank was looking back like he wanted to murder him there and then.

"Incontinentia Buttocks!" shouted someone from the other side of the room.

The room erupted in laughter, as if everyone was simultaneously wondering when someone was finally going to say what they were all thinking.

"We need to go now," said Chaz, not even laughing a little.

At first, Dave thought maybe Chaz didn't get the reference. Then he thought about the bigger context and realized that not only did Chaz understand the reference, but that it had been more than an insensitive joke. Whoever said that meant it as a warning. Frank might actually murder Dave if he didn't take this opportunity to run.

Dave and Chaz backed away from Frank and started creeping toward the door.

"Whewa do you fwink youwa going?" said Frank. "Wonda, put 'em to sweep!"

Rhonda turned her back to Dave and Chaz and faced Frank. "Just let them go."

"She's with them now," said Tony the Elf. "Right before you got here, she was planning to desert."

As puffy as Frank's face was, there wasn't a whole lot of physical difference between his expression of rage and his expression of despair, but Dave could see it in his eyes.

"Wonda? Is that twoo?"

"I'm not going anywhere, Frank. I'm going to stay here and take care of you. But you're becoming unhinged. You haven't slept in two days."

"They betwayed us! They took owa onwee webewage! How can I sweep?"

"I'll help you." Rhonda raised a hand, palm out, toward Frank. "Sleep."

Frank fell on his side, his giant red face smacking against the bar top.

Dave and Chaz continued inching toward the exit. Tony the Elf glared at them like he was deciding whether it would be best to jump over the bar or run around it.

"We can't turn this place into a prison," said Rhonda. "That's only going to keep people's minds focused on how they can escape, and we've got more important things to focus on."

"Like what?" said Tony the Elf.

"We've got a Mordred."

Tony the Elf looked at the man with the bag over his head. He was sitting calmly and patiently, his bagged head held high. Gilbert hovered over him like an overprotective mother.

Dave and Chaz made it to the door. Dave felt for the handle.

"We might have more leverage than we think," said Rhonda. "If we use our imaginations, who knows what kind of information we can get out of him? We can coerce the truth out of him with magic. We can find out where the other Mordreds are. We may even be able to find out where Tim and the dice are."

Tony the Elf kept his eyes on Dave. "If Mordred knew where Tim and the dice are, we'd all be dead already."

What Rhonda was saying was starting to make some sense.

Dave stopped feeling for the door handle."Tim's not dumb enough to walk right up to Mordred and hand over the dice. Neither of them have any reason to trust the other. If Tim really means to screw us all over to get himself and his sister back home, he and Mordred are going to have to set up some sort of arrangement. They'll have to relay messages through neutral third parties, agree on drop off locations, whatever. If we can get this Mordred talking, we might be able to intercept Tim."

Tony the Elf thought for a moment, then nodded.

"You need a fresh mind," said Rhonda. "Go do your meditation thing."

"Thanks, Rhonda," said Tony the Elf. "I'm sorry things got so heated before. I'm glad you're staying." He retreated to the corner of the room where the elves hung out at night.

"Does this mean we're not leaving?" asked Chaz.

Rhonda looked at Dave, as if she were also interested in the answer to that question.

"I guess that depends," said Dave. "Is the bar reopening?"

Rhonda smiled. It was by no means a pretty smile, but it lightened some of the tension in the room just the same. "I think we could all use a drink right about now."

CHAPTER 16

"So you want to tell everyone we've been shacking up for the past couple of days?"

"Of course not," said Stacy. "I just want them to think it."

"Subtle hints, then." Julian thought for a moment. "Hey, Frank. No sign of Tim at the Starlight Motel for the past two nights, if you know what I mean." He wiggled his eyebrows.

"Yeah, real subtle. Maybe I should go in alone and say you got eaten by wolves or something."

"I'm sorry," said Julian. "I just need some clue as to what you want me to say."

"Say nothing. The less either of us say about what we've been up to, the more people will assume we've been sweatin' up the sheets."

"And why do we want them to assume that?"

"Because it shields us from any suspicion, and keeps us from having to report back on what we've actually been up to."

"You mean looking for Tim."

"Correct."

"Which is what we're supposed to have been up to."

Stacy sighed. "Also correct, but –"

"I understand that our goals for finding Tim are different from theirs," said Julian. "But wouldn't it be safer to agree on some false information to report, rather than take for granted that they're all going to think that we snuck away to boink for two days straight?"

"Not at all. A lie might come back to bite us in the ass later on if we get caught. Silence is just that. And Tim already plant-ed the seeds in everyone's heads that we're boinking. That's what made him go all stab happy on Mordred. But aside from that, most people would assume that when two young attractive people run off together for a couple of days, that it's going to involve some boinking, even if the reality is that they haven't boinked a bit."

In truth, this is why Julian was averse to the sex story. The two nights they'd just spent together had been uncomfortable to say the least.

"Listen," said Julian. "About that, I –" Sudden panic hit Julian in the gut. "Ravenus!"

Stacy rolled her eyes. "Oh please. You can send him out scavenging for half an hour."

"No, that's not what I meant!"

"Wait a minute. Are you... and the bird..."

"NO! Something's wrong with Ravenus."

"Oh thank God."

Julian turned and ran in the opposite direction, away from the Whore's Head Inn. Ravenus had flown this way after sniffing out what he'd referred to as a 'major score'. Might Mordred have lured him into a trap with a chunk of spoiled meat? Might Julian himself be running into the same trap?

He ran past the redeveloped area into the section of the Collapsed Sewer District which still looked like its name. He slowed down to a walk and scanned the area. Wherever Ravenus was, he was still panicking.

"Slow down, Julian," said Stacy, running to catch up to him.

"Careful. It could be a trap. This is the same feeling I had when Mordred captured Ravenus before."

Stacy wrinkled her nose as she drew her sword. "Do you smell that?"

Julian nodded. The air was thick with the stench of death. "This isn't normal, even for this part of the city. Come here." He walked behind a crumbling, half-buried section of stone pipe.

Stacy followed. "What are we doing?"

"Playing what cards we've got," said Julian. "I'm going to walk ahead. You hide back here. If I can get Mordred to chase me, I'll lead him right past you so that you can Sneak Attack him. If that plan doesn't work out and I get killed or captured, you can at least give the others what information you gather on him."

"It's not a great plan, is it?"

"I'm making it up on the spot."

"Well this hiding place sucks," said Stacy. "There's no visibility. I'm going to hide on that pile of rubble over there."

Julian looked at the pile of rubble, then back at Stacy. "That's barely knee high. How are you going to hide behind that?"

"I didn't say behind it. I said on it." Stacy pulled a black cloak out of her bag and wrapped it around herself. It instantly lightened to the same shade of grey as the surrounding dirt. The Cloak of Elvenkind Mayor Merriweather had given her. Like a blurry gazelle, she bounded toward her indicated rubble pile and disappeared into it as her cloak took on shadows and texture.

Julian remembered that Stacy wasn't the only one who'd received a gift from the mayor of Port Town. He dug around in his pocket until he felt a ring, which he slipped onto his finger. "Fade."

Being invisible bolstered his courage to step into what he still had every reason to believe was a trap, but he didn't let himself get overconfident. The game had means for detecting invisibility, and Mordred was probably powerful enough by now to have easy access to those means. Julian proceeded invisibly, but unarmed and with his hands held high.

"Ravenus?" he called out. There was no answer, but he could still feel that his familiar was terrified. He walked further out into the open. "Ravenus!"

"Fuck!" cried a voice from behind a wall, where the epicenter of the smell seemed to be located. Ravenus rocketed out over the wall and flapped frantically in Julian's general direction. "Where are you, sir?"

With Ravenus safely in the air, Julian remained silent, not wanting to give away his position until he saw who was on the other side of the wall which Ravenus had just flown over.

As silently as he could, Julian took a careful step toward the wall, then stopped. In all the commotion, it was just now registering to him that the voice which said "Fuck!" had sounded a lot like... "Cooper?"

Slowly, cautiously, Cooper's head rose up behind the wall until his eyes were visible. "Julian?"

"Cooper!"

Cooper turned toward him, but seemed to look straight through him. "Julian?"

"Oh yeah," said Julian. "Hold on a sec." He put his hand in his pocket and slipped off his ring.

"Holy shit, dude." Cooper stood straight, revealing a fresh bleeding cut on his upper arm.

"There you are, sir," said Ravenus, flapping down to rest on a bent iron bar sticking out the top of a garbage pile.

"What happened to your arm?" asked Julian.

"Your fucking bird happened."

Julian looked at Ravenus. "Did you do that to Cooper's arm?"

"He's gone mad, sir! I mean, more so than usual. He captured me and wouldn't let go. He was growling and drooling and spitting in my face! Truly, I thought I was done for."

"I'm sure he was just talking and you didn't understand him."

"Is he talking about the growling and spitting?" asked Cooper.

"As a matter of fact, he is. I assumed... Were you actually growling and spitting in Ravenus's face?"

Cooper laughed. "Yeah. He hates that."

"Of course he hates it!" said Julian. "Why would you do that?"

"I needed him to start freaking out so you'd come find me."

"My Empathic Link to my familiar is not meant to be used as a beeper!" Julian had to admit, however, gross it was, that Cooper's idea had actually worked. "We were looking for you. What are you doing here?"

Cooper looked rapidly from side to side. "Are you here alone? Were you followed?"

"I don't think so," said Julian. This didn't seem to reassure Cooper, whose bloodshot eyes kept darting in random directions, like they were trying to stay constantly focused on all of his surroundings at once. He added, "Relax, Cooper. We're here alone."

Cooper's eyes widened, locking in on something behind Julian. "The fuck you are!" He stood straight, raising a severed human arm above his head by the hand, like he'd just given someone an all-too-enthusiastic handshake.

"Jesus Christ!" said Julian. "What the –"

"Fuck you, you Predator motherfucker!" Cooper flung the arm hard at whatever he was shouting at.

"OW!" cried Stacy. "My nose!"

Julian looked back to see Stacy removing the hood of her cloak, her head becoming fully visible over her shimmering, semi-transparent body. In fairness, the Cloak of Elvenkind did have a Predator-like quality to it when she was moving. Still, that didn't explain the arm.

Cooper called out to Stacy, "Sorry about that."

"Sorry?" said Julian. "You just threw an arm at her!"

"You said you were here alone."

"We!" corrected Julian. "I said we were here alone."

"I thought you were talking about you and Ravenus."

"Fair enough. A simple misunderstanding. But I'm less curious about why you attacked Stacy, and more curious about –"

"Who the hell's arm is this?" asked Stacy, kicking the arm forward as she approached Julian and Cooper.

Cooper shrugged. "I don't know. One of these guys."

"These guys?" Julian walked around the wall, dreading

what he was going to see on the other side. His fears were justified. Human bodies and severed parts were piled up against the inner corner of the crumbling wall. Julian was no forensic scientist, but most of them looked to have been axed to death.

"This isn't what it looks like," said Cooper.

Julian tried for a moment to imagine something he might be mistaking for a pile of dead bodies, but came up empty. "Really? Because it looks like a pile of dead bodies."

"I suppose, in a strictly literal sense, it's exactly what it looks like."

Stacy rounded the corner and gasped. "Cooper! What have you been doing here?"

"I was looking for Tim and Katherine."

Julian and Stacy glanced at each other.

Julian swallowed and nodded at the pile. "Do you have reason to believe that they are in there somewhere?"

Cooper looked at the corpses, then at Julian. "Of course not. We wouldn't have killed them."

There went Julian's last hope that Cooper hadn't just stumbled upon these corpses. "So you killed all of these people?"

"No," said Cooper. "That's what I was trying to tell you before. "It was Knobby."

"Knobby?"

"Something like that. She's particular about how you pronounce it."

"Who the hell is Knobby?" asked Stacy.

Cooper unstrapped his axe from his back and held it out. "This is Knobby."

Julian and Stacy took a step back.

"Okay," said Julian. "Just take it easy and lower Knobby."

Cooper closed his eyes like he was suddenly suffering from a migraine, then opened them again. "She asks that you stop calling her Knobby."

"That's what you told us to call her," said Stacy.

His eyes closed again, Cooper nodded slowly. "N-A-B-I."

"Oh," said Julian. "Nabi, as in the Old Sylvan word for butterfly. Wow, how do I know that?"

Cooper opened his eyes. "She says you are correct."

Julian sighed, unsure of where this conversation was headed. "That's a pretty name."

"It's a hell of a lot better than Knobby," Stacy agreed.

That was exactly the sort of flippant remark Julian feared might trigger an episode in his unstable friend. He grabbed Stacy firmly by the arm and smiled warmly at Cooper.

"Do you mind if I speak to Stacy in private?"

Cooper shrugged. "Sure, I guess."

Julian led Stacy to the other side of the wall where they both crouched down.

"Your Charisma score is one point higher than mine," whispered Julian. "But I have more ranks in the Diplomacy skill. While engaging my homicidally insane friend, how about we let me do the talking?"

"What makes you think he's crazy?" asked Stacy.

"Are you fucking kidding me? He's talking to a goddamn axe!"

"You talk to a bird."

"The bird talks back. You can understand Ravenus, so don't even compare the two. Cooper has gone full Cast Away, except Willis never sent Tom Hanks on a murder spree."

"Wilson," corrected Stacy.

"Whatever!"

"I believe Cooper."

Julian rubbed his temples. "You're a sweet girl, Stacy. But don't be willfully naive. We have a mountain of evidence that Cooper's psyche has cracked, and he's dangerously unhinged right now. We have very little evidence that he has a telepathic axe."

Stacy's glare hardened with each word Julian spoke, but she kept her lips firmly pressed together until he was finished.

"You're a sweet boy, Julian. But don't be a condescending

prick. If you were paying attention, you'd see that we have all the evidence we need that Cooper is telling the truth."

"Oh? And what evidence is that?"

"Cooper can't spell."

Julian thought. N-A-B-I. Cooper's not insane. At least, not necessarily. "You're right. I'm sorry for being a condescending prick."

Stacy smiled. "It's okay. We're all under some stress right now."

They stood up and walked back around the wall to find Cooper picking his nose.

Julian cleared his throat.

Cooper looked at Julian, but continued picking his nose. "Hey."

"So why have you and Nabi been killing all of these people?"

"Because they're evil."

"That's a good reason, I guess."

"What makes you think they're evil?" asked Stacy. "Did they greet you with Nazi salutes or something?"

"They were wererats," said Cooper. "Nabi said the curse of lycanthropy darkened their souls. The way she explained it, I think she means it changed their alignment."

"And what about Tim and Katherine," asked Julian. "You said you were looking for them here. Why are you expecting to find them here?"

"Tony the Elf and I chased them into the sewer. I thought they might come out here."

"There are a lot of places the sewer lets out. They could have gotten out anywhere."

Cooper shrugged. "It was the best place I could think of." He looked at the tunnel entrance and frowned. "I'm starting to get worried."

"We've got some good news for you," said Stacy. "We have reason to believe they escaped the sewer somewhere else, and we think we know where they're headed."

"Sweet!" said Cooper. His piggy eyes lit up. "Let's get the fuck out of here. This place smells like ripened assholes."

"Ravenus!" called Julian.

Ravenus poked his head out from between a leg and an ass cheek in the corpse pile. His beak dripped with ocular fluid. "Here I am, sir."

"Get out of there. It's time to go."

Ravenus squeezed his way out and tumbled down the pile. "I may have overdone it, sir. I'm not sure I can fly just yet."

"You can perch on my staff. You're not riding on my shoulder until you've had a bath."

CHAPTER 17

One of the nice unrealities Katherine appreciated about the game world is that there was no such thing as insomnia. When she was ready to go to sleep, she could turn that shit on like a switch. No Ny-Quil or Xanax required.

It didn't work quite the same way for staying awake, however, as she'd recently found out in the swamp. So she took the calculated risk of letting her brother further his lead while she rented a room as close to Eastgate as she could find.

The cute dwarven couple who ran the little inn she decided on stood in the doorway and looked her up and down warily until she demonstrated that she had money. When she offered five gold pieces for a room she and her wolf could spend the night in, and a hot bath, they welcomed her in like she was part of the family.

They literally sat her down at the family table for dinner. Mama Dwarf gave her a warm damp cloth to wash her face and hands with, then set an extra bowl and spoon on the table in front of her.

Katherine needed to work out the approximate dollar value of a gold piece.

"Papa lost his eye fighting off a bandit who was going to kill us all in our sleep," volunteered the couple's young son before shoveling a spoonful of whitish lumpy glop into his mouth.

Katherine wasn't going to ask about her host's eye patch, but there it was.

"Hush, Jesper," said Papa Dwarf. "Don't make me out to be some kind of hero in front of our guest."

"I think it's plenty heroic," said Mama Dwarf, having returned to boil another kettle of water for Katherine's bath. "You saved your family, and paved an honorable path for our son on his way to manhood." She smiled at Katherine. "How's your gruel, dear?"

To keep from staring at the woman's beard, Katherine forced herself to look into her nearly empty bowl. "It's delicious, thank you." In truth, it tasted like warm Elmer's glue with chunks of eraser in it. Hopefully it was at least nourishing.

"There's plenty more where that came from. Would you like another helping?"

"Oh, no thank you," said Katherine. "Honestly, I couldn't eat another bite." Not without a nearby bucket to puke in.

Katherine was also uncomfortable sitting at the table and eating while this woman, rugged as she was, hauled heavy kettles of water around to prepare her bath. Neither her husband nor her son seemed to be bothered in the least by this. Maybe it was a dwarf culture thing.

When Mama Dwarf informed her that the washtub in her room was full of piping hot water, Katherine thanked her hosts and retired to her steam-filled room, where Butterbean was eagerly waiting for her.

The room was the very definition of sparse. If she hadn't specifically requested a bath, the only furnishing would have been the wicker mat and threadbare sheet on the floor. There weren't even any windows. But that was probably for the best, seeing as how she was planning to bathe.

Her sensitive half-elven ears picked up the sound of a chair scooting softly against the floor in the next room over. That was strange, as she didn't think there were any other guests staying there.

Maybe she was being paranoid, but Katherine decided it couldn't hurt to inspect the wall for secret peepholes before she started taking her clothes off.

It wasn't a big room, and so there wasn't a whole lot of wall to inspect. She poked and prodded at knots in the wood, finding them all to be natural and solidly in place.

Satisfied, she undressed next to the washtub. The water was still far too hot for her to get in, so she decided to take care of laundry first. She bunched up her clothes and her big black cloak and shoved them to the bottom, clouding the water with swamp filth. When she pulled her arms out, they were red like boiled lobster claws. She wished she hadn't lost her scythe in the swamp.

Taking one last look around the room to see if there was anything else that could use a wash, she spotted the bedsheet that came with the room. Who knew who might have used it before her, or when it had last been washed? But without a fast means of drying it, she'd just be rendering it useless for her to sleep under. And peepholes or no peepholes in the walls, she didn't fancy the idea of sleeping completely bare-ass naked.

"Purify," said Katherine as she quickly touched a finger to the scalding hot water. It did the trick. The water was suddenly crystal clear, and all her clothes were spotlessly clean.

After hanging up her clothes on wall pegs to dry, she tested the water again. It was still really hot, but she thought she could take it. Once it cooled too much, it would be on a fast path to unpleasantly tepid.

Easing her feet in first, she bent over and splashed a bit of water on her arms and breasts to acclimatize herself.

Hearing another chair-scooting from the direction her naked ass was pointed at, she couldn't shake the feeling that someone was watching her. It gave her a chill that prompted her to kneel down and submerge herself as far down into the water as she could.

With her arms crossed over her breasts, she glanced behind her. The wall was still as solid as before. Could there be some kind of sliding window that she'd missed? She didn't think so, but the point of such a window would be to remain hidden beyond careful scrutiny.

Katherine would neither enjoy her bath nor willingly go

to sleep until she had satisfied herself that she wasn't being peeped at. How to proceed?

She could whip her head around quick and try to catch the open window, but then she might spook whoever was behind it, and they might just wait for a while and watch her while she was sleeping. Somehow, that thought creeped her out way more than someone watching her bathe. Another idea suddenly occurred to her.

"Butterbean," she said. "Come here, boy."

Butterbean hopped to attention, trotted over, and placed his front paws on the tub rim.

Katherine stroked the fur on his head and neck. "That's a good boy!" She leaned in close and whispered the incantation in his ear. "Speak."

"Hello, Katherine," said Butterbean.

"Is this uncomfortable for you?"

"Not at all."

"I mean, me hugging you while naked."

"It wasn't until you just said it like that. I mean, I'm always naked. Why are we whispering?"

"I need you to look at the wall behind me. Do you see a hole?"

"Yes," said Butterbean. "Someone appears to be watching you. It smells like the dwarf with the eye covering."

"Figures. I'm starting to develop an alternative theory as to how he lost that eye."

"Shall I bark at him?"

"No. Do you have to pee right now?"

"I wouldn't mind, but I can wait for a more convenient time."

"Is the hole too high for you to pee through?"

Butterbean wagged his tail. "It's higher than I usually go, but I believe I'm up to the task."

"Good boy. Casually walk around the room, sticking close to the walls. I'll keep him distracted. When you have a clean shot, take it."

"With pleasure."

Butterbean disengaged and began circumnavigating the room and sniffing at the walls.

Katherine didn't know how this would play out, but she was determined not to waste this opportunity to get clean. She sat in the washtub, lifted her feet out, and submerged her torso and head.

Underwater, she bubbled out another incantation. "Purify." She felt instantaneously cleaner, more than she'd ever felt in her life. Every pore on her body soaked in clear hot water. It was at the same time invigorating and almost painful.

She wished that she could linger in the bath a bit longer, but she had a rat to flush out. She sat up, careful not to look in the direction of the secret peephole, but offered a bit of sparkly-clean side boob that way as she started to wring out her hair with both hands in a manner which she hoped was distractingly sexy.

"WYOW!" cried a voice from the next room, accompanied by a chair-scooting and followed immediately by a loud crash.

Katherine hopped out of the tub, wrapped herself in her sopping wet cloak, ran out of her room to the next one over, and kicked in the door. She was still reflexively thinking like a vampire, which made for a more-than-powerful-enough kick to swing the door in, but also for a sore foot.

Papa Dwarf was writhing on the floor, trying to scrub wolf piss out of his eye and pull up his pants at the same time. His genitals were slathered with a bright orange paste, which Katherine recognized as having come from crushed kavi nut, known for both its soothing and lubricating properties. It was a popular masturbatory aid among dwarves who, through years of working with stone, tended to have considerably rougher skin on their hands than they had on their junk.

Katherine resolved then and there to put no further ranks in any Knowledge skills.

"How dare you invade my privacy!" cried Papa Dwarf. "Get out of here at once!"

"Don't even try to turn this around on me, Purvy Smurf. You've been caught red-handed and orange-dicked." Katherine stomped across the room, ignoring the tenderness in the bottom of her right foot.

Papa Dwarf abandoned his attempts to pull his pants up, and reached up for a two inch square hole in the wall.

Katherine slapped his hand away. "You move another muscle, and I swear to God I'll crush your kavi nuts." She was more curious than angry though. How had she missed such a big hole? How was it hidden? Feeling around the edge of the hole, she was surprised to find that it peeled away like an old Band-Aid, turning black as it lost contact with the surface. When she was done, she was holding an ordinary-looking piece of black fabric.

"That's mine!" said the dwarf.

"What the hell is it?"

"It's my son's future."

Katherine looked down at him, still struggling to pull up his pants. "You're purposely raising your son to be a sad old pervert?"

"No, I meant that I plan to sell that to contribute to my son's education."

"Good news, Papa," said Katherine. "Today's the day you cash in."

The dwarf got to his feet and pulled his suspenders over his shoulders. "Do you know how much that's worth? What have you to pay for it?"

"It's one of those long-term investment things," said Katherine. "Think about it like this. If I let you keep this... whatever this is, sooner or later you're going to lose your other eye, effectively making you more useless than you already are, unable to work and a burden to your family. So I'm going to do the opposite. Think of all the money you'll save on medical bills and jerk-off cream."

The dwarf smiled and held out an open palm. "Very funny, young lass, but I'll be having my hole back now."

"You'll be shutting your hole, you fat one-eyed shitbag."

"Now take it easy, Miss Mouthy." The dwarf pulled a long, thin-bladed dagger out of his boot. "Just hand over the hole, and we can pretend that none of this ever happened."

Katherine put her hands on her hips. "With all the shit I've been through, you think that little blade scares me?"

"It ought to, unless you're hiding a bigger one under that wet cloak." His single eye was wide, staring at the cloak where it clung to her breasts. "Doubtful."

"I've got something better. Something you'll never have."

"Is that so, Missy? And what might that be?"

"Depth perception, motherfucker!" Katherine kicked the dwarf's wrist, sending the dagger flying straight up, where it stuck in the ceiling.

She was relieved that had worked, because she was pretty sure she'd just flashed her cooch at him. It was worth it because she'd disarmed him. But failure would have meant showing this little creep even more of the goods than he'd already seen right after having delivered an action movie quip, which might have been more humiliation than she could handle. And she probably would have gotten stabbed in the foot as well.

But for now, all the humiliation in the room was squarely on the shoulders of her host as he made repeated futile efforts to jump up and grab his dagger. A dwarf's body wasn't made for high jumps. His boots were barely leaving the floor.

"Please stop," said Katherine. "You're embarrassing yourself." She was tempted to sidekick him to the floor while he was in the air, but she found herself feeling a little sad for him after this little display. "You know what? Here, let me help." She reached up and plucked the dagger out of the ceiling.

Papa Dwarf pulled a coin purse out of his pocket. "Please, m'lady. Those are the two most valuable things I own. Take my gold, but leave me the dagger and the hole. My son's future."

"In the future, you should try offering the money before you threaten to murder a person."

"Yes ma'am." He nodded humbly.

In spite of everything she knew about this dwarf, Katherine felt herself growing even more compassionate toward him. "Set your chair upright and take a seat. I want to talk to you."

The dwarf did as he was told, then looked up at her attentively with his one sad eye.

"You keep bringing up your son's future. Given the circumstances, a lot of people would dismiss that as the desperate Hail Mary pleading of someone staring down the barrel of certain defeat. But I truly believe that your son is the most important thing in your life."

"He is."

"I know. I could see it in your eye when he retold your horseshit tale of fighting off the bandit who was going to murder your family."

The dwarf lowered his eye, but made no attempt to defend the truth of his story.

Katherine continued. "Your little boy sees a hero in you. He's still young enough for you to become the man he thinks you are before he discovers you for the piece of shit you are now. With regard to his future, that's worth more than anything gold can buy."

"You're right, m'lady," said the dwarf. "I want to be the man he thinks I am. I'm going to change."

"I believe you. Now toss over the gold."

The dwarf held his coin purse close to his chest with both hands. "How can I trust that you won't just run off with my gold and my possessions?"

Katherine smiled. "On the contrary. You can trust that that's exactly what I'm going to do." Without taking her eyes off the dwarf, she leaned back and called out, "Butterbean!"

In less than five seconds, her wolf was standing by her side, looking formidable and growling softly.

Papa Dwarf scowled as he tossed the coin purse to Katherine. “After all that talk about being a good person, you’re nothing but a lowlife thief.”

“How can you say that after all I’ve done for you?” asked Katherine. “I’m taking this hole thing to help you avoid temptation. I’m taking your dagger because you threatened to murder me with it. I think we can agree that that’s fair.”

“And my gold?”

“I need it to rent a room in a nicer inn. My room here smells like wolf piss.”

CHAPTER 18

Randy threw another stick on the fire, which crackled and flared as it greedily began to consume the new wood. One thing this desert didn't lack was plenty of fire wood. Randy and Denise were on the edge of what looked like a small mummified forest. Being bone dry, the wood burned pretty quickly, but that also made it easy to start. Randy guessed that these dead trees had been called to life the same way their pissberries had been, only on a much larger scale. Something must have dumped a ton of water onto this spot at some point in the past. But when that something moved on, the desert sucked out all the moisture.

"This desert fuckin' sucks," said Denise. "Why ain't we seen a snake or a lizard or some shit we can kill and eat? I'm so goddamn sick of piss-flavored fruit. I feel like I got the runs, but I ain't got enough liquid left in my body to let it go."

"We only been walkin' a few hours now, and this ain't so bad, as deserts go. Sure it's hot during the day, but it ain't so cold at night. I prefer this to all the humidity back home."

"Jesus Christ, Randy. How is it that you got your head in the clouds when there ain't no clouds for hundreds of miles from here?"

Randy lay on his back and looked up at the cloudless night sky. "I ain't never seen so many stars in all my life."

"And you ain't never likely to again, on account of we're gonna die in this goddamn desert."

"Have some faith, Denise. Jesus spent forty days in the desert. We ain't gonna die in just one night, and once we get back to the city, you're gonna regret not having taken the time to appreciate all this natural beauty. Take a look at that moon, so big and full."

"I'm tired, I'm thirsty, I'm hungry, and I got sand all up in my vag. When I get back to the city, all I'm gonna appreciate is a hot bath and a cold beer. That moon can suck my big and full dwarf titties." Denise raised two middle fingers toward the moon. He slowly lowered his hands as his jaw dropped open. "Holy shit, Randy. I don't fuckin' believe it!"

"Well that's quite the sudden turnaround."

"No, you dumb shit. Get up off your ass and take a look at this."

The dark barren landscape didn't offer a lot of distractions, so Randy was able to spot what Denise was so worked up about almost immediately. The moon appeared to have a twin at ground level... a reflection.

"You don't s'pose..."

"I do s'pose!" shouted Denise. "That's fuckin' water!" She ran as fast as her short thick legs would take her.

Randy walked briskly after her, keeping up with relative ease. "Hang on, Denise! It might just be a mirage."

Denise shook her head. "You are one dumb motherfucker. You know that, Randy? A mirage is what you call an optimal allusion."

"You mean an optical illusion?"

"What the fuck ever, Mr. Rand McNally."

"Don't they make maps?"

"Goddammit, Randy! Would you shut the fuck up and listen for a minute? The point is that a mirage is caused by sunlight. Everybody knows that. Ain't no mirages at night."

"I still don't feel good about this." In truth, Randy felt almost as good as Denise seemed to about this. He hadn't realized how parched he was until there was actually some promise of water. But this seemed like one of those too-good-to-be-true things, and he didn't want Denise to get her hopes up. "Why didn't we see this during the day?"

"We just wasn't lookin' hard enough. Think about it. We ain't really seein' it now. We's just seein' a big fat fuckin' moon reflection on the ground, and that ain't too hard to spot."

Randy supposed that made some kind of sense. Denise was probably right, and Randy certainly hoped she was. But there wasn't any harm in playing Devil's Advocate if it occasionally kept them out of any potential... Oh shit.

"Denise," said Randy. "Stop right there."

Denise stopped dead in her tracks. "Oh man, what is it? Do I got spiders on my back?"

"No. I just had a thought is all."

"Well I'm real fuckin' proud of you, Randy. But I'm thirsty as shit and I got a coochie full of sand."

"Just hear me out, will you? Think back to when we took a piss on the ground earlier, and all them berries grew out of the dirt."

"Yeah? So what?"

"If that's really water over there, then why's it just sittin' there, instead of bringing forth a forest full of fruit trees or somethin'?"

"Don't ask me, Randy. You was the one who dismissed my magical piss theory so quickly."

"I didn't dismiss it. I tested it scientific like. My piss also made plants sprout out of the ground."

"Well maybe we both got magical piss," snapped Denise. "Or maybe it don't work with water. Maybe there's a chemical in piss that causes the phenomenon. You ever think of that, Professor?"

Randy hadn't thought of either of those theories, but he remained skeptical.

"You stay here and drink sand if you want," Denise continued. "But if you fancy a drink of water before I scrub out my hoo-ha, you best not lollygag too long."

With a refreshing oasis mere yards away, Randy knew he wasn't going to stop Denise. He plodded along behind her toward the palm tree lined pool of glistening water, ready for the worst.

Sure enough, as soon as Denise stepped into the water, the whole oasis vanished. In its place stood a large red pavilion-style tent, three camels, and two grinning scorpion people.

"Aw shit!" said Denise.

Randy silently agreed with Denise's assessment of their situation, but was surprised to find that he wasn't afraid. He should have been afraid. With the lower half of giant scorpions, and the torsos and heads of muscular humanoids, these creatures looked like fear incarnate. They had a set of normal human-like arms at the shoulders, with which they brandished large scimitars. But much more frightening – at least objectively – were the massive scorpion claws extending from where the two body styles met. They wore plated metal armor on their upper halves which matched the exoskeleton on their lower halves. A single drop of what Randy confidently assumed to be venom glinted at the tip of the stingers at the end of their raised tails.

Even for someone like Randy, who often stretched suspension of disbelief to the point of tearing in order to try to see the good in people, their grins couldn't be interpreted as anything but malicious. He had every reason to believe he and Denise were seconds away from certain death, but somehow he just couldn't muster up any fear. He stood tall, ready to draw his sword, but not before the creatures had made their intentions plain.

The scorpion person on the right looked down at Randy, then at Denise, then past them into the part of the desert through which they'd traveled to get here. He shrugged with something like bemused satisfaction, then they both lowered their scimitars. That was a step in the right direction, Randy supposed, but the scimitars may have been the least threatening things about them. Their scorpion claws looked like they could take the heads off Randy and Denise's shoulders in one snip, and their stingers would probably pierce through their hearts and out of their backs, killing them long before the venom had time to do anything.

The one on the left stroked the neck of one of the camels with its human-like hand. "Fortune smiles on my camel this night."

That was probably an ancient proverb in their culture. Randy did his best to respond in kind.

"A penny saved is a penny earned."

The scorpion people glanced at one another briefly.

Denise turned to Randy and mouthed, "The fuck?"

"For my camel is wiser than some who roam the desert."

Were all their proverbs about camels? Randy hurriedly tried to think up another response.

"A rolling stone gathers no moss."

Denise buried her face in her palms, which Randy didn't appreciate. He was doing his best.

"An open flame on flat ground may attract predators."

That one was a little more helpful at least. Practical advice.

Randy offered a polite bow before responding. "You are what you eat."

The scorpion people grinned again. The one with the fondness for camels gave his wisest a little squeeze on its deflated hump. "Then tonight we shall be fools rather than camels."

It took a few seconds, but Randy finally grasped the implication.

Denise shook her head. "Goddammit."

The larger of the scorpion people snapped its claws eagerly. "We offer you the option to choose which one of you will take our camel's place."

Randy knew they were outmatched. If it came to a fight, he and Denise would most likely both die. Running away was even less of an option. These creatures were almost certainly faster than either of them, and better equipped for the terrain. More importantly, Randy was much faster than Denise, and he couldn't leave her to be slaughtered and eaten, even if it was only moments before he was slaughtered and eaten himself. There was only one option.

Randy stepped forward. "Take me."

Denise glared at him. "Are you fuckin' retarded? He was asking us to choose which one of us they gonna eat."

"I know what he was asking." Randy looked the scorpion person in the eye. "If you promise to release my friend, I will gladly give my life for your nourishment."

The scorpion person nodded. "Very well. Your bravery exceeds your intelligence."

"Thank you."

"Hold up!" said Denise. "Fuck that. At least let me make a counter offer."

The scorpion people spoke for a moment in a language that sounded like a recording of two arguing gibbons played in reverse. When their deliberations had concluded, the one doing the negotiations looked down at Denise.

"We shall hear your offer."

Denise placed both hands at the hem of her battleskirt and slowly lifted it. "What if I offer my own body, not as a meal, but as a woman?"

Randy looked away. "Come on, Denise. Just this once, show a little bit of dignity."

"Fuck you, Randy. I'm tryin' to save your life."

The scorpion people were making sounds that were neither laughter nor gagging. It almost sounded like... discussion?

He turned back toward them. They were speaking in their own language, but they actually seemed to be having a serious conversation about Denise's offer. Randy didn't know whether to feel relieved or horrified. The code of ethics which had guided Randy's conscience ever since he became a paladin was failing him now.

"Are you sure you want to do this?" he whispered to Denise.

Denise gave him a wide smile. "I've never been this sure

about anything in my life."

"We accept your terms, dwarf," said the larger of the scorpion people. "My name is Raslan." It gestured to the other one. "This is Azhar." Then it backed up to the tent on its eight legs with a grace that confirmed Randy's suspicion that he and Denise had no chance of outrunning them.

Denise rubbed her palms together. "All right! So how we gonna do this? One at a time? Rotisserie style? If Randy wants in we can do it like one of his goofy proverbs. How about it, Randy? One in the hand and two in the bush."

"Please, Denise," pleaded Randy. "Just let them eat me."

"Uh uh, my friend. Tonight's menu is pulled pork and tender loins."

Raslan pulled back one of the flaps. "Please accompany Azhar into the tent."

"Don't mind if I do." Denise walked into the tent, followed by Azhar.

Raslan let the tent flap fall back into place and scuttled over to Randy. It must have sensed his concern. "Your friend will not be harmed."

Randy sat on the ground and tried not to pay attention.

"Azhar, is it?" said Denise from inside the tent. Randy could hear her more clearly than he would have liked, considering what he expected to hear very shortly. "My name is Denise, and for the record I ain't never been with one of your kind before. So let's maybe try to ease into it a bit, take it one step at a – Goddamn!The fuck is – Oh my God!"

Randy started to stand, but Raslan placed one of his huge open pincers on Randy's shoulders, ostensibly to comfort him, but the fact that his head was between the open pincer jaws was not lost on him.

"Oh Jesus, Mary, and Joseph, you're really up in there." Denise groaned and panted. "Whoa, easy now. There you go. Holy shit! Is that... Oh my God! Wait, no. Give me some time to... Did you just... OH MY GOD! How can there still be any more...

Dear Lord, that's enough! Please! Have you never whacked off in your life?" She let out a long sigh. "Hey, man. Don't sweat it. We can try again in a few minutes if you like. I don't s'pose you got a cigarette?"

Azhar exited the tent looking no different than before. Denise, on the other hand, stumbled behind like she'd just survived getting hit by a bus. Her clothes were disheveled, her hair and beard clung to her face with sweat, and she didn't appear to know which way she wanted to walk.

"Denise," said Randy. "Are you all right."

Denise nodded, and her eyes grew more focused.

Raslan likewise approached Azhar, the former placing one of its human-like hands on the latter's shoulder. "Did all go well?"

Azhar nodded. "My burden is relieved."

"You bet your ass it is," Denise muttered softly enough (hopefully) such that only Randy could hear. "Son of a bitch relieved about eight gallons of burden into me over the course of five seconds." She sounded more annoyed than revulsed and horror-stricken, which Randy thought more appropriate responses. "I'll give him a few minutes to recharge, and see if he wants to have another –"

An animal scream rang out in the night, something like a cross between a donkey and a goat on fire. When Randy turned to look, Raslan and Azhar both had their tail stingers buried in the neck of their wise camel. The scream turned into a gurgle as blood dripped out of the camel's neck. Tiny plants sprouted where each drop of blood splattered on the dry ground. Larger plants grew where it coalesced into pools.

When the camel was dead beyond all doubt, Raslan and Azhar removed their stingers, and the camel fell sideways with a thud. As if it was the most routine thing in the world, Azhar scuttled to the other side of the camel, reached over with his pincers, and lifted the animal's left hooves, leaving its underbelly vulnerable to Raslan. Raslan made a swift and powerful swing with the pointed tip of his right pincer, slicing the camel open from it's junk to its neck. A gush of entrails, blood, and other organs and bodily fluids spilled out, prompting the sudden growth of shrubs, vines, and small fruit-bearing trees.

The camel's body started to deflate like a leaking balloon as the earth sucked the moisture out of its body. Raslan and Azhar snipped and tore at the loosened skin, exposing bare muscle onto which they sprinkled freshly growing herbs and squeezed the juices of whatever fruits were in reach. As they watched, the meat shrunk and hardened as it detached from the ligaments and bones.

"Hot damn!" said Denise. "Camel jerky!"

Randy slapped her lightly on the side of the face with the back of his hand.

"Shit, Randy! The fuck was that for?"

"I appreciate you savin' my life like you done, but I ain't gonna tolerate any more of those racially disparaging remarks."

"You stupid asshole. I said jerky, as in dried meat."

"Oh," said Randy. "I misinterpreted your meaning. I apologize."

"Come, new friends!" Raslan called to them. "You must be hungry after all your travels. Let us dine together."

Randy and Denise walked around to the head of the mummifying camel, where the plants were less dense, and accepted long dry strips of dried camel meat. Randy had to admit that camel tasted better than he would have given it credit for. The juices and herbs were a nice touch.

"Bring out the wine," said Azhar.

Raslan pulled a large glass bottle full of dark purple liquid out of a saddlebag on his back. He took out the stopper, swigged a bit, then passed it to Randy. "Try this."

"That's very generous," said Randy, accepting the bottle. As much as he appreciated the meat, it hadn't done anything to sate his thirst. He smelled the wine before putting it to his mouth. It was bitter.

"It's distilled from our own venom," said Azhar

Randy sprayed wine all over the plated mail on Raslan's chest.

Raslan frowned. "The distillation process renders the venom harmless."

Azhar covered his mouth with his hand to hide a smile. "Perhaps I should have mentioned that."

Raslan looked at him and smiled. "You did that on purpose."

"Come on, Randy," said Denise. "Don't hog the whole bottle. Give it here and let me try some."

Randy passed the bottle. He'd try another sip later.

As Denise put the bottle to her lips, Azhar and Raslan's smiles disappeared.

"What's wrong?" asked Denise. "Y'all Muslims or somethin'? Women ain't s'posed to drink?"

Azhar gave Raslan a small reassuring smile. "Perhaps one sip wouldn't hurt. She is a dwarf, after all."

Raslan took a deep breath, then nodded. "One small sip."

Denise took her sip while Azhar and Raslan watched with anxious eyes. When she was finished, Azhar quickly relieved her of the bottle.

"So," Denise said to Raslan, breaking the uncomfortable silence following the booze situation. "How 'bout after dinner you and me go in the tent and you pump me full of scorpion sauce?"

If the short silence following the booze situation had been uncomfortable, the silence that hung in the air now was burlap-and-broken-glass underwear as all eyes were fixed on Denise.

Raslan smiled awkwardly. "That will not be necessary. The eggs are already fertilized."

"My eggs?" said Denise. "I don't think so. Your buddy drops a big load, I'll grant you that. But we ain't even close to the same species."

Raslan cocked his head to the side and narrowed his eyes.

"Not your eggs. Azhar's eggs."

Azhar lowered the bottle after having taken several deep gulps. "Aaahhh, that's so nice. I haven't been able to have a drink in weeks."

Denise's eyes and mouth switched sizes. "The fuck are you talking about?"

"How is this unclear?" asked Raslan. "You offered us your womb to carry my wife's scorplings to term."

"I did no such motheruckin' – Hang on, Azhar's a woman? But she had a dick as big as my goddamn arm!"

Randy held his breath, hoping he was correct in thinking that Denise had the best possible defense against being murdered right now. Raslan's furious eyes suggested he was on the fence about it.

"Relax, dearest," said Azhar. "They are obviously unfamiliar with scorpionfolk. The dwarf meant no insult. Have a drink."

Raslan took the bottle and drank deeply, never taking his eyes away from Denise.

"What you mistook for a penis," Azhar explained to Denise, "is actually an extension of my vagina. Scorpionfolk eggs adapt easily to foreign hosts."

Randy hadn't seen that look on Denise's face since she found out her balls had been eaten.

"I f-f-feel so v-v-v-violated."

"I'm sorry," said Azhar. "We thought you knew. Do try to relax though. Stress is bad for the babies."

Raslan"s mood seemed to have lightened since he had a bit of wine in him. He grinned down at Denise. "Have some more camel, dwarf. You're eating for nine now."

CHAPTER 19

As Frank climbed from stool to tabletop to address what residents remained at the Whore's Head Inn, Dave and Chaz inched closer to the door. Frank looked more composed than he had in days. His head and hands still looked like pink half-deflated balloons, but the swelling had gone down considerably and he was finally able to talk somewhat normally. After a couple of nights of magically induced sleep, courtesy of Rhonda, he no longer had that crazy bloodlust in his eyes. But it didn't hurt to be prepared for the worst.

There was no need to hush the crowd. Being early morning, no one was feeling particularly chatty yet.

"I'd like to begin," said Frank, "by apologizing for my behavior over the past couple of days. I was frustrated and angry. And I still am. But perhaps I was a tad overzealous with my response to the situation."

"Fuck that!" shouted a dwarf at the back of the room. "I can forgive a lot, but I've got a family to get back to. I still say hang the little prick!"

Murmurs of agreement reverberated around the room.

"Better yet," said Stuart's wife, Rose, thereby doubling the amount of words Dave had ever heard her speak. She stood on a chair, a cloak covering her revealing armor, and held up one of the many wanted posters that Dave had noticed on display around the city. "I say we hand him over to the authorities."

She'd opened strong, standing above the crowd and dramatically thrusting the paper into the air, but her follow through was lacking. The crowd grumbled their disappointment.

"My husband nearly died helping him rescue his sister from

a vampire," she continued. "A quick hanging isn't good enough for me. I want to return to my real life knowing that he's stuck back here, languishing in a prison within a prison for the rest of his miserable life."

The crowd was more receptive now. A change of phrasing made all the difference.

"He's a weasely little bastard," argued the dwarf who'd suggested hanging Tim. "He'll just find a way to escape."

"Escape to what?" asked Fritz, the creator of the masterwork dildo stake. "He'd be friendless, penniless, the most wanted fugitive in the kingdom. He'll spend the rest of his life blowing bugbears for shots of stonepiss. That's even better than –"

Frank banged hard on the table with Rhonda's staff, which he appeared to have borrowed exclusively for that purpose.

"Everyone please listen!" said Frank. "You're all missing the point, just as I did. Instead of focusing on revenge fantasies, we should be focused on getting back those dice. If we catch Tim in the process, we can discuss then what form of justice is most fit for him to serve. What we need now are ideas."

"What have you been able to get out of Mordred?" asked Stuart.

Frank frowned. "Not a lot. I'm beginning to doubt if the guy we've got tied up in the cellar even is Mordred."

"Of course he's Mordred," snapped Gilbert. "I'd bet my life on it."

"That's fine. But you can't bet all our lives on it."

"What makes you think he isn't Mordred?" asked Chaz. Dave cringed. He wanted as little attention brought their way as possible.

"Nothing he's told us suggests that he's anything but an NPC," said Rhonda. "And he's been extremely cooperative in answering our questions."

Gilbert scoffed. "I'd be cooperative too, if you were lapping up every last drop of bullshit that I was feeding you."

Rhonda put on her shitkicking face as she glared at Gilbert.

"There is further evidence that he's not Mordred. We've been observing him around the clock, and not once has he gone into one of those catatonic trances. Do you really think that all of Mordred's other avatars are hanging around in comas just so we don't get suspicious about this guy?"

"Who knows? It sounds pretty brilliant to me. Keeping us all in the dark while he picks up bits and pieces of information from our conversations here. Besides, the other Mordreds might be able to move about freely while this one sleeps. Whatever happened to that... free-spirited... female dwarf? We know that Mordred is quick to slip into a coma when he gets a good beating."

"You need a woman to do your torture for you?" asked Rhonda. "Why not grow a sack and do it yourself?"

Gilbert balled up his fists. "She claimed to be an experienced interrogator!"

"Enough!" Frank banged on the table again. "Denise left a few days ago, and nobody has seen or heard from her since. And we're not torturing anyone. Next."

A thick meaty hand bounced up and down, barely above the heads of those around him.

Frank rolled his eyes. "Derek, you don't need to raise your hand. Just spit it out."

"Remember just before Tim killed the other Mordred?" It was the same dwarf who had suggested hanging Tim. Dave made a mental note to remember that his name was Derek.

"Yeah?" said Frank.

"Dave said he could use a Command spell to force him to say our names while we forced his hand to roll the dice. Maybe we could use it to force the truth out of whoever we have tied up in the cellar."

Dave felt bad that Derek knew his name but he hadn't known Derek's. He felt even worse that all eyes in the room were suddenly fixed on him. But he felt worst about what he was about to confess.

"After further research, I've discovered that the Command spell is very limited in what commands it allows. It wouldn't actually have worked the way I suggested it would."

"Suggestion!" cried Gilbert.

Everyone turned to him, much to Dave's relief.

"Let's hear it," Frank said after a few seconds of silence.

"No, I meant the spell Suggestion."

"If a Command spell isn't going to compel him to talk, what makes you think a Suggestion spell will?"

"Command is a first level clerical spell," said Gilbert. "Suggestion is more powerful. It's a third level wizard spell."

"Okay," said Frank. "Now we're getting somewhere. Can you cast Suggestion?"

Gilbert shifted his weight. "No," he admitted. "I'm only a third level wizard. You need to be fifth level before you can cast Level 3 spells."

"Do we have any fifth level wizards here?" Frank asked the crowd. Everyone shook their heads. Their strategy of lying low wasn't presently earning them dividends.

"I can do it!" said Chaz.

There were a few snickers from the crowd, but they did little to diminish Chaz's enthusiasm.

"Suggestion might be a Level 3 wizard spell, but it's only a Level 2 bard spell. I've seen it in my options."

Dave felt a little sorry for Chaz. His excitement over having something so improbably helpful to contribute only highlighted how useless he was in general.

Frank took Chaz, Rhonda, Gilbert, and Tony the Elf down to the cellar. Tony the Elf closed the door behind them.

"What the –" Dave couldn't tell whose voice it was, as the sound was muffled by the closed door. After a few seconds more of confused shouting, a few articulate shouts rose to the surface.

"NO!'

"STOP!"

"GET HIM!"

The cellar door opened, letting out a puff of thick blue smoke. A foot-long wooden stick popped out from the smoke cloud and landed on the wooden floor, spewing more of the same blue smoke from the end that was sparkling like a lit fuse. It smelled like spent fireworks. The door closed again.

"DYNAMITE!" someone shouted, prompting everyone to flee to the edges of the room, turn over tables, and take cover behind them.

Dave was still the closest to the door, but was forced to make a split-second decision between ducking behind a nearby wooden table, or making a run for the door. Frozen for a moment in indecision, he forced himself to make a choice and went for the table. How embarrassing would it have been to have his remains splattered against the door as evidence that he was trying to leave everyone else there to die?

As everyone waited in silent anticipation of their fiery deaths, the room failed to explode. Instead, it merely continued filling up with blindingly thick blue smoke.

The confused shouting from the cellar suddenly grew louder and clearer, as if the door had been opened, but it still sounded as if it was coming from beyond the staircase. As the voices grew louder, presumably ascending the staircase, the confused shouting turned to shouts of pain, then rapidly retreated back downward.

In a moment of clarity, Dave had a sudden revelation.

There's no dynamite in C&C. That's just a smokestick.

"Don't let him escape!" cried Frank from downstairs.

Dave made out a shadow in the smoke, gunning for the door. He wasn't much of a jumper, but he sprung at the shadow with as much force as his thick dwarven legs had in them. It wasn't much of a dive, and he was glad nobody could see it, but it was enough. Both of his hands gripped an ankle.

"HA HA!" cried Dave.

CLANG! Something hard smashed against the top of Dave's

helmet. He was dizzy with pain as lights twinkled in the darkness.

"Fuck!" Dave realized that he had lost his grip on the prisoner's leg and scrambled to regain it, hoping he might have tripped the guy or something. His hands found something in the smoke, but it was no leg. As the dissipating smoke and his probable concussion slowly relented, allowing his vision to return, he confirmed his suspicion as to what he was holding.

Tony the Elf was the first one to make it out of the cellar. He was limping, and frantically scanning the room. When his eyes found Dave on the floor and the open door behind him, he gasped.

Dave's head hurt like a son of a bitch. He held up the giant wooden dildo. "Why the fuck do we still have this?"

CHAPTER 20

Katherine's early-to-bed-early-to-rise plan hadn't worked out quite like she'd planned. The pervert innkeeper had cost her precious time, between her confrontation with him and the subsequent need to sort herself out at a different inn, but the money she'd taken from him might make up for it if she could procure another horse, another weapon, and other traveling supplies.

Her clothes were still too wet and tight for her to squeeze into. The cloak was even wetter, the thick wool barely having let go of any of the water overnight. But at least it was loose-fitting enough for her to cover herself with. It was scratchy and uncomfortable, clinging to her skin. She added dry clothes and a new cloak to her mental shopping list.

But as large a city as Cardinia was, there didn't seem to be any equivalent of a 24-hour Super Walmart where she could pick up a horse, a weapon, and equipment at four in the morning.

She and Butterbean prowled the empty streets near Westgate, where she peeked into store windows, trying to find shops near the stable that would provide what she needed, minimizing the time it would take her to get on the road once everything opened.

Magically illuminated streetlights provided enough light for Katherine to identify shops without having to get too close. It didn't take her long to find a general goods store and an armory. Provided they and the stable all opened for business at the same time, she could be on the road moments thereafter.

In the meantime, frustrating as it was, she had no choice

but to wait. She walked to a nearby park from which she could still see the shops, sat on a bench, and tried to think of some way she could distract herself. The obvious answer came to her almost immediately. She could play with her magical hole.

While digging into her pocket, she made a mental note to never use that turn of phrase around Cooper.

She pulled the silky smooth patch of black fabric out of her pocket and unfolded it. Neither side stood out as the obviously correct one to apply to a surface. Both were completely and identically black.

Wondering if she'd be able to see through to the other side of the world, she placed the fabric on the ground. It remained black and featureless. Poking at it cautiously, she found that her finger went right through the hole. That freaked her out a little, and she jerked her hand back, relieved to still have a finger.

She scooped up a handful of dry dirt, sprinkled it into the hole, and listened carefully. The dirt made no sound. It was silently absorbed into the void. Not quite satisfied that she had exhausted all the possibilities of that particular experiment, she bulldozed a larger pile of dirt with both hands, stood over the hole, and thrust the dirt down into it. The dirt that fell on the square perimeter outside the hole made noise, but the bulk of the dirt which got absorbed was silent. Now Katherine felt silly. She glanced around to make sure no one was watching her. Aside from Butterbean, it appeared she was alone.

She peeled the hole off the ground, held it up in the air, and poked at it again with her finger. This time it just moved the same way a normal piece of silk would, not absorbing her finger.

That was interesting. If nothing else, she learned that the magic is only activated when the hole is applied to a surface.

But what was the difference between applying it to the interior wall of an inn, or to the ground? Both triggered magical properties of the hole, but the results were different. Maybe it had something to do with being applied horizontally or vertically. With nothing better to do, it was worth investigating.

Katherine walked to a nearby tree and applied the hole to the smooth bark. It projectile-vomited a cloud of dust and grit right into her face.

"Ow! Fuck!" Katherine said, suddenly blinded as grit stung her eyes. She dropped to her knees and tried to blink the dirt out. Maybe she'd been mistaken about how the innkeeper had lost his eye. It could have been an infection from this stupidly random magical effect.

"Goddammit, that hurts." Her vision returned, teary and blurred, but both eyes seemed to be functional. She continued to blink until the pain lessened and her vision started to clear. She could still feel the dirt on her face, and she knew she was filthy. So much for that bath.

When her vision had more or less fully cleared and she'd regained some of her composure, she noticed that the dirt on her freshly cleaned cloak was identical, in color and texture, to the dirt that she'd just recently dumped into the hole.

Very interesting.

Also interesting, though perhaps not quite as much, was that she couldn't see through the tree trunk. The hole was just black.

She stood up and poked at the hole with her finger. It went right through, though she could feel nothing inside. She tried to put her whole hand in, but couldn't squeeze it into the opening.

Instead, she found a long stick on the ground and inserted it until she was sure it should have been poking out the other side of the tree. It wasn't. She pulled the stick back out and dropped it on the ground. The dirt thing was more interesting, and she had an idea for further experimentation.

Within a few minutes, Katherine had gathered a few dozen stones, ranging in size from a marble to a golf ball. She stood about ten feet away from the tree and hurled the stones, one by one, into the hole. She guessed she had maybe a 20% success rate.

She peeled the hole off the tree trunk, stood to the side, and prepared to reapply it with outstretched arms. If her hypothesis was correct, a shotgun blast of stones should fly out of the hole.

Her hypothesis was incorrect. There was once again just a plain old black magical hole in a tree, and it was starting to piss her off.

"What's with this fucking thing?" she asked herself, peeling the hole off again. She returned to the bench to think up some other experiments she could fail at.

She didn't come up with much about the dirt/rocks situation, but she had a new idea about the seeing-through-walls thing. Maybe it had to do with the thickness of whatever you were trying to make a hole in.

That had to be it. She should have thought of that immediately after the preposterous idea of making a hole through the world occurred to her. Fortunately, the perfect means to test this new theory was right under her ass.

The polished wooden plank that formed the seat of the bench was only about an inch and a half thick, probably similar to the thickness of the walls at the inn.

Katherine excitedly spread the hole flat on top of the bench. An eruption of rocks flew upward, all of which would have pelted her in the face had she been holding her head directly over the – Shit.

"Watch out, Butterbean!" Katherine cried as she huddled on the ground with her hands covering her head.

"Ow. Shit. Fuck. Ow." The success rate of the falling stones hitting her was considerably higher than 20%, but they didn't really hurt that much.

When she stopped hearing the thuds of stones hitting dirt, Katherine stood up and looked at the hole. It was a proper hole now, and she could see straight through the bench to the ground below it. One mystery solved. One remained.

She picked up one of the fallen stones and dropped it into the hole on the bench. It fell straight through to the other side.

The other side. The other side!

Excitedly, Katherine peeled the hole off the bench and set it back on the ground. She scooped dirt, rocks, twigs, whatever she could find, into it. When she was satisfied, she peeled the hole off the ground, flipped it over, and applied the opposite side to the tree. All the shit she had just dumped into it spewed down the trunk.

"Hell yes!"

She wanted to test the rock experiment one more time. Standing five feet back from the tree, she gathered five of the nearest fallen stones. She tossed them lightly toward the hole, and it took her four tries before she got one in. She dropped the fifth, went back to the tree, and peeled off the magical hole. When she flipped it over and reapplied it, the rock dipped upward for a split-second before dropping back down, right into Katherine's waiting hand.

As incredibly cool as that was, Katherine could think of no practical application for this item outside of party tricks and peeping at naked people. If it was bigger, it might come in handy for escaping a cell or something, provided she was willing to part with it. She didn't know if she'd be able to retrieve it from the other side of the wall without losing her hand, or getting it stuck in solid stone or something. She could think of ways to experiment with that later. There wasn't much point as long as it was only big enough to fit her hand in... unless she used it to open a locked door from the other side.

That might come in handy for breaking into a place as well as out of one. Say, for example... a weapon shop or general store... perhaps even a stable...

Katherine felt a little hypocritical after having lectured the dwarf about not using this thing for nefarious purposes, but this wasn't the same as whacking it to a woman taking a bath.

Katherine was trying to rescue her brother, and time was a factor. Anyway, she could always leave a few coins on the counter. That wouldn't be stealing at all. It's just shopping after hours.

She debated whether it would be best to hit the weapon shop or general store first. On one hand, the weapon shop seemed like the wiser option. That way, if any shit went down at the general store, at least she'd be armed with something more substantial than the dwarf's dagger.

On the other hand, the general store seemed far less intimidating. If she was going to make mistakes that she could learn from, she wanted to learn from them before breaking into a shop full of weapons and pissing off a shopkeeper who was intimately familiar with how to use them all.

The general store also had a nice row of hedges out front, and Katherine let herself believe that the concealment they would provide was what swayed her in that direction.

She looked left and right before darting across the road in front of the general store. It was partly instinctive, but she was more concerned about patrolling guards than oncoming traffic.

Satisfied that the coast was clear, she led Butterbean to the front entrance, crouched down behind the hedges, and placed the magic hole on the door next to the latch. She sat her Bag of Holding at the ready next to her, and wondered how honest she'd been with herself when she considered leaving behind enough money to pay for all the shit she was about to take.

Her hand hadn't quite fit through when she'd tried shoving it into the tree, but she hadn't tried very hard. She didn't need it to go through all the way anyway. She just needed her fingers to be able to find and reach the locking mechanism. It would be so much easier if this hole was just a little bit bigger.

Her fingertips grazed what might be the lock. If she still had her longer slimmer vampire hands, this wouldn't have been a problem.

"Come on, mother–"

"You there!" demanded a familiar voice with the confidence of authority.

Fucker.

"Turn around slowly and raise your hands." The voice came from behind, and considerably above, where Katherine was crouching. It was either from a freakishly tall person or a man on horseback. Either way, she might be able to conceal the fact that she was removing the magic hole from the door, but she'd definitely be caught if she tried to slip it into her pocket. She peeled it off the door and stuck it to the front of her cloak. A perfectly square hole might be a curiosity if it was pointed out, but she didn't think it looked all that conspicuous. Only after the fact did it occur to her that she might be opening a massive cavity in her body where her lung should be. Fortunately, that didn't seem to be the case.

"Stay," Katherine whispered to Butterbean. He was lying down closer to the hedges, and it was possible he hadn't been seen. She raised her hands above her head and slowly turned around.

Captain Righteous and his younger, less-physically-imposing partner looked down at her from atop white horses. The captain had a crossbow pointed at Katherine. The other one had a piece of paper pointed at her. With the light of a nearby street lamp, Katherine could make out the sketch of Tim that she'd seen posted throughout the city.

Both guards looked annoyed and disappointed as the younger one rolled up the paper.

"Couldn't have been farther off the mark," he said. "Neither male nor halfling."

"Lower your hood and state your business," demanded Captain Righteous.

Katherine lowered her hood. "Hello. I was just tying my shoes while I waited for this shop to open."

Both she and the guards looked down at her feet. Her boots didn't have laces.

Shit.

The captain scrutinized Katherine for a time, like he wasn't sure if he recognized her or not. Finally, he said, "And what is that?"

Shit shit. Did nothing get past this guy? Who was he, fucking Columbo?

"It's nothing," said Katherine. "Just a hole in my cloak."

The two guards exchanged impatient glances.

"You are testing my patience, half-elf. What do you have in your hand?"

Katherine looked up at her fatiguing right hand and realized that she was holding up her Bag of Holding. Force of habit. It's not the sort of thing you want to leave lying around.

"Oh. Um... It's a bag." She honestly wasn't trying to piss these people off.

"And what, exactly, do you have in the bag?"

"Nothing. Just stuff. Normal stuff."

"Stolen stuff?"

Katherine scoffed. "I'll have you know, sir, that I am a druid." That sounded a lot less stupid in her head just before she said it.

"Go on, Bingam. Check her bag."

"Gladly, sir." The one called Bingam dismounted while Captain Righteous kept his crossbow leveled at Katherine's heart.

Katherine couldn't think of many options, but as Bingam approached, she knew that whatever options she had were rapidly disappearing.

Bingam smiled, holding his hands out to take the open bag from Katherine's hands. "Let's see what we've got in – Wha!"

As soon as she'd flipped the bag over Bingam's head, she heard the dreaded click and twang of the captain's firing crossbow. She winced, but felt no pain.

"Blast!" shouted Captain Righteous. He was already loading another bolt.

Butterbean jumped out and bit down hard on Bingam's

thigh, which caused his arms to flail even more, preventing Katherine from being able to completely enclose him in the Bag of Holding.

"Stay back, Butterbean!" said Katherine. "I've got this under control."

That may have been a slight exaggeration. Katherine didn't want to kill these two guys who were doing their job to protect the people of this city, but she had shit to do.

She didn't have much of a plan worked out, but she knew she couldn't continue to rely on the captain's shitty aim. When he raised his weapon to fire, Katherine jerked Bingam's body to the left. His bleeding leg surrendered to her just in time.

CLICK!

TWANG!

THUNK!

The only sound missing was Bingam's reaction to suddenly having an unexpected crossbow bolt in the back. Katherine didn't have anything against the guy, but she needed him to put his hands down.

"Sorry," she whispered just before kneeing him in the nuts.

Bingam's hands immediately went to his crotch, and Katherine pulled the bag down hard.

By the time the captain had reloaded his weapon, Katherine had scooped Bingam into the bag and was holding it in front of her.

"Do you know what happens if you puncture a Bag of Holding?" The question was kind of a bluff. Katherine didn't know the answer herself.

Captain Righteous scowled at Katherine as he slowly lowered his crossbow. "Everything inside will be forever destroyed."

"That's right!" supposed Katherine. "Now drop your weapon."

"Take it and go." He leaned over on his horse and set the crossbow gently on the ground. "Bingam has a family."

"Bingam has ten minutes before his air runs out." Katherine had gained a slight upper hand, but the clock was ticking. She thought out loud, hoping the captain might help her think of an idea that could work out for everyone. "I can't let you go, or else you'll round up a posse and hunt me down. What if we rode together through Westgate. Once we've traveled far enough, I'll take both your horses and let you two walk back home or something."

"That's very thoughtful of you. But you won't get through the gate riding a Kingsguard horse."

Katherine thought. "I might if I'm dressed as a Kingsguard."

"And where do you intend to get a Kingsguard uniform in the next ten minutes?"

Katherine reached into the Bag of Holding. "Guard's clothes." Bingam's entire uniform spilled out of the bag all together, as if a body had been sucked right out of it.

She worked at separating the layers so she could put them on in the proper order. A yellow tabard with the city's emblem, the Cardinian Rose, on the front and a pair of baggy green pants made up the outermost layer. Under that was a chain suit that reminded Katherine of giant metal baby pajamas. The innermost layers consisted of a set of what looked like thermal underwear, and then a pair of actual undershorts. Those smelled as if they'd been sweated and farted in quite a bit since their last wash.

Her own cloak would be suitable padding for the length of time she needed to wear the armor. She shoved the undergarments back into the bag so that poor Bingam wouldn't have to float around in extradimensional space completely naked.

Bingam's body was considerably larger than Katherine's, so the armor was easy to slip into, but it sagged like the skin of an obese person who lost a bunch of weight way too quickly. Lifting her arms up and down and taking a short walk, Katherine also found that normal movement was cumbersome.

"You're one of them, aren't you?" said Captain Righteous

while Katherine slipped the uniform tabard over her head.

"One of who?" she asked, playing dumb.

"I don't see many half-elven women walking around with wolves at their sides. You're one of the group I chased here from Algor. A companion of that murderous halfling."

"He's not a murderer!" Shit. So much for playing it dumb.

"The posters all over the city say otherwise," said the captain. "I will take great satisfaction in bringing him to justice this time, Miss..." He raised his eyebrows expectantly.

There wasn't much point to keeping her name secret. If things went south, she was in deep shit whether or not he knew her name.

"My name is Katherine." She tightened Bingam's belt to the very last hole, but it was still a little loose. "How do I look?"

"You look ridiculous," said Captain Righteous. "If you get stopped even for a moment, Bingam is as good as dead. It may be too late for him already."

"Good point." Katherine put her hand inside the Bag of Holding. "Carbon dioxide." A rush of warm air blasted past her hand.

"What is this carbon dioxide? Is it an incantation?"

Neither Katherine nor Bingam had time for her to explain. She held the bag open wide and started spinning around.

"What manner of spell is this? Never have I seen magic performed in such an undignified manner."

Between the weight of the armor and her self-induced dizziness, Katherine found she could no longer keep her balance. She fell over on her side, crashing into the street. For something that was supposed to protect her, the chains in the armor pinched her arm, hurting her more than if she had fallen without wearing it.

"By the gods, woman!" said the captain. "Have you lost your mind?"

Katherine stood and steadied herself against Bingam's horse. The world around her hadn't quite stopped spinning yet. "I just reset the clock. We've got ten minutes to get the hell out of here. You ready, Butterbean?"

Butterbean barked and wagged his tail.

Captain Righteous frowned. "The wolf is going to arouse suspicion."

Katherine bit her lip. "Without him, can we be out of here in five minutes?"

"We can try."

On one hand, Katherine saw this as a disadvantage. The insurance policy that she'd been considering was to keep a dagger held close to the bag to make sure the captain didn't rat her out at the gate. He'd be much less likely to buy her threat if her own wolf was in the bag with Bingam.

On the other hand, she was relieved that she wasn't going to have to be that big a bitch.

She placed the Bag of Holding gently on the ground and lifted up the lip. "Get in the bag, Butterbean. I promise it won't be for long."

Butterbean's tail lowered, but he walked toward the bag, gave it a sniff, and looked up at Katherine with his sad doggy eyes.

"Speak," said Katherine. She hadn't wanted to use up the spell so early in the day, preferring to have it available for when she could make time for some more meaningful conversation with her Animal Companion. But she needed information.

"I know it's no fun in there, but I promise it'll just be for a few minutes."

Butterbean nodded. "As you wish, Miss Katherine."

"Don't attack Bingam, okay? He's had a rough day."

"I understand."

Katherine set the Bag of Holding gently on the ground and lifted the lip. "I'm going to pull you out after a few seconds. I need to know how Bingam is doing, and if the air is breathable."

Butterbean walked into the bag and disappeared.

"I suppose this is what's meant by the phrase 'barking mad'," said Captain Righteous.

That made for one more curiosity solved. Katherine had wondered what she sounded like to other people when using the spell.

"I told you, I'm a druid. I cast a spell so that I could talk with my wolf." She put her hand in the bag. "Butterbean."

The wolf tumbled out of the bag, rolled over, and stood up wagging his tail again. "It's quite a ride when you're not concerned about dying."

"Is Bingam okay?" asked Katherine.

"He's alive, but crying. And he appears to have urinated."

"Good enough. How's the air in there?"

"Fresher than I remember it being last time I was in there. I mean, aside from smelling like human urine."

"Okay. I'll get rid of the pee. Now get back in there... and be nice."

Butterbean stepped back into the Bag of Holding, then Katherine put the tips of two fingers just inside the lip. "Pee." A yellow stream trickled out over her fingers. When it was done, she wiped them on the front of her Kingsguard uniform.

Captain Righteous gasped, and Katherine realized she was wiping piss on the royal emblem.

She looked up at the captain. "I'm sorry. Was that disrespectful?"

"Did you command your wolf to urinate in the bag with Bingam?"

How to answer that? The truth might lead to further humiliation down the line for Bingam. Verifying the wolf story would only serve to make Katherine out to be even more of a cruel and heartless bitch. The bitch thing was really the only card she had to play.

"Yes, I did. Both of you need to understand who's in charge here. Are we clear?"

Captain Righteous narrowed his eyes. "Indeed."

Katherine reset the clock once more, this time opting to hold the bag open while running in a straight line, about ten yards one way, then ten yards back. The encumbrance of the armor made even such a short run exhausting, but that should have been enough to fully replenish their air supply.

She looped a stirrup around her boot and pulled herself onto Bingam's horse. "Let's get this over with."

"Not too quickly," said Captain Righteous as Katherine's horse pulled ahead of his. "The object here is to look as casual as possible. If we're lucky, the shifts won't have changed yet, and the guards at the gate will be tired and weary. Your best bet is to slump over and feign illness. That might cover your ill-fitting armor, and it will make them think twice about getting too close to you. I am your commanding officer, so let me do all the talking. Are we agreed."

The captain spoke calmly and rationally, and everything he said made sense. This both reassured and concerned Katherine. The man had some cunning in him. Had he developed this plan so quickly with the means of securing his and his fellow guard's safe release? Or was he putting himself in a position of total control in order to spring some surprise on her at the gate? He had her bested on strategy, and she had neither a counter-plan, nor the time to think of one.

"Just don't try anything stupid." Though she tried to sound tough, she could hear the surrender in her own voice.

"We're in too deep to go back now."

Westgate was just ahead of them. Katherine slumped over, making it impossible to see where she was going, but at least it had the advantage of hiding her face.

The horses walked for what seemed like an eternity while Katherine waited anxiously to play her role. If it helped the performance, she felt like she might be able to vomit at will without a whole lot of effort. She was sweating through her cloak. They weren't going to make it in time.

Just when she was going to say something, Captain Righteous's horse stopped walking. Katherine's stopped beside it.'

"Utterly shameful," said the captain.

"What?" whispered Katherine.

"Two guards sleeping. Two more not even at their posts. And neither of the other two gave a second glance at your embarrassment of a uniform."

"What?" whispered Katherine again.

"Congratulations, half-elf. You've made your daring escape."

Katherine looked back. They were a good thirty yards beyond the gate. "Sweet!"

"Now be true to your word and release my partner."

"Not yet," said Katherine. She looked at the road ahead. "I'll let him out once we get around that bend."

"We've used up too much time as it is. Think of your wolf!"

"It's cool." Katherine once again removed all the carbon dioxide from the Bag of Holding, held it open, and let her horse drive fresh air into it.

Once they were around the bend, Captain Righteous's tone soured. "I have held up my end of the deal, half-elf, betraying both my station and my king. We are well out of sight now. I demand you release my partner at once."

"I was just about to." Katherine stopped her horse and dismounted. "You hop down from yours too. I promised to let you go, but not on horseback. I need to keep my lead."

"I understand." Captain Righteous dismounted.

Katherine held open the bag. "Butterbean."

Butterbean came out panting, though Katherine couldn't tell if it was from excitement or oxygen deprivation.

"A final insult to poor Bingam," said the captain, shaking his head. "You release the dog first."

"He's a wolf," said Katherine. "You'd do well to remember that. I couldn't release Bingam first, and risk having you two jump me, could I?"

"You make a fair point. It was a wise decision on your part.

Now, if you don't mind."

Katherine looked at Butterbean. His gaze was fixed on the captain. That was good.

She reached into the bag. "Bingam."

A pale naked man spilled out of the bag, curled up into a fetal position, and resumed crying. Katherine tried not to stare.

"He's my sister's son," Captain Righteous volunteered, in spite of Katherine having given no conscious signal of giving a shit. "He's fragile. I hoped a stint in the Kingsguard might toughen him up a bit." He knelt by his nephew and leaned down to whisper. "Please stop crying, Bingam. Come on. Get on your feet."

"Why are you naked?" asked Katherine.

Bingam's head jerked toward her with a teary glare. "Because you stole my clothes, you evil bitch!"

"I put your underwear back in the bag for you."

Bingam sniffled. "They kept flying past me, always just out of reach."

"I'm sorry about that." Katherine reached into the Bag of Holding again. "Bingam's underwear." As soon as she felt it, Katherine jerked her hand back and let it drop on the ground, aiming to minimize how much of the man's ass sweat she had to touch.

Bingam snatched up his long underpants and stood up with his ass facing Katherine. He put both feet in the leg holes and hurriedly began to tug them upward.

"Put your hands in the air," demanded a deep, stern, and not entirely unfamiliar voice from behind Katherine. "We have you surrounded."

Butterbean snarled and bared his teeth, and Katherine looked to Captain Righteous for guidance as to whether they were going to fight or not. When he shook his head and slowly raised his empty hands, her heart sank. She'd been the one who'd disarmed him. Her heart sank even further at the sight of Bingam hopping up and down, trying desperately to pull his underwear up before surrendering. In his haste, he fell forward, planting his face into the hard-packed earth.

Katherine raised her hands above her head and turned around to face her captor.

"You people again?" she said when she saw the jet black skin and snow white hair of the two slender figures pointing bows at her.

"We people?" asked one of them.

Katherine covered her mouth with her hands. "Oh my God! I totally didn't mean it like that."

"Vile thugs!" snarled Captain Righteous.

"Whoa!" said Katherine. "Not cool, man."

The other black elf lowered his bow slightly as his jaw dropped open. "It's her! She's the one who killed Lady Vivia's cat, mangled its body, and wrote a mocking apology on the wall with its blood."

"Is that true?" Captain Righteous whispered.

"I didn't have a pen and paper."

"I don't think so," said the first elf. "That one was more sleek and slender. Almost pretty by half-elf standards."

Katherine gasped.

"So she's let herself go a bit. But I'm telling you it's her."

"What did you say, you long-eared fuck?" Katherine took a step forward, but stopped as the two black elves tensed their bowstrings. Butterbean growled.

The first elf nodded. "That's her alright." A sinister grin spread across his face. "And she has herself a little pet now. Won't Lady Vivia be pleased to hear that."

"No." Katherine couldn't bear to think what that sadistic woman would do to Butterbean in retaliation for what was really a very simple misunderstanding.

"Bag them," said the elf in charge.

More black elves emerged from their hiding places in the trees. Three of them lowered their weapons and opened head-sized woolen bags, which they pulled over the heads of Katherine, Captain Righteous, and Bingam.

The bag fit loosely over Katherine's head, but breathing was still a chore. Designed to prohibit sight, the threads were woven tight, forcing her to breathe in much of the same air she was breathing out. It didn't help that the inside of the bag reeked of sweat and vomit.

"We will bring the prisoners to the holding cells. Have Zibon draw up the usual Kingsguard ransom demands for Lady Vivia's approval. And inform the Lady that I, Stavros Shadowblade, have apprehended Mittens's killer, and her pet wolf."

"The prisoner's pet wolf, sir?" asked one of the others.

"Yes, of course the prisoner's. Who else's wolf would I be referring to?"

"Just wanted to be clear, sir. It sounded like you might be referring to Lady Vivia's pet wolf. The her threw me off."

"Would it kill you to think before you speak?" said Stavros. "Lady Vivia doesn't have a pet wolf."

"You might have meant that we were presenting this wolf as a new pet for Lady Vivia, as a replacement for her recent loss of Mittens."

Stavros sighed. "I suppose that is not an entirely unreasonable interpretation. You did well to seek clarification. I meant the prisoner's wolf."

"I was way off," a third voice laughed. "I thought you were referring to Mittens's pet wolf."

"That's just preposterous."

"Yes, sir. I see that now. That's why it gave me a chuckle."

"This is exactly why I'm taking charge of the prisoners," said Stavros. "Can you two idiots be trusted with the task of taking this wolf down to the kennels?"

"Shall we feed him to the deathhounds, or begin his training to become one?" asked the elf in constant need of clarification.

"Just put him in one of the cages for now. His fate will be decided by Lady Vivia, whom I imagine will have more creative ideas as to what to do with him."

"And the horses, sir?" asked one of the elves behind Katherine. "They're too big to fit through the tunnel."

"Lead them off the road and kill them. Chop them up and put the pieces in the Bag of Holding. Help yourselves to the choicest cuts of meat, and feed the rest to the deathhounds."

A murmur of excitement among the black elves suggested that even more of them had come out of hiding since Katherine's head had been covered. Captain Righteous had probably suspected as much, which was why he'd surrendered so easily.

"But the Bag of Holding is to be returned to me," continued Stavros. "And a small dish of horsemeat would not be unappreciated."

"Of course, sir!" said one of his subordinates.

"I like mine medium rare."

"You blackhearted fiend!" said Captain Righteous. "Touch one hair on Melody's beautiful mane, and I'll tear you apart!"

"Melody? That's a pretty name. Perhaps I'll share a piece with you. How do you like your horse?"

"The gods were too merciful when they banished you people from the Light!"

"Hey!" said Katherine. "No need for that." She turned her head as best she could, without being able to see, toward the black elf leader. "He meant specifically you people who are kidnapping us."

"No I didn't!"

"Come on, man. You're better than that."

"Perhaps," said Stavros, "you would be wise to stop bickering and pay attention to your pudgy naked friend. He's the only one of you who seems to understand the gravity of your current situation."

The air was silent but for a sniffle and a couple of choked back sobs.

"Mercy of the gods, Bingam," said Captain Righteous. "Please stop crying."

CHAPTER 21

By the time evening rolled around, Stacy, Julian, and Cooper had followed the westward road out of Cardinia through a lot of what Stacy now thought of as 'conventional' forest. The farther west they traveled, however, the taller and wider the trees grew. Massive pines left the forest floor carpeted with brown needles as long as her legs and pine cones roughly the size and shape of Dave.

"It's incredible," said Stacy, marveling at the magnificence of it all. "Doesn't it make you feel so tiny and insignificant?"

Julian smiled. "I feel like an ant marching home after raiding a picnic."

"I feel like taking a dump," said Cooper.

Stacy stopped walking. Julian gave Cooper a 'Was that really necessary?' look.

"Sorry. I thought we were sharing our feelings."

"It's fine," said Stacy. "I've got to go too. Men's room on the right, ladies' room on the left. Do you need some of those big leaves I collected?"

Cooper shook his head. "Keep them. I'll just use a fistful of pine needles. It gets kind of rough down there, and those leaves just disintegrate in my hand when I try to wipe. Plus, the pine needles leave behind a pleasant scent to help mask the –"

"A simple 'no thank you' would have sufficed."

The bathroom rules had been established earlier in the day. Everyone got their privacy, but made sure not to wander beyond shouting distance.

Stacy walked around the other side of one of the big trees and swept aside some pine needles with her foot. She unbuckled her pants, and held her balance by keeping a hand on one of the tree's giant roots. It was an ideal situation to be in when she spotted a wild boar about the size of a short bus. Cooper's frequent needs to relieve himself ensured that Stacy never had to wait too long for a pee break, but her bladder let go like she'd been holding it in for a week.

A few years ago, she'd witnessed a boar run out of the woods and charge a moving Range Rover for no discernible reason beyond 'Fuck that Range Rover.' It popped one of the tires with its tusk, and then ran back off into the woods like it had just needed to blow off some steam. Those things were tough and dangerous. How much more so would a twelve foot long version of them be?

The giant boar was a good forty yards away from her, rooting through some dirt, but Stacy still wrapped up her business as quickly as she could. When she was done, she tiptoed around the tree and spotted Julian and Cooper coming back toward the road from the other side. She waved to get their attention.

"I'm not claiming it's the end of the world," grumbled Cooper. "I'm just saying, why isn't it ever 'just a fart' when I'm talking to people?"

When Stacy finally caught Julian's eye, she waved them both over to her.

"Look," said Julian. "Stacy wants to show us something."

"She probably wants to show off the massive log she dropped."

"Somehow I doubt that's the case."

Stacy put a finger over her lips, and the guys crossed the road in silence. When they got to her tree, she pointed at the boar.

"Sweet pig," said Cooper.

Stacy elbowed him and pressed her finger even more firmly on her lips just long enough to make her point, then whispered, "That's all you've got to say?"

Cooper poked his bottom lip out. "Sorry, I don't know what

you... Wait, is today your birthday?"

"What? No!" Stacy couldn't believe that neither Cooper nor Julian seemed the least bit impressed by a two thousand pound boar. She glared at Cooper. "Are you not awed by the size of that thing?"

Cooper looked back at her with his lips pressed tightly together, like he was holding his breath. Little snorts escaped from his nostrils. More snorts came from Julian's direction. He was turning blue in the face. They looked like two tea kettles trying not to boil. It was like they were trying not to...

"Is this because I said 'awed by the size of that thing'? You two need to grow up."

Julian let himself laugh and his face returned to its original color. "I'm sorry. I was just laughing at Cooper trying not to laugh."

Cooper also released the pressure he'd been holding in, except he did so through the other end. Stacy grimaced. It was a wet one.

"Goddammit," said Cooper. He bent over and scooped up a large handful of pine needles. "I'll be right back." He stomped around to the other side of the tree.

An angry squeal echoed through the massive trees.

Julian's jaw dropped. "Um... Cooper?"

"Dude, give me a minute. I'm fucking wiping."

By the time Stacy turned around, the boar was charging straight at her. Its snout was caked in fresh soil and its wild eyes burned with rage. She pulled out her sword, bent her knees, and focused her mind. Timing would be everything.

"Magic Missile!" cried Julian. A golden bolt of magical energy flew out of his hand to further mildly annoy the beast still charging directly at Stacy.

Stacy thought of an aerial diagram showing everyone's position on the battlefield. Cooper, whose shart had been the catalyst for the boar's sudden rage, was on the opposite side of the tree from her, putting her directly between him and the boar.

It thought she was the one who'd produced the odor which had so offended it. Interesting.

She stepped to her left, spun around, and raked the tip of her sword across the animal's cheek, neck, and shoulder as it smashed its face hard into the great pine.

"Cooper!" cried Julian. "Hurry the –"

CRASH

Julian had been taken out of the fight by a giant pine cone.

The boar grunted as it thrust its two foot long tusks at Stacy. She dodged and weaved as she backed up, but it came at her even harder. She could use that.

She ducked under its sweeping tusks and jabbed at its snout. The tip of her sword penetrated the soft tissue. The boar reeled back, squealing in pain and rage, and Stacy ran back to her tree.

When the boar charged her again, demonstrating an inability to learn from its past mistakes, she sidestepped the charge once more. But instead of attacking, she hopped up on the beast's back and grabbed hold of its mane with her left hand, while she raised her sword hand to thrust her blade down into its skull.

The boar bucked hard. Nope. This is definitely a two-hand job.

Stacy let go of the sword and held on for her life with both hands. "COOPER!"

In retrospect, as the furious pig squealed and did everything in its power to throw her off, this felt like a poorly thought out plan. Her high Wisdom score had let her down, and her Strength and Dexterity felt like they were getting ready to fail her as well.

Then it stopped suddenly, still as a statue.

Stacy looked down as she caught her breath. The right side of the boar's face, from eye to tusk, was coated in a blob of pine needles and greenish-brown paste. Both the boar and Stacy turned their heads toward the tree to find Cooper standing ready with his axe.

The forest filled with a deafening porcine scream as Stacy's ass hit the ground. She looked first at the two fistfuls of mane she was clutching, then at Cooper bringing his axe down hard on the raging beast he'd just half-blinded with shit.

They slammed into each other like idiots, neither making any visible effort to avoid the other's attack. Cooper's axe stuck deep into the back of the boar's head, but it didn't even seem to notice as it plowed its tusks into Cooper's abdomen without even slowing down.

"Cooper!" cried Stacy. She picked up her sword and chased after them.

"Fuuuuuuuuck," said Cooper. Stacy lost sight of him as the boar carried him behind a tree, but she heard him invoke his Barbarian Rage. "I'm really angry!"

Stacy ran around the tree and got back within visual range of them just in time to see Cooper's metamorphosis. The added weight from his suddenly increased muscle mass was too much for the boar. Cooper hit the ground and used the boar's inertia to flip it over himself. The boar's scream upon landing seemed like a bit of an overreaction to landing on its back on a soft bed of pine needles. Had Cooper hurt its pride?

When the boar got back on its feet, Stacy saw the axe still sticking out the back of its head. Yeah, that would have hurt.

Cooper wasn't looking so hot either with two tusk wounds bleeding out of his abs. As soon as they were both standing, they charged at each other again, squealing, grunting, bleeding, and drooling. Truly, Cooper had found his equal.

They weren't far enough away from each other for the boar to get another good gore in. Cooper caught it by the tusk and punched it repeatedly in the snout.

"FUCK! YOU! PIG!"

It looked like a stalemate, but Cooper's Barbarian Rage had a limited duration. Stacy was sure she could finish the beast off if she could make use of her Sneak Attack power. She approached from its blind side, looking for a path to the heart that didn't go directly through the rib cage.

When the boar reared up on its hind legs, trying desperately to swipe Cooper with its front hooves, Stacy found her path. She lunged forward, grabbed the boar by its front leg, and drove her blade deep into its fleshy armpit, all the way up to the hilt.

The resulting agonized squeal turned into a wheeze, and blood spurted out of the animal's mouth. She'd missed the heart but punctured a lung. Not ideal, but hopefully she and Cooper could keep it from ripping them to shreds with its tusks before Cooper's Barbarian Rage –

"Oh shit," said Cooper. His voice didn't sound particularly enraged.

The boar, on the other hand, was as pissed off as ever. It was overpowering them. Stacy grabbed its unclaimed tusk with both hands, letting go of both its leg and her sword. But even with their combined Strengths, the boar pinned them both to the ground.

"Push back!" said Stacy. The boar's massive head loomed over her, practically vomiting out lung blood at this point.

"I'm trying!" said Cooper. "I'm fucking fatigued!"

The boar was drowning, but not quickly enough. Bloodmist from the beast's ragged breaths made the tusk slippery in Stacy's hands. If she lost her grip, the boar wouldn't need to find an alternative route to her heart. Her rib cage would be about as effective as tinfoil.

The porcine wheezing came to a halt as the giant boar suddenly froze, as if it had just had some life-changing epiphany. Two seconds later, its legs gave out, and it collapsed harmlessly on top of Stacy and Cooper.

Stacy squirmed out from under the boar's head, then withdrew her sword from its armpit. She looked down at Cooper. "Are you okay?"

Cooper lay back in the pile of pine needles that had resulted from the boar's advancement. He was covered in blood. "Define okay."

"Hey!" said the boar. It's voice was a little muffled, but positively eloquent for a dead pig.

Stacy frowned. "Is that normal?"

Cooper groaned in pain as he sat up and shoved the boar's head sideways by the tusk. "Define normal." He wrapped his hand around a cluster of black feathers sticking out of the eye socket and pulled.

"Gently!" cried Ravenus.

Tail was followed by talons, then wings, head, beak, and finally a long dripping trail of optic nerve.

"Thanks for stealing my kill, you Kamikaze asshole," said Cooper.

Ravenus slurped up the rest of his meal and shook the gore from his feathers. "Would it be out of line to request giving the other eye a rinse?"

"Holy shit!" said Julian, awake again and on the scene. "Cooper, are you okay?"

"No thanks to you losing a fight with a goddamn pine cone."

"Oh come on. You can't blame me for that. Did you see the size of that thing?"

Cooper winced as he laughed. It must have been excruciating with two tusk holes in his gut, but he just couldn't help himself.

After a pause for thought, Julian started laughing too.

Stacy shook her head. "Unbelievable. It wasn't funny the first time." But that only made Cooper laugh harder, subsequently causing him more pain. Her resistance eroded, and it didn't take long for her to succumb to the contagion as well.

CHAPTER 22

Desperate times call for desperate measures. And when a person's desperate enough, there's only one place to go. Arby's.

Going on what Dave had overheard Professor Goosewaddle's acquaintance boasting about a few days earlier combined with the fact that the Whore's Head Inn's most recent prisoner had mentioned a place called the Crescent Shadow, the remaining inhabitants of the Whore's Head Inn placed their bets on the only lead they had, however much of a longshot it was.

Business had slowed down since Cardinia's only fast food restaurant had opened, but Dave was surprised to see a line of people waiting outside the open door. It was nothing like opening week, but old Goosewaddle must have done something to get business booming again.

Somewhere in the stink of a crowd of people and vaguely humanoid creatures in a world where deodorant had yet to be invented, Dave identified the familiar scent of Arby's roast beef. His stomach longed to be filled with the sweet taste of home.

"Should we wait in line?" asked Chaz.

"Nah," said Dave. They were VIPs at this place. "When you think about it, Goosewaddle owes his success to us. Besides, we're not here to eat. We just need to –"

"Uh uh!" Jennifer, the recently promoted manager of Arby's shoved her way through the line of customers at the front door and wielded a broom at Dave and his crowd. "Nope, nope, and double nope. You freeloaders are cut off. Do you hear me? Cut. Off. Go on back to wherever you came from."

"But we're VIPs," said Dave. It felt so douchey to say out loud.

"You're V.I.Shit, Department Store Santa. I can't turn a profit with you mooching lowlifes occupying all the tables and helping yourselves to free soda refills."

"Are the soda refills free?" asked a lizardman waiting in line.

"NO!" Jennifer snapped back at him.

Chaz stepped up next to Dave. "Hey lady. We just want to talk to Professor Goosewaddle."

Jennifer raised her eyebrows and looked Chaz up and down. "And who the hell are you, Lady Gaga? You think you're gonna go over my head? You best turn around if you know what's good for you."

Dave reassured himself that this was just an ordinary young woman with an ordinary broom, and he shouldn't be as frightened of her as he was. He cleared his throat.

"We're not going anywhere until we talk to the professor."

Jennifer's angry face trembled, and Dave thought she might lunge forward and beat the shit out of him with her broom at any second.

"I'll call the professor alright. I'll tell him to Fireball your freeloading asses from here to Kingdom Come. You see if he don't listen to me." She leaned inside the door. "Professor!"

After a moment of intense glaring on both sides, Professor Goosewaddle floated out the door and hovered next to Jennifer.

"Oh, it's you." The professor eyeballed Dave and his companions like they were a bunch of hemorrhoids. "I'll take care of this," he said to Jennifer in an apologetic tone.

"Don't you let those people in my restaurant." Jennifer spoke to Professor Goosewaddle in a tone that Dave would never have dared.

"What the fuck, lady?" said Chaz.

Jennifer pointed her broom at him. "You shut that filthy

mouth of yours, or I'll shut it for you."

"Please go back inside," said Professor Goosewaddle. "You're doing such a fine job. I'll get rid of them."

Jennifer looked at Dave and Chaz, then thrust her broom forward, causing them both to jump. Satisfied, she went back into the restaurant.

Professor Goosewaddle hovered toward the Whore's Head crowd, gesturing for them to move back, which they did. "Sorry about that. Jennifer has established some new rules in the restaurant."

"I can't believe you let her talk to us that way," said Chaz.

"I can't believe you let her talk to you that way," said Dave. "You're this super-powerful wizard, and she's just an ordinary girl."

Professor Goosewaddle shrugged. "She's an effective manager. A tad unconventional, that's for sure. Can you believe she's making me pay the goblins who work in the kitchen?"

Dave frowned. "Yes, you've mentioned that."

"A silver piece an hour! She calls it a 'living wage', as if I wouldn't replace them when they die. It's ludicrous!" Professor Goosewaddle was beginning to sound a lot like Dave's racist Uncle Jimmy when he got a few drinks in him at Thanksgiving. "But she runs a tight ship. As you can see, business hasn't been this good since our opening week."

"Congratulations," said Chaz.

The professor broke eye contact and fidgeted with his beard. "So I'm afraid I'm going to have to ask you folks not to come back here. It's nothing personal. She showed me the numbers, and the cost of potatoes alone –"

"We're not here for curly fries, Professor," said Dave. "We need a favor."

Professor Goosewaddle narrowed his eyes at Dave. "Jennifer says I've been too generous with you folks, and that you're taking advantage of me. I'm beginning to wonder if she's right."

Dave wished Julian was here to use Diplomacy. He knew the

Arby's card was a strong one, but he wasn't sure if this was the right time to play it.

"You wouldn't even have this restaurant if it wasn't for us," said Chaz.

Fuck.

"Now you listen here!" The professor was putting his foot down. Metaphorically, of course. He was actually levitating about a foot higher now. The bottom of his Arby's uniform shirt hung below his toes, making him look like an angry bearded Pac-Man ghost. "I don't know what you think I owe you, but remember that when you introduced me to your strange world, it was I who was doing you a favor."

Now that Diplomacy was off the table, Dave used what little leverage he could muster. "We paid you for that."

"Ha!" cried Professor Goosewaddle. "You call that payment?"

"That was a big pile of gold!"

"It was a pittance! Have you any idea what the going rate for a Teleport spell is?"

This line of arguing was only digging Dave deeper into the hole. It was time to beg. "Please, Professor. This is important. Just one last favor, and we'll never ask you for anything again."

Professor Goosewaddle folded his arms and scowled at Dave. "What is it?"

Dave wished he'd gone with begging from the get go. He hung his head low. "A Teleport spell."

The professor shook his head. "You've got a lot of nerve. I'll give you that."

"We believe there's something big going down at the Crescent Shadow. Something that involves my friend Tim."

"He's the halfling drunk?"

"Yes, and Mordred."

"He's the naked man who summoned four young boys before he fell out of the hotel window?"

"Yes, and your friend who was in here the other day," said

Dave. "The one with the black and white forked beard."

"Murkwort." The way Professor Goosewaddle spat out the name suggested that he thought even less of Murkwort than he did of them.

"We need to get there as soon as possible, figure out what's going on, and try to stop it."

Professor Goosewaddle stroked his beard thoughtfully. "Murkwort acts like a pompous fool, but he's no one to double cross or take lightly. He'll fry you with Lightning Bolts just as soon as look at you if he suspects you're trying to steal from him."

"We'll be careful. We might not have to steal from him. Maybe we'll steal from one of his buyers or something. Our first priority is making sure that Mordred doesn't get his hands on those dice."

"And my first priority is this restaurant," said Professor Goosewaddle. "I'll grant you this favor just for the sake of putting some miles between us."

"Thank you, Professor!"

"But only on the condition that this is indeed the last favor you'll ever ask of me. Are we agreed?"

Dave nodded enthusiastically. "Yes!"

"Very well. I can take two of you."

Dave frowned, fearful of pushing his luck. "I was kind of hoping you'd take all of us. We don't know what we'll be up against."

Professor Goosewaddle's little face reddened with frustration. "Unless I have specific reason to do otherwise, I prepare precisely two Teleport spells a day. One to get me out of potential danger, and the other to take me back home."

"And the spell limits you to only two fellow teleportees?"

"The more people I try to bring along, the less accurately I'll be able to focus on a point of destination."

"If we're a couple of miles off, we can walk the rest of the way from there."

Professor Goosewaddle smiled at Dave like a teacher patiently explaining why we're not supposed to feed pencil shavings to the class fish. "Have you any idea what or where the Crescent Shadow is?"

"No."

"It's an island, four miles wide at its widest, which floats five hundred feet above the Fertile Desert. If we're a couple of miles off, I don't expect you'll be walking out of the craters you make when you hit the ground."

"Two it is." Dave turned to face the rest of the crowd. "Who wants to go? Frank? Rhonda? Hey, Tony the Elf's a good tracker."

"It's got to be you two," said Frank. "If Tim sees any of us, it could spook him into doing something monumentally stupid. You and Chaz are the ones he's most likely to trust."

Fuck.

As much as Dave hated to admit it, Frank was right. For once in his life, he wished Cooper was there with him. Cooper was closer to Tim, and might actually have enough Hit Points to survive a five hundred foot fall.

"Are you even more accurate with just one person?" asked Chaz. "I don't really see why Tim has any reason to trust me. I barely know him."

"The accuracy is marginally higher with only one companion than it is with two. But two is still well below the threshold of danger I'm willing to risk your lives on."

"Your lives?" said Chaz. "Not our lives?"

Professor Goosewaddle looked at the ground, then back at Chaz. "I can fly. You can't."

Chaz nodded. "That makes sense. And what exactly is the danger threshold you're willing to risk our lives on?"

"Chaz," said Dave. "Stop being such a pussy. You're coming." It felt good to have someone around more cowardly than himself. That was reason enough for Dave to keep Chaz by his side.

“Fine.”

Professor Goosewaddle descended and reached his hands out to Dave and Chaz. “Hold on.”

Dave took the professor’s left hand. Chaz grabbed hold of his right.

“Focus, Professor,” said Chaz. “Focus on the center of the island.”

The professor smiled. “Then you’d surely be dead. It’s called Crescent Shadow for a reason.”

“Shit.”

Dave only caught the beginning of an incantation as a crackle of electricity and a flash of white light rendered him suddenly deaf and blind.

CHAPTER 23

If Katherine remembered correctly, this was the same cell she had sprung Tanner and Chaz from. She thought she could still see a little smudge of cat blood on the wall next to where Bingam sat on the floor weeping.

"She was a big sturdy horse," said Stavros, the leader of the band of black elves who had ambushed them in the woods. He stood just outside the cell, his face visible in the flickering torchlight through the small barred window of the cell door, popping a small chunk of horsemeat into his mouth. "She tastes as though you kept her properly exercised. Well done."

Katherine knew he was just trying to get a rise out of Captain Righteous. These guys could see in the dark. The only explanation for him having bothered to light a torch was that he wanted them to be able to see him. What a dick.

The captain was doing a commendable job of ignoring his taunts. But Katherine hadn't eaten anything since that glue shit at the inn the night before, and the horsemeat smelled really good.

"Where are my manners?" Stavros continued. "She was your horse. Surely, you are entitled to a bite."

Captain Righteous continued to stare stoically at the center of the stone floor, not wanting to give his captor the satisfaction of losing his cool. But when a chunk of meat landed on the exact spot he was staring at, he finally snapped. He jumped up and thrust his arm through the window bars.

"You fiend! I'll tear you limb from limb!"

Stavros, of course, had been well prepared to leap out of the way. He laughed at Captain Righteous. "Don't be so greedy.

Perhaps I'll give you another piece once you've finished your first one. We don't want to be wasteful."

While they were talking, Katherine licked her lips and glanced down at Bingam. He was still cradling his head in his hands.

She snatched up the chunk of horsemeat and popped it in her mouth. It was fucking delicious.

Captain Righteous shook the bars hard, but that door wasn't going anywhere. He turned around and looked despairingly down at the floor. Then he looked up at Katherine, who stopped chewing.

She offered him a tight-lipped grin and a reassuring shrug.

Stavros stopped laughing as footsteps approached rapidly from down the dark hallway.

Captain Righteous turned back to the cell door, and Katherine swallowed the meat.

Lady Vivia's face appeared in the window. Her cold violet eyes glared at Katherine through a thin black veil.

"So the reports are correct." She sneered with naked contempt and disgust. "She really has let herself go."

Katherine held in her anger. She knew she was very attractive by half-elf standards. Anyone who had only ever known her as a vampire was now holding her to unfair standards of beauty. And considering the woman's recent loss, Katherine decided to let this one slide.

"I'm really very sorry about your cat. That was an accident."

"An accident!" cried Lady Vivia. "You accidentally murdered Mittens, mangled her body, and scrawled a message on the wall with her blood?"

"Of course not. But I didn't know she was your cat."

"Your groveling will not save you, half-elf."

"Shall I send for the Extractor?" asked Stavros.

"No. I have a more fitting fate in store for this one. We shall starve her wolf until it is driven mad with hunger. Either she will be devoured, or she will be forced to murder her companion. She will feel my loss before she dies."

"He hasn't eaten in a while," said Katherine. "He's probably on the brink of madness right now."

"Nice try, half-elf, but I think we'll wait a week or two."

"Weeks? I don't have that kind of time. I need –"

Lady Vivia shook her head. "This one, always worried about time. On the contrary, dear. Weeks are all the time you have left."

"Listen," said Katherine. "I know you're upset, but –"

"Do you know that I have not shared a bed with a man since Mittens's death?"

That was more information than Katherine felt she needed to be privy to. "Oh?" What else does one say to that?

"Now that her death shall soon be avenged, I once again crave the pleasures of the flesh." She turned to the side. "You have done well, sweet Stavros, and you shall be rewarded."

"Would you like to satisfy your cravings here, where the half-elf can see, or would you prefer someplace more private?"

"An interesting, if not entirely appropriate question. I shall ask Alessandro what he prefers."

"But I thought... You said I shall be rewarded."

"And you shall. The Bag of Holding is yours to keep, and you shall face no disciplinary measures for trying to keep it from me."

After a short pause, Stavros spoke again. "Yes, Lady Vivia."

With that, the black elf lady walked away.

When the sound of retreating footsteps had faded away entirely, Katherine went to the window. "Tough break, Stavvy."

Stavros jerked his hand away from his crotch and whipped his cloak around to cover his front. "Back away from the window!"

"Feeling a little blue... in the balls area?"

"Be quiet!" Stavros's voice faded as he continued to grumble. "Is it too much to ask for a minute of privacy? I'm surrounded by fools, idiots, empty-headed..."

Katherine joined the other two prisoners on the floor. "He's not going to last very long, so we don't have much time. We need ideas on how to bust out of here. What have you got?"

"Impossible," said Captain Righteous. "The crossbar holding the door in place is much too thick to break through. The best we can hope for is that the king agrees to pay a ransom for us. We'll be demoted for sure. Possibly kicked out of the Kingsguard altogether. But at least..." He looked at Katherine and decided against finishing his thought.

"At least it's better than what Butterbean and I have in store, you mean?"

The captain shot her an annoyed glare. "Your poor choices led to us being captured by Drow. Your fate is regrettable, but you have no one to blame but yourself."

"Bullshit," said Katherine. "There's always a way out. I've busted out of this cell before. I can do it again."

Bingam stared quizzically at Katherine through watery eyes. "What? You mean this particular cell that we're locked inside of?"

"Yes."

A glimmer of hope shone in Bingam's eyes, and Katherine felt really bad about having to answer the question he was about to ask.

"How'd you do it?"

Katherine shrugged but couldn't meet his gaze. "I was a vampire then. I turned into mist and slid through the window."

Bingam's lower lip quivered. He was trying hard to keep from crying again, but that dam was about to burst.

"You were a vampire," said Captain Righteous. "You were an undead abomination, living outside the Light's grace, and that's since cleared up like a mild case of the pox, has it?"

"I can explain that later. We're wasting valuable brainstorming time."

"Brainstorming?" The captain actually cracked a smile. "There is clearly a tempest raging in your brain, Miss Katherine. In my whole career as a –"

"That's it!"

"What's it?"

"My hole!"

Bingam lost his composure and started sobbing again.

Captain Righteous frowned sympathetically at Katherine. "Miss. I appreciate the desperate nature of your situation, but our Drow captor has already stated that he's not particularly attracted to you. Besides, I believe he's currently... self-administering any needs you could hope to satisfy with your... hole. Might I suggest you die with at least a little bit of dignity?"

"You need to get your mind out of the gutter, creep." Katherine pulled the small square of magical fabric from her cloak. "How good are you with a crossbow?"

The captain squinted at her. "Do you ever have more than one coherent thought in a row?"

"Forget it," said Katherine. "We'll find out soon enough." Careful to keep aware of which side of the hole she'd had stuck to her cloak, she placed the black cloth on the door just below the window. With the iron bands holding the vertical planks of the door together, the hole it opened was just shy of penetrating through to the other side of the door, but it was deep enough to allow Katherine to wrest one of the three iron bars loose. Unfortunately, the bar slipped through her fingers, fell outside the door, and landed noisily on the stone floor.

"What in the Abyss!" cried Stavros from a short distance down the hall.

Katherine backed away from the door as footsteps quickly approached.

"What are you doing?" whispered Captain Righteous. "Grab the Portable Hole!"

But it was too late for that. Stavros's face was in the window, sweating and seething. His wild eyes examined the perfectly cubic extension of the interior of the window.

"What happened here?" he demanded. "How did you do

this?"

"It just fell," said Katherine. "Looks like termite damage."

Stavros ran a finger along the edge of the hole. "Termites that eat through solid iron?"

Katherine shrugged. "Rust, maybe?"

"All I needed was one more minute. Is a single minute too much to ask?" Stavros continued to explore the edge of the hole in the door with his fingers.

Katherine raised her eyebrows at him. "Did you wash your hands?"

"Shut up, half-elf! When Lady Vivia is done with you, I shall spill my seed upon whatever is left of your corpse!"

"That's kinda fucked up," said Katherine. "Does Alessandro talk like this? Your weird fetishes might have something to do with why Lady Vivia prefers a man like him."

"I told you to shut –" The rage vanished from Stavros's eyes, and was replaced with fascination as one of his fingers caressed the bottom right corner of the hole. "Is this what I think it is?" His fingers found the corner of the hole, and he slowly peeled it off. Aside from the missing bar in the window, the door was once again whole.

"That's mine!" said Katherine angrily.

Stavros smiled. "Not anymore, my dear." He retreated from the window in the same direction he'd come from.

"It was a good effort," said Captain Righteous. His voice sounded sympathetic. "I apologize for what I said earlier. Your mind is sharp and resourceful." He glanced at the window. "For what it's worth, none of us could have fit through that window even if you'd removed all the bars."

"Is he gone?" asked Katherine.

The captain looked out the window, then spoke in a whisper. "He's wandered off. I imagine he has some unfinished business to attend to. Why? Do you have another plan?"

Katherine shook her head. "I'm all tapped out of ideas." She didn't bother to whisper. "But I need to pee. Would you and

Bingam mind turning around?"

"Of course, Miss Katherine." Captain Righteous turned around to face his wall. Bingam did likewise.

"No peeking," said Katherine. "Can I trust you to be gentlemen worthy of your station?"

"On my honor as a servant of His Majesty."

"Okay. Stay turned around. I'm going to hang my cloak over the window in case that little pervert comes back. I'll tell you when I'm decent again."

"Very well, ma'am."

Katherine peeled off her still-damp cloak. As dank as the air was in this place, it felt good to have some air against her bare skin. She hung the cloak by the hood on two bolts poking out of the iron band that ran across the top of the window, covered her private areas as best she could with only two hands, and walked to the filthy chamber pot at the back of the cell. As much as she really did have to pee, she couldn't bring herself to squat over the pot just yet.

THUNK

"Unnnnnggggggg..."

"Miss Katherine?" said Captain Righteous. "Are you quite all right?"

"Just keep looking at the wall, buddy." Katherine relieved herself in the chamber pot while she watched Stavros through the small square hole in the door, collapsing with the back end of a crossbow bolt poking out of his right eye socket. When she was done, she retrieved her cloak and got dressed again. "Fucking pervert."

"I can assure you, Miss, that neither I nor Bingam so much as glanced at –"

"It's cool. You can turn around."

While Bingam was turning around, his gaze fixed onto the hole in the door. "What's this?" He bent over to peek through it, then stood bolt upright. "I don't believe it, sir. She's killed the guard!"

Captain Righteous pressed his face to the window bars and looked down. "Incredible! Where did you... How did you..."

Katherine smiled. "It was a team effort. You're a pretty good shot with that crossbow of yours after all."

The captain puzzled through in thought until the pieces fell into place. "By the gods, I knew I didn't miss you."

"Very clever, Miss Katherine," said Bingam, who finally seemed to be over his crying. "Now how do we get out of here?"

"Come on, guys. Team effort, remember? Maybe you could contribute to the next part of the plan."

Bingam frowned. "So we're really no better off than before. The only difference is that we've got a dead Drow with his cock in his hand lying right outside our cell."

"Quiet, Bingam," said Captain Righteous. "Get a hold of yourself."

"We're worse off than before," Bingam continued blubbering. "You can forget about being ransomed. They'll kill us now for cer–"

Katherine slapped Bingam lightly on the cheek, to which he responded with wide-eyed bafflement.

"Shut up. We need to think."

Bingam stuck out his lower lip and looked more like he was concentrating on not crying than thinking of an escape plan, but at least he was quiet.

"You don't think you could just bash through the door, huh?" Katherine asked Captain Righteous.

The captain shook his head. "With a weapon and enough time, I could chop through it, but the crossbar is too thick."

Katherine squeezed her head through the gap in the barred window. Bingam hadn't been kidding about Stavros. Sure enough, his dead black hand was firmly wrapped around his dead black dick.

To her left, she could see the Bag of Holding sitting on the floor next to a stool by the wall.

She pulled her head back into the cell and put her arm out

through the window. She could just barely reach the crossbar with the tips of her fingers, but she wouldn't be able to move it. The Portable Hole, as Captain Righteous had referred to it, was below the crossbar, well out of reach.

Even from inside the cell, if she'd wanted to risk having her hand fused together with the door by trying to peel off the hole from the opposite side of where it had been applied, her hand wasn't quite slender enough to fit through the thickness of the wood.

Low on ideas, she turned around to examine their inventory inside the cell. Not a whole hell of a lot to work with.

"You claim to be a druid," said Captain Righteous. "Can you not simply turn into a bird and fly through the window?"

Katherine put her hands on her hips. "Well fuck. Why didn't I think of that?"

"No need for sarcasm. I merely want to exhaust any possibilities that come to mind. Have you any druidic magic that could be of use?"

Katherine thought about what spells she had prepared. "I could summon a monkey."

Captain Righteous sighed. "A monkey would not be able to even reach the crossbar, much less have the strength to move it."

A light went on in Katherine's mind. "But it could grab the Bag of Holding!"

"Do you have anything in the bag that might help us escape?"

Katherine frowned. "I don't know. Probably not. But it's a step in the right direction, right?"

"It's worth a shot, I suppose."

Katherine pointed her finger out the window to ensure that the monkey would appear outside the cell. "Monkey!"

With a near inaudible poof of magic, a small white monkey appeared on the floor outside the cell. It stared up at Katherine.

"Go get the Bag of Holding," Katherine commanded.

The monkey continued to stare at her.

"Shit. It doesn't understand me." She tried speaking more slowly and loudly, pronouncing her words as clearly as she could. "Go. Get. Bag." She jerked her head to the side to indicate direction.

"Eeee! Eeee!" replied the monkey.

"Damn it." Another idea occurred to her. She repeated the command in a British accent.

The monkey scratched its ass.

"What would lead you to believe a monkey could speak the Elven tongue?" asked Captain Righteous.

"It works with birds, doesn't it?"

"I don't... No, of course it doesn't. Have you gone mad?"

Bingam resumed crying again.

"Shut up!" they both shouted at him.

Katherine looked outside the cell again just in time to see the monkey disappear. "Goddammit, that spell sucks."

Captain Righteous frowned. "Perhaps it is the will of the gods that we meet our ends here."

"Fuck the will of the gods. We're getting the hell out of here. Take off your cloak and tear off a few strips of it."

"I will do no such thing. If I am to die, I shall die proudly as a servant of His Majesty, with my uniform in-tact."

"Would it be more honorable to force me to tear my own cloak to shreds, knowing that I'm naked under it?" The captain's answer would play a large part in how Katherine viewed this man's character in the future.

"I suppose you have a point. The Drow will most likely desecrate it anyway." He unhooked the clasp of his cloak and took it off.

"Even better," said Katherine. "I'll need the clasp as well."

Three torn strips of fabric later, she had herself a nice length of rope with a hooked and weighted end. Tanner would be proud.

There wasn't enough room to fit both her head and her arm through the window, so Katherine was forced to fish blindly. She swung the clasp around on the end of the rope a few times, then released it. Metal clanked against stone. She started pulling it back and felt no resistance, meaning she had not successfully hooked it on the drawstring of the Bag of Holding.

"You are indeed, creative, Miss Katherine," said Captain Righteous. "But I'm afraid that this is a ridiculous waste of time. The odds of you successfully retrieving that bag are –"

"Twenty to one," said Katherine, tossing her hook again and missing.

"I find that to be at the same time oddly specific and naively optimistic."

"I've been forced to sit through a few sessions of this game. If you roll a 20 on any theoretically plausible attempt at anything, no matter how stupid, you'll succeed."

"I don't know what you're talking about, but –"

"You're from here," said Katherine. Another swing and a miss. "This world, I mean. How often have you seen ordinary people do extraordinary things in desperate situations?"

"Often enough, I suppose," said the captain. "Then again, I think I've seen competent soldiers stab themselves in the leg in the heat of battle just as often."

"Mark my words, Captain. I'll have that bag in less than seventeen more tries."

She was wrong. It took twenty-three more tries, but statistics could kiss her ass. She pulled the Bag of Holding in through the window and turned around triumphantly.

"Impressive," said Captain Righteous. "Would you care to check the inventory?"

"Fuck no." Katherine had no intention of going back in that bag. "No disrespect intended, sir, but I don't like the idea of being at your mercy, considering the rocky start of our relationship."

"I feel the same way."

They both looked at Bingam.

Bingam choked back a sob. "Fine." He stood up and put his arms down flat at his sides.

"I'll pull you back out after a minute. Tell us if you see anything useful." Katherine pulled the bag down over Bingam's head, and it swallowed him whole.

"I hope he finds some weapons in there," said the captain. "If we can't find a way through the door, we may be able to surprise our captors when they open the cell to retrieve us. And even if we do get through the door, we may still need to fight our way to the surface."

Katherine shook her head and smiled. She was having a lot of Dr. House moments today. "Brilliant."

"Thank you, Miss Katherine. But it's the possibility of having to fight when escaping one's captors is something I believe would occur to most people."

"Not that, silly. Through the door."

The captain frowned. "Again, the door of a cell is the most obvious point of entry and exit. It doesn't take a military genius to –"

"Just shut up and watch this." Katherine shoved the Bag of Holding through the gap in the window with her left hand, and squeezed her right hand through the remaining bars and into the bag. "Bingam."

"Oomph!" cried Bingam as he tumbled out of the bag and onto the hard stone floor outside the cell. Tears streamed down his face as his cheeks shook with sobs.

"Bingam!" said Captain Righteous. "For the Light's sake, what's wrong with you?"

"Horse... parts... *sniff* floating... around me... *sniff* everywhere." He looked up at the window and suddenly stopped crying, then jumped to his feet and pressed his face against the bars. "How'd you escape? Don't leave me in here, uncle! I promise not to cry anymore!"

Captain Righteous flicked Bingam hard on the nose. "Stop

your blubbering and let us out of here, you fool!"

Bingam's eyes focused past his uncle, into the interior of the cell. Then he looked left and right down the hallway. "Oh."

"Hurry!"

Bingam bit his lower lip and looked down. Katherine didn't know what he was thinking about. She'd dealt with the wooden crossbar holding the door shut when she rescued Tanner and Chaz. It wasn't all that complicated a mechanism.

Finally, he seemed to figure it out. He grabbed the beam by one end and tried to lift it with both hands.

"Hnnnnnnggggggg," he groaned until his face turned red, but the beam didn't move.

Super vampire strength notwithstanding, Katherine didn't remember the beam being quite that heavy. If these skinny-ass black elves could move it...

"I can't move it, uncle," said Bingam. "I need your help."

The captain shook his head. "My sister had to marry a bard." He faced Katherine and put his arms flat by his sides. "Would you mind?"

A sudden feeling of fear and suspicion came over Katherine. She looked at Bingam, who was practically drooling with anticipation, then back at Captain Righteous. "How do I know you won't just ditch me in here?"

"You have my word of honor as a captain in the Kingsguard."

"I'd like to believe that means more to you than it does to me, but –"

"You don't have much of a choice, Miss Katherine. The only other alternative is for you to go in the bag, after which there would be nothing to stop me from following you in there and having my nephew pull only me out on the other side... if I were an honorless scoundrel. I'm afraid you'll just have to trust me."

Katherine found little comfort in the fact that the captain had so quickly come up with a plan for betraying her trust, but after having given the logistics of the plan some consideration, she determined it feasible. She really didn't have much of a choice.

She could have pleaded with him not to leave her in the cell, but he might take that as a sign of weakness.

She could have threatened to hunt him down like a dog if he betrayed her, but if he was the betraying sort, she'd only provide him with smug satisfaction at her empty threat.

She could have reasoned that they needed her, but he might scoff at the idea of needing help from a half-elven woman, and leave her there just to show her otherwise.

Instead, she sighed and pulled the bag down over his head.

Holding the bag outside the cell, she pulled the captain out again.

"By the gods!" said Captain Righteous upon landing on the floor. "It's horrifying in there. Sweet Melody. She was too good for this world."

Bingam snatched the Bag of Holding from Katherine's hand. "Let's go, Uncle!" He started to run, and Katherine's heart skipped a beat.

Captain Righteous, still on the floor, spun on his ass and kicked his retreating nephew in the shin. Bingam went down like a sack of dog snot.

The captain stood over his cowering nephew and shook his head. "We are not thieves and swindlers!" He leaned over, picked up the Bag of Holding, which Bingam had abandoned in order to shield his face, and ripped off the clasp of Bingam's cloak. "And you are not fit to wear this cloak."

He turned to the cell and removed the crossbar without so much as a grunt. When the cell door swung open, he held out the bag to Katherine.

"Thank you," said Katherine, accepting the bag.

"No need to thank me. What's yours is yours, at least until I arrest you properly and confiscate it as evidence."

"How generous of you." Katherine peeled her Portable Hole

off the door and slapped it back onto her cloak.

Captain Righteous looked away and cleared his throat.

"What?" Katherine looked down at the hole. The cloak had dried out a bit, and the fabric wasn't clinging to her body anymore. Consequently, the hole didn't recognize body and cloak as one unit. So instead of a square of dark emptiness that was camouflaged by the blackness of the fabric, she just had what appeared to be a normal square hole in her cloak showcasing the top of her right tit.

"Shit. Sorry about that." She removed the hole and placed it lower on the cloak, down by her calf. "Now help me get this elf body into the bag." She lifted Stavros's lifeless head and slipped the lip of the bag underneath it.

"Why in the Light's grace do you want to put a dead Drow in your bag?"

"It might come in handy."

"For what?"

Katherine huffed in exasperation. "I don't know. Use your imagination. What if we have to fight a dragon or something? Come on, man. Think."

The captain reluctantly helped Katherine shove the rest of the body into the bag. "Very good. You are now the proud owner of yet another festering corpse. Now would you please lead the way to the exit?"

"Not before we go to the kennels. I'm not leaving here without Butterbean."

"We're in serious danger down here!" whined Bingam. "We're not putting our lives on the line to rescue your pet wolf!"

Katherine whirled around and glared at him. "Butterbean is not my pet. He's my Animal Companion." Jesus Christ, she sounded like one of those PETA nutters. "You go if you want, but I'm not leaving without him."

"It would appear the criminal is more honorable than some," said Captain Righteous.

"Oh snap!" Katherine smiled at Bingam. "Should I cast a Create Water spell? 'Cause you just got burned, son."

"That will not be necessary," said the captain. "My nephew could do with some lessons in courage and honor. We shall accompany you in finding your wolf."

Katherine made a half-hearted effort not to come off as too smug. "Thank you."

"Which way to the kennels?"

"Fuck if I know."

Captain Righteous sighed. "So we're to wander around aimlessly until we stumble upon them?"

"I was thinking more like we'd start opening doors and beat some directions out of the first Drow we find."

"How very honorable," said Bingam.

"Shut up, Bingam!" said Katherine and Captain Righteous.

CHAPTER 24

Randy woke up feeling rested and refreshed. Looking past the fact that they took Randy and Denise prisoner and impregnated Denise with baby scorpion people, Raslan and Azhar were very hospitable hosts. Raslan had even gone so far as to sleep outside so that Randy and Denise would be more comfortable.

Judging by the light shining through some holes in the worn tent fabric, it was well into morning. Randy yawned and rubbed his eyes. "Denise?"

"God fuckin' dammit!" Denise sounded like she was crying. "Son of a – BLAAARRGGGHHHHH!" That was the unmistakable sound of vomit forcefully hitting dirt.

Randy got up and stepped outside the tent to find Denise on her hands and knees a few feet away, her face hidden by three enormous heads of lettuce.

Azhar greeted him with a warm smile. "Well well. Look who decided to wake up."

"Mornin'," said Randy. "What's wrong with Denise?"

"Nothing to worry about. Her body is going through some adjustment. It's perfectly natural."

Denise spat out some residual vomit. "I got fuckin' morning sickness! Ain't nothin' natural about – BLAAARRGGGHHHHH!"

"Prepare your belongings," said Raslan, already taking down the tent. "We've wasted too much time as it is."

Randy rubbed his eyes. "I'm sorry I slept so long. I didn't know we was in such a hurry."

Raslan removed the center pole, collapsing the whole tent. On the other side of it, a stone statue of a camel lay on the ground where a real camel had stood the night before.

"We had a visitor in the night."

"Was he a sculptor?"

Raslan snapped his claws, got up in Randy's face, and narrowed his eyes. "It might well have been me who was turned into stone, and you make jokes? You would do well to consider who will replace the camel once we've finished eating his brother before you speak again."

Randy hadn't been making a joke. At least, not intentionally. He was still a little groggy, and unclear as to what was going on, but it sounded like he might be in danger of being eaten again.

"Stop it, Raslan," said Azhar. "What's done is done. There's no harm in trying to lighten the mood a little. It's not his fault you tried to fight a basilisk alone. You should have woken me up."

"I'm surprised I didn't. You should have heard the beast scream when I stabbed out one of those damned petrifying eyes."

"Did you at least wear your mask?"

Raslan waved dismissively at her and smiled. "I kept my eyes closed."

Azhar was not amused. "You can't go taking those kinds of risks anymore. Think about our children!"

"BLAAARRGGGHHHHH!" said Denise, producing a tomato plant with fruit that almost certainly looked better than it tasted.

Raslan moved in close to his wife and cradled her face with his hands. "I would never let any harm come to you or our children. That's why I drove it away instead of killing it. Now that you're awake and no longer with child, we can follow its trail and kill it together."

Azhar gave him a pouty look. "Wear your mask this time?"

"Of course."

The two of them packed up their camp with unbelievable

efficiency, moving heavier objects with their giant scorpion claws and performing more delicate tasks with their human-like hands. They had everything packed up and ready to go in no time.

"Climb onto our backs," demanded Raslan. "The beast moves slowly, but the desert wind is quick to cover tracks."

Randy climbed on to Azhar's back, figuring that Denise was still harboring some ill will toward her, and would be less likely to try to provoke Raslan.

The plates on her back were hard, but not without a little flexibility, like a cross between plastic and steel. Sharp spikes protruded from the sides at regular intervals. Nature had no doubt intended them for defense, but Randy found the largest ones at the front to be a good place to hold onto like motorcycle handlebars.

Denise climbed sluggishly onto Raslan's back. She didn't look like she was up to the task of doing any provoking anyway.

"This is pretty exciting, ain't it Denise? A real live basilisk, just like in Harry Potter."

"I don't even want to know how many times you whacked it during them movies," said Denise.

Randy stuck out his chin. "I'll just attribute that comment to the hormonal changes your body is going through right now."

The scorpion people moved as fast as horses, their eight legs a black blurring in a cloud of dust.

"The tracks are getting clearer," shouted Raslan. "We'll be upon the beast soon!"

"There it is!" said Azhar a short time later.

Randy turned away quickly. Azhar looked back at him and smiled. "You can look. Its gaze isn't dangerous beyond a distance of thirty feet."

That was good to know. Randy peeked over Azhar's shoulder, and Denise peeked around Raslan's torso. Something was crawling on the dirt ahead of them, but it certainly didn't look like the basilisk from Harry Potter. This thing looked like a fat, orange, eight-legged alligator.

"I thought they was s'posed to look like a big snake."

"Perhaps you're thinking of nagas?" said Raslan.

Denise giggled. "Once you go black, as the sayin' goes. Ain't that right, Randy?"

Randy shot her a warning glare. At least she seemed to have gotten over the worst of the morning sickness.

Raslan slowed as they approached to within a hundred feet of the basilisk. "Don't use your stinger. Stick to the spears."

The basilisk had turned to face them. Its mouth was open wide, displaying its hundreds of sharp white teeth. It glared angrily at them with its one remaining eye.

"Why toy with it?" asked Azhar. "Put the poor beast out of its misery."

"I can't help but wonder if the venom in the camel meat is what made the dwarf ill."

Azhar smiled. "You're being silly. Like I said, it's perfectly natural for a woman's body to have difficulty adjusting."

"You also said we shouldn't take any unnecessary risks." Raslan set down his pack and pulled out a black strip of cloth.

Azhar nodded. "Very well, but it's going to take more time." She pulled an identical black strip of cloth out of her pack, and they both tied the strips around their heads over their eyes.

"Not as long as you think," said Raslan. "The human and the dwarf can guide us."

"Excellent idea!" Azhar turned to Randy. "Tell me where the beast is in relation to me. And remember to stay more than thirty feet away from it."

Azhar and Raslan held up their spears and started walking slowly in opposite directions to flank the basilisk. Randy and Denise followed behind them.

"Alright," said Randy. "I'll keep you between it and me. Just move away from the sound of my voice."

"Yeah," said Denise. "Ditto for me."

The basilisk swung its tail back and forth, creating a massive cloud of dust, as the two scorpion people closed in from either side of it.

"Easy does it," said Denise. "Yer gettin' close."

"Steady, steady." Randy didn't really know what to say, but he felt he should keep talking.

The basilisk cowered back slowly, instinctively trying to look at each of them, but it only had an eye on Raslan's side.

"Alright!" cried Denise. "Give him a poke!"

Raslan thrust his spear forward, catching the basilisk in the fatty tissue hanging below its neck. The basilisk made a sound like an Auto-Tuned duck.

"Hot damn!" Denise was more excited than Randy thought such a minor wound should warrant. "You just took out that scaly sonofabitch's other eye!"

Randy took a second to process what he'd just heard. "Wha–"

"Ha!" said Raslan, pulling off his blindfold. "Now we've – NO!"

The basilisk's eye shone like the glint of a mirror in the sun. Raslan dropped his spear and tried to shield his eyes, but it was too late.

The whole petrification process only took about two seconds, starting from his eyes and spreading through his body to the tips of his fingers and claws, the feet of his arachnid legs, and the stinger of his tail. It sounded like cracking ice. His final pose made for a beautiful statue, a masterpiece of terror.

"What have you done?" cried Azhar, having removed her own blindfold. "Rasla–"

CRACK

Whatever bug exoskeletons are normally made of is strong enough for those thin legs to support the weight of their enormous bodies. Stone didn't seem to hold up as well with the same proportions. The legs all snapped at once, letting the body crash to the ground. The two scorpion claws snapped off at the shoulder on impact. Raslan now looked like a statue of a terrified merman with a pointy tail.

The basilisk turned its attention to Azhar. She didn't even try to shield her eyes as she furiously thrust the tip of her spear into the eye that had just killed the father of her children. It howled and jerked its head away, leaving a tendril of eye goop hanging between socket and spear tip.

"Shit!" said Denise. She waddled quickly around Raslan's remains, stepping over his shattered stone legs toward his abandoned spear.

"STOP!" Azhar held her spear up with both hands, ready to throw. Tears streamed down both sides of her face as she glared at Denise. "Why?"

"The fuck you mean why?" Denise held her hands up, but inched closer to the spear.

Azhar cocked her spear back like she was about to throw it. "Don't take another step, dwarf, or by the Dark Gods I'll kill you where you stand!"

Denise spread her arms wide. "Take your best shot." After a moment of Azhar's hesitation, Denise continued to taunt her. "Come on, you spear-chuckin' half-bug whore! Why ain't you chuckin'?" She feigned surprise and stroked her beard. "Oh my... Could it be on account of me havin' your little cockroach babies inside me?"

"Denise!" said Randy. He could understand Denise being upset, but using a mother's unborn children as human shields – or something like that – might have been a new low.

Azhar lowered her spear. "You're right. I can't kill you." Her frown turned into a wicked grin as she shifted the tip of her spear in Randy's direction. "But I can kill your friend."

"What?" said Randy. "I ain't had nothin' to do with –"

"You think I give a good goddamn about Randy?" Denise laughed and looked at Randy. "Bend over, buddy. She's 'bout to give it to you like you ain't never had it before."

Randy couldn't tell if she was bluffing or not. He didn't know what she'd have to gain by bluffing, though, as he couldn't see what Azhar would have to lose by calling the bluff. As far as he knew, the scorpion people had only been keeping him alive as a courtesy to their surrogate mother. Randy was fucked.

"On second thought," said Azhar. "I'll spare the paladin. His healing powers will be useful."

"That's right." Denise nodded at Randy, as if he had known all along that she wasn't going to murder him, which Randy didn't believe for a second. "The world just got a lot more dangerous without your big man to protect you."

Azhar smiled at Denise. "I can protect myself just fine. You'll be the one in need of healing. You are an incubator for my unborn children. As such, I can't kill you. But I can remove those parts of you unnecessary to the health of my babies. The fingers, the toes, move up to the hands and feet, then the arms and legs. And then we'll get creative. Your friend will keep you from bleeding out, and the three of us can eat the pieces. When my children are born, they can devour whatever remains."

Denise frowned. Her little insurance policy didn't cover maimings. She dived for the spear.

Azhar's eyes were still red and moist with tears, but she couldn't help but laugh at Denise's pathetic effort. "So eager to get started, are you? Very well, dwarf. What would you like to lose fir–"

The blind basilisk reared up on four of its eight legs and wrapped Azhar's torso in a fierce bear hug, taking her head and right arm into its mouth.

Azhar's spear fell out of her hands, but she resisted with fist, scorpion claws, and stinger, punching, pinching, and piercing the beast.

They seemed pretty evenly matched. Randy stood frozen in indecision, not knowing which side, if either, he should try to assist.

Denise had no such quandary. "Fuck you, lobster bitch!" she cried as she shoved the tip of her spear up into the less heavily plated underbelly of Azhar's scorpion body.

Azhar's arm and claws went limp. Her tail flailed wildly for a moment, then fell flat against the barren earth.

"What'd you go and do that for?" asked Randy.

"Don't nobody impregnate me with scorpion babies without my consent."

"The way I saw it, that was a misunderstanding. She thought she had your consent."

"They was gonna eat us, Randy. You ought to be thanking me. I just saved your life again."

"You was gonna let Azhar kill me!"

"Psh," said Denise. "I was bluffin'."

"It didn't sound like no bluff to me."

"That's the fuckin' nature of a bluff, dumbass. She's dead, and we's alive, so I guess I know what I'm talking about."

"Oh we's alive all right. But how long can we make it out here? You just done killed two people who know how to survive in the desert and had a vested interest in keeping us alive."

"So we're back to square one," said Denise. "We ain't no worse off now than when we first arrived."

"You're pregnant, Denise! Do you know how long of a gestation period these things have? What if you go into labor out here. I don't know nothin' 'bout delivering no scorpion people babies."

WAAAAARRRGGG

The exhausted basilisk looked like it had seven feet in the grave. Thin vines with bunches of small yellow berries grew out of the dirt where the envenomed blood of the creature's many wounds spilled on the ground. It had released its hold of Azhar's body, which spilled enough blood to grow a nice shrub full of what looked like blue citrus fruits.

The beast lay on the ground and groaned.

Denise frowned. "I reckon we should put that big bastard out of its misery."

"I seen all the killin' I want to see today," said Randy. "It ain't gonna hurt us if we just leave it be."

"You think it's better to just let it suffer? Look at it, Randy. It's fuckin' done for. Puttin' that thing down is an act of mercy."

"There's other ways to show mercy," said Randy. He carefully approached the basilisk from behind and placed a hand on its tail. "In Jesus Christ's name, I heal you." He felt the healing power flow out of him. The basilisk's wounds stopped dripping blood as they closed up, but it was still in pretty bad shape. Randy's healing powers were limited.

"The fuck you go and do that for?" asked Denise.

"I was showing mercy, just like you said."

"You wasted your power. What if we need that later on? And what good's it gonna do this motherfucker? You ain't grew its eyes back. How's it gonna hunt? All you done is ensure it's gonna starve to death."

The basilisk curled its tail around Randy and pulled him toward its mouth.

"Oh shit!" said Randy. "Denise, help!"

Denise shook her head and pulled the spear out of Azhar's dead body. "I s'pose it might be able to survive on a diet of bleedin' heart retards."

Randy was staring into the nostrils of the giant beast. It sniffed him, but didn't bite. Instead it stuck out its reddish orange tongue and licked Randy's face.

"Stop making out with the goddamn thing, Randy," said Denise. "Pull away so I don't accidentally pin your heads together."

Randy stroked the side of the basilisk's head and gently pushed it away from his own. "Put that spear down. It's friendly." The basilisk resumed eating Azhar's arm.

Denise lowered the spear. "You're just puttin' off the inevitable. How long you think that thing's gonna last once it runs out of scorpion lady?"

"Maybe we'll just take it with us and look after it until we can find a zoo or a wildlife refuge or something."

"Jesus Christ, Randy! Are you hearing the shit coming out of your mouth? This ain't no fuckin' kitten. It's a goddamn man-eating eight-legged dinosaur."

"Come on, Denise. That's just a little bit dramatic, don't you think?"

"Are you not seeing what I'm seeing?"

Randy looked down. The basilisk had devoured Azhar's arm up to the shoulder, and was now going to work on her head.

"While that's unpleasant to witness, it's just nature taking its course. You said it yourself. Basil is a defenseless creature now that they done stabbed out his eyes. You and I are the only ones who stand between his life and death."

"Basil? Who the fuck is Basil?"

Randy smiled. "It's short for basilisk. I thought that would be a good name for him."

Denise shook her head. "You have officially checked the fuck out, my friend. How do you even know it's male? Did your dick get hard when it licked you or something?"

Randy crouched down and tried to peek through the creature's forest of legs. He didn't spot anything immediately recognizable as genitalia. "I s'pose if it turns out to be a female, we can call it Lisa."

"Why Lisa?"

"It's Basil spelled backwards, only without the B."

Denise looked suddenly panicked.

Randy frowned. "If you have a different girl name you'd prefer..."

"I don't give a shit about the name, Randy." Denise looked into Randy's eyes. "I think I forgot how to read."

CHAPTER 25

While Stacy used the Decanter of Endless Water's geyser setting to get Cooper as clean as anything short of a Charisma-boosting magical item was likely to get him, Julian was assigned to the task of building a fire.

"One of those big pine cones should burn nicely," Stacy had suggested, and Julian had just the one in mind.

By the time they'd slain the dire boar, the sun had set, Cooper had been hurt pretty bad, and they had two thousand pounds' worth of fresh dire pork waiting to be cut up and eaten. If ever there was a perfect time to call it a day and set up camp, this was it.

They had moved a little farther off the road to avoid calling attention to themselves, but if Stacy and injured Cooper could drag a dead boar with them, then Julian could roll a pine cone.

Big as it was, the weight was less of a problem than the shape. Being conical, it kept wanting to roll off to the left of where Julian tried to push it. And the scales were pointed at the tips, forcing Julian to push from under his serape, which made maneuvering the thing even more difficult.

But after more time and effort than resentment toward a pine cone should have warranted, Julian had his assailant back at the campsite and was ready for vengeance.

The ground was nothing if not a vast carpet of kindling, so much so that Julian spent more time clearing away pine needles in a wide enough radius around the pine cone than he did stuffing them under it.

As expected, the dry needles lit up with ease, producing big orange flames, copious amounts of white smoke, and a nice smokey pine scent. When the flames began to settle down, however, the pine cone itself didn't seem to be catching.

Julian sent Ravenus off to gather up any fallen twigs or branches that he could carry back, hoping they might burn longer and hotter than pine needles. In the meantime, he kept the fire going by scooping up armfuls of pine needles from the perimeter and piling them on top of the cone until they started falling down the sides and catching. No harm in widening the safety zone, after all. When the new needles caught, the flames were impressively large, and gave off a lot of heat. But the flare-up didn't last long, and that stubborn pine cone still mocked him with its refusal to submit to the flames.

"You'll burn, you big bastard," Julian said as he scooped up another armful of needles. "You can't hold out forever."

"What are you doing?" asked Stacy. She and Cooper stood at the edge of the safety zone. Cooper's abdomen was bandaged up nicely, and he looked like he was feeling better.

"I'm getting a fire started, just like you said."

"I said that an hour ago."

Julian dumped his new load onto the fire, and watched the needles flare up. "It's just taking a little time to catch."

"That's because you're using the worst pine cone you could have possibly picked. That one's way too green and dense. All the scales are still pressed together. It doesn't have any air flow."

"It'll burn. Just give it a minute."

Stacy walked off into the woods. Cooper helped Julian dump more pine needles onto the fire, probably not as a show of solidarity, but just because he enjoyed watching shit burn.

When Stacy returned, she was dragging a shorter, wider, browner pine cone with her. The scales were very wide apart from each other. She set it upright near Julian's effort. When she started stuffing needles between the scales, Julian understood immediately that his efforts had been bested.

"Nice idea," said Cooper. "That thing's gonna light up like

a motherfucker."

Indeed, it lit up like a motherfucker. The flames spread quickly around the loosely packed pine needles at the base, then up to the more densely packed needles at the top. It was a perfect cone of flame, as if these giant cones had evolved toward the goal of being set on fire.

This small victory was enough to raise everyone's spirits, except for Ravenus, who was worn out from dragging back an impressively large branch, only to discover that his efforts had been unnecessary.

Conversation was next to nonexistent. Everyone's attention was fixed on the flames and the intense red glow of the smoldering pine cone scales.

When it was hot enough, Stacy asked Cooper to tip the burning pine cone over with his axe.

Cooper asked the axe's permission first, which was weird. But 'Navi' apparently had no objections to being shoved into a fire. She was tough that way.

Stacy led Cooper into the woods and came back with two more dry cones, which they laid on either side of the burning one, wide bottoms adjacent to its pointed top. When they pushed the cones toward each other, their scales interlocked with the one in the middle, and the fire soon tripled in volume.

Standing back with her hands on her hips, Stacy gave the fire a satisfied nod. "Do either of you know how to slice up a boar?"

Julian shook his head.

"How hard could it be?" asked Cooper. He walked over to the giant pig carcass and swung his axe down hard into the beast's side. After a few more whacks, Stacy interjected.

"Cooper!" When Cooper stopped swinging, she continued. "Just in case the goal was unclear, we're trying to eat this thing."

"I know that," said Cooper. "I was trying to remove its ribs." He licked his lips. "Can you imagine grilled dire pork ribs?"

"That does sound good. Let me give it a try." Stacy took a more surgical approach with her dagger, tracing a line around where she thought she should cut the hide. Actually cutting through proved a greater challenge. She sawed furiously with her dagger for at least five minutes, but didn't get more than six inches before giving up. "Okay, this isn't happening. Cooper, just chop a hind leg off. We'll throw it onto the fire and see what happens."

Spreading the boar's hind legs apart for Cooper to get a better chopping angle, they discovered the beast was male. At least it was until a few of Cooper's less careful chops. The bone proved a real bitch to get through, and Cooper had to use up his remaining Barbarian Rage for the day in order to hack through it. Even then it took quite a few whacks, not all of which were delivered with pinpoint accuracy. By the time he finally succeeded in separating the leg from the body, the boar's genital area was such a minced and mangled mess that future discoverers of the body would no doubt suspect its killer's motivations as having been deeply personal.

Cooking provided its own set of challenges. There wasn't time to build a spit and slow roast the beast, so they simply hefted the big leg onto the fire. The smell of scorched boar hair was nearly enough to sour Julian's appetite, but it didn't last too long.

The meat didn't cook evenly at all. The line between charred and raw leg muscle was a thin one, and the few edible bits they managed to tear away were so chewy that they were almost certainly spending more calories digesting than the meat was providing.

"Okay, I'm done," said Stacy, her voice heavy with exhaustion and defeat. She scooped up a big bundle of pine needles to use as a pillow, snuggled down against a giant root, covered herself in her Cloak of Elvenkind, and all but disappeared into the tree bark.

Cooper stayed up a little while longer to throw more pine

needles on the fire and watch them burn. Together, he and Julian threw the soot-blackened cone which had fallen on Julian's head onto the fire. It once again produced a ton of white smoke, but still didn't appear to be getting consumed.

Cooper eventually drifted off to sleep as well, lulled there either by the mesmerizing flickers of flame or smoke inhalation.

Even Ravenus lay snoring in a soft bed of pine needles.

Being the only elf in a party was lonely at night. Not being able to sleep, it was expected that Julian would keep watch over the others. His nightly meditation killed half the time, but those other four hours were brutally dull. He whiled away the hours preparing his spells and throwing more pine needles onto the fire. By the time dawn finally broke, he'd widened the fire safety perimeter by 150%.

As the twinkles of stars faded, new twinkles took their places in the sky. Billions of dew drops hung in mid-air until they coalesced into larger drops which were apparently too heavy for the invisible force which kept them suspended. And when they finally did fall, they fell sideways, like they were traveling on invisible rail lines. It was a mystery well worth checking out.

After taking a few minutes to find a tree which he judged most easy to climb, Julian got to climbing. He was about fifty feet off the ground when he came to the first line of strangely suspended dew drops. The line they hung from wasn't invisible after all, but only very nearly so, much like spider silk.

Taking into account how many such threads lined the forest canopy, this place could be crawling with giant spiders at any minute.

Julian ran a finger along the thread. It wasn't sticky like a spider's web should be to catch prey. And now that he thought about it, there wasn't really any web-like formation of threads. All of them were running parallel.

Feeling the thread to where it met the tree trunk, he felt a small bulge and a trail of line dangling down from it. He wound the dangling line around his finger and gave it a little tug. The entire line of dewdrops fell to the forest floor.

Oops.

These nigh-invisible threads were all tied to the trees. Who would go to that kind of effort? And for what purpose? Definitely something to discuss with Cooper and Stacy. It was probably a good time to wake them up anyway. Not knowing how much ground they had to cover, it was best to get as early a start as possible.

Julian climbed down the tree and discovered that Cooper and Stacy were already awake, and that they weren't alone. Five centaurs stared sternly down at them. They were impressive specimens, their human-like and horse-like halves both lean and muscular. Three males and two females, made evident enough by their lack of clothes or armor. Each of them held spears twice as tall as themselves. Julian could imagine any one of them being able to charge down a dire boar at full gallop and skewer it through the heart with no effort at all.

Stacy was likely having similar thoughts as she stared blankly back at the visitors. Cooper also stared blankly, but Julian strongly suspected his thoughts were completely composed of centaur tits.

The last thing Julian wanted was to surprise or alarm these... people. If they thought he was trying to sneak up on them, it might instigate retaliatory action before he was able to use his Diplomacy skill. Staying on his low branch, he addressed the centaurs.

"Good morning!" he said loudly and clearly. All five centaurs looked at him in unison, their expressions no less stern.

The largest of the male centaurs stepped forward and pointed his spear at Julian. "You there. Come down from the tree." He was at least half a foot taller than any of the others, and his broad shoulders and chest made him look like one of those people who actually look forward to going to the gym.

Julian climbed the rest of the way down as non-threateningly as he could. When he reached the ground, he spread his arms wide and gave them a friendly smile. "How may we assist you gentlemen?" His lips twitched as he felt a sudden jolt of panic. Ravenus had just woken up and taken in the scene.

"State your purpose for being in the Great Wood," demanded the spokesman of the centaurs.

So captivated was he by centaur breasts, Cooper had no reaction to the term Great Wood.

"We were merely passing through, sir," said Julian, "in search of the..." What was the name? "Desert of Fertility?"

Stacy cleared her throat. "The Fertile Desert."

"Oh, right," said Julian. "That's the one."

The lead centaur exchanged glances with his companions, then looked back at Julian. "The Fertile Desert is half a day's walk west of here."

Now they were getting somewhere. Stacy nodded encouragingly at Julian.

Julian bowed. "Thank you, kind sirs. We are grateful for the information."

"We are on our way to the Fertile Desert ourselves," said the lead centaur. "We can gallop there in a quarter of the time it would take you to walk. May we offer you a ride?"

Julian seemed to recall hearing or reading somewhere that centaurs almost never allowed people to ride them, and were extremely offended at being treated in any way like a horse. He must have had a hell of a Diplomacy roll. He looked to Stacy and Cooper for their reactions.

Stacy was nodding enthusiastically with a wide-eyed expression that screamed, How many opportunities does one get to ride a centaur?

Cooper was still gawking at the female centaurs' boobs.

Julian turned to the centaurs. "We gratefully accept your offer."

All five centaurs formed a circle, facing each other, and

pounded their front right hooves on the ground. Four of them repeated the process again. Then three, then two. Julian wasn't sure exactly what they were doing, but going on their reactions, he suspected it was some centaur version of Rock-Paper-Scissors.

A female centaur, one of the two who had competed in the final match, brushed back her light green hair and smiled at Julian. "I'll take the elf." She lowered herself until her horse-belly touched the ground. "Climb on and take hold of my breasts."

Julian climbed onto her back as he was ordered, but hesitated before following the rest of her 'instructions. Where was he supposed to put his hands? Palms over nipples? Underboob? He awkwardly attempted a few different holds and felt her heart beating faster in her chest. This was not the reaction he'd been going for, and wasn't helping his efforts to control his own body's reactions at all.

Ravenus landed on his shoulder. "I don't know what's come over me, Master Julian. I suddenly feel lightheaded and tingly around the clo–"

"You're fine. Shut up."

The lead centaur knelt before Stacy. "You may ride upon my back."

"Don't mind if I do," said Stacy, smiling at Julian.

"Take hold of me wherever it please you. But hold tight, for the ride may be rough."

"Thank you. I'll feel around for the most comfortable grip."

As Stacy groped him from his bulging chest down to his rock-hard abs, the centaur stood up. His massive horse dong was nearly touching the ground, and he seemed not the least bit ashamed of it.

"I think you're a fine fellow indeed," said Ravenus.

"Thank you." Julian wasn't sure what his familiar's motivations were for complimenting him out of the blue like that, but he welcomed the distraction.

"Don't burden yourself with these feelings of jealousy and

crippling inadequacy."

"SHUT UP, RAVENUS!" Everyone's gaze turned to Julian. Everyone except the centaur he was riding, who moaned as his grip on her breasts inadvertently tightened, and Cooper, whose attention was still shifting between the other female centaur's breasts and the leader's giant horse dick. Julian composed himself and loosened his grip. "I mean, why don't you go scout ahead?"

The riderless female centaur kept her head turned at an awkward angle to avoid meeeting Cooper's hopeful gaze. "I'll stay behind and put the fire out."

"I"ll help!" said the loser of the second match of the centaur game.

Cooper and the remaining centaur hung their heads low. Neither of them spoke as Cooper climbed onto the centaur's back and awkwardly gripped him by the shoulders.

Cooper's mount glared at his snickering friends. "Let's get this over with."

CHAPTER 26

By the light of Stavros's torch, Katherine led the way down the hall until it stopped at a T intersection. She thought she remembered having come this way before, and that there should be some doors to the right. After a few minutes of walking in silence, aside from the sound of Bingam's whimpering, she found one.

As delicately as she could, Katherine tested the handle. "It's locked," she whispered.

"Excellent," Captain Righteous whispered back. "That means it's occupied by someone who won't be ready for visitors. Stand aside."

Katherine stepped to the side, unsure of the captain's logic, but satisfied that he was at least trying to help.

Captain Righteous pressed his fingers on various parts of the door for a few moments while Katherine and Bingam kept looking left and right for signs of any wandering Drow.

"Dead center it is," said the captain. He took a step back, then slammed the sole of his boot into the center of the door, which seemed to offer almost no resistance as it swung wide open. "They should have hired dwarves."

He and Katherine stormed into the room, and Bingam followed and closed the door behind him.

A handsome naked Drow sat bolt upright in a large bed. His junk was covered by a silk sheet, but he was pitching a pretty good tent. His face showed a mixture of terror and confusion, and his gaze darted toward a sword sheathed in a belt on a nearby chair.

Captain Righteous's face, meanwhile, showed an expression of 'Just give me an excuse.'

"Alessandro?" called a female voice from behind a closed door in the interior of the room. The door opened, revealing a female Drow in an open satin robe. "Are you talking to –" Upon seeing the intruders, she pulled the sides of her robe together.

Katherine glared at the elf on the bed. "You're Alessandro?"

The elf nodded. "I am."

"And who the fuck is that whore?" asked Katherine, pointing at the woman in the robe.

"That is Shava."

"Do you know that Lady Vivia is looking for you right now?"

Alessandro suddenly appeared a more appropriate level of concerned for his well being. "It would be best if she did not hear of this."

Katherine shook her head. "That's what I thought. You should be ashamed of yourself."

"I have needs! She and I have not shared the pleasures of the flesh since her cat died."

"She's in mourning, Alessandro! Mittens wasn't just any cat. That was her familiar! You couldn't give her a couple of weeks to grieve for her loss without poking your dick into some bimbo?"

"Hey!" said the bimbo.

"I'm sorry," said Alessandro. "Who are you, exactly?"

"I'm the one who killed Mittens, asshole. So I think I know what she's going through. Do you know why she's looking for you?"

"No, I –"

"She wants to share the pleasures of the flesh with you right now."

"She does?"

"You bet she does. She got all horned up by the thought of starving my wolf and having him devour me alive. Stavros put the moves on her, but she only wanted to share the pleasures of the flesh with you."

"She –"

"And here you are, having your fleshy pleasures with this strumpet. What have you got to say for yourself?"

"I'm sorry?"

"Fuck your sorry!"

Alessandro waited for a moment before speaking again. "Did you come here just to reprimand me for my indiscretions?"

"No," said Katherine. "I need directions to the kennels. I've got to spring my wolf and get the fuck out of here."

Alessandro's eyes shifted to his sword again, then back at Katherine. "I cannot help you. Lady Vivia may forgive my lack of fidelity. We've been through that before. But if I willingly assist Mittens's killer, it will be I who gets fed to the death-hounds."

Katherine couldn't believe what she was hearing. "Do you think I'm fucking around?" She reached into the Bag of Holding. "Stavros!" The dead Drow body spilled out onto the floor, crossbow bolt still poking out of one eye socket, and cold dead hand still firmly wrapped around cold dead dick.

Shava screamed.

"By the Dark Gods!" cried Alessandro.

"Now where the fuck are the goddamn kennels?"

"Up the hall a ways and down the spiral staircase."

Katherine turned to Captain Righteous, not bothering to hide her smugness. "You see? I told you it would come in handy."

Captain Righteous grimaced at the body on the floor, then looked at Katherine. "And what shall we do with these two?"

Katherine thought about it for a moment. She didn't have it in her to straight up order anyone's death, but she also couldn't leave them alone. She turned to Alessandro. "Are the kennels guarded?"

"No," said Alessandro. "The hounds are all kept in uncomfortably small cages, deprived of food and light to the constant brink of starvation and madness. Even the cruelest Drow would soon be driven mad as well by their constant howling."

Katherine felt a little less queasy about murdering these people, but Captain Righteous might have moral qualms about it. She was already in enough hot water with him as it was.

"You stay here and keep an eye on them. I'll run and get Butterbean, then meet you back here."

"It could be dangerous," said the Captain. "Would you like Bingam to accompany you?"

"Fuck no."

Katherine let Bingam hold onto the torch so that they'd be able to see. She produced a Light Stone from her Bag of Holding, opened the door, and peeked left and right. The coast seemed clear enough.

She ran on her toes and the balls of her feet past a dozen more doors, some closed and some open, until she found a doorway with no door. Sure enough, though, there was a spiral staircase leading down.

Tiptoeing down the stairs, she found that there was a door at the bottom. She tested the handle. It was unlocked. As soon as the door opened outward just a crack, a cacophony of barks and snarls bellowed out from the room on the other side.

"Shit!" said Katherine, pushing the door shut. The barking stopped instantaneously. It was perfectly silent. This door must be soundproofed like a motherfucker. Concerned that someone may have heard the noise, she tucked the Light Stone into an inner pocket of her cloak.

In one quick motion, she opened the door just wide enough to slip inside and shut it behind her.

The barking was indeed maddening, as was the powerful stench of shit and scorched hair. The complete and utter darkness didn't help. She pulled the Light Stone back out.

Being able to see didn't make the place any less horrific. More than two dozen emaciated wolves growled and snarled at her, pawing the doors of their tiny cages lined up along the perimeter of a black iron circular floor about half the size of the Whore's Head Inn's common room. The bottoms of the cages were matted with the wolves' filth. Only poor Butterbean, lying down in his relatively clean cage, didn't look as though he wanted to tear Katherine's body to ribbons with tooth and claw. Through the bars of an iron gate on the right side of the circular room, Katherine saw a stone stairway that led along the wall to a larger cage, about the size of the Chicken Hut's bathroom, standing behind and above the wolves' cages. The big cage was unoccupied, much to Katherine's relief. She didn't even want to know what kind of beast the Drow normally kept in there.

Katherine undid the latch on Butterbean's cage to the howling protests of the other wolves. He leaped out of his cage and licked her like she was made out of heroin-flavored ice cream. The other wolves stopped their snarling and growling. They stared at Katherine and Butterbean with what seemed like bewilderment. Had they never seen this kind of affection between a person and a wolf before?

Katherine felt sorry for the rest of the wolves, but didn't trust that they wouldn't kill and eat her if she opened the cages.

"Sorry guys," she said, and stepped toward the door.

Butterbean whined, and Katherine realized that he wasn't following her. He sat in front of the other cages and continued to whine.

Shit.

Katherine knelt in front of Butterbean and spoke her Speak With Animals incantation. "Speak."

"I'm sorry, Katherine," said the wolf. "I beg you to set these wolves free. The stories they've told me. It's beyond cruel."

"I just don't know if I can trust them," said Katherine. "They're starved out of their minds. Who's to say they wouldn't kill and eat us as soon as we open the cages?"

Butterbean barked and growled at the other wolves, who

all turned toward the large black wolf Katherine assumed must be the alpha. The alpha responded to Butterbean with a short series of barks.

Butterbean turned to Katherine. "He says they promise not to eat us."

"That's just not good enough. They'd probably say anything to get me to open their cages." Then Katherine had an idea. "I've got some chopped up dead horses in my bag."

"Since when?"

"It's a long story, and this spell isn't going to last forever. Ask them if they'll agree to spare me in exchange for horse meat."

Butterbean relayed her proposal and translated the alpha's reply. "He says they'll spare you, but the other denizens of this place are fair game."

The alpha wolf's counter-offer convinced Katherine that he wasn't just agreeing to anything she asked, and would likely honor his part of the bargain.

"That's between them and the Drow. But I'm traveling with a couple of friends, so tell them not to kill any non-Drow."

Butterbean wagged his tail excitedly. "Excellent. But who are the Drow?"

"They're the black-skinned elves with the white hair. They're the ones who live down here and are keeping them prisoner."

"So you want me to tell them to only hunt down black people."

Katherine grimaced. "Could you possibly word it any differently than that?"

Butterbean cocked his head to the side and barked at her.

Shit. The spell had timed out.

Against every moral impulse in her being, Katherine nodded, hoping that Butterbean would understand. "Yes."

Butterbean seemed to understand. He exchanged some barks with the alpha wolf, then barked sharply back at Katherine as he wagged his tail.

Katherine wasn't thrilled about gambling her life on a tail wag, and the more she thought about serving the Drow up unaware, however much they may deserve it, the more it felt like straight up mass murder. But a deal was a deal, and Butterbean would certainly hold his ground if she tried to ditch them all now.

She reached into her Bag of Holding. "Horse." Nothing happened.

She thought for a moment, then concluded that since the horses were all chopped up, they no longer qualified as horses. She tried again.

"Horsemeat." Something slick and fleshy materialized in her hand. She pulled out a long thin slab of what she assumed to be leg muscle and let it flop on the floor.

The wolves barked and yipped at the bloody scrap on the floor. Though Butterbean was free, and almost certainly hungry, he dared not eat in front of the other caged wolves.

Katherine put the tips of her fingers into the bag. "All the horsemeat." As soon as she felt the first sticky bit of flesh, she yanked her hand out of the bag, which proceeded to vomit out chunks of meat, organs, and two horse's worth of everything aside from skin, bone, and hoof. A massive pile of gore piled up at her feet while the wolves watched, tongues hanging out of their open mouths.

Now came the question of how to release them. Should she release the alpha first or last? Should she just start on one end and work her way around? Each cage was about the same distance from the exit, so there was no clear advantage in starting from one side or the other.

How did the Drow open the cages when they fed prisoners to the wolves without getting attacked themselves?

Katherine's eyes drifted up to the larger cage above the rest, then it clicked. That was no holding cell. It was an observation platform.

Butterbean whined at her, no doubt wondering what was taking so long. The other wolves started to growl.

"Follow me," Katherine said to Butterbean. She opened the gate to the staircase, closed it behind her and Butterbean, and latched it. As she suspected, the floor of the big cage was completely clean of monster shit, and had a nice view of the floor below.

Three chains with engraved wooden handles hung from the ceiling at the front of the cage. The engravings read from left to right:

OPEN

CLOSE

HEAT

The first two seemed obvious enough. They would open or close all of the cages simultaneously. HEAT was more of a mystery. Katherine supposed it might get uncomfortably cold down here in the winter months, but having the climate control switch here next to the kennel controls seemed stylistically off. She pulled the chain to see what would happen. It came down about a foot lower, then raised up an inch, leaving the handle nearly a foot below the other two.

The wolves' barks and growls grew in intensity, and Katherine felt like a jerk for letting them continue to starve while she screwed around experimenting with chains.

"Sorry guys!" she called down to the cages below. "Here you go. Dig in." She pulled the OPEN chain, which came as far down as the HEAT chain had, but retracted to its original position when she let go of it. She could barely make out the squeal of rusty cage doors swinging open over the noise the wolves were making. To her surprise, not a single wolf jumped out. They just kept on barking and growling.

Katherine peered down at the cages to make sure the doors were open. Every single one of them had swung out. There was nothing between these stupid wolves and a mountain of horsemeat, but not a single one of them moved.

"What are you waiting for?" Katherine said, but she couldn't even hear herself over their noise. "Stop barking and go eat already!"

Then she caught a whiff of something other than horse entrails and wolf shit, and dots tried to connect in her head, but she couldn't even hear herself think for all the goddamn barking.

"SHUT THE FUCK UP!" she shouted. The wolves became silent.

"What is that?" She sniffed the air. "Is someone cooking something?" On the floor she could see tendrils of steam rising out of the pile of horsemeat, and some of the more liquid parts were beginning to bubble.

The floor was a giant skillet. What the hell was that for? Did they routinely cook piles of horsemeat down here? Then it hit her, and she yanked again on the HEAT chain. It retracted to its former position, aligning with the other two handles.

Those evil sons of bitches. The floor wasn't for cooking. It was for forcing the wolves back into their cages once feeding time was over.

"Sorry about that!" Katherine called down to the wolves.

The wolves poked their heads out the front of their cages, fixated on all of the semi-cooked meat in front of them. Drool dripped from their mouths and sizzled on the still-hot floor. Some of the more impatient wolves tested the floor with their paws, only to jerk them back with a yelp.

Finally, the alpha wolf made a break for it. He bounded out of his cage, leaving little sizzling paw prints as he touched the floor, then dove straight into the pile of gore. He tore into the horsemeat like it had personally killed his mother.

The other wolves soon followed, yelping as they ran, but

seemingly delirious with joy once they dove into the pile of horse innards.

"We should go now," Katherine said to Butterbean.

Butterbean stared longingly at the other wolves as they ripped apart and rolled around in horse gore. Katherine didn't know if he was hungry, or just longed to be with his own kind. But they could talk that out later. Right now, they had to get out of there.

"Come on."

Butterbean snapped out of his funk and followed her down the stairs. Katherine was wary about opening the gate, but none of the wolves gave her or Butterbean so much as a passing glance as she slowly opened it and inched along the curved wall to the spiral staircase leading out of the kennel chamber.

They'd made it to the top of the stairs and out into the hallway when Katherine had another hard decision to make. Should she shut the door and keep the noise inside? Or should she leave it open so that the wolves could roam free once they finished their meal.

She didn't have time for hard decisions right now. Safety was her primary concern. Some poor unsuspecting sap would be along soon enough to let them out. She closed the door, and the hallway was suddenly dead silent.

Somewhere far in the distance, a door slammed shut. Shit. Had Alessandro escaped?

Katherine cupped the light stone in her hands, allowing only enough light to peek through so that she could see where she was going. Just before she and Butterbean reached Alessandro's door, she heard another door slam. This one was closer, but still a good ways off.

"Keep looking!" Lady Vivia's voice echoed out from one of the side corridors perpendicular to this one. "He's around here somewhere, and may the Dark Gods have mercy on his soul if I find him in the company of another one of the kitchen staff."

Katherine took that as an indication that Alessandro had

not escaped, but it also meant that the clock was ticking. She thought about doubling back and releasing the hounds, but there was a fair chance that they were still so preoccupied with rolling around in horse guts that they wouldn't respond. Besides, the exit she knew of wasn't far from the cell they'd been locked in.

Katherine opened the door, slipped inside after Butterbean, and closed it behind them.

Alessandro and Shava sat up in bed, covered by the sheets from the waist down. The latter had her arms crossed over her breasts, and the former rubbed what appeared to be some swelling on the side of his face.

Captain Righteous sat in the chair next to the bed, rubbing Alessandro's sword with Alessandro's clothes. The little bit he'd shined was no longer black, but shone like normal steel. "You were gone too long. I feared the worst."

"I was fine," said Katherine. She was still distracted by the sword blade. "What are you doing?"

"I'm rubbing the bladeblack off this blade."

"Bladeblack?"

"A tool for cowards and criminals. They smear it on their blades to keep them from reflecting light. It helps them to sneak up on unsuspecting people in the dark."

"Neat," said Katherine. Her curiosity sated, she focused on more important matters. "What happened here? Where's Bingam?"

The captain glanced annoyedly at the bathroom door. "Bingam needed to answer Nature's call." He nodded at Alessandro. "Then this one decided to take his chance while the numbers were more in his favor. But numbers mean little compared to training and experience. A lesson he learned the hard way."

"That's fantastic," said Katherine. "But we really need to move. Lady Vivia is on her way here right now." She knocked on the bathroom door. "Pinch it off, Bingam. It's time to bounce."

"I'll be out in a minute!" Bingam called back at her.

"We don't have a minute. We need to go now!"

"Alessandro!" called Lady Vivia from out in the hall. She was closer than Katherine had expected. Interestingly enough, Alessandro didn't look any less frightened.

"We're too late," said Katherine. "They"re checking the rooms pretty hastily. If we hide in the bathroom, they might pass us by. Help me get Stavros back in the bag."

Captain Righteous gave the two Drow in the bed a warning glare, then helped Katherine shove the dead one back into the Bag of Holding.

Katherine grabbed Alessandro's and Shava's clothes and turned to Captain Righteous. "They're coming with us."

All it took was another look from the captain for Alessandro and Shava to fall in line behind Katherine.

"Oh, Shava... Oh, Shava... Oh SHIT!" said Bingam when he turned his head back and found Katherine, Shava, and Alessandro watching him choke the bishop in the corner. He jerked his hand out of his pants, but remained facing the wall. "It's not what it... I couldn't help... I was enchanted by her bosom."

"Bingam!" snapped Captain Righteous. "What in the Light are you –"

"Everybody shut up!" Katherine whispered harshly. "They'll be here any second."

Captain Righteous kept Alessandro's sword pointed up and toward Alessandro. "If we're discovered, you die first."

The bathroom was small, and more crowded than it needed to be due to Shava wanting to keep her naked body as far away from Bingam as she could. Bingam, as usual, was trying desperately to hold back sobs.

Katherine heard the door to the hallway swing open and slam into the wall. Several sets of footsteps marched into the room.

"It's empty," said a male Drow voice.

"The air is warm in here," said Lady Vivia. "And there is a peculiar smell in the air."

"We are getting near the kennels." The third voice was also male. "The air doesn't circulate so well this far back."

"Very well. Move on to the next – Wait, what was that?"

Everyone glared at Bingam, but none quite so disgustedly as Shava. His fart had barely been a squeak, but it might as well have been an air horn for Drow ears. His lower lip quivered as his face turned purple from trying not to cry. Something had to give.

"Who's in there?" demanded Lady Vivia. "Show yourself!"

Captain Righteous grabbed Alessandro tightly by the upper arm and whispered in his ear. "Get rid of them." Pressing the tip of the sword against his neck, he continued. "If it comes to a fight, I'm coming after you first." He pulled the door open slowly and nodded for Alessandro to go through. Alessandro complied.

"Ah, there you are," said Lady Vivia. "And without a scrap of clothing. How interesting. Were you alone in there?"

"I was."

Bingam blew a wet sob out through his nose.

"... not," said Alessandro, making as good an effort to improvise as anyone could have asked for.

Captain Righteous nodded for Shava to exit as well. Terror in her eyes, she shook her head. Then she glanced at Bingam, who was staring at her tits, and reconsidered. She walked out of the bathroom, covering her body as well as her skinny black arms would allow.

"Just as I suspected," said Lady Vivia. She had the same joyous yet hateful tone in her voice as she had when she'd been telling Katherine what she planned to do with her. Shava was fucked.

"Lady Vivia, you need to look in the –"

"SILENCE!"

Katherine didn't know if that was an incantation or just a regular shout, but it succeeded in the task of shutting Shava the hell up.

"Take her to the kennels," Lady Viva commanded her subordinates. "Prepare her to beg for her life on the hot plate."

"Very good, Lady Vivia."

"I must have some words with Alessandro. I'll be along shortly. Close the door behind you."

After the door closed, Captain Righteous looked at Katherine and held up two fingers.

Katherine shook her head. Yes, there were only two of them out there. But one of them was a wizardess. It was better to wait and see if Alessandro was going to get rid of her or betray them.

"M'lady," said Alessandro.

"Don't you m'lady me! Why don't you give me one good reason I shouldn't try you on the hot plate as well?"

"Do you want to hear me beg?" asked Alessandro, his voice full of confidence and sleaze. "I can do that here."

"Your skills are not as unique as you seem to believe. I could train any of the clan to perform the acts of love as you do, and there are many who would love to take your place. Why even today, Stavros demonstrated an uncharacteristic boldness in his advances. How would you feel being replaced by Stavros?"

"Disturbed."

Katherine smiled to herself. Nice one, Alessandro.

"I'll give you one last chance, Alessandro," said Lady Vivia. "Share the pleasures of the flesh with me, then we shall go watch your whore burn together."

"Yes, Lady Vivia."

"I just need a moment to freshen up."

"NO!" cried Alessandro.

Katherine's eyes met Captain Righteous's. It was preferable to avoid a fight, but if Lady Vivia discovered them hiding in the bathroom, shit was going to go down. Katherine shrugged. At least she wouldn't have to listen to them fuck.

"What is wrong with you, Alessandro? I must make water."

"Then make water on me!"

Wow. Way to take one for the team, Alessandro.

"I beg your pardon?" said Lady Vivia.

Come on, Vivia. You're thinking about it. Sell it, Alessandro!

"Shower me with your sweet golden water! I long to feel its warmth on my bare chest... and... face."

He wavered a bit with that last bit. Rein it in a little, buddy.

"Is that what the young Drow are doing these days?" asked Lady Vivia. Her tone was pouty but curious. "Do you continue to stray because I've not yet urinated on your face?"

"Um... yes."

"How was I to know? You've never even asked me."

"I've been meaning to bring it up, but the timing never seemed quite right."

"Hmmm..."

Holy shit. She was really considering this.

Captain Righteous gestured at his own crotch, rolling a finger outward to simulate peeing. Then he ran his fingers down the front of his face. Finally, he pointed at himself and Katherine.

That fucking sleazebag. For all his "righteousness", he was just as bad as Bingam. Katherine mouthed the words "Fuck no!"

The captain rolled his eyes and continued his pantomime. He went from pointing his finger between himself and Katherine to pointing outside, then punched his fist into his open palm.

Katherine rethought the whole performance from the beginning, altering her interpretation. While Lady Vivia is pissing on Alessandro's face, we attack. That sounded much better. Katherine nodded her consent, hoping like hell that this new interpretation was the correct one.

"I'm sorry, Alessandro. Perhaps when I'm feeling more adventurous. Today, you shall love me as I've trained you." Her voice was getting closer to the bathroom.

"Please!" cried Alessandro.

"Compose yourself! You can't just spring this sort of thing on a woman and expect her to be as aroused by the idea as you are. Now get on the bed and wait for –"

Lady Vivia stood in the open doorway in a semi-transparent purple silk robe which was untied and hanging open. Her whole body froze, except for her eyes which moved from the sword pressing against her neck, to Captain Righteous, to Bingam, who may or may not have still been trying to rub one out in the corner. When her gaze fell on Katherine, her eyes widened, then widened more still when they found Butterbean. Katherine could practically see the dots connecting in her mind.

"No!" Lady Vivia gasped. She turned to run. "Stop! Don't open the –"

Katherine caught a handful of Lady Vivia's robe and jerked her back, landing her hard on her bony black ass.

Captain Righteous stood over her with his sword. "Not another word."

It was too late anyway. The sounds of barks, howls, and screams were beginning to echo down the hallway, and they were quickly growing louder.

Captain Righteous looked up at Katherine while he tied Lady Vivia's hands behind her back with the belt of her robe. "You opened all the cages?"

"I had to," said Katherine. "They were being treated cruelly. They were all cramped and starved half to death."

"How many were there?"

Katherine shrugged. "A couple of dozen."

"We can't risk going out there now. They'll tear us apart."

The howls and screams seemed to have settled just outside the door. The panicked Drow screams were now accompanied by new Drow shouting orders. Reinforcements had arrived, and they were making a stand.

"No," said Katherine. "Now is the best time to go. I made them promise not to attack –" She stopped just short of saying us. "... me."

"You made them promise?"

"Well... Butterbean made them promise."

Captain Righteous looked at Butterbean, who was wagging his tail and looking very proud of himself. "And we're to bet our lives on the promise of starving dogs? They'd say anything to get out of those cages, and I've witnessed many a man break a promise for lesser motivations than an empty stomach."

"Their stomachs aren't empty," said Katherine. "I fed them."

"With what?"

Shit.

Katherine looked at the floor. "Melody."

Captain Righteous sighed. "A fine horse, she was. I'll put my trust in her to save my life this one last time. Let's go."

"Not so fast," said Katherine. "With all those Drow and wolves out there, we should still try to call as little attention to ourselves as possible. I know of an exit not far from here, and we'd do well to reach it without any confrontations."

Captain Righteous nodded. "Agreed. What do you have in mind?"

Katherine looked at Lady Vivia. "I want you to know that I'm really sorry about this, and that I have nothing but respect for you and your people."

Lady Vivia glared at Katherine with pure hatred in her violet eyes. "No amount of your groveling will make me forgive what you did to Mittens."

"I'm sorry for that as well, but that's not what I was talking about."

"What are you talking about?" asked Captain Righteous.

Katherine shook her head. "I can't even bring myself to say it. I need the sword."

"I will not let you murder a restrained and unarmed prisoner in cold blood."

"Please," Katherine scoffed. "As if I would ever do that. Just hand over the sword please."

Captain Righteous presented the sword, palms up under the flat of the blade, the pommel to Katherine, but he shifted his stance to be between her and Lady Vivia.

Katherine rubbed two fingertips on the black blade. The substance coating it was thick and oily to the touch. Her fingertips were pitch black. She rubbed her blackened fingertips on the back of her other hand, and the bladeblack transferred just as she hoped it would. After giving the blade a good rubbing up and down with both palms, she smeared the substance all over her face, hands, and forearms where her cloak left them exposed. When she was as done as she could be without a mirror, she turned to Captain Righteous.

"How do I look?"

"Like a damned fool."

Katherine sighed. "I mean, could I pass for Drow?"

"Is that meant to be a joke?" asked Lady Vivia.

"Absolutely not. I honestly mean no offense by this."

"It's not offensive, you stupid mongrel. It's simply preposterous."

"See now, that's offensive."

"I'm afraid I have to agree with Lady Vivia," said Captain Righteous. "There's more to being Drow than black skin."

"I'm not trying to infiltrate their government or anything. I just need to fool them for as long as it takes for me to run by with a wolf chasing me."

"Your hair is the wrong color. By the Light, you're not even a full-blooded elf!"

Katherine raised her eyebrows at Captain Righteous. "You're walking a line there. And I'm telling you, none of that is going to matter. I'm going to be another black blur in the darkness. I'm sorry. That came out wrong."

"Even if you could pass for Drow, where does that leave me and Bingam? Our body styles are even farther removed from that of the Drow than yours is."

"That's why you two are going to ride in the Bag of Holding."

"Are we now?"

"Do you have a better idea for avoiding confrontation?"

"Fine. Give me back the sword, and we'll agree to ride in the bag."

"I'm about to charge out into a bunch of Drow. What if I need to defend myself?"

"If your disguise is as effective as you seem to believe it is, you shouldn't need a sword."

"I didn't say it was foolproof." Katherine didn't know why the captain was being so stubborn on this particular point. Why would he trust her enough to pull him out of the Bag of Holding, but not enough to let her hold onto the only weapon they had between the three of them? Unless...

"Running away while holding a sword while the others stand and fight may call even more attention to you," he said. "If your disguise fails, you can quickly pull me out of the bag. I would imagine that I'm more dangerous with a blade than you are."

... unless that motherfucker was still planning to arrest her once they got out of immediate danger. Well played, Cap'n.

"Fine," said Katherine. "Take the goddamn sword. You guys ready to go?" She held open the bag.

Captain Righteous stood tall and erect with his arms flat by his sides. Bingam followed his uncle's example.

Katherine scooped up both men, then smiled to herself and reached inside. "Sword." She pulled Alessandro's black-smeared blade out of the bag.

"Good luck," said Lady Vivia. She was actually smiling. That provided little reassurance for Katherine.

"Ready, Butterbean?"

Butterbean let out a sharp bark and wagged his tail.

"On three, let's go. One, two... AAAAAAAHHHHHH!" She screamed as she opened the door, both to aid the being-chased-by-a-wolf scenario and to cover Lady Vivia's cries for help. She and Butterbean slipped outside, and Katherine slammed the door shut behind her.

Both wolves and Drow paused in their fighting to stare at her. Then all hell broke loose.

Two of the wolves she'd made the pact with snapped at her, catching the bottom of her cloak in their teeth. At the same time, one of the Drow shouted, "That's Lady Vivia's prisoner! She killed Mittens!"

Fuck! This plan sucked. Her disguise had fooled the wolves, but hadn't even come close to fooling the Drow.

She smacked one wolf on the muzzle with the flat of her blade and yanked her cloak free from the other one. She and Butterbean ran like hell down the corridor.

"Get her!" cried the Drow who had identified her. Wolves and Drow were both hot on her trail. Butterbean barked as they ran, Katherine glanced back to find that the wolves had stopped chasing her, and had instead chosen to gang up on one of her pursuing Drow. That guy was fucked. Four more Drow were still hot on her trail, and one of them was nocking a bow as he ran.

A well-timed duck sent the arrow ricocheting off the wall in front of her, but she couldn't keep that up forever. She needed to think of something quick.

Think, Katherine. What else do you have in that bag? Stavros's body probably wouldn't slow them down much, and would likely piss them off even more. What else did she have in there? She supposed there must still be the skin and bones of two horses, but that was even less useful than Stavros.

There was always Captain Righteous, but that was an absolute last resort. If Tim could accidentally take down a minotaur, then she could take on four skinny – Goddammit, Katherine.

She held the Bag of Holding upside down as she ran. Reaching up into it, she whispered, "All the caltrops." No point in giving them any warning. The spiked metal doodads clattered onto the floor behind her, but not quite as spread out as she would have liked.

"Caltrops!" shouted one of the sword-wielding Drow. So much for whispering. Katherine glanced back. Three of Katherine's pursuers slowed down to step carefully through the trap, but the archer's attention was focused on nocking his next arrow.

"YEEEOOOOOOOOWWWW!" he cried, falling forward onto his bow and snapping it in half.

Katherine had bought herself a little bit more of a lead. She just hoped it would be enough.

By the time she and Butterbean reached the stairs, the three Drow had nearly caught up to them again.

The stairs led nearly all the way up to the surface, but the exit was higher still, hidden in a nook between the branches of a massive elm tree. Accessible by a ladder running up a narrow chute bored through the trunk.

She had two choices. Pull everyone out of the bag and fight the Drow, or put Butterbean in the bag and start climbing. It was a gamble, but she needed to think beyond just the next few minutes. Escaping the Drow wasn't going to get her any closer to her brother if Captain Zero-Tolerance was just going to take her into custody as soon as they surfaced. She shoved her sword into the Bag of Holding, knelt in front of Butterbean, and held it open. "Hurry up. Get in."

By the time she'd scooped up Butterbean and started climbing, the Drow were right on top of her. Or rather, she was right on top of them, in a more literal sense. Her progress was slow, as she spent more time jerking her ankles away from grabby hands and trying to stomp fingers than she did climbing. Once she reached the top, she was still going to need to open the hatch and climb out. The Drow underneath her finally got a solid grip on Katherine's leg that she couldn't shake off. Her knuckles strained to maintain their grip on the ladder rung. But he was strong, and had gravity and both of their combined weight on his side. She had made it all the way to within three ladder rungs of freedom,

His white teeth grinned up at her through the darkness. He knew he had her. "The game is over, half-elf. You will pay for Mittens's death!"

Mittens's death? Seriously? This guy didn't give a shit about Mittens. He was just trying to get into Lady Vivia's pants, just like – That's it!

"Okay," said Katherine. "I'll pay." She redoubled her effort to maintain her grip on the rung with her right hand and let go with her left. "Can you break a Stavros?"

"What?" The Drow looked genuinely confused, but it didn't affect his grip.

Katherine pressed her body back against the wall, and held the bottom of the Bag of Holding between her teeth. She reached inside and carefully pronounced the word "Stavros" through the corner of her mouth.

The dead elf spilled out of the bag and onto the Drow holding Katherine's ankle.

"Wha!" he cried, and Katherine felt him let go.

The two Drow below him also shrieked as they all fell down the chute and crashed onto the hard stone floor. It probably wasn't enough to kill them, but they were going to feel it.

Katherine removed the filthy bag from her mouth and resumed climbing. "Keep the change, asshole."

The fresh evening woodland air was rejuvenating, and made her wonder how the guys were doing inside the Bag of Holding. First things first, though. She had to make sure this hatch stayed shut. It only locked from the inside, but Katherine had a spell prepared that she hoped would do the trick.

"Entangle," she said, then watched with fascination as vines snaked their way down branches and wrapped the hatch shut.

She was a good twenty feet off the ground, but the big tree had strategically grown knots, made by driving spikes into the trunk and letting the tree heal itself over them, to use as hand

and foot holds. Kind of a dick way to treat a tree.

She reached into the Bag of Holding. "All the armor." Captain Righteous and Bingam's armor spilled out of the bag and into the weave of vines holding the hatch shut.

She felt a small pang of guilt as she put her hand in once again. "All the clothes." Both men's clothes piled into a dirty sweaty heap atop the pile of armor, as did a couple of Katherine's things, which she hurriedly picked out and shoved back into the bag.

After scurrying halfway down the trunk and jumping the rest of the way to the ground, she reached into the bag and said, "Butterbean."

Butterbean rolled out onto the ground and started panting.

"Sorry," Katherine said, reaching into the bag again. "Sword." The whole point of all this was to maintain the upper hand and escape without being pursued any further.

"Bingam."

Bingam fell out of the bag gasping for air and covering his junk with his hands. "What's... wrong... with... you?"

"Captain Righteous."

The captain was also breathing heavily, but didn't bother to cover his junk. Instead, he used his hands to aim a Kingsguard-issue crossbow at Katherine.

"Shit," said Katherine. Only now did she remember having shoved Bingam's weapon into the bag. Double crossing him on the sword issue suddenly felt a bit less clever.

Butterbean growled at the captain, but Katherine hushed him.

"Where are my clothes?" asked Captain Righteous.

"In the tree." Katherine looked up to indicate more specifically where she was talking about, and to avoid checking out the captain's junk. She admired his commitment to professionalism, and thought she could at least pay him that respect.

"Why are our clothes in a tree?"

"So you can't follow me."

"My oath to enforce His Majesty's laws means far more to me than modesty. Drop the sword, place your hands atop your head, and step away from the wolf."

"No."

The captain narrowed his eyes. "You are in no position to –" A banging noise came from up in the tree. Katherine's spell was timing out, and it was only a matter of time before the Drow would be able to break through the now-inanimate vines. Captain Righteous glanced up, but kept his aim fixed on Katherine. "What was that?"

"Some shit you're about to have to deal with." She didn't want to part on a sour note. "Good luck. And listen, thanks for all your help down there. You're a good man."

Katherine ran off into the woods, and Butterbean followed. She didn't even bother worrying about direction. She'd figure that out after she put some distance between herself and the law and the Drow.

Captain Righteous had had plenty of time to shoot her and reload his crossbow before the Drow managed to open the hatch, and Katherine thought it was sweet that he didn't. She was growing on him.

CHAPTER 27

The ride through the Great Wood was an exhilarating one. Talirius, the centaur Stacy rode, was swift but gentle as he galloped gracefully along the center of the road. Though there was plenty of room on the road for the centaurs to travel two abreast, Julian's ride, Nadia, made her way through the rougher area beside the road the side of the road. Jumping over roots and pine cones, she seemed to enjoy the experience much more than Julian did as he clutched onto her boobs for dear life.

Cooper rode behind them. Whenever Stacy glanced back, Cooper and his mount, Dyril, both looked like they were plodding toward their own executions.

A few hours passed by like a few minutes, at least for Stacy. As they traveled, silver threads in the forest canopy grew more and more visible as they concentrated closer together. Finally, the centaurs slowed to a stop in front of a tall iron gate, overgrown with vines. On either side of the gate, a fence stretched north and south as far as Stacy could see. The farther away from the gate the fence stretched, the thicker the vines tangled around it. Beyond twenty feet in either direction it became just a wall of vine. Beyond the gate lay a village in the most un-desert-like terrain she could imagine. It was like a botanical garden juiced up with an illegal version of Miracle-Gro.

"Welcome, travelers, to Minswater," said one of two elves with tufts of silver hair growing from their chins.

"Thank you," said Stacy. "But actually, we were looking for the Fertile Desert."

"You've found it!" said the other elf with the strange beard. "Minswater is but one of many ancient settlements along the edge of the Fertile Desert."

"Oh, okay then." Stacy climbed off Talirius's back and stopped herself just short of gasping at the sight of his raging horse boner. She looked up at Julian, who met her gaze with an 'Oh right. You're only now just noticing that' kind of smile until Nadia reared up on her hind legs and dumped him off her back.

"I can wait no longer," said Nadia. "I must be satisfied at once."

Talirius placed a gentle finger on Stacy's cheek. "Thank you for the ride. I sincerely hope we cross paths again." He turned to Dyril. "Take care of this, will you?"

Dyril pouted. "Yes, of course, damn my cursed hooves."

Nadia and Talirius trotted off into the Great Wood.

"Would it be possible to hurry this up?" Dyril asked one of the silver-bearded elves. "I'd rather not stick around to watch this anymore than I have to."

"I'll run and fetch Whistlewood right away." Without warning, the elf shrank rapidly, morphing into a small brown bird, then flew over the gate and into the village."

"Whoa!" said Julian. "Is he a weresparrow?"

The remaining elf smiled at him. "We are the Druids of Minswater. The Wild Shape is but one of the many gifts Nature bestows upon us after years of devotion and spiritual –"

"YES!" cried Nadia.

Stacy whirled around. She'd assumed that Talirius and Nadia had run into the woods seeking privacy, but that was clearly the least of their concerns. Apparently, all they were seeking was a low-enough-hanging branch for Talirius to hold himself up with as he impaled Nadia from behind.

Stacy turned back to the bearded elf, but Julian and Cooper continued to gawk like they'd just discovered their dads' porn stashes.

The Druid of Minswater cleared his throat. "Come, allow me to show you to your guest quarters. Please step through the side entrance." A curtain of vines parted next to the main gate.

Stacy sensed something was off. Why was this guy treating them like they'd called ahead and booked reservations at this place? "Guest quarters?" she said. "We didn't plan to stay that long."

The elf looked at Stacy with a hint of sternness in his eyes. "I'm afraid your plans will have to be postponed, young miss. You're a guest here. At least until you've served your sentence."

"Okay, that's it. We're out of here. Julian and Cooper, it's time to go."

"Hang on a sec," said Cooper. "I want to see what kind of load this guy shoots."

"Guys! It's time to – Hey!"

Something wrapped tight around Stacy's ankle and jerked her back so that she fell to the ground. Vines. They grabbed Cooper's and Julian's ankles as well, pulling them all through the side entrance they'd been instructed to go through.

"Oomph!" said Julian.

"What the fuck?" said Cooper.

Stacy struggled to free herself, but more vines grabbed her wrists and continued pulling.

Those vines which weren't pulling her caressed her body from toe to head as she passed through the curtain.

Once they were on the other side, Stacy felt something like a pin prick on her neck. "Ow!" she, Cooper, and Julian said simultaneously. The vines released their hold and retreated back to their original hanging position. Stacy ran a finger over the spot on her neck where she'd felt the prick, and found it had a small smear of blood on it.

"What did that vine just do to me?" Stacy demanded from the elf who'd walked in unmolested by the vines hanging from the main gate. "Did I just get poisoned?"

The bearded elf smiled his disconcertingly warm smile again. "Of course not, dear. The vines just needed a small sample of your blood with which to identify you as guests. Welcome to Minswater. My name is Gildon. Please follow me." He turned around and started walking down a quaint red brick path between a thick patch of cucumbers on the left and an equally thick patch of eggplants on the right.

Stacy looked at the curtain of vines hanging from the main gate. As if they could read her mind, they started spontaneously growing long thorns with barbed points.

"Hey asshole!" Cooper shouted at Gildon's back. When the elf ignored him, continuing to walk farther into the village, he plucked off a large cucumber and cocked his arm back to throw. "I'm talking to you!"

"Cooper, no!" said Stacy. There was a reason this elf didn't seem in the least bit threatened by them, even as he allowed them to remain armed, and she didn't want to find out what that reason was the hard way.

But Cooper had already committed to the throw. "Eat a dick pickle!" The cucumber hurtled end over end until Gildon snatched it out of the air without even turning around.

To Cooper's credit, he succeeded in getting Gildon's attention without getting them all beaten to within an inch of their lives. Their host stopped walking, turned around, and took a small bite of the cucumber. "Your questions will be answered once you're settled in."

Cooper and Julian looked to Stacy for guidance. She was stumped. "I guess we follow him."

Minswater was a beautiful little village. Every house was painted a different vibrant color, and all of them were surrounded by gardens positively bursting with vegetation. Their occupants cheerily picked ripe fruits and vegetables and put them in large wicker baskets, never seeming to put so much as a small dent in the available fruits and veggies left to pick.

Two identical steel towers stood tall above the one-and-two-story buildings that populated the rest of the town. They looked like chalices with cones rising up out of the cups. All the threads from the Great Wood converged at the points of these cones. Billions of dew droplets ran down the cones and filled the cups with water, where there was presumably a system of pipes distributing the collected water into the ground.

"That's quite an irrigation system you've got set up," said Stacy, hoping she might be able to get something useful out of their host if she could get him to first say anything at all.

Gildon gazed fondly at one of the towers. "Aye, 'tis that."

That was less of a response than Stacy was hoping for, but it was something. She decided to try a different angle. "It seems like a lot of effort for something that could easily be done magically."

"The Druids of Minswater frown upon the arcane arts."

"Oh?" Stacy looked back at Julian to make sure he was paying attention, then spoke very deliberately. "It's fortunate that none of us practice arcane arts."

"Julian!" cried Ravenus, flapping down to land atop Julian's staff.

The host elf turned around and frowned at the big black bird.

"Um..." Julian stammered. "Hello, strange talking bird. How do you know my name?"

"Are you okay, sir? I sensed you were being gripped and stroked, but it felt somehow different than when you send me away so you can have your Julian time."

Stacy needed to know if these weirdos were going to try to burn Julian at the stake and, if necessary, adjust her strategy. "Is magic forbidden here?"

"Not forbidden, no," said Gildon. "Merely frowned upon. We believe the gods favor those who work hard and don't take shortcuts."

"So you're, like, Amish?" asked Cooper. "Is that what those beards are all about?"

Stacy gave Cooper a look which she hoped successfully conveyed the message, "Shut up," then quickly thought up something to say before their host could ask Cooper what the hell he was talking about. "Do you like... toast?" Shit.

"At long last, here we are," said Gildon, pretending to not have heard either of them. He'd led them to a quaint little cottage just like so many they'd passed along the way, if not a little larger. This one was pink, with a pale yellow door.

"Shit," said Cooper. "What kind of prison is this? This place is nicer than my house back home."

"Please don't think of this as a prison." Gildon led them into the sparsely furnished but very clean house. "Make yourselves at home. An elder shall be along shortly to pass sentencing."

"Sentencing for what?" asked Stacy. "We didn't do anything."

"It's not my place to judge. You will be given the opportunity to present evidence refuting the centaurs' accusations."

"The centaurs! Those hornballing horsehumpers threw us under the bus?"

Gildon frowned. "I don't... I'll be leaving now. Please enjoy your stay with us." He stepped outside and closed the door behind him.

As soon as the door closed, the light inside the room grew darker as vines crawled up the windows.

Stacy tried the door. She saw no locking mechanism, but it was held firmly shut from the other side. "Don't think of this as a prison, he says."

During the hours that passed, Stacy, Julian, and Cooper discussed their options. A number of ideas were proposed. The most ridiculous, Cooper's idea of Raging out and hurling Julian over the fence so that he could go for help, inspired what turned out to be the best they could come up with, Julian's counter-proposal of sending Ravenus off for help. The bird had flown into town without a problem. He could presumably fly back out.

A gentle knock on the door preceded a flood of light into the house as the vines drew back from the windows.

"Good evening," said an old man's voice. The door opened

slowly, and two elves walked into the house. A strong young elf held a much older elf by the arm and escorted him to a humble wooden chair in the corner of the room. Both elves had the same tufts of hair growing from the bottom of their chins, but the old elf's silver beard grew down past his chest.

Stacy made eye contact with Julian, inviting him to take the Diplomacy lead.

"Hello," said Julian. A natural-born diplomat, he was.

"Greetings, travelers," said the old elf. "And how are you this fine evening?"

Julian had gotten off to a shaky beginning, but Stacy nodded at him encouragingly to try again. Their freedom was on the line.

"Kinda shitty, now that you mention it," said Julian. "We've spent the past two hours trying to figure out the best way to escape this dump."

As shocked as Stacy was, the expression on Julian's face suggested that he was even more so.

"What the fuck kind of Diplomacy was that?" asked Cooper.

The old elf smiled, then looked up at his younger companion. "The half-orc."

"You." The younger elf extended his right hand toward Cooper and spoke in a no-nonsense tone. "Would you like to kiss my ring?"

Stacy could only imagine how Cooper might have responded under regular circumstances, but trusted him to suck up his pride and do what was best for all of them.

"I'd rather shove my foot up your ass." Cooper clapped his hands over his mouth, then gave them a small sniff.

"What is wrong with you two?" asked Stacy.

"Now the human girl," the elder said to his companion.

The younger elf looked at Stacy. "Is it true you wish to leave our village?"

"Badly enough to consider jerking off your grandpa's ancient withered elf dick." Stacy gasped. "Hey! What the..."

The old elf raised his bushy white eyebrows and smiled at Stacy. "I shall take that under advisement."

"I'm so sorry!" said Stacy. "I don't know what... I would never... I..."

"Do not be alarmed. We must be certain the Zone of Truth is effective before we begin our interrogation. As long as we're all being honest, pre-interrogation is my favorite part of the process."

Stacy crossed her arms. "That's fine. Keep the questions relevant and on point, and you'll see that we've committed no crimes."

"Interesting." The elder held out his hand. "Fallion, the charges, please."

The younger elf placed a rolled up piece of paper in the elder's hand.

The elder unrolled the paper and cleared his throat. "Let's begin with setting an unattended fire in the Great Wood. How plead you?" He looked up from the paper at Stacy.

"We didn't know that was a crime. There weren't any signs posted about fires being prohibited."

"Fire is a gift from the gods. Its power is great, however, and must be respected and wielded with responsibility."

"We were being responsible," said Julian. "We cleared out a safety perimeter, and there was always someone near the fire."

The old elf looked back down at his paper, then at Julian. "The centaurs' report states that when they found you, two of you were sleeping, and one of you was up in a tree. Yet the fire remained burning. Do you deny this?"

Julian looked hopefully at Stacy. She knew the Zone of Truth would prohibit her from lying, but maybe she could lawyer her way out of the charge with her high Intelligence score.

"If you don't mind me asking," she said, "what is the exact wording of the law my friends and I have allegedly broken?"

The elder smiled. "Our laws are not written, young lady. We judge what is right or wrong as the situation is presented to us."

"So you just make it up as you go along?"

"You could choose to look at it like that if you like. Now, do you deny the charge leveled against you?"

Stacy looked down. "No."

The elder turned to Julian. "And you?"

"No."

"And you, half-orc?"

Cooper pulled his finger out of his nose. "Huh?"

"How do you plead?"

Cooper got down on his knees and folded his hands. "Please let me ride on your back and hold on to your titties."

The elder narrowed his eyes curiously at Cooper, then looked back down at his paper. "Let us move on to the next charge, shall we?"

Stacy sighed. "Sure."

"Very well. Tampering with the city's water supply." He looked up sternly. "This is a very serious crime."

"That is some very serious bullshit!" said Stacy. She raised her hands defensively. "Excuse my language. That's the Zone of Truth talking. We did no such thing."

Julian raised his hand timidly. "I might have."

"What are you talking about? We've been together since we got forcefully pulled into this backwards-ass elven hillbilly nightmare." Stacy looked at the elder. "No offense. Zone of Truth and all that. The point is, none of us have had the time or the privacy to go take a dump in a well or anything."

"I untied one of the threads," said Julian. "While I was up in the tree. It was an accident."

The old elf looked at him sternly. "Accident or not, it is a costly mistake to remedy. Of the three of you, you should know best how difficult it will be to find the fallen strand. Elven silk is nigh-invisible."

"Whoa!" Julian's reaction seemed disproportionate to what the old elf had said, and inappropriate for having charges leveled against him. He looked at Stacy. "I know all about Elven silk. That's what your cloak is made of!"

Stacy supposed it was one of those game things, when you suddenly realize that you have knowledge that you didn't possess in the real world, like how to use a sword more effectively than just clanging it against your opponent's. Stacy had already had many such revelations during her short time in this world. And sure, it's exciting. But now was a time to remain focused.

"Is there anything else?" she asked the elder.

The old elf squinted at the bottom of the page, then looked up at Stacy, then Julian, and finally at Cooper. "Brutal mutilation of a dire boar's genitals?"

Cooper looked out the window. "That was also an accident."

"It is clear to me that you have little to no remorse for your wrongdoings," said the elder. "Your atonement shall come when you've filled fifty thousand sacks in the citrus orchard."

Holy shit. They'd just been sentenced. It was finished. What the hell is fifty thousand sacks?

The younger elf was assisting the elder to stand up. They were leaving. Stacy couldn't let this be the end. She had to say something.

"What about our stuff?"

The old elf paused. "Your stuff?"

"Yes. Our belongings. You're just going to let us keep them?"

"We are not thieves, young lady. If your possessions will help you harvest vegetables more efficiently, I recommend you use them. In the meantime, I recommend you learn to live in peace with nature, lest you rest in peace as you return to it." With that, the two elves walked out the front door, which failed to close behind them. No vines grew over the windows.

Stacy walked out the door, just to see if she could. Once outside the house, she turned around and looked through the doorway at Julian.

"Julian! Your serape is covered in spiders!"

"FUCK!" cried Julian, whipping the garment over his head and throwing it as far away from himself as he could. He shivered and brushed his hands down both sides of his tunic while Stacy and Cooper laughed at him.

He stopped brushing, looked down at his bundled, spider-free serape, then up at Stacy. "What's going on?"

"I was just messing with you. Honestly, I can't believe you fell for the old 'There's a spider on your shirt' line."

"I saw a man turn into a sparrow today. These guys could have spider-summoning powers for all I know. Do we really have nothing better to do than play grade school pranks on each other?"

"Keep your skirt on," said Stacy. "I needed to see if the Zone of Truth worked out here. Looks like it's confined to the house."

CHAPTER 28

The benefits to being a fighter were obvious. Katherine didn't kick quite as much ass as she had when she was a vampire, but she felt confident about holding her own in a brawl. But outside of a couple of lousy spells and the companionship of a wolf, Katherine hadn't noticed a lot of benefits to being a druid, at least until now.

She was running through brambles and thick forest underbrush like none of that shit was there. She scarcely touched a leaf as she passed. The best tracker in the world wouldn't be able to follow her trail, and even if they could, they wouldn't be able to move nearly as quickly as she could. Still, as fantasy superpowers go, being able to run through the woods at normal speed was kind of lame.

And the benefit didn't last as long as she'd hoped. The briers and brambles thinned out as the pine trees grew taller and thicker the farther west she traveled. Also, she still didn't know where she was going.

Katherine was running past the biggest goddamn trees she'd ever seen. A shin-deep layer of brown pine needles covered the forest floor. Pine cones the size of cars dotted the landscape as well. Getting hit by one of those falling from a branch might well kill a person.

She slowed her pace and kept a wary eye on the branches above her to watch for falling cones. The sharp crack of a fallen branch brought her attention back to ground level.

A centaur stood leaning casually against a tree, staring at Katherine with one eyebrow cocked. It was like he was going for some kind of James Dean suaveness which he couldn't quite pull off due to his being half barnyard animal.

His front left hoof was positioned forward on top of the recently cracked branch. It wasn't a failed Stealth check. He was purposely alerting her to his presence.

"Why do you cover your skin in bladeblack?" The centaur's expression changed from one of curiosity to one of amusement. "Are you trying to impersonate a Drow?"

Katherine couldn't answer truthfully, lest she have to do more explaining than she had time for. Also, the centaur's amusement at the idea reinforced Captain Righteous's and Lady Vivia's opinion on just how stupid trying to impersonate a Drow had been in the first place. She racked her brain for some semi-plausible alternative explanation.

Camouflage?

Religious cult?

Coal mining?

Football!

"It keeps the glare out of my eyes."

"Oh," the centaur said disinterestedly. He stood up straight and took a step toward her. "The Great Wood can be a dangerous place for a young lady all alone."

Not this shit again. Katherine restrained her eye-rolling instinct. "It might be just as dangerous for a centaur all alone."

The centaur smiled and held up a wineskin. "Lucky for us, we're not alone anymore." He tilted back his head and drank deeply from it, spilling some of the purple wine down his chin and muscled chest. This may not have been his first skinful. He cocked an eyebrow at Katherine. "Care to have a drink with a lonely centaur?"

"I'd really love to." Katherine wasn't just being polite. Even if this guy was leering at her like she was the one he'd finally drunk enough to settle for at last call, she could really go for some wine. "But I'm in kind of a hurry. I need to get to a place called The Fertile Desert. Do you know it?"

"Sure I do. And I can get you there a lot faster on four legs than you can on two."

"Are you offering me a ride?"

"In exchange for the pleasure of your company over a couple of drinks, yes."

That sounded very reasonable to Katherine. "You've got yourself a deal,..."

"Call me Dyril."

"I'm Katherine. It's nice to meet you, Dyril."

"The pleasure's all mine. Please, have a seat." He gestured at an exposed root, then twisted his torso to dig around in one of the saddlebags he wore on his horse half.

"So... Do you live around here?" Katherine didn't have a lot of experience making small talk with people in this world.

"Ah, here we go!" said Dyril, producing a glass bottle full of Windex-blue liquid and a silver cup. He poured the contents of the former into the latter until it was nearly full, then swirled the drink around. "Give it a moment to breathe. Let the flavors mingle."

"You didn't need to go to all that trouble," said Katherine. "I would have been fine with whatever you were drinking before." She didn't have the most refined tastes in the world. She was more utilitarian with her drinking, not the sort to let a drink 'breathe' or allow time for 'flavor mingling'. But as long as this guy was buying, she'd endure a little snobbery. She only hoped he wouldn't ask her to describe the bouquet, or whatever kind of bullshit those wine aficionados said to each other.

Dyril waved the cup under his nose, breathed in deeply, then smiled. "Perfect." He bent down to offer the cup to Katherine.

Katherine accepted the cup. The drink appeared a shade purpler than what was in the bottle, but light reflecting off the silver might account for that. She took a sip.

"Oh, that's good." It tasted like store brand grape juice and Robitussin. But Katherine had tasted worse. Hell, she'd knowingly bought worse when times were especially lean at the

Chicken Hut.

"It pleases me that you like it." Dyril drank from his wineskin, keeping his eyes on Katherine.

Katherine took a bigger sip, relishing the soothing effect of alcohol coursing through her bloodstream, thankful once again for no longer being a vampire. Now that she was getting accustomed to it, she didn't find the taste as off-putting as she had initially.

"Do you always wander around alone in the woods carrying around a stocked bar and an extra cup?"

"One never knows when or where one might make a new friend. I find it's best to be prepared. May I fill your cup?"

"Can I at least have another drink first?" Katherine laughed at her own joke. Dyril stared blankly at her. Cooper would have gotten it. She thought of another one. "Let's not go putting the cart before the horse!"

Dyril's left eye twitched. At least, Katherine thought it did. Her vision was suddenly a little blurry.

She blinked until Dyril came into focus, a look of disapproval on his face. "Perhaps you've had enough."

"Oh shit," said Katherine. "Was that racist? I didn't mean... Holy shit that stuff sneaks up on you." She grabbed a knot on the root to keep herself balanced as she stifled a yawn.

"Are you quite all right?" asked Dyril.

"I'm good. I just need a minute to – Jesus Christ!" Leaning sideways, Katherine caught sight of Dyril's eight dicks. She blinked.

Only four dicks. She blinked again.

Okay, just the one dick. But wow, was it just hangin' free. That was probably natural for a centaur. He'd have looked pretty goofy wearing pants. Katherine laughed at the thought.

"Does my masculinity amuse you?"

"Huh? No. I was just picturing you in jean shorts. Don't ask me why. I think I'm a little drunk."

"Perhaps you won't find it so funny when I'm inside you."

"Ha!" said Katherine. "I'm not that drunk, Ponyboy. Can you just give me a ride back to the dorms. I don't feel so good." She shook a sudden wave of dizziness out of her head.

Dyril narrowed his sixteen pairs of eyes at her. "Don't you mean the Fertile Desert?"

"Yeah, that's cool. If it's on your way."

"Of course. Climb on my back." Dyril knelt until his massive horse dong was sandwiched between his belly and the ground.

"I really appreciate that." Katherine put a leg over Dyril's back, wrapped her arms around his chest, and whispered in his ear. "Can we stop at a 7-11? I want some nachos."

"I don't know what any of that means, but please keep talking."

Katherine suddenly found herself moving really fast. She held on tight, willing herself to focus. "Take it easy, man. My I.D. was good enough for the bartender, but it's not going to fool a cop." Trees whirring by her on either side were making her nauseous, so she looked down. "Hey, did you know your lower half is a horse?"

"You'll know my lower half very well soon enough."

Katherine felt a wave of distress wash over her. "Dude. Stop the car. I think I'm gonna –" She threw up all over Dyril's head and back. "Oh my god, I'm so sorry."

Dyril slowed to a stop. "You disgusting half-elven bitch!"

"It's not that big a deal," said Katherine. She had an idea. "I know how to fix this." With clumsy fingers, she opened her Bag of Holding.

Dyril wiped slimy purple vomit from his shoulders, then felt the back of his head. "It's in my hair!"

"Take it easy," said Katherine, wobbling to stay balanced on his back while she lifted the bag. "I've got this."

"Oh, you'll get it all right. You'll get it so hard you'll wish you never –" The forest was calm and silent again when Katherine pulled the bag down over Dyril's head. His head, arms, and torso disappeared into the bag. She was about to reach in and call forth 'all the vomit' when Dyril started bucking.

Katherine flew off and landed hard on the ground. "Ow! Shit, that hurt. What just happened?"

A large grey wolf approached her, but she wasn't frightened. It seemed somehow familiar.

"Butterbean?"

Butterbean looked past her. Katherine followed his gaze to find a headless horse jumping around like a crazy asshole. A leather bag covered the top of its severed neck.

"What the fuck is up with that horse?" Katherine asked Butterbean. "I'm so fucking wasted. Wake me up in an hour, will you?" She snuggled up against Butterbean, closed her eyes, and went to sleep.

CHAPTER 29

Julian spent the non-trance hours of the night preparing his spells for the coming day. He didn't have anything that seemed particularly useful for picking citrus fruits, so he stocked up on Mount spells as it was the spell he'd come to find most versatile in any number of situations.

That hadn't taken up as much time as he'd hoped, so he spent the remainder of time alone with his thoughts again. He wondered where Tim was, and hoped that he was having at least as much trouble making it to the Crescent Shadow as they were. Maybe he'd also gotten picked up by centaurs for a stupid crime, and they'd see him picking lemons tomorrow. He'd be pissed, for sure, but it might have saved his life if it kept him from falling into whatever trap Mordred no doubt had waiting for him.

If Tim had made it to the Crescent Shadow, Julian hoped he was being careful, and that he would make good use of his rogue skills. He was smart. Maybe he would anticipate a trap and turn it around on Mordred. But then at least one of the Mordreds was probably smart as well, and would take Tim's brains and rogue skills into account when setting the trap. This line of thinking was exhausting. Julian wished he could sleep.

The sky was just beginning to lighten when Cooper, Stacy, and Ravenus woke up. When they went outside, Julian was surprised to see so many other residents of the town busily about their day picking vegetables out of their gardens, or headed somewhere with various kinds of harvesting tools.

Julian approached a dwarf with a set of long-handled pruning shears resting on his shoulder.

"Excuse me, sir. You're not, by chance, headed toward the citrus orchard, are you?"

"Indeed I am," the dwarf said cheerily. "A fine day for picking, it is."

"Would you mind if we followed you there? We don't know the way."

"Not at all! The more, the merrier! My children have already beaten us there, I'm afraid. We'll be lucky if there's fruit left to pick."

"Your children?" said Stacy.

The dwarf grinned. "I'm only joking!"

"Oh." Stacy forced a smile. "So your children aren't doing slave labor to work off your prison sentence."

The dwarf ceased grinning. "I was joking about there not being any fruit left. The Fertile Desert never fails to provide. And there aren't many trees in the world fit for the short arms and legs of a dwarf child to climb, so please forgive them if they happen to knock down an orange or two while they're playing."

Stacy had struck a nerve. Time for Julian to step back in and smooth it over. He would show humility by being open with his and his friends' flaws.

"Glad to hear there's a lot of fruit," said Julian. "We're in for fifty thousand sacks each."

The dwarf raised his eyebrows and whistled. "That's quite the sentence. What did you folks do, rape a unicorn?"

"It was a dire boar," said Cooper. "And it wasn't rape."

The dwarf stopped walking and looked up at Cooper. "You're saying she consented?" Leave it to Cooper to make not raping a unicorn sound as bad as possible.

"It was he, and no."

Julian had been naive to think 'as bad as possible' was a truly attainable goal as far as Cooper was concerned.

"What he's trying to say," explained Julian as quickly as he could in order to get Cooper to stop talking, "is that he chopped up its genitals." This wasn't helping.

The dwarf shook his head. "After bumraping it? Are you folks in some sort of cult?"

"There was no bumraping!" said Julian, perhaps a little too loudly. A few passersby took a couple of steps to the side as they passed. Even their new dwarf friend seemed to be looking for an escape route.

Julian took a deep breath. "At no point did anyone, besides you, mention sexual intercourse, consensual or otherwise, with an animal. We were attacked by a dire boar in the Great Forest. After killing it, we tried to roast and eat one of its hind legs. My friend Cooper here is not exactly a surgeon when it comes to butchering animals. He missed the mark a few times, and it was kind of a grisly sight."

The dwarf thought for a moment, then nodded. "My name's Ollie."

"It's a pleasure to meet you, Ollie. I'm Julian, and this is Cooper and Stacy."

"We're really nice people," said Stacy.

Cooper put his thumbs up. "Heeeyyyyyy!" Julian wasn't sure that a Fonzie impression was appropriate here, but it was better than continuing to speak, he supposed.

Ollie continued walking. "I'm willing to give you the benefit of the doubt. If my time in Minswater has given me anything, it's renewed faith in the inherent good of most races."

Julian smiled. "Oh? That's... loaded."

"But know this. If you betray my faith and lay so much as a finger on one of my children, pray that the elves of this town take you before I do."

"We're totally not like that," Stacy reassured him.

"That's true," said Cooper. "I don't give a fuck about your kids."

"Nice!" said Julian. Time to change the subject. "So, how much farther to the citrus orchards?"

"Just beyond these beanstalks. We're at the tail end of Minswater. Beyond the orchards is vast, bone dry desert as far as the eye can see."

They were walking through an arbor covered in vines. Fat juicy blackberries grew up the sides, and plump bean pods hung from above.

"Is it cool if we pick stuff off and eat it?"

"Help yourselves!" said the dwarf. He was back to his old jovial self. "That's the best part of living here. Behave yourselves, and you'll want for nothing."

Julian tasted a blackberry. It was very sweet, almost too much so, and practically exploded with juice in his mouth. Next he tried a bean pod. It was crunchy on the outside and juicy on the inside, with just the right amount of sweetness. It was a different kind of delicious than the blackberry. More subtle. Julian couldn't remember ever having enjoyed the taste and texture of raw beans before. Maybe it was an elf thing.

He plucked off handfuls of pods and stuffed them into his pockets to snack on while he worked.

"And here we are!" said the dwarf once they'd passed through the arbor and reentered the sunlight. "The citrus orchards."

The trees were lined up and cultivated like modern orchards, but they were much bigger, and different-looking than citrus trees that Julian had seen back home. The branches hung low to the ground, weighed down with ridiculous amounts of oranges, lemons, limes, grapefruits, as well as several other fruits that, while certainly citrusy, Julian couldn't readily identify.

Between the bean trellises and the citrus orchard stood a line of tables with folded sacks lying on top.

Ollie grabbed a sack and smiled at Julian. "Best get started. You've got fifty thousand of these to fill. I find it best to work as a team. Good luck. I've got to run along and find my children."

With the trees bursting with fruit as they were, maybe fifty thousand sacks wasn't such a tall order.

"How long do you think it would take to fill that many sacks?" Julian asked Stacy.

"More time than we've got. But we'll need to fill a few before I can make any calculations."

"We can fill more sacks faster if we use our heads," said Julian. He grabbed a few sacks. "Ravenus, I'm going to hold the bag open, and you fly up into the tree and cut oranges loose."

"As you command, sir."

Julian followed Ravenus to a tree and the process began. Ravenus clipped oranges loose with his beak, and Julian caught them in the sack.

Julian smiled at Stacy. "Not bad, eh?"

Stacy, who'd been examining the fruit-laden branches, shrugged. "I might have a better idea." She wrapped both hands around the tree trunk, took a deep breath, then shook the shit out of the tree.

Oranges rained down, littering the ground densely in a wide circumference at the base of the tree. Ravenus squawked and flew off his branch, and Julian thought he might have heard some giggling through the noise of falling fruit and rustling leaves.

"Let me try," said Cooper. Stacy let go of the tree and Cooper took her place. "I'm really angry!"

His muscles expanded until he was fifty percent larger.

"Hold on!" said a child's voice high up in the branches. "This is going to be a good one!"

Shit! Ollie's kids! "Cooper, don't –"

"FUCK YOU TREE!" Cooper shook the tree so hard that Julian thought he might either uproot it or snap the trunk. But miraculously, the tree held together as oranges piled up on the ground.

"Aaaahhhhh!" cried a small voice which stopped suddenly as a dwarven child smashed into a fruit pile. Then another, and still another. It was now raining oranges and dwarf kids.

"Cooper!" cried Julian. "Stop shaking the –"

*

Julian awoke some time later on a bed of squashed oranges. His head hurt, and he was wet and sticky with orange juice, but he was able to wiggle his fingers and toes. Stacy, Cooper, Ollie, and six dwarven children stood over him.

"What happened?"

Ollie grinned. "You found Ollie Jr." He nodded at one of the kids, the largest one by a wide margin. Ollie Jr. was nearly as large as Ollie Sr., his fat oily face showing the humble beginning of what was sure to be a big bushy beard someday.

"Sorry," said Ollie Jr.

"Don't be," said Julian. "It wasn't your fault." He looked up at Ollie Sr. "I'm sorry about Cooper shaking your kids out of the tree. Are they all okay?"

"Elia sprained her wrist, but that's nothing to worry about. It'll put hair on her chest."

The littlest of the dwarf children, presumably Elia judging by the sling holding up her left arm, picked up an orange and put it in her father's sack.

"You put that back right now!" Ollie scolded her. "We don't take what's not ours."

"Please," said Stacy. "Take all you want."

Cooper's fatigued eyes widened. "What the fuck? I just used up one of my goddamn –"

Stacy grabbed Cooper by the arm. "I'd like to talk to my friends alone. Please feel free to collect as many oranges as you can. It's the least we can do." With her other arm, she helped Julian to his feet, then led them deeper into the orchard.

"My arm hurts," said Cooper. "Loosen it up a little."

Stacy stopped walking and turned to face Cooper and Julian. "I had a little chat with Ollie while you were out. I noticed that Ravenus could come and go from this town as he pleased, so I figured the place isn't as completely escape-proof as I thought."

"I'm sorry," said Julian. "I'm still a little groggy after having a fat adolescent dwarf kid fall on my head. You realize that none of us can fly, don't you?"

"Yes. But I kept digging. I asked him if he knew of anyone ever having escaped before, and he said it happens occasionally. Every now and then a wizard or sorcerer will fly or teleport out of here."

Julian shook his head. "I'm nowhere near high enough level to –"

"I wasn't finished." Stacy's expression suggested she was about to get to the good part. "He also mentioned that some desperate souls just wander off to die in the desert."

"You look far too pleased about... Hang on. You mean there's nothing preventing us from just walking into the desert?"

Stacy smiled now that Julian was finally catching on. "Ollie says the desert is barrier enough to keep all but the most desperate or foolhardy folks from trying to escape that way. He said that even on horseback, taking all the fruit you can carry, you'll only be putting off the inevitable."

Julian felt a renewed sense of hope. "Not inevitable if you're carrying your own endless supply of water."

Cooper grinned stupidly and tapped on the side of his bag. His claws clinked against something metallic inside, the Decanter of Endless Water. "Let's get the fuck out of here."

CHAPTER 30

Katherine woke up with a splitting headache, a stiff neck, and a faceful of wolf slobber. It was morning, and she was in a forest.

"Butterbean? Where are we? How did we –" Her first clue was a headless horse lying on the ground next to her. Memories started creeping back. "Dyril!"

She crawled over and pulled the Bag of Holding off Dyril's torso. His blue face and bulging eyes suggested he'd been dead for quite some time.

"Shit!" What had happened? How did she get so drunk from that one cup of wine? No. She hadn't just been drunk. She was whacked out of her mind. The memory was mostly a blur, but the bits and pieces she recalled couldn't be attributed to mere alcohol. She didn't remember putting the bag over his head, or why she'd want to. She really hoped she'd had a good reason.

With little to go on, she looked inside the dead centaur's saddlebag. She found four bottles of Windex booze, several locks of hair, and a row of small corked test tubes. It was all very organized. The bottles had their own compartment. There was a place for the silver cup, though it appeared they'd left that behind.

The test tubes were lined up along the side, held in place by leather holders stitched into the inner lining of the bag. All but one of them were filled with a red liquid. Katherine remembered the purple tint of the drink in her cup.

Had he spiked her drink? Impossible. She saw him pour it. Unless he spiked the cup beforehand.

Katherine opened the half-empty bottle of blue booze and

took a small sip. It tasted like gin, with not even a hint of Robitussin.

She looked down at Dyril's rigor mortis stiffened arms, then at his pre rigor mortis stiffened dick. That thing would have been coming out of her mouth. "You sick motherfucker." She was tempted to kick him, but decided against it. No point in beating a dead horse. Ha!

Katherine also saw no point in letting good booze go to waste, so she started putting the bottles into her Bag of Holding. The sleeping potions might have applications outside of date rape as well. Hell, saddlebags are probably worth something. She would have taken the corpse too if the lip of the bag had been wide enough to accommodate the horse half. No time for chopping up bodies today. She had somewhere to be.

Unfortunately, she had no idea how far, or even in which direction, Dyril had taken her. But she was still in a forest, so it stood to reason that she should keep heading west.

She and Butterbean ran past the massive pine trees, jumping over roots and staying alert for falling pine cones.

After half an hour of running, their path was blocked by what appeared to be a solid wall of tangled vines running as far north and south as she could see. Her recently discovered druid power of being able to pass through thick underbrush should apply here as well, but there must be some sort of structure holding the vines up. There was probably a fence or wall under all that vegetation. That still wasn't a problem. Katherine laughed to herself and felt some pride in recently beginning to give a shit about nature. The irony of going to all that effort to build a wall, only for nature to come along and provide an easy means to climb over it.

The wall was too high for her to throw Butterbean over it, but she'd figure something out. First she wanted to see what was on the other side. She was supposed to be heading toward some kind of desert, and hoped to see some cacti or sand dunes or something, but she expected the change in environment wouldn't be as sudden and severe as all that.

She grabbed the two sturdiest looking vines she could find, and started seeking a foothold when she felt a piercing pain in her hands.

"FUCK!" Katherine cried as she jerked her hands away, lost her balance, and fell on her ass. Her hands were bleeding profusely from the palms. She looked up at the blood prints on the vines where she'd taken hold and found the vines to be covered in sharp thorns. Those hadn't been there before, she was sure of it. Those vines had just purposely attacked her. She felt so betrayed. She was a druid, after all. Why was nature being an asshole to her?

Instinctively, her mind tried to summon a swarm of rats for her to bite the heads off of. But she was no longer a vampire. She couldn't summon rats, and biting their heads off wouldn't do her any good anyway. Now that she thought about it, it was actually kind of gross.

As a poor substitute, she used up one of her first-level spells to heal her hands, then wiped the blood off as best she could against the trunk of one of the massive pine trees.

Remembering the road she'd purposely avoided, Katherine followed the wall northward, hoping that no one was stupid enough to build a road leading to nothing but an impenetrable wall of vines.

There was nothing but big stupid wall to her left and big stupid trees to her right for miles until she and Butterbean finally came to the last two people she wanted to see.

"Goddammit," said Katherine.

Bingam looked obnoxiously smug. Captain Righteous looked stern, but professional. Both of them were wearing their uniforms and looked to be very well rested. They stood in front of a large iron gate with a loose curtain of vines hanging over it, and were accompanied by two elves with strange silver beards jutting out of the bottoms of their chins.

"We thought you might show up here eventually," said

Captain Righteous.

"Dear child," said one of the elves. "What's happened to your skin?"

The other one smiled. "I nearly mistook her for a Drow." Their shared laugh at that made Katherine feel even dumber.

"It's medicinal," said Captain Righteous. "She has a skin affliction."

The two elves took a step back. "My apologies, Miss," said the one who'd made the joke.

Katherine appreciated Captain Righteous's attempt to spare her dignity, even if it did involve telling people she was a leper. She glared at the stupid-bearded elf.

"Your little Drow comment. Not funny. And frankly, I found it a little bit offensive."

As long as the captain was feeling uncharacteristically empathetic, Katherine thought it was worth making a token attempt at reasoning with him.

"We've just been through a lot together. I know you're a hard-ass for the law and all that, but we've saved each others' lives. I need to get to the Crescent Shadow and find my brother before he gets himself hurt or killed."

Captain Righteous's eyes betrayed what Katherine hoped was a hint of sympathy for her. "Even if I were to let you go, how do you propose to locate the Crescent Shadow? It flies erratically over the Fertile Desert. A well-equipped traveler might wander for months without seeing it. You won't last two days. And even if, by some miracle, you were able to find it, it floats five hundred feet in the air. Have you wings under that cloak of yours?"

Katherine frowned. "No."

"Without a guide, you and your wolf will die in the desert without ever catching a glimpse of the Crescent Shadow."

Katherine tried to summon some tears to milk that little bit of sympathy. She found it wasn't difficult, given how travel-weary and worried she was, especially now that the captain had laid out just how hopeless her quest was. "He's my little brother. I've got to try."

"Careful," said Bingam. "Your medicine is running."

Katherine wanted so badly to kick him in the dick, but Captain Righteous was stroking his mustache thoughtfully. Was he actually thinking about letting her go?

"I'm sorry," the captain finally said. "I know not what trouble your brother is in, but it makes no sense to betray my oath and let you wander off into the desert to die on a fool's errand. I'm afraid I'll have to take you back to Cardinia."

Shit. He was actually on the fence for a second there. And he mentioned a guide before. He knew of a way to get her to the Crescent Shadow. He just needed a nudge in the right direction.

"My brother," said Katherine. "He's the one you were looking for when you found me, the one on the poster that your nephew was looking at."

Bingam laughed.

Captain Righteous even smiled a bit. "I appreciate the effort you're going to, but your sneaky little halfling friend is the fugitive on the poster."

"He's not my friend. He's my brother."

"Impossible."

"I know it sounds strange," said Katherine. "And I don't have time to explain it right now, but I need you to believe me."

Captain Righteous looked at her with now nakedly sympathetic eyes. "Against all logic and reason, I nearly do believe you. But your claim is preposterous."

"I also sense no falsehood," said one of the bearded elves. "There is a way to verify the truth of the young half-elf's claim."

After a twenty minute walk through a quaint little village, past gardens practically bursting at the seams with fruit and vegetables, they came to a pleasant little cottage. The elf who'd led them there guided them through the door, then followed them inside and shut the door behind him. Butterbean and Bingam remained outside.

The elf looked at Katherine, his wizened eyes stern and serious. "What do you think of my beard?"

"It looks like your face is trying to shit out a squirrel tail." Katherine gasped in horror at what she'd just said. "What the fuck is wrong with me? I'm so sorry! I didn't..." The words slurred in her mouth until she finally spat out, "I meant every single word of that. It truly gives me the creeps, and I totally want to reach over right now and rip it off your chin." She clapped both hands over her mouth.

The elf smiled. "Excellent. It would appear the Zone of Truth is in working order." He turned to Captain Righteous. "Is there something you want to say to the young lady?"

Captain Righteous looked into Katherine's eyes. "With every ludicrous word that comes out of your mouth, I inexplicably find myself more and more attracted to you."

Katherine had thought she couldn't be more uncomfortable than she was right after the squirrel tail thing. She was mistaken.

The elf frowned. "Perhaps a question? Something about her brother?"

Captain Righteous's panicked eyes regained their seriousness. "Is your brother the halfling pictured in the poster?"

"Yes, he is," said Katherine. "Now you know I'm telling the truth. Please don't waste any more of my time asking me to explain it right now."

"Very well. But if you're so worried about your brother, why would you lead me straight to him?"

"Because I believe you have the means to get me to the Crescent Shadow, and because I have every intention of giving you the slip again once I've rescued him." Katherine didn't mind semi-voluntarily vomiting out these truths. The captain should expect that much from her, and this was his best shot at nabbing Tim.

"My heart is torn between love and duty," said the captain. "And I really want to get out of this house."

Katherine nodded vigorously. "Agreed."

The elf, Captain Righteous, and Katherine shuffled silently in single-file through the door like it was a fire drill.

"Looks like rain," said the captain, peering up into the cloudless expanse of blue sky.

"Indeed it does," said Katherine. Both of them breathed a sigh of relief.

Bingam glanced up confusedly at the sky, then looked at his uncle. "That didn't take long. What did you talk about?"

"NOTHING!" said Captain Righteous and Katherine simultaneously.

"Gildon," Captain Righteous addressed the elf. "In the name of King Winston, I demand escort to the Crescent Shadow."

The elf nodded. "Yes, I thought you might." He started walking and waved for them to come along. "Follow me to the stables."

Half an hour later they were up to their waists in pineapples in a giant wicker basket.

"Must we fill the basket with pineapples?" Captain Righteous asked Gildon. "They are very uncomfortable to travel with, and we would like to waste as little time as possible."

Gildon continued to gesture for his farm workers to dump their sacks of pineapples into the basket. "We have the best chance of the Crescent Shadow coming this way if we offer the inhabitants a shipment of pineapples."

"Why can't we just go to them?" asked Katherine.

"Even unburdened, the pegasi would be unlikely to find the island before falling out of the sky from exhaustion and dehydration. The only way to get there is for them to come to us. The best way to make that happen is to offer them pineapples."

"They're itchy!" whined Bingam. "Why can't we just make the offer, then explain that we had to deceive them on account of this being an emergency?"

Gildon glared severely down at Bingam. "The Druids of Minswater spread no falsehoods. And the wizards who inhabit the Crescent Shadow are valued customers. They pay triple what the Cardinian's pay for produce."

"What's a pegasi?" asked Katherine.

Gildon pressed his lips together like he didn't have time for her silly questions. "A pegasi is nothing. The word is the plural form of pegasus."

"Oh right. Like a winged horse?"

Gildon raised his eyebrows down at her. "I don't recommend you let them hear you refer to them as such while they're carrying you five hundred feet above the ground."

"Oh shit, sorry." Katherine knew that the next question out of her mouth was going to come off as another stupid one, but she needed to know if it was stupid because the answer was Of course! or Of course not! "So... they can talk?"

"They have a language of their own," said Gildon, surprisingly non-condescendingly. "They can't speak like you or I can speak, but they understand much of our language. Sometimes more than they let on, so mind your tongue."

When the last sack was dumped, they were up to their chests in pineapples. Butterbean, being forced to lie naked on top of them in order to not be buried alive, had the worst of it until Captain Righteous offered what remained of his cloak as a cushion. Katherine was touched by the gesture, but kept her 'thank you' as formally polite as she could.

The stable doors opened, and four pegasi strutted out toward the basket. Two were black, and two were white. Even folded up on their backs, their wings were enormous, boasting feathers as long as Katherine's forearms. They were magnificent and proud creatures. Katherine was completely awed by them. She had to stop herself from objecting when two of those bearded elves strapped offensively ordinary-looking leather harnesses around their shoulders, backs, and bellies.

A large steel ring hung from the bottom of the harnesses,

identical to the large steel rings at the top of each corner of the basket they were standing in. Katherine's guts twisted inside her as the realization of what was about to happen really hit home. She was about to be lifted into the air in a wicker basket by four goddamn flying horses. She really hoped they weren't telepathic as well.

"The Crescent Shadow says your offer pleases them greatly," said a bearded elf younger than Gildon who'd just walked into the stable area through a curtain of grapevines. "They shall arrive momentarily."

Gildon nodded. "Excellent." He stroked one of the black pegasi's manes and fed it a carrot. "This is an extra special delivery, Darius. Slow and steady, understand?"

The pegasus whinnied what Katherine hoped was a yes. He stretched his wings wide and looked eager to take flight. The others seemed restless and ready to go as well.

"I'm having second thoughts," said Katherine. "I don't know if I love my brother this much. I think I want to get –"

A sharp crack of thunder threatened to stop Katherine's already overtaxed heart, and the sky suddenly grew darker.

"What the fuck was that?" Painful as it was half buried in pineapples, Katherine turned around and stood on her tiptoes to peek over the lip of the basket. The barren landscape to the west, beyond the lush orchards, was bleak and featureless except for a wide round shadow. It looked like the opposite of a solar eclipse. A small circle of light at the edge of a larger circle of darkness.

"The Crescent Shadow," said Captain Righteous. He looked up. "I've never seen it in person before."

Katherine followed his gaze to see what was making the shadow. Though she'd already been told, she wasn't prepared for something quite this amazing. It was breathtaking. It was glorious. It was... really fucking high up there.

"Five hundred feet is a lot higher than I imagined. Fuck that. My brother's a big boy. He can take care of himse– SHIT!"

The two black pegasi started flapping at once each of them towing thirty foot long ropes connected to diagonally opposed corners of the basket, which jolted upward about a foot when the slack ran out.

Katherine frantically started trying to dig herself out of her uncomfortable tropical tomb while pleading with the two white pegasi. "Please don't go. Please don't go. Please don't – FUCK!"

The white pegasi launched themselves into the air and flapped their massive wings hard. The basket jerked up again, then began to rise more steadily. It lifted out of the surrounding platform and that was that. They were officially in the air.

"You look nervous," said Captain Righteous.

"No shit."

"Would you like to hold my hand?"

Katherine grabbed the captain's hand and squeezed it. The same logic that told her that these pegasi had probably hauled this giant fruit basket up to that flying island a thousand times without incident also told her that holding Captain Righteous's hand would provide her zero additional safety. And yet she was still terrified and desperately wanted something to hold on to.

"Will you hold my hand too?" asked Bingam. Katherine hoped that he was talking to his uncle, but Captain Righteous was looking at her. Shit. She turned to Bingam, who had an equally terrified look on his face and his hand stretched out to her. He had some nerve, after the way he'd treated her. She had half a mind to tell him to stick his hand up his ass. But she accepted his plump sweaty meatglove.

Her contempt for Bingam had just about fully distracted Katherine from her flying anxiety, but as soon as she took his hand, the basket started turning over. The top layer of pineapples rolled and collected in the corner opposite Katherine's.

"SHIT! SHIT! SHIT! SHIT! SHIT!" Katherine cried as the rolling pineapples piled closer and closer to the top of the dipping corner of the basket. "WE'RE GOING TO DIE!"

"Please, Miss Katherine," said Captain Righteous. "It's just one of the pegasi conserving its energy by flying closer to the center. See?" He looked directly up.

The black pegasus in the front was flying almost directly overhead, while the other three remained wide apart.

Katherine looked back at the captain. "Conserving energy?"

He smiled at her reassuringly. "We're going to be fine. Though I may never use a sword again."

Katherine looked down at his hand, which she was squeezing the shit out of, but didn't ease up on it in the slightest. "How is that conserving energy? It's still carrying the same amount of weight."

"I'm afraid the technical aspects are beyond my ability to explain. Perhaps you can ask the pegasi once we land."

"I think I know more physics than a goddamn horse," said Katherine. "And I think they're just trying to fuck with us because they're –"

A large blob of grass-speckled shit splattered on the piled up pineapples in the corner.

"That son of a bitch!" Katherine looked up as the basket started to even out again. The pegasus which had been 'conserving its energy' was now returning to its original place in the formation. "That was meant for me, wasn't it?"

"Gildon warned you that they don't like to be called horses."

Katherine shouted at the pegasus who tried to shit on her. "You missed me, asshole!"

The basket immediately started tilting again, and Katherine remembered her circumstances. She grasped at straws for a way to spin what she'd just said into something less offensive.

"I was talking to your actual asshole, so there's nothing to get offended about!"

The pegasus neighed and started flying outward again. Katherine couldn't believe that worked. She'd have to tell Julian about that feat of Diplomacy if she lived to see him again.

Almost just as soon as the basket finished fully evening out, it began to tilt in the opposite direction. Katherine was losing altitude. Her corner was dipping now.

"NO! NO! NO! NO! NO! NO!"

To make matters worse, all the pineapples that were piled up in the opposite corner were now barreling right at her.

Because she'd apparently pissed off a vengeful god, those pineapples were now splattered in pegasus shit.

"NO! NO! NO! NO! AAUUUGGGHHH!" She could have shielded herself from a significant amount of prickly shit-covered pineapple skin punching her in the face, but that would have involved letting go of her death grip on Captain Righteous's and Bingam's hands. She endured the pineapples.

When the pegasus in Captain Righteous's corner took its turn, the captain got a little green in the face, but held his shit together admirably, even if he did return Katherine's hand squeeze to the point of nearly cracking her bones.

Bingam's turn was not so dignified. He slathered the pineapples near his face with vomit. Katherine suspected he'd probably also soiled the ones underneath with urine, but she couldn't blame him. The only one who seemed to be calmly enjoying the ride was Butterbean, who seemed blissfully unaware that he was flying several hundred feet in the air as he rolled back and forth on a wave of pineapples.

After a few more dips, swings, turns, and lurches, Katherine felt a small jolt from below. Something had jostled the basket. Katherine hoped that it wasn't some angry-ass dragon or something. Not being able to see anywhere but straight up, she looked for a clue as to what was going on. The pegasi were tightening their formation, flying as closely as they could without batting their wings against each others'. It didn't look like a defensive formation to Katherine, but she didn't know shit about what a defensive formation was supposed to look like.

The basket hung low beneath them, the four ropes it was

suspended from hanging nearly vertical. And then Katherine saw the last thing in the world she expected to see. A tree branch. Unless this was the tallest fucking tree in the world, that had to mean they were close to solid ground.

The basket jolted again, harder this time. It came to rest with a thud that really pushed the pineapple spikes hard through her cloak and into her skin. The pain was a price she was more than happy to pay for a safe landing.

The ropes slackened as the pegasi descended to a landing platform very much like the one at the elf village five hundred feet below them.

A group of humans and elves, all dressed in vividly colored robes, approached eagerly from all sides of the platform. They're expressions faltered as they looked down into the basket. Their produce orders were no doubt usually cleaner and less infested with people and wolves than this one.

"Hello," said Katherine, which prompted no change in the puzzled looks on their faces. "Were you not expecting us?"

"I was expecting you!" said a cheerful half-elf, peeking over the edge. He was dressed in sequined blue robes and a matching floppy hat. "As is your halfling friend!"

"Tim! He's here?" Katherine squeezed Captain Righteous's hand again, then realized that she no longer needed to be holding it, and remembered his relationship to her brother. She let go of his hand.

"He's been eagerly awaiting you. Please follow me."

Bingam, naturally, was the first one out of the basket. Katherine was a little more surprised to see that Captain Righteous climbed out before she did. That was until he knelt and offered his hand to assist her. Even if he was actively trying to arrest her brother, Katherine thought a lot of guys back home could learn a lot from him. She accepted his offer with her right hand, and picked out a relatively clean pineapple with her left.

The original greeting team busily got to their tasks of rinsing off and unloading pineapples.

While Captain Righteous helped Butterbean out of the basket, Katherine walked over to Darius, the pegasus which had tried to shit on her head.

"I'm sorry about that horse remark," she said.

Darius sighed through his nostrils.

"I was scared. I didn't mean anything by it. Even among other pegasi, you're a beautiful creature. I want to thank you for taking care of us." Katherine raised her hand to stroke his face, but waited for permission.

He pressed his face against her hand and nickered softly.

"I've got something for you." Katherine held up the pineapple she'd swiped from the basket.

Darius was clearly interested, but glanced back at the people unloading the rest of the pineapples.

Katherine smiled. "Don't worry. I stole it. You didn't."

That was all the rationalization he needed, apparently. He bit into the fruit, his teeth tearing through the tough rind with ease.

"Please hurry along, miss," said the half-elf in the blue robes. "The halfling requires your assistance."

Katherine gave Darius's nose a final rub, said a quick goodbye, and followed the half-elf out of the pegasus landing and into a luxuriously lit corridor lined with smooth white granite. "Is he okay?"

"He's quite well, miss. Just in a spot of legal trouble."

"I can believe that," said Captain Righteous, but there was no hint of pleasure in his tone. He was still torn.

Katherine didn't want to use his feelings for her as leverage, but she felt she owed him her sincerity. "I appreciate you helping me, but I want you to know it's every man for himself from here on out. I don't want to fight you, but I didn't come all this way for you to arrest my brother."

Captain Righteous gave a small nod as he continued looking and walking forward.

The half-elf stopped and sniffed the air. He turned around

and grimaced in Katherine's direction. "Perhaps you'd like to freshen up before we proceed?"

"Yes!" said Bingam. Katherine and Captain Righteous nodded politely.

The half-elf turned a corner and led them into a large circular room lined with doors at the far end. Each door had a glowing stone above it. All glowed green but the two on the far left, which glowed red. "This is the lavatory chamber. You will find everything you need inside. Running water, chamber pots..." His smile flickered when his eyes landed on Katherine. "Soap."

"This is pegasus shit, just so you know." As soon as she said it, she realized he might have been referring to the bladeblack.

"Feel free to use any of the green-lit rooms. The red light means it's occupied."

Bingam hurried to a green-lit door, slipped inside, and shut the door behind him. A few seconds later, the light above the doorway changed from green to red.

"You are most generous, sir," said Captain Righteous. He stepped into a room, and the light above his door changed colors shortly afterward.

"That's really cool," said Katherine. She led Butterbean into one of the unoccupied rooms. It was the first bathroom she'd found in this world that wasn't completely primitive by her modern standards. Most of them were just a hole in the floor. But this had what appeared to be an actual sink with a faucet. There were no knobs, but there was a chain hanging from the ceiling. She gave it a tug.

The entire bathroom disappeared around her, leaving behind a steel cage about the size of two refrigerators. A breeze blew through the bars. All sides but the one she'd walked in through were exposed to the outside. The bars making up the floor of the cage were closer together than the bars making up the walls and ceiling, but five hundred feet of open space was clearly visible between herself and the desert ground below. She was on the underside of the Crescent Shadow.

"What the fuck?" Katherine turned around. The door was still there, unnaturally smooth and white against its rough stone surroundings. She tried the handle, but the door didn't budge. It didn't even rattle. It was as though it wasn't even a door, but merely the form of a door carved into the rock and painted white.

Suddenly, with a loud mechanical churning sound from above, the door handle began to rise in her hands. No, that wasn't quite right. Taking in the larger picture, it became clear that she was being lowered.

What also became clear was that the side of her cage facing the door had no bars at all. There was nothing on that side to keep her and Butterbean from splattering all over the desert floor. She let go of the handle like she just realized it was a snake.

As the cage continued to descend, Katherine pressed her back against he barred wall opposite the open lack of wall and kept her left arm wrapped tight around Butterbean as she kept her right hand gripped on one of the bars.

Wanting to look any way but down, she looked left and right. There were chains on either side of her. Following one of them down about twenty feet, she saw that it ended supporting a cage identical to the one she was descending in. The same was true for the cage on her other side.

When her cage reached the level of the others, it stopped. Captain Righteous was likewise caged on her left, as was Bingam one cage beyond him. On her right, interestingly enough, was...

"Chaz?"

His eyes were glazed over, like he had been here so long that he was now too exhausted to continue being terrified. When Katherine spoke his name, his eyes focused on her.

"Kat?" He blinked a couple of times, then squinted at her. "Are you wearing blackface?"

"No!" said Katherine. "Kinda. But it was for a good reason.

I'll explain later. Who's that in the cage on the other side of you?"

Chaz glanced back at the cage Katherine had indicated. "Oh, that's... DAVE!"

The figure who Katherine hadn't been able to identify sat bolt upright. It was indeed Dave. "Wha? Fuck!" "You have got to stay awake, man!" said Chaz. "If you roll over in your sleep, you're not going to fucking wake up again."

"How long have you two been here?" asked Katherine.

Chaz shrugged. "About a day, I think. Maybe two. It all kind of blurs together when you're dying of dehydration, sleep deprivation, and constant terror."

"Who did this to you?"

Chaz nodded past the open side of his cage. "He did."

Katherine looked through her missing wall and saw the half-elf in the blue robes stepping out from a hole in the rock onto a small rocky platform.

"Good evening!" the half-elf called out. He was only about thirty feet away from them, but the wind was blowing strong.

"Who are you?" shouted Katherine. "Where's my br–" She stopped herself. "Where's my halfling friend?"

"He'll be along shortly. Just as soon as the rest of your friends arrive."

"Do you know who I am?" said Captain Righteous. He didn't need to shout. His natural voice cut through the wind.

"No," the half-elf responded casually.

"My name is Righteous Justificus Blademaster. I am a captain in the Kingsguard. Imprisoning me is an act of treason against the crown."

"Oh!" The half-elf feigned being impressed. "Well do you know who I am?"

"No," admitted Captain Righteous.

The half-elf waved a hand over his face. His eyes were wider apart. His nose turned up slightly higher. His lips were thinner. Even his skin tone was considerably darker. He was still a half-elf, but seemed to be a completely different one. “Then it seems I have nothing to worry about.”

CHAPTER 31

"Before we wander too far into the desert," said Julian, "maybe it would be a good idea to test just how fertile this Fertile Desert is."

They'd already been speedwalking through the desert for about half an hour, anxious about one of those bearded elves catching up to them and dragging them back into their little slave camp. But no one had followed them, and the village was a hazy blur on the eastern horizon.

Stacy took off her bag and set it down on the dry sand. "I wouldn't mind a drink. It's amazing how the climate goes from tropical to arid just like that."

Julian shrugged. "Magic."

Cooper pulled the Decanter of Endless Water out of his bag, held it over his head, and let water flow into his giant gaping mouth until he'd had his fill, then passed it to Stacy.

Stacy drank the water greedily, letting it spill down her chin and the front of her clothes. It was hot out there.

Julian had a few sips, but he wasn't feeling the thirst like his friends were. "You too, Ravenus. All that flying is bound to dehydrate you." He held the silver pitcher up to the top of his quarterstaff, where his familiar was perched, and tipped it forward, letting water flow out of it so that Ravenus could drink from it like a water fountain.

"Whoa!" said Cooper.

"Hot damn," said Stacy.

"What?" said Julian. They were looking at his feet. Julian looked down and found that he was standing knee deep in a small watermelon patch. Dark green melons were growing like balloons on vines that were likewise growing like... well, like really fast-growing vines. He stopped pouring, and the melons stopped growing.

"They weren't fucking around with that name," said Stacy. "This place is more fertile than an Alabama middle school."

Julian and Cooper winced at the implication, then Cooper got distracted by something. Judging by the look of bafflement on his face, Julian guessed it was a thought.

"Give me the jug," said Cooper. "I want to try something."

Julian handed over the Decanter of Endless Water.

Cooper turned it over, and the watermelons and vines continued to grow and flourish. Gripping it tight with both hands, he said, "Geyser."

With a sudden rush of water, Julian found himself suddenly tangled in vines, barely able to move or see.

Then the explosions started. They were louder than popping balloons, but not so loud as artillery fire. Maybe they were like landmines; they were immediately followed by an accompanying splatter.

"Cooper!" cried Stacy. "That's enough!"

"Fuck that. This is awesome!"

"We're losing Julian!"

"What? Oh shit."

When the sound of rushing water stopped, so did the explosions. Julian lay still in the darkness of his cocoon of watermelon vines, unable to move his arms or legs.

"Come on, Cooper," said Stacy. "You can do better than that. Why don't you go at those vines like you went at all of those people you had piled up by the sewer?"

"That wasn't me. It was Nabi. If these were evil watermelon vines, she might be a little more motivated."

Wait a second. Was he...

"Cooper!" cried Julian. "Are you trying to chop me out of here with an axe?"

"Um... yes."

"Well please stop that. The vines are loosening up on their own." They were. It hadn't been but a minute since he'd been immobilized by vines, but he'd already regained quite a bit of mobility in his arms and legs. Sunlight was peeking through from above as well. The vines were withering around him.

After a few more minutes of struggling, He had torn himself completely free and was able to peek out the top of the nest of vines and leaves that had swallowed him up.

Cooper and Stacy were a good ten feet away from him, so Cooper wasn't actually within threat-of-dismemberment range. They were covered in pink slime and chunks, which Julian first thought was the remains of whoever had been stepping on all the landmines. Then he saw the withering husks of watermelons which had grown to the size of Volkswagen Beetles before the rinds had reached their thresholds of rapid expansion. Cooper was right. That would have been pretty badass to watch.

"Can we try that again?" asked Julian. "But this time, I want to stand over –"

Thunder cracked in the sky, like a lightning bolt had hit Julian directly in the eardrum. He dropped to his knees with his hands clapped over his stupidly sensitive ears.

He regained his vision before his hearing, and saw that there was something big between himself and the sun. It was moon-shaped. But it couldn't have been a moon. It was only five hundred feet off the ground, and moons aren't moon-shaped anyway.

Had Randy's New God sent them a massive holy crescent roll for wandering the desert for forty minutes? Stop thinking stupid things, Julian. Get your head in the game.

" – THE FUCK IS THAT?" asked Cooper as Julian's hearing returned.

"What do you think it is?" said Stacy. "It's just what we've been looking for. It's the Crescent Shadow."

That seemed painfully obvious now that she mentioned it.

Julian was happy he hadn't voiced his holy crescent roll theory aloud.

"How the hell are we going to get up there?" asked Stacy.

"HEY!" Cooper shouted at the island in the sky. "COULD YOU COME DOWN HERE FOR A SECOND?"

"There's no way they can hear you all the way up there," said Julian. "Maybe they've got a rope or something? I could ask Ravenus to fly up there and get them to drop something down."

Cooper shook his head. "I can't climb a goddamn five hundred foot rope."

"Well maybe they've got something set up so we just have to hold on and they can reel us in. I mean, people have to get up and down from there somehow, right?"

"Maybe they use four pegasi towing a basket," suggested Stacy.

Julian sighed. "That's not super helpful. You see, a rope is a thing that people sometimes actually have. Let's start with the simplest potential solutions first, then work our way outward to – Oh, look at that. That's actually a thing."

Looking past Stacy's smug expression, Julian saw four winged horses launching out of Minswater with a large basket hanging below them.

Cooper waved his arms. "HEY! WE NEED A LIFT!"

"Maybe we can get a ride up in one of those?" Stacy sounded doubtful.

"We don't have time to go back," said Julian. "Think about it. Those pegasi were all hitched up and ready to go. The island showed up here specifically to receive whatever is in that basket. Once the delivery is made, it's going to go back to wherever it came from." That was, of course, the situation they had just been in a few minutes ago, but it seemed somehow a lot more hopeless now.

Cooper and Stacy frowned, sharing Julian's sense of hopelessness. Then Cooper's eyes lit up. Was it even possible that he could have two profound thoughts so close together?

"We can set the watermelon vines on fire!"

Julian supposed that, no, it wasn't possible. He also mused that he may have been generous in referring to Cooper's idea of making giant watermelons explode as "profound".

"They're all dried out now," Cooper continued to try to justify his idea. "They'll light up easily."

"But what's the point?" asked Stacy. "How is burning watermelon vines going to get us up to that island?"

"Smoke signal," said Cooper. "If we can get those fuckers to look down here, we might be able to get them to throw down a... Oh right. Shit. Sorry."

Julian shook his head. "Don't be sorry. We're brainstorming and the clock is ticking. Spit out whatever you've got. No idea is too stupid. No thought too –" Julian bit his lower lip and looked up at the chunk of rock flying so high above them, then down at Cooper. "Cooper, you're a genius."

"Fuck you, dude."

"No, I mean it!" Julian dug deep into his pockets and pulled out fistfuls of bean pods. "Look at this!"

Cooper frowned. "Yay."

Stacy's eyes widened in sudden realization and terror. She looked up at the Crescent Shadow. "No fucking way."

"It's the only fucking way," said Julian. The pegasi had reached the island. The cargo was no doubt being unloaded. Their time was running out. "You can't honestly tell me you want to live the rest of your life knowing you didn't at least try this."

"Goddamn, Julian," said Cooper. "How good could those fucking beans be? Let me try one." He reached out to grab one.

"No!" said Julian, yanking his hands away.

"Fuck you, dude," Cooper said again. "I'm gonna fart whether I eat the fucking beans or not."

"They're not for eating. Think Jack."

Cooper snorted.

Julian sighed. "My fault. Poor choice of words. How about this. Jack and the..."

"Jackin' the taco with sour cream," said Cooper. "I fucking get it, man. There's only so much privacy I can give you two out here. You want me to turn around or something?"

Stacy looked mortified. "Jacking the taco with sour cream? Is that a thing people say?"

Julian spread his beans out on the dirt, and dug through his pockets to find any he'd missed. "Cooper, I need you to use your Decanter of Endless Water and hit these beans with everything you've got."

Cooper frowned at the circle of beans on the ground, then looked at the withering mass of watermelon vines, then up at the Crescent Shadow. "Oh fuck yes!"

Julian smiled at Stacy. "See, Cooper thinks it's a good idea."

"It's like that story," Cooper said excitedly. "You know, the one with the giant and the duck that shits gold. I can't remember what it's called."

The Crescent Shadow might disappear at any second. It was now or never.

"Come on, Cooper," said Julian. "Hurry up!"

Cooper held the Decanter of Endless water over the beans. "You guys ready?"

Julian and Stacy shook their heads.

"Do it," said Julian.

Cooper turned the decanter upside down. As the first of the water hit the seeds, he shouted, "GEYSER!"

The ground trembled beneath their feet. Then something like a green leafy dick shot out of the ground and into the air. Two dozen or more stalks, all twisted together, wrapping around and supporting each other. Julian grabbed a stalk and shot skyward. Leaves and pods sprouted out of the vines, some growing bigger than he was, as he climbed higher and higher into the air.

"This is the best thing ever!" cried Stacy, a few yards below

Julian and climbing up to meet him. "I want to do this every day!"

They'd made it to about sixty percent of the way to the Crescent Shadow when the conglomeration of stalks began to tilt sideways.

"Oh shit!" said Julian. "Oh shit! Oh shit! Oh shit!"

"Wrap your arms up in the vines!" said Stacy. "We'll be okay!"

She was right. It wasn't a free fall. They were falling fast enough for it to hurt when they landed, but at least they'd probably survive. Still, it was frustrating. They were so close!

"I should have grabbed more beans," said Julian.

Stacy smiled at him sympathetically. "You couldn't have known."

They were upside down and heading straight down toward the desert floor when they passed Cooper heading in the opposite direction on the still-growing beanstalk.

"What the fuck?" asked Cooper. The spray from the Decanter of Endless Water almost knocked Julian off the stalk. "You're going the wrong way!"

"Look!" said Stacy. She was looking at the ground.

Before Julian had a chance to figure out what she was referring to, she let go of their part of the stalk and leaped onto the part which was still heading upward and started climbing after Cooper.

"Well, shit." Julian had no intention of trying to make a jump like that. He was still confident that he wasn't falling fast enough to die when he hit the ground, especially with all the new vegetation growing in a wide circumference at the base of the stalk. The higher Cooper took the Decanter of Endless Water, the wider the spread and gentler the spray. Where Julian was now, it just felt like a summer shower, rather than a fire hose.

"FUUUUUUUUUUUUUUUCK!" Cooper's voice grew louder from above as Julian prepared for impact.

"YEE HAAAAW!" cried Stacy.

Julian looked up and saw Cooper and Stacy sliding down the stalk toward him. Stacy was holding the decanter, which had been deactivated.

When they reached Julian, Stacy re-wrapped her left arm in vine from wrist to elbow, then turned to Julian and Cooper. "You're gonna really want to hold on this time." She took aim at the massively thick base of the stalk. "GEYSER!"

Dust clouds erupted around the base as new stalks sprouted and wrapped themselves around the rest, further reinforcing the structural integrity of the collective multi-stalk.

The top of the stalk, on which they were riding, slowed in its descent until it stopped altogether, then started ascending.

"FUUUUUUUUUUUUUUUCK!" cried Cooper again.

"Cooper wasn't keeping the full force of the water on the beanstalk," Stacy explained as they continued to climb higher and higher. "The higher up he went, the more water sprayed all over the place, and the less fed into the stalk." As they climbed, Stacy kept the Decanter of Endless water focused on the center of the stalk, so that most of the water flowed down its length and continued to feed it.

"We're actually going to make it!" said Julian. The stalk had straightened itself and they were still climbing, albeit slower than they had been.

"I don't know," said Stacy. "It's going to be close. Even at geyser setting, this thing isn't putting out enough water to keep us going up indefinitely."

The rocky bottom of the island was almost close enough to touch, but they were climbing more and more slowly. Julian felt the the tiniest hint of a sway. The ride up had been anything but steady, and the tilt was only a few centimeters. It was nothing he would have noticed under normal circumstances, but riding a beanstalk at four hundred and fifty feet in the air had given him an acute sensitivity to such changes.

"We're not going to make it."

"Like fuck we aren't!" said Cooper. He'd pulled a coil of rope out of his bag. "Julian! Get Ravenus to tie us off on that guard rail."

"He's a bird!" said Julian. "He doesn't know how to tie knots!"

"Then what the fuck good is he?"

"We're going to fall!" cried Stacy. "Hurry up!"

"Ravenus!" Julian called out.

"Right here, sir." He perched on a curl of stalk hanging down near Julian's head.

"Do you know how to tie a knot?"

"I don't think so, but I'd love to learn."

"Another time maybe. I need you to take the end of Cooper's rope and try to secure it to that railing up there. Can you do that?"

"I can do my best, sir!" Ravenus flew up to Cooper and snatched up the end of the rope in his talons while Julian prepared for another nosedive toward the ground.

When Ravenus reached the railing, he didn't have enough slack in the rope to tie a knot even if he knew how.

"It was a good try," said Julian. "But he can't pull us up there."

"He might not have to." Stacy's eyes looked surprisingly hopeful as she stared at something beyond Julian. "Look!"

Julian looked up. The uppermost part of the stalks, too thin to support their weight, found Cooper's stretched out rope and began to twist around it like a pack of snakes scurrying up a tree. They braided themselves all the way up to the railing, then wrapped around it, sprouting new leaves and pods.

"Do you think that will hold us?" asked Julian.

Stacy wrapped her legs around her section of stalk, deactivated the Decanter of Endless Water, and drew her sword. "We're about to find out." She hacked at the stalk below her. One by one, individual stalks made snapping sounds as her sword relieved their tensile stress.

Cooper grabbed Julian's wrist. "Guys, I know I'm not too bright. But this feels like a really dumb thing to do."

Julian grabbed Stacy by the decanter-holding arm, leaving her sword arm free to continue hacking. He looked up. The vines looked like they'd support their weight, but it wasn't something he was keen to test.

HACK HACK SNAP

And just like that, they were hanging from a flying rock five hundred feet in the air by the will of a few bean vines. The stalk fell away and began a slow-motion collapse.

Julian's arms were stretched between Cooper and Stacy. He supposed he was grateful that Cooper wasn't the one below him, lest his arms be pulled out of their shoulder sockets. He voiced a concern which he sincerely hoped Stacy had thought of before chopping away their best chance of not dying. "So... What happens now?"

"I'll have to climb up," said Stacy. "Sorry, Cooper. But I need to drop the Decanter of Endless Water."

"Fuck that," said Cooper. "I've got a better idea."

Three ideas in a row from Cooper was just asking for trouble. As Julian's eyes focused on a small leaf, it withered and died in front of him. Oh fuck. "Cooper, no!"

"I'm really angry!" shouted Cooper. His grip on Julian's arm felt like a malfunctioning blood pressure monitor.

Before Julian knew what was happening, he and Stacy were flung upward like a couple of rag dolls. Completely weightless. Falling free. Landing hard on polished marble.

"Ow," said Julian.

"Cooper!" cried Stacy, scrambling to her feet then running for the railing. Julian got to his feet and ran after her.

The vines holding the rope to the railing were drying out and turning brown. Their leaves were wilting and the pods were dropping off one by one.

Just as the vines started to snap, Stacy grabbed the rope with both hands. Julian grabbed her.

"Cooper!" Stacy grunted. "You're too heavy! Come out of your rage!"

"I'm cool!" said Cooper. "Cool cool cool. Totally fucking cool. Never been calmer."

Stacy breathed easier and pulled back on the rope. Satisfied that Cooper wasn't going to send her flying over the side, Julian let go of her and helped pull the rope. Cooper climbed over the impressively well-crafted railing, and onto the relative safety of the flying island.

"That was quite the entrance," said a young half-elf in blue sequined robes standing casually by a doorway on the other side of the little patio area they now found themselves in.

"You could have helped," said Stacy.

"The Crescent Shadow is an exclusive community. The wizards who live here are not often receptive to intruders. If your halfling friend hadn't intervened on your behalf, or if you hadn't been so entertaining to watch, they might have Fireballed you out of the sky."

"Our halfling friend?" said Julian. "Tim's actually here!" He suddenly realized he'd just gone through a whole lot of effort to now be surprised that it wasn't all for nothing.

"Oh yes," said the half-elf. "He's been hoping you'd arrive. Would any of you care to use the lavatory before you meet him?"

"Thank you," said Julian. "That would be lovely." He hadn't had a lot to drink, but after a traumatic experience like the one they'd just gone through, he'd take whatever kind of release he could get.

"I could stand to freshen up," said Stacy. She was still sticky with watermelon juice.

"I relieved myself quite a bit on the way up here," said Cooper. "As a matter of fact, I may never need to shit again."

Julian, Stacy, and the half-elf who greeted them stared blankly at Cooper.

"I guess I could wash my hands or something."

CHAPTER 32

Katherine had no doubt that the beanstalk gambit was the work of someone she knew, but it was happening too far away for anyone to see who was on it, or if they had successfully managed to make it onto the Crescent Shadow. But she remained optimistic. The odds of them being rescued had just taken a sudden spike.

Those odds took another nosedive a short while later, however, when Cooper, Julian, and Stacy were lowered down in cages.

"Katherine!" said Julian through the bars of the right side of his cage. "Dave! Chaz!"

Dave and Chaz nodded. Katherine said, "Hey."

Stacy looked at Katherine with unmasked disgust. "Why do you look like you just got out of a minstrel show?"

"Whoa!" said Cooper before Katherine could repeat an explanation that sounded dumber every time she said it. "Let's not go there, huh?"

Katherine hadn't expected Cooper to stand up for her like that. "It's okay, Cooper. It was a fair question."

"It's just part of your nature. It's nothing you need to answer for."

Cooper's enthusiastic support was beginning to turn sour.

"I'm surprised at you," Stacy told Cooper. "I know you're friends, but –"

"Seriously, Cooper," said Katherine. "What's wrong with you?"

"What the actual fuck is going on here?"

"You see nothing wrong with me covering my face and

hands in black makeup?"

Cooper frowned. "Now that you mention it, that is kind of fucked up. But what does that have to do with menstruating?"

The wind filled a sudden lull in the conversation.

"Can we get back to more immediate concerns?" asked Julian. "In case none of you have noticed, we're in open cages hanging from an island flying five hundred feet above the ground."

Katherine hugged Butterbean. "We might have more immediate concerns than that. Chaz and Dave have been here for a day or two already, and they may be dying of thirst."

"Coop's got you covered, guys," said Cooper. "Open wide, Dave!"

For what must have been the hundredth time, Julian shouted, "Cooper! No!" just a little too late.

Dave took an initial blast of water to the face, but the stream went wild very quickly, giving everyone a nice showery mist. Steel clanged against steel as Cooper's cage slammed into Stacy's, knocking her out the open side.

Julian pressed his face against the bars and screamed, "Stacy!"

Fortunately, Stacy had managed to grab hold of the bottom of the cage.

Julian's shoulders sagged with what looked like exhausted relief. Then he tensed up again and screamed, "Shit!" as the spray of water swung counter-clockwise, and Cooper's cage came at Julian's like a speeding freight train.

CRASH

Katherine felt something besides mist on her face. She wiped some of the moisture from her cheek and rubbed it between her fingers. Grit. She looked up and saw tiny pieces of rock shaking loose from the hole Cooper's chain fed out from.

"Cooper!" shouted Katherine. "Turn that thing off!"

The water stopped gushing, and Cooper held on tight to the bars of his cage until the swinging lessened. He tipped the Decanter of Endless Water over and poured a normal stream onto the bars making up the floor of his cage. The water dripping from the bottom of the cage was distinctly browner.

"I honestly thought I'd gotten it all out of me."

While Stacy climbed back into her cage, Katherine shook her head at Cooper. "If we survive this, I'm taking that back."

"That's a big if," said a high pitched voice from the observation platform that faced the open sides of their cages. Halfling? Tim?

She had one guess out of two correct. A halfling stood in front of the hole leading into the interior of the island. He wore a bright red hooded cloak. Katherine was reminded of Little Red Riding Hood, and she'd had just about all the fairy tale references she could handle for one day.

"Who the fuck are you?"

"Is this the halfling who's been expecting us?" asked Captain Righteous. He sounded disappointed.

The halfling curtsied. "You may call me Wister."

"Mordred!" Dave wheezed through his dry throat.

Wister rolled his eyes. "Fine, if you insist on breaking the fourth wall. You know, if you'd remained in character from the beginning, you might not be in the mess you now find yourselves in."

Cooper snorted. "And if your dick had stayed in your mom for half a second longer, you might have a twelve-fingered kid."

"Whoa!" said Julian. "Hey now. Let's everyone just calm down a little."

"Don't count on your Diplomacy skill to get you out of this one, Julian," said Mordred. "Given what we've been through, do you have any idea what the Difficulty Class for a Diplomacy check is between you and me?"

"You and me specifically? I thought we were cool."

Mordred smiled. "We are most certainly not cool. Some day you will learn that your actions have consequences."

The last thing Katherine needed was a dad lecture from a pompous nerd. "Where is my brother, asshole?"

"He's right back there," said Mordred, gesturing into the hole behind him. "He's been waiting for his friends to come find him. Frankly, I'm surprised any of you bothered to show up."

"That's what friends do, fuckhead," said Cooper. "You might find that out for yourself if you ever have any."

"So says Cooper, the wonderful friend who abandoned Tim on the road south of Cardinia. Oh yes, I know all about that. Tim and I have been doing a lot of talking since he's been here."

"He abandoned me." Cooper frowned. "Well, it was kind of mutual."

"I want to see my brother!" said Katherine.

Mordred sneered at her. "Blood is thicker than water. It was an especially nice touch to bring a captain of the Kingsguard with you to hunt down your fugitive brother."

"It's not like that. I needed his help getting up here. I was going to ditch him as soon as I found Tim." Katherine had no idea why she felt compelled to explain herself to this bag of dicks. She hoped Tim could hear her.

Mordred had already lost interest in her, turning his attention to Julian. "And his good friends Julian and Stacy, constantly parking the beef bus in Tuna Town while poor Tim's been held prisoner here all this time."

Stacy gave him a 'What the fuck?' kind of look. "Does nobody just say fucking anymore?"

"Why are you giving us shit about Tim's woes?" asked Katherine. "What's it to you?"

Mordred rolled his eyes. "You know how he is. Get a little drink in the guy, and you can't shut him up. We've gotten pretty well acquainted over the past few days. I'm almost sorry to have to kill him." He snapped his fingers.

The blue-robed half-elf who'd tricked them into these cages escorted a halfling out onto the observation platform. The halfling was wearing a bag over his head, but those were Tim's clothes all right, down to the pants with the semi-permanent piss stain around the crotch area. He stumbled as they dragged him forward, dropping to his knees at the edge of the platform when they stopped.

"Don't you fucking touch him!" Katherine screamed. She balled up her fist, filled with frustration at her inability to back up the threat.

Mordred stood behind Tim and yanked the bag off his head, removing Katherine's final hope that this all might just be a big bluff. He was gagged, and bruised, and bleeding from his swollen nose. But he was Tim. His wild, terrified eyes locked pleadingly on Katherine's.

She mouthed the words, "I'm sorry."

"What do you want, Mordred?" asked Stacy. She was smart and capable, and Mordred had a thing for her. Katherine would forgive her general bitchiness a thousand times over if she could save her little brother.

Mordred smiled at Stacy. "Interesting. What would you be willing to do to save this little parasite's life? Would you sit by my side as my queen and rule over this world with me?"

Katherine glared at Stacy, prepared to leap from cage to cage and throw that bitch out of hers if she gave the wrong answer.

Stacy looked directly into Mordred's eyes. "Yes, I would."

"Well forget it! You had your chance and you blew it!" He pulled a jewel-hilted dagger out from under his cloak, which Katherine recognized as the one that Tanner had given Tim in the sewer. What the hell had happened to Tanner. If he was here, he'd know what to do. All Katherine could do was try to talk him out of it.

"Tim has a lot of problems," said Katherine. "He's petty, and selfish, and shallow, and generally an all around piece of shit."

Mordred frowned. "Are you sure these are the last words

you want him to hear you say?"

Stay focused, Katherine. This isn't for Tim. This is for Mordred, so that these won't be the last words Tim hears you say. You have to go all in.

"Look at him. He's pathetic. He's a good-for-nothing self-loathing drunk. He's more dried piss and vomit than man. He's never done a worthwhile thing in his entire wasted life. It's all been a series of fuck-ups, each one a little more self-destructive than the last."

Julian cleared his throat. "Um, Katherine..."

Katherine ignored him, staying focused on Mordred. "But you've got everything. You're rich and powerful. You've got a whole world that you're going to rule. You're literally living the fucking dream. You can do anything you want. Do you really want to stoop down to his level? Because let me tell you, that path does not lead to greatness. With an entire world at your fingertips, do you really want to go through life knowing that, when you had to choose between being the bigger man and making Tim continue his life of misery while you ascended to glory, or being a cowardly piece of shit who was so afraid of a drunk man-child that you murdered him in cold blood, that you chose the latter?"

Mordred pursed his lips and thought for a moment, then looked back up at Katherine. "Yes, I think I can live with that." He grabbed Tim's hair and pulled his head back.

"I'm warning you, halfling," said Captain Righteous. "Your prisoner is a wanted fugitive. He is to be taken to the king alive. If you –"

"Can it, Captain Cockface. I created you and your stupid king. You'd better keep your mouth shut if you don't want to meet the same fate." Mordred brought the tip of Tanner's dagger to Tim's throat.

Katherine screamed, "NOOOOOO–"

"HORSE!" Julian shouted. A large brown horse appeared on the platform next to Tim and Mordred, silencing everyone for a moment.

Mordred hissed at the horse, which reared up on its hind legs and neighed excitedly. It backed away from Mordred, lost its footing on the edge of the platform, and fell off.

When the sound of equine scream had faded, Mordred cleared his throat. "Let this be a lesson for all of you." He raked the dagger blade across Tim's throat.

Tim's eyes rolled back. Blood spilled down the front of his clothes and spurted out of his neck like crimson ribbons unspooling in the wind.

"TIM!" Katherine cried.

"Do not fuck with the Cavern Master." Mordred kicked Tim in the back as his half-elven companion let go of him. Tim fell forward, right off the edge of the platform.

Katherine squeezed Butterbean as her dead little brother fell out of sight. Hot tears spilled down her cheeks as she considered the final words he'd heard spoken about him. Did he know she was just trying to save him? Or did he die feeling completely and utterly alone?

She felt everyone's eyes on her, watching her cry. But Mordred stared at her with a little smirk on his face.

The tear-well had run dry. Katherine felt her chest seizing up like her heart was turning to stone. She felt her fingernails digging into her palms. She glared at Mordred with dry eyes.

"I'm coming for you. I'm going to kill you so fucking hard that it's going to make today worth it."

Mordred raised his eyebrows as his smirk disappeared. "I hope for your sake that you don't," he said. "Your brother killed me, so I killed him. Now we're square. I'll leave you here to think about whether or not you really want to re-tip the scales." With that, Mordred and his companion walked through the hole in the rock at the back of the platform.

Katherine willed herself to turn into a bat and fly after him. She almost felt like she could, and she came close to trying even though she knew she couldn't.

"Katherine," Dave whispered in his raspy dehydrated voice.

Katherine whipped her head to the right. "What? You want to talk now? I noticed you didn't make a fucking peep while that nerd was murdering my brother."

"Tim will be fine."

Katherine stared at him, dumbfounded by the stupid coming out of his mouth. "Fine? Did you not just see what the rest of us saw?"

"I didn't want to say anything while Mordred was listening. We can take Tim to a temple and get him resurrected."

Katherine's heartbeat quickened like she'd just woken up from a bad dream, and wasn't quite sure if it was real or not. Was Dave right? Didn't they bring that fat chick at the Whore's Head back from the dead? Was it just a matter of money? She could sell her Bag of Holding and her Portable Hole and her Decanter of Endless Water. Tim would be good as new, and they'd have enough left over to get good and shitfaced. She could tell him that she loved him, that she understood he was going through a hard time, and that she'd always be there to protect him like a big sister should.

"Mordred would have anticipated that," said Stacy. "And why did he just kill Tim but not the rest of us? Why would he walk off like a Bond villain and leave us all here in these easily escapable cages?"

Julian looked alert. "Does that mean you have a plan for getting out?"

"Well, no." Stacy leaned back in her cage. "But come on, how hard could it be? We'll think of something."

Katherine's instincts were to lash out at Stacy, but she didn't have the energy. Instead, she thought about what Stacy said. It was peculiar that Mordred would just leave them hanging there, and that he'd overlook something as obvious as them being able to get Tim resurrected. Her heart softened a little as Mordred's motivations started to make sense to her.

"He was just blowing off steam."

Cooper wiped some tears away from his eyes. "That's uncharacteristically understanding of you."

"He wants us to live," said Katherine. "Even Tim. He was just being a dick by killing him, flexing his nerd muscles and all that. But he needs us. All of these people he created, Captain Righteous and Bingam here, none of them are real. No offense."

"None taken," said Captain Righteous. "I honestly have no idea what you're talking about."

"Mordred needs real people, Earth people, to dominate for it to be satisfying. Otherwise he's just the same lonely fat kid he's always been, playing alone with his Star Wars figures in his cat shit-riddled sandbox."

Julian frowned. "That's a very specific image."

Katherine smiled and scratched the back of Butterbean's neck. "I was thinking back to when Tim was a kid."

"Okay," said Stacy. "Now, who's got an idea for getting us the hell out of here?"

Responses were slow-coming. Surprisingly, Cooper was the first one to blurt out an idea.

"We could ride a pegasus."

Julian shook his head. "Why is that everyone's knee-jerk reaction to – Well I'll be damned. Another goddamn pegasus."

Black wings spread wide, the majestic figure of a pegasus glided down from further along the Crescent toward their cages, toward Katherine's cage.

Katherine pressed her face against the bars. "Darius!"

"Oh," said Stacy. "You're acquainted. That's nice."

Darius flew up to Katherine's cage and held as steady as a flying horse was able.

Katherine stroked his cheek. "You came to rescue me?"

Darius neighed and jerked his head sideways.

"Back in the bag, Butterbean." Butterbean, for once, seemed more than happy to comply as she pulled the Bag of Holding down over his head.

Gambling her life on being able to interpret pegasus gestures, Katherine reached around his neck and climbed onto his back.

"I'm going to get Tim's body!" Katherine shouted to everyone.

Dave stood up and grabbed the bars of his cage. "Could you maybe let us out first?"

"I'll be right back!" Katherine hugged Darius around the neck. "Take me down."

CHAPTER 33

"I can't go on no more, Randy! Just go on without me. Leave me here to die."

"You ain't going nowhere anyway," said Randy. "Basil's doing all the work. What difference does it make if you sit on his back or sit on the ground?"

Basil wasn't looking much better than Denise claimed to feel. For an eight-legged lizard, he wasn't a fast mover, but he seemed even more sluggish than before. Randy had healed him as much as he could, but wasn't able to bring his eyes back. He was getting skinnier too.

"I just can't take it no more. I got these little monsters crawlin' around inside me. I can feel their pincers ready to tear me apart from the inside."

"It's only been a couple of days. I don't think their pincers are developed yet. You're just dehydrated is all."

"Then why don't you give me some goddamn water?"

Randy understood Denise's temptation. He wanted nothing more than to guzzle what remained of their water supply right then and there. He'd wrapped his pants around his head like a turban to soak up his sweat, and he was running out of sweat to soak.

"We need to conserve what little water we got. We don't know how much farther we got to walk. Finish those grapes, then I'll give you some more water."

"I can't eat another fuckin' grape that tastes like my own piss. I got special needs now, Randy. I'm having hot flashes and menopauses and shit. Without medical attention, I'm gonna die."

"I'm doing my best, Denise. Just as soon as we get back to town, I'll take you to a healer."

"I don't need no fuckin' Crusades-era witch doctor. I need a goddamn OBJIM."

"Objim?"

"I need ultrasounds and pap smears and epidermals."

"Epidermals?"

"I got eight fuckin' scorpion babies inside me! You best believe I'm gonna be pumped full of drugs when they're ready to –" Denise leaned over and vomited down one of Basil's right middle legs. When it touched the ground, a small plant sprouted up and produced a single jalapeno pepper. For some reason, this prompted Denise to start sobbing.

One puke-flavored pepper between Randy, Denise, and Basil wasn't going to stave off starvation, and something about it had triggered Denise, so Randy decided to let that one go and continue leading Basil across the desert.

"You all right, Denise?"

Denise choked back her sobbing. "Yeah, I just got sand in my eyes is all. Let's talk about something else."

That sounded just fine to Randy. He'd heard as much of Denise's unfamiliarity with gynecology as he could take. "I'm worried about Basil. He ain't ate nothing since Azhar. You complain about the pee grapes, but I can't hardly taste the pee in them. I wouldn't think a basilisk would be so picky."

"This here beast's a carnivore. He don't want no grapes, piss or otherwise. He needs meat."

"Oh, so now I s'pose you're an expert on fantasy wildlife as well. How do you know he's a carnivore?"

"'Cause he ain't eatin' the goddamn piss grapes!"

Randy frowned. Denise made a good point. "I'm sorry, Denise. My tone was out of line. The desert's starting to mess with my head, making me irritable."

"You ain't gotta tell me. If I never set foot in another desert, it'll be too fuckin' soon."

"I'm worried about you, and Basil. And I'm worried on account of what if we been walking in the wrong direction all this time?"

"You ain't got to worry 'bout that," said Denise. She sounded more confident than her previous reasoning should have accounted for.

"I ain't trying to get an attitude with you again, but what makes you so sure we're going the right way."

Denise shrugged. "I ain't. But if we start backtracking now, we'll die long before we get back to where we started. If we made a mistake, it's one we got to stay committed to."

That sounded like a philosophy Dennis had followed throughout his whole life. While Randy questioned that logic in most circumstances, it made sense in this case. There was no point in worrying about things they had no control over. Randy decided to turn the conversation in a more optimistic direction.

"What's the first thing you want to do when we get back to civilization?"

"I'm gonna drink the Whore's Head Inn dry as a fuckin' bone for starters."

Randy frowned. "I don't know if that's such a good idea, considering your condition and all."

"Bullshit," said Denise. "My mamma was drunk as a rat in a gin bottle all through her pregnancy with me, and I turned out just fine."

Randy kept his thoughts on that to himself. "I think being a mom might do you some good."

"Jesus Christ, Randy. Don't say shit like that. I thought we was gonna talk about something other than –"

A sound like the crack of a bullwhip echoed down from the sky as a sudden gust of wind blew dirt into Randy's eyes. When he could see again, there was something in the sky to the east that hadn't been there before. It looked like a flying island. The bottom was rough and rocky, but Randy could make out trees and structures on top of it.

"What is that?" said Randy.

"I don't give a good god damn what it is," said Denise. "It's something other than desert, and that's good enough for me. Get this future luggage set moving."

Randy stroked the loosening dry skin on the basilisk's shoulder. "Come on, Basil. There's something up ahead. We might find you something you can eat."

Basil groaned and kept plodding forward. At the rate they were moving, the floating island didn't seem to be getting any closer. But they must have been, because after a while, Randy thought he could see something beyond the island through the desert haze.

"Denise! I think that's a village up ahead!"

"Sweet." Denise was clearly still more interested in the flying island.

Randy tried to focus on the village, but it was really hazy. He had a sudden worrying thought. "Say, what if this is just another mirage?"

"Clear the shit out your brain, Randy. When folks hallucinate in the desert, they see palm trees and oasises and shimmering pools of water. Or maybe they see their traveling companion turn into a fried chicken leg or some shit. They don't see nothin' like this."

"But what if it ain't a real mirage. What if it's another magic one, and there's more scorpion people trying to lure us in?"

"Then we'd be seeing something more along the lines of a refrigerator full of beer, or big-tittied hookers or something. Ain't no point in tricking us into seeing a giant goddamn island in the sky. We might just as soon run away from it for all they know."

A few seconds later, a massive beanstalk exploded out of the ground, the tip of which was gunning straight for the island.

"On second thought," said Denise. "Maybe we are hallucinating. That's fee-fi-fo-fucked up."

The stalk grew and grew like it was giving all it had to give to reach that island in the sky. But it wasn't quite enough. The desert floor bloomed with all manner of colorful flora around the base of the stalk as it started to wilt.

Then a few minutes later, having got a second wind or something, it shot straight up again. The top of the stalk grow closer and closer to the island.

It was too far away for Randy to tell if it touched the island or not, but a few minutes later it started to fall away. Slowly at first, then faster and faster and –

"Oh shit," said Denise as the shadow of the stalk covered them.

"Come on, Basil!" cried Randy. "Move! Move! Move!"

Basil followed Randy's change in direction, but didn't move any faster.

"FUUUUUUUUU–"

Denise was cut off with an earth-shaking crash and a splatter of lima bean green. She'd been hit with a pod.

"Denise!" cried Randy. "Are you okay?"

The pod split open. The beans inside it had liquefied on impact. Denise was covered in green goop, which flowed out of the pod onto Basil.

"No, I'm not fucking okay. I feel like I just got bukakked by a room full of Jolly Green fuckin' Giants." She spat out liquid bean and wiped it out of her eyes, then tore away the husk of the pod.

They followed the fallen stalk. As they got closer to the base, the village beyond it became clearer through the desert haze. It was real, all right. They'd done it. They were going to survive.

"We're almost there, Basil," said Randy. "You just hang on a little longer and we'll find you a chicken or a rat or something."

"Randy," said Denise. "I don't feel so good."

"Come on, Denise. Hold it together. Don't you go having no scorpion babies out here in the desert. We're almost there."

"It ain't that. I think I just gotta take a shit is all. I ain't had this much fruit in a while, and them piss grapes is doing a number on my insides."

"I reckon we can make it there in under an hour at the pace we're going. You sure you don't want to hold it?"

"Yeah, I'm fuckin' sure. It's not like they gonna have any finer facilities in that shithole village than I got out here. There's enough leaves on this goddamn beanstalk to wipe an army's worth of asses."

"That's true enough. All right. Go take care of business."

"Well thank you for the permission, your holiness." Denise slid down off Basil's back and waddled quickly over to the stalk, pushing her ass cheeks together with her hands. She hadn't been fooling around about needing to go. She stopped when she passed a giant bean pod, much like the one that had landed on her. After a moment of staring at it, she leaned over it and plunged a fist through the top.

"Come on, Denise," said Randy. "One bean pod falls on your head, and now you wanna take it out on all of them? We gotta get you and Basil to town."

"I'm using my head for something other than cock storage. You might want to give that a try some day." Denise shoved her arm elbow deep into the top of the bean pod and wiggled it around. It didn't look particularly violent, but Randy had no idea what she was up to.

When she was done with whatever she was doing, Denise pulled her arm out of the pod and smiled, satisfied at her handiwork. "Now take a look at that. A nice cushioned toilet. I reckon there's no better place in this whole godforsaken world to drop your little brown babies in the well."

Randy put his hands on his hips. "What'd I tell you about that racist talk. Just because you're pregnant don't mean I'll –"

"The fuck you talking about? I was just talking about taking a shit. If you wanna make something racial out of that, maybe that says more about you than it does me. You ever think of that, Saint Randy?"

"Just hurry it up. I'd like to get to the village before dark."

"I don't need an audience. Why don't you go pick some fruit or something?"

Once again, Denise made a solid point. This wasn't something Randy cared to witness. And though many of the plants had withered during their walk, there were still quite a number of shrubs and small trees this close to the base of the stalk, bearing ripe fruits in a variety of shapes and colors. Randy left Basil's side and sought out fruits he'd never seen or tasted before.

If Denise was shy about being watched, she wasn't so much about being heard. No amount of humming to himself could drown out her grunts and groans, or the gushing splatter of shit into hollowed bean pod in prolonged bursts between deep breaths. Those piss grapes really had done a number on her insides.

When she made a sound like a screaming horse, Randy grew concerned. Piss grapes or no piss grapes, that just wasn't normal.

"Denise? Are you o–"

"JESUS FUCKING CHRIST!" screamed Denise.

Randy had turned around just in time to see Denise leaping off her makeshift toilet as an actual horse smashed into it from above. The pod exploded its green and brown liquid contents all over Denise, who appeared otherwise unharmed. The horse, on the other hand, disappeared on impact.

"Denise?"

Denise spat out a cocktail of liquefied bean and shit. "Not a fuckin' word, Randy. Not a goddamn fuckin' word. Just go about your business and let me clean myself off."

Randy nodded and turned around, focusing harder than ever on his search for indigenous fruits while Denise started sobbing again. Sometimes a person just needs time to be alone. He'd be there for her if she needed to talk about it. That was the best he could do.

A few minutes later, while Randy was examining something that looked like a purple artichoke, he was distracted by a distant thud, like something else had fallen from the flying island above them. It sounded too small to be another horse, but Randy would feel safer once they got out from underneath the island.

He didn't bother asking if Denise was okay. She was still crying, but it was consistent with the crying she'd been doing before he heard the sound.

Scanning the area where he thought he'd heard the noise, Randy didn't see anything out of the ordinary, except that Basil appeared to have found something to eat. Maybe he was an omnivore after all, and just didn't care for the taste of piss grapes.

Randy frowned at an alternative theory that popped into his head. Maybe he'd grown so hungry that he was now eating things his body wasn't meant to digest. Given Denise's gastrointestinal issues with grapes, Randy feared Basil might shit himself to death.

"Hey buddy," said Randy as he approached. Basil was friendly toward him, but he was still a man-eating monster, a blind man-eating monster, so it was prudent to stay calm and give him plenty of warning that he was nearby. "What do you got there? Did you find something you like? A pumpkin? Or an avocado? Maybe a – Oh, dear God." When Randy got close enough to see what Basil was eating, all that remained of it was a forearm and a hand lying on a large cabbage leaf. A child's forearm and hand. Before he had time to react, Basil scooped up the poor child's final remains and swallowed.

"Denise?"

"Leave me alone, Randy!" Denise called back through sobs. "I need a little more fuckin' time, okay?"

"Denise!" Randy shouted. "You need to get your shit together right now, man. We got bigger problems."

Denise waddled out wearing what appeared to be a pair of underpants made out of one end of a giant bean pod, and a top made from a leaf. She'd cut a hole in the middle for her head, and tied the ends down her front and back around the waist with a length of vine. Most of the bean-shit mixture had been wiped from her face, but it was still thick in her hair and beard.

"What are you wearing?"

Denise gave Randy the finger. "My other clothes are pretty well done for. This'll have to do until I can find something else. Now what the fuck else kinda problems we got now?"

"A little kid. I think it was a boy, but I ain't sure. He just fell off the island."

Denise rolled her eyes. "Well surely that's his fuckin' problem, ain't it?"

"That ain't all," said Randy. He looked up to make sure the coast was clear, then whispered. "Basil ate him."

"There you go. One less problem than we had before."

"This is serious, Denise. What are we gonna do?"

"I'm gonna try to wipe some more shit out of my beard, then we're gonna walk to that village over there and I'm gonna see about getting a change of clothes and a stiff fuckin' drink. What you and your goddamn lizard are gonna do is up to –" Denise looked up. "What the fuck is that?"

Randy turned around and saw what he at first mistook to be another horse falling out of the sky. But this one wasn't falling. It was descending slowly and steadily, on account of it having big black wings. As it flapped down toward them, Randy saw that it also had a rider. Her skin was as black as her cloak. Randy thought she might be the Angel of Death. Had she come for him or Denise? Was he supposed to fight her, or let her do God's bidding?

His paladin instincts had prevented him from lying even when reason told him there was moral justification to do so.

It seemed strange that these same instincts provided no guidance on the etiquette involved in meeting a holy – or possibly unholy – messenger.

The flying horse and rider had nearly touched ground when Randy understood why his paladin instincts were crapping out on him.

"Katherine?"

The black flying horse landed, and Katherine dismounted. "What the fuck are you two doing down here?"

"We got lost in the desert." Randy nodded toward the village. "We found our way out now."

Katherine looked down at Denise. "What happened to you? You look like you just lost a game of Jumanji."

"And you look like Mary J. fuckin' Blige!"

Katherine smiled. "Do you really think so?"

The conversation was taking a very uncomfortable direction. Randy decided to change the subject. "That's a nice-lookin' horse your rode in on."

The horse huffed at Randy through his nostrils.

"Darius is a pegasus," Katherine snapped at him. "They don't like to be called horses."

Denise shook her head at Randy. "Fuckin' racist."

Randy was taken aback as the most racist person he'd ever known, a woman in blackface, and a winged horse glared judgmentally at him. "I didn't mean nothin' by –"

"I don't have time for your hillbilly bullshit," said Katherine. "Have either of you two dorks seen my brother?"

Randy felt a strange mixture of relief and grief. He'd been wrong about it being a child. That was something. But poor Tim. Poor Katherine.

"Katherine, I –"

FWOOOSHHHH

The sunlight was suddenly much brighter as a gust of wind blew upward. When Randy looked up, the flying island wasn't there anymore. It had disappeared just as suddenly as it had appeared in the first place.

"Ah, shit," said Katherine, staring up at the empty sky. "I should've let them out first." She looked back at Randy. "What were you saying?"

Randy removed the pants from his head and held them to his chest with both hands. "Katherine, I'm really sorry."

The End

ABOUT THE AUTHOR

Robert Bevan took his first steps in comedy with The Hitchhiker's Guide to the Galaxy, and his first steps in fantasy with Dungeons & Dragons. Over the years, these two loves mingled, festered, and congealed into the ever expanding Caverns & Creatures series of comedy/fantasy novels and short stories.

Robert is a writer, blogger, and a player on the Authors & Dragons podcast. He lives in Atlanta, Georgia, with his wife, two kids, and his dog, Speck.

Don't stop now! The adventure continues!

Discover the entire Caverns & Creatures collection at
www.caverns-and-creatures.com/books/

And please visit me on Facebook at
www.facebook.com/robertbevanbooks

73005992R00192

Made in the USA
Middletown, DE
09 May 2018